THE
DATING
Equation

HarperNorth
Windmill Green
24 Mount Street
Manchester M2 3NX

A division of
HarperCollins*Publishers*
1 London Bridge Street
London SE1 9GF

www.harpercollins.co.uk

HarperCollins*Publishers*
Macken House
39/40 Mayor Street Upper
Dublin 1
D01 C9W8

First published by HarperNorth in 2024

1 3 5 7 9 10 8 6 4 2

A catalogue record for this book
is available from the British Library

ISBN: 978-0-00-862185-8
Printed and bound in the UK using 100% renewable electricity at
CPI Group (UK) Ltd, Croydon

This novel is entirely a work of fiction.
The names, characters and incidents portrayed in it are the work
of the author's imagination. Any resemblance to actual persons,
living or dead, events or localities is entirely coincidental.

MIX
Paper | Supporting
responsible forestry
FSC™ C007454
www.fsc.org

This book contains FSC™ certified paper and other controlled
sources to ensure responsible forest management.

For more information visit: www.harpercollins.co.uk/green

THE
DATING
Equation

Emily Merrill

Harper
North

*For anyone who feels terrified of, and fascinated by,
the idea of falling in love.
And for Adam, who showed me that sometimes
it's the easiest thing in the world.*

Also by Emily Merrill
Heartbreak Houseshare

1

The big screen on the wall read three minutes and thirty-seven seconds, and I knew that it was impossible, but the seconds felt like they were slipping by faster with every minute that passed. My heart fluttered as we hit three minutes thirty.

'This is *way* more exciting than New Year's Eve.' Maeve clapped her hands. 'How big was the firework budget?'

Rory shot her a look. 'About as big as the budget was for bourbon biscuits.'

Maeve pulled her hand out of the tin, empty but for a sea of crumbs by this point. 'Sorry, I'm a stress eater. You guys know this!'

'No shit. I really hadn't noticed that in the eight years we've known each other.' He nudged her. 'Just like I would bet my life that Penny is staring into space and coiling her hair around her finger right now.'

They both tore their eyes away from the countdown and stared purposefully at the knot in my hand. I unravelled it, tossing it over my shoulder. I was predictable, who cared?

Dexter burst into the office, laden with bags of Tesco cava. 'How long have we got? If I accidentally miss this because big boss lady told me to go get fizz, I'm entitled to take her glass, right?'

Ella, our Managing Director, rolled her eyes. 'One, if I'm big boss lady, what does that make those two?' She gestured to Rory and me. 'And two, we've still got two minutes and seven seconds. Stop being a drama queen and pass me a glass!'

She jumped into action, popping a bottle and pouring it into plastic flutes (we were a start-up – cava and plastic glasses was about as far as we could stretch when we hadn't yet had a single download).

Rory turned to me, eyes frantic. 'What if nothing happens?'

One minute and twenty-nine seconds until our lives change forever.

I tried not to show how desperately I wanted that *not* to be the case. 'We're 26 years old. If nothing happens, we'll pick ourselves up and try again. But it will.'

'Well, you would say that, wouldn't you? My birthday's before yours, and time, dear Penny, is a-ticking.'

Maeve, ever the optimist – and also the one with least genuine investment, as a non-employee – piped up. 'Relax, guys. Someone, somewhere, is about to download the app that will help them find the love of their life. You should get an invite to the wedding, if you ask me.'

I bit my lip and took a sip of wine. Yes, feasibly our brand-new dating app could lead to a wedding. Or a breakup. A stream of breakups. Divorce. If I thought too hard about it, nervous hysteria bubbled to the surface.

'I think I'll settle for a successful first number of downloads.'

Dexter raised his pint glass. 'Now *that* is something to toast to.'

Ella put her hand out. 'One minute to go, everyone.'

There was a collective intake of breath, all of us refreshing our phones repeatedly. Everyone had stopped speaking, instead giving the countdown their undivided attention. Maeve was on my right-hand side, squeezing my fingers so tight that she threatened to cut off my circulation. Rory was to the left, biting his fingernails, a habit he'd brought with him from our university days.

My best friend did have a point. If this was a failure, it really *was* easier said than done to start over. This app was our baby. Literally since *we'd* been babies, studying for our Computer Science Masters in Edinburgh. A lot of Pot Noodles and instant coffee had gone into this project, but there'd been nothing instant about any other part of the process. We'd been in London since we graduated, on a mission to make it work. And maybe it could.

'Thirty seconds!' Maeve whisper-shouted in my ear. She might not have been a direct member of the team, but she was our own personal cheerleader and the feeling was mutual. We'd been known to pull all-nighters during uni, flicking the kettle on for Maeve as she got up to study just as we finally went to sleep. And she was the one who'd dragged us out to karaoke bars when she declared that we needed a break (Rory's karaoke song had been, and always would be, 'Copacabana'). She'd also been the one administering pep talks backstage before our crowdfunding pitch two years ago. I'd been a hyperventilating mess, throwing up my wild waves in approximately fifty different versions of a messy bun before we went onstage. Rory had been eerily silent, running through his cue cards at breakneck speed. It was potentially the only time I'd ever known him to have nothing to say, and it had freaked me the hell out. Maeve had been the glue, pinching our skin hard enough to bring us back to reality, forcing us to have a bit of self-belief. She'd always been our rock, and as a recently qualified psychologist, pep talks were kind of her thing.

'I think I'm going to be sick.' Rory grabbed my hand now, bringing me back to reality.

'Please don't.' I nudged him with my hip. 'It would be a really inconvenient time to have to deal with you spewing. I told you last time, Ror, I'm not holding your hair back again.'

I felt the side-eye before I saw it. We'd been friends long enough now that I knew every single combination of his facial expressions and what they meant. And this one, this particular blend of a slightly scrunched up nose, ruffled hair and gritted teeth, said 'not now, Penny'.

Fifteen seconds. I allowed myself to feel something other than nerves. In fifteen seconds, Level would be out in the world for anyone to download. I was a deeply pragmatic person, had been the only person to take Further Maths in sixth form. I had always searched for a way that numbers could make sense of life, and now we might actually have cracked it.

'Ten!' Around the room, people started to chant.

'Nine!' Rory grabbed my hand.

'Eight!' Maeve squeezed even harder, eyes bright with excitement.

'Seven! Six! Five! Four!'

'Three!' I took a breath, holding it.

'Two!'

'One!' Rory's eyes met mine, the nerves suddenly disappearing and morphing into something more like elation. His eyes were bright, and I could see my own excitement reflected back at me. This might have been a team effort from over thirty people, but at its core, it was a dream concocted between the two of us in our university bedrooms.

'We did it.' I finally exhaled, resting my head on his shoulder.

Feeling his head lean on mine, I could imagine him smiling to himself. 'Yep, we made an app.'

Everyone in the room had their phones out, checking the app store and typing in the word 'Level'. Shouts went up almost collectively as it appeared: our little green logo, painstakingly designed (and redesigned and redesigned). Just one of the many elements that had taken us four years to get right. But it was real, and it was there. Life started now, and I couldn't wait.

★★★

'I was just telling the barmaid that my best friends are going to change the world,' Maeve said as she came outside with a white wine spritzer for her and a pint for me, placing them on the wooden table in front of us and shimmying onto the bench, pulling her jacket closer to her body. It was that time of year, early spring, when it was definitely not warm enough for a beer garden yet, but everyone still gave it their best shot because the thought that pints in the sunshine might be just around the corner made the cold weather that bit easier to bear.

'Does your world-changing best friend not deserve a pint?' Rory leaned behind me to shoot her a look. 'I'm dying of thirst over here.'

'Dexter has everyone else's.' She pointed at our lead programmer, who was balancing five glasses in his hands.

'Should I just change my job title to programmer/bartender?' He looked down at Rory and me through the huge Nineties-style glasses he had always worn. 'This balancing act was definitely not in my job description.'

We helped pass pints down the table, Rory clinking his against mine for an initial private cheers, just between us.

'To the most organised, picky programmer I know.'

I snorted. 'And to the messiest, most argumentative one *I* know.'

Ella held up her glass for the official toast. 'To a year of incredibly hard work, and the brilliant team that we couldn't have done it without.' Rory held up his pint, and the rest of us reciprocated. Maeve planted a big drunken kiss on my cheek, putting her arms around Rory and me to pull us close.

'I'm very proud of you guys. Extremely so.'

Tonight, she was wearing her favourite dangly earrings that looked like boobs, and a bright orange crop top. It was one of her tamer outfits. I wished I had the confidence to take full advantage of her bulging wardrobe in the room adjacent to mine, but I had a love affair with neutrals. Brown, beige, white, black. I had a system.

'It's a pity you'll never get to be a guinea pig for Level.' I grabbed her phone, gesturing to the missed call from Adrian, her long-distance boyfriend of two years. 'It's a symptom of my control-freak nature that I'm saddened by the fact we couldn't be responsible for finding the love of your life.'

She grinned. 'There are so many things that I could unpack there, but I'm off the clock.'

'You're right.' I took a swig from my glass. 'And trust me, we don't have the time *or* the money to dig into that.'

Dexter interrupted the mini conversations going on down the table, calling out another live update from his phone. 'One hundred downloads! And it's only been' – he checked the time – 'one hour and thirteen minutes.'

I tried to tamp down the excitement that bubbled inside of me whenever someone checked the stats. We'd had some expectation that the app would get a good initial reception – our crowdfunding success had generated some publicity for us in the last couple of years – but there was no guarantee that it wouldn't just fizzle out after a few days. People might download the app, but would they actually use it? And more than that – would it actually work?

'Level is on its way up.' Harriet was the oldest, wisest, and chicest member of our team, least likely to ever need a dating app (although she did threaten a test run when her husband forgot to take the bins out), but one of the most enthusiastic about its success. She'd been in communications for over a decade; taking a chance on a start-up was an unnecessary risk. But she had twin daughters in primary school, and the thought of them as teenagers downloading unsafe apps was enough to swerve her career trajectory. 'The hashtag "Level" is trending on Twitter.'

There was a whoop from somewhere at the bottom of the table.

'Tell the story again.' Maeve was stirring her spritzer with a bamboo straw that she never failed to pull from her bag. 'The Level origin story.'

Rory grimaced. 'It's not a superhero.'

'Not *yet*.' Maeve stuck her tongue out at him. 'And you're lying if you say you haven't pictured yourselves in Lycra.' She turned to me. 'If you can't tell that story tonight, of all nights, when can you?'

She had a point. I relented, tucking my hair behind my ears and taking a big swig. 'Fine. But if you get bored because you've already heard this a million times, it's on you. Help me out, Ror?'

'What? Sorry, I'm still stuck on picturing certain team members in Lycra . . .'

I shoved Rory, who was smirking at me.

He shoved me gently back. 'I'm talking about Dexter, *obviously*. Anyway, let us begin.'

My cheeks warmed. 'Okay, so it was six months into our fourth year, when we were in the middle of applying for our Masters. I'd been on a really bad date —'

Dexter interrupted. 'How bad are we talking?'

'Fifteen minutes into our date, he revealed that he'd expect his tea on the table when he got home from work. Just like his mum had always done.'

Maeve tutted, fiddling with a boob earring and psycho-analysing subconsciously.

'We'd been talking for a week or so, about surface-level stuff, and there'd been no sign of his glaring misogyny and obvious mummy issues. It really annoyed me, how carried away I'd got believing that we were on the same level. When clearly, a week of conversations about dream holidays and favourite cocktails does not a connection make.'

'She moped about it for a full week.' Maeve flicked a droplet of condensation from the side of her wine glass in my direction.

It was true, I'd moped. But not because I'd thought that particular date was going to be *the one*. I'd never been close to finding the one, and I didn't care. It was what that date had represented. How was anyone supposed to find someone that they genuinely connected with when the entire talking stage was an act in pretending that the reason the conversation was happening in the first place was *not* because of a shallow set of photos? How was I supposed to avoid fuckboys and subpar stretches of time in dive bars after work, if every conversation was meaningless and began because of how someone rated my face in a few snapshots? I said as much.

'Hence the moping.' Rory gestured to me in a sweeping motion. 'She had a point, though. I was going through the same thing. Pointless dates, boring dates, dates where the other person wouldn't stop staring at my eyebrows like I'd somehow tricked them in the photos.'

They really were one of his best features, but took people by surprise. Rory had incredibly bushy eyebrows. Tweezers cowered in fear.

'So, after my week of moping . . .' I let Rory finish.

'We mapped out our dream dating app. One where you couldn't access someone's profile photos until you'd reached a certain level of conversation. Then you could figure out if you were attracted to them on more than just that surface level.'

We sat back in our seats, grinning at each other. Level was the product of the angst of our early twenties, but we also thought it was a genuinely good idea. And we weren't alone, judging by the array of people in front of us who'd been working tirelessly on the app to reach this launch date.

Maeve had been recording our speech, and she brought her phone down now, beaming with pride. 'We're going to watch this back when you're both famous.'

'You know,' Ella said, tilting her head, 'you might have saved a lot of time and energy if you'd just dated each other.'

Rory rolled his eyes, and I wasn't far behind. As if we hadn't heard this suggestion a hundred times before. Maeve, Rory, and I had been a set of three since our third night in first year university halls. We'd bonded over our mutual disgust for a fellow flatmate, who'd reheated his rice three nights in a row. Mum had drilled food hygiene into me before she sent me off to live alone, so I'd been horrified. As an experimental amateur chef with boundaries, Maeve had also been aghast.

Rory, I'd since learnt, would have done the exact same thing and reheated his rice for a fourth night. He'd just been craving friendship. It only took one night of free-flowing conversation, a bottle of rosé and little to no self-consciousness for the bonds to form. We'd all been stuck with each other ever since.

'And then all of you would be out of a job.' I cradled my glass.

Ella nodded and raised her glass. 'Fair point. Here's to our brilliant CEOs. Let the single people of London start walking in twos like they're boarding Noah's Ark.'

Everyone followed suit, laughing around the table. It was the kind of thing that Isla, my brother's girlfriend, would have called kismet. Or for regular people, destiny. We were crammed outside a busy pub near our office in the middle of Shoreditch, only a five-minute walk from the hub that Rory and I had started renting two years ago.

'Just a thought' – Maeve had leaned in conspiratorially – 'now that you've created a dating app, you might want to actually consider dating.'

I didn't bite. It was a weekly thing, this lecture from my best friend. Sure, I'd dated. My dating escapades were the whole reason that this venture had begun. But somehow, I'd never *actually* had a boyfriend. Not even one of those sixth-form relationships where you held hands on the bus. There was always an excuse – I was too busy, they'd been leaving Edinburgh whilst I'd been staying on, there wasn't a 'spark' – why my situationships had fizzled out. I knew how to debrief a bad date like the back of my hand, but I'd never returned with rosy cheeks and a gushing story about how he'd held the door open and everything changed. Maeve had met Adrian whilst doing her doctorate in Leeds, after a string of very questionable exes that I'd been *very* vocal about. Rory had also had a couple of girlfriends, including Lottie, the girl he'd met two weeks after we'd moved to East London post-graduation. They'd bumped into each other at a bar when we'd been out for Maeve's birthday, and for a while it seemed like he'd cracked the romance thing. She was the one, until she wasn't. So for both of my best friends, I'd watched the cycle from hopeful beginnings to the bitter end. It didn't exactly appeal. I'd grown up with two households for Christmas, and two birthday dinners, since my parents had split when I was 11 years old. I'd seen first-hand the fallout of two people completely wrong for each other, so whilst it wasn't that I wanted to be alone forever, I would just rather be alone than with the wrong person. Joe brought enough romance to the family for both of us. He and Isla had been together since they were 15, walking home from school with their hands entwined and playing footsie under the dinner table when they thought Mum and I couldn't see. They were the reason that the pressure was off for me.

I said as much to Maeve, who smirked. 'You're so predictable, Pen.'

Rory heard us, chiming in. 'I have a secret conspiracy that she uses AI to talk to us.'

I shook my head, smiling down at my drink. These were my people. If anything, this — celebrating the launch of Level with both of them beside me — was kismet.

2

After the first initial flurry of excitement, it really was a waiting game. No one was meeting the love of their life overnight. We turned up to work each morning, checking the app for bugs and glitches, pouncing on Harriet as soon as she arrived to see if there was any media noise. Of good dates, bad dates, *any* dates. And then, two weeks later, it started to happen.

The concept of Level was this: you answered short, introductory questions about yourself first. Some of the questions were light-hearted – What is your idea of a dream first date? How would you spend an ideal weekend? – and some were heavier and asked about your political inclinations and whether you planned on trying for children. The app then paired you with six potential matches based on their answers, your answers, and proximity. You could start chatting to all of them (or just one of them), using prompts if needed to move the conversation along. Once you'd reached a level of chatting that hit our programmed target, you unlocked their photos. At that point, you could take it off the app and start dating – technically, you could start dating whenever you wanted, but research showed that people were 80 per cent less likely to go on a true blind date. If you kept chatting on the app after the photos were unlocked, the final level was an added extra. Your meet-cute. Despite it being part of daily life, people still got embarrassed about meeting their significant other on a dating app, preferring to make up their own story about how they met. So, at the final level, the app would spit out a meet-cute. An idea, based on prompts and conversation, for how you might have met in real life. You could use it as a cover story, or as your actual first date idea. Programming this last level had been a logistical nightmare, but it was worth it. Nothing was more stressful than planning a first date. Getting it delivered on a silver platter to you? Incredibly helpful. Or so we hoped.

★★★

I shoved the phone in Joe's face whilst he fought back tears, his knife deep into a red onion. '*Look.*'

Credit to my big brother, he didn't snap, instead taking in the tweet.

'Tapas at St Katharine Docks, huh? Level isn't sending people to KFC, then.'

I beamed down at my phone, and the girl who'd posted about her experience with Level. She seemed to be in her mid to late twenties, and she had a sausage dog in her profile photo. From the looks of things, she was a dating blogger. And she'd been for a *very* successful first date last night.

'Our first success story.' I leaned back on the bar stool with a happy sigh. 'Or at least, our first *hope* of a success story. There is always time for it to go tits up.'

'My sister, ever the optimist.' Joe blinked back a fresh wave of tears. 'Good God, are these onions radioactive? I'm surprised that people are even tweeting about their dating life – I would rather die.'

He did have a point. The issue with needing public noise for success was that people were kind of hesitant about sharing their dating app experiences online. @dateaholic97 was a rare gem.

'I bet Rory is bouncing off the walls.' He went back to his chopping, finishing it up before crouching to root around in his and Isla's kitchen cupboards. I was bracing myself for crisis; the recipe that Isla had left him unattended with – an Ottolenghi recipe for sweet and smoky chicken – was beyond both of our repertoires. We'd been left in charge of dinner *once* when I was 15, and Mum had never quite managed to get the scorch marks out of her worktop.

'He was quite excited, to say the least.' In reality, he'd stood in the middle of our shared office and done an improv dance to 'Love is in the Air', pulling me in until I had no choice but to dance along with him. Never a dull day. I described this to Joe, who snorted.

'Sounds like Ror.'

I could hear him banging around below. 'What are you actually doing down there?' I pinched a salted cashew from the tiny dishes that Isla had placed on their dining table. It was either that or a pumpkin seed – something that I maintained only belonged in a bird feeder.

'You'd think turmeric would be easy to spot, wouldn't you?' My brother's head finally appeared again, his hairline damp with the stress of being left alone whilst Isla had dashed out for emergency couscous. He wasn't coping well with the responsibility. Having people's lives in his hands, he could handle. Being responsible for roasting a chicken had tipped him over the edge.

'I would ask you to help, but I think that might actually make the whole thing worse.'

I rolled my eyes. 'And technically, that would be cheating.' I raised my can of Diet Coke. 'And I am many things, but I am not a cheater.'

Joe, who had disappeared again for another attempt, appeared from below deck, clutching a jar of bright yellow spice. 'Aha! Victory is mine. So, what else are people saying online?'

Social media made launching a new product simultaneously way more difficult and a lot easier. Easier, because you could instantly reach thousands of users at once. Harder, because you were trying to break through the traffic of hundreds of brands doing the exact same thing. I scrolled through Harriet's work online, wincing as I passed a promotional video Rory and I had done to introduce our app. In general, I preferred to leave most of the activity that required charisma and confidence to Rory, since he had both in abundance. In this rare video that they'd managed to squeeze out of me, we were sitting in the library in Edinburgh – Harriet had maintained that one of our strongest USPs was that we'd started Level as students, and I cringed at my accent. *Did I really sound like that?* It was a culmination of growing up a Londoner and then spending five years in Scotland before returning home. Sometimes, when I was distracted, I accidentally let out an 'aye', much to my family's amusement.

'Humiliating publicity aside,' I said, scrolling past the video, 'people seem to be enjoying the experience. A few men complaining about the blind–date element. Imagine my surprise.'

My brother scoffed. 'If I'd been able to hook Isla in with my charm alone, and not the teenage overbite and the acne, things would have been a lot less stressful.'

I shoved another handful of cashews into my mouth. 'Oh, look, here are some comments telling us that the female CEO has a weird nose.'

Joe paused to take a proper look at me before returning all attention to his chicken, poking it with a fork. 'It's not weird. Slightly crooked, maybe, but I've seen a lot of messed up noses. Yours isn't weird.'

Given that Joe was training to specialise in Accident and Emergency, most of the people he saw on a daily basis probably weren't feeling their *best*. It wasn't much of a compliment. I brought up my phone camera, staring at the alignment of my nose. *Was it weird?*

He worked in silence for a few minutes peeling potatoes into neat wedges with expert precision whilst I responded to some of the comments from our Level profile. Joe had been the toddler who immediately stacked up building blocks in a perfectly aligned tower on his first try whilst the other children threw them on the floor and wailed. He'd taken some of his GCSEs early and had been reading brick-sized books whilst I'd still been getting my head around Biff, Chip, and Kipper. I hadn't always been this close to my brother.

With only two years between us, we'd been arch-nemeses during childhood. But in the wake of an emotional divorce, siblinghood had become a tag-team effort. When Joe had gone off to university in Bristol, I'd had to do the dashing between Mum and Dad's houses alone. Things had become a whole lot more complicated when I'd fled to Edinburgh. Teaching them how to FaceTime had been a bloody nightmare.

Although our parents's divorce had been a blessing – there were only so many arguments two children could listen to from the top of the stairs – they'd both reacted to it in entirely different ways. Dad, realising his part in the breakdown of their marriage, had never quite recovered. Mum had blossomed, finally getting the time for herself that she'd craved. It made for awkward conversations ('no, Dad, I *promise* Mum is finding it hard too') but at least it had meant we only needed to worry about one of them. It had strained my relationship with Joe for a little while, but we'd survived the ordeal, and now as adults we were closer than ever, and our parents had found their way to civility too. My big brother had always been older than his years, obsessed with his routine of drinking a black coffee and reading the newspaper on Sunday. Every week he sent me a photo of the crossword, and we'd race to finish it first. The current tally was 11–17 to me, and I planned to never let him forget it.

'How's the ring?' I gestured to the cupboard with the first aid kit in it. It was an ingenious place to hide an engagement ring; with a doctor in the house, I'd never seen Isla so much as *think* about trying to find a plaster. He'd bought it five weeks ago in a tiny jewellery shop, taking me with him for moral support and making us trek all the way to Balham to choose the ring that he knew Isla would fall in love with. There'd been a slightly awkward moment when the jeweller asked when we were planning on getting married, but other than that it had been a success.

'Christ, Pen, shout it louder why don't you.' He jerked his thumb towards the front door, even though it was directly in my line of sight and the others definitely weren't home yet. Especially couscous-laden Isla. 'We're too close now to give the game away.'

The ring was a simple, elegant solitaire, with a sizeable diamond that he must have been saving up to buy for years. As someone with over twenty different loyalty cards in her purse, and who had been scraping out jars of knock-off Nutella until they were practically sparkling, I was perplexed by the amount people were willing to fork out on engagement rings.

'Can you go round and light our incense?' Joe looked down at his handwritten list. 'If she gets home and the whole place doesn't smell like patchouli, my guts are for garters.'

Hearing words like 'incense' come out of my brother's mouth had taken some getting used to. I hopped up, grabbing their jar of matches, and headed towards the mantelpiece. Joe and Isla had been living in their one-bedroom flat that was about a ten-minute walk from Dad's since Joe had finished his foundation programme. Although it was cramped, they'd managed to make it completely their own. There were photos *everywhere*, with enough lamps to sink a ship (Isla had a life-long aversion to the 'big light'). I'd spent a *lot* of time on their hammock/loveseat hybrid. It paid to monopolise your own little area of London.

It had been a no-brainer for Maeve and me to choose Greenwich. I'd been staying with Mum in my childhood home in Blackheath, waiting for Maeve to finish up her training in Leeds so we could live together again (when you found someone you could live with without tearing each other's hair out, you clung on *tight*). As soon as she'd found a job here, we'd haunted the local letting agencies. Rory had slowly followed suit, finding a new flatshare and moving a fifteen-minute walk away, leaving his Hoxton house that he'd shared with his group of climbing friends. Joe and Isla lived in Deptford, with an easy route to the hospital. It was our own corner of the city, with just enough green to pretend that we weren't clogging up our lungs.

For years, Joe had maintained that he wasn't going to propose until they'd managed to buy instead of rent – but in London, that was borderline impossible, and so eventually he'd caved. He'd decided that at 28, after thirteen years together, the time was right. Isla had the patience of a saint. The plan was as follows: he was proposing *not* on their actual anniversary (too predictable), but on the anniversary of the date that they'd first become official during year six, when they were 10 years old (because normal people remember these kinds of dates, right?). They'd walked to the park after school, where he'd asked her to be his girlfriend on the swings. Even though their first attempt at a relationship had been short-lived, my brother was convinced that it was where their story began.

'Are you nervous?' I swigged the bottle of beer I'd helped myself to from their fridge. 'Thirteen years is quite the build-up.'

He looked frustrated; at me, or at the size of the oven as he tried to cram the chicken in, I wasn't sure.

'Are you sure that you –'

'I can do this.' He cut me off, brow furrowed. 'And stop trying to make me nervous about the proposal or I'll tell Isla not to make you a bridesmaid.'

'Pfft. Like she'd listen.'

'It's inconvenient how much she loves you. *Finally*. Thank God for that.' He turned away from the oven, satisfied with a job well done. 'I've nailed this. You may as well bow out now.'

I pulled a face. Tonight, it was Joe and Isla's evening in our group's *Come Dine With Me*. Rory had hosted last month (a seaside theme with homemade fish and chips that had scored a very commendable 36/50) and my brother was up second. Even though Maeve was my flatmate, I'd agreed that Adrian could partner with her when it came to their turn, and then clearly they were saving the best until last. *Heavy* on the sarcasm. Rory and I were technically at a disadvantage – it was harder to turn around a three-course meal *and* host an evening when you were a party of one – but I could hardly register a formal complaint, since Joe was currently doing everything single-handedly anyway. And because I'd already suggested that Rory and I team up, but he'd rejected the offer on the basis of not wanting to be 'dragged down'. Charming.

We heard them before we saw them, Isla's key turning in the lock and the rest of them clomping up the stairs to the second-floor flat. 'And the *best part*' – the door opened, Maeve's voice carrying – 'is that I think we're nearing a breakthrough. I saw it in their eyes, we're getting somewhere.'

Adrian was hot on her heels, throwing us a wave but clearly caught up in her joy. It was his turn to visit London from Hull, and Maeve had been counting the days down on her calendar. Rory and Isla were last to come in, Rory carrying Isla's floral tote bag and a bottle of wine in his other hand.

'So yeah, a great week. The best in a while.' Maeve beamed. Being around my best friend was a bit like constantly being at the top of a wave, never feeling it crash onto shore. I could tell immediately from the conversational snippet that she was talking about work. She was a newly qualified clinical psychologist, working with 12–18-year-olds for the NHS. In the entire time she'd been working with patients, I'd only ever heard her give the baseline facts. She took confidentiality incredibly seriously, which is why I'd always trusted her as a true confidant.

Rory headed straight for me, squeezing my shoulder and placing the tote on the counter. 'See the review?'

I nodded, halfway through combing my fingers through my waves. 'Hallelujah. Did Dexter figure out what was happening with the bug?'

We'd been informed three days ago that there was a minor blip in the process; some users were automatically getting set back a level if they didn't reply in twenty-four hours. People had – very understandably – pointed out that a slightly longer reply time did not mean disinterest. The expectation of an immediate response was the norm now, but that didn't mean people had to give it.

'He sorted it this afternoon. Back on track, baby, back on track.' He chose a pumpkin seed, grimacing when he crunched it. 'Wow, grim. I'm docking three points immediately.'

'I heard that.' Isla smiled at Rory. 'It's not my fault that you wouldn't know nutrition if it punched you in the face.'

'I hope it doesn't.' Rory rubbed his nose. 'I bruise like a peach.'

My soon-to-be sister-in-law shook her head, laughing. You couldn't help but laugh at Rory; he had that effect on people. She gave as good as he did – for someone that looked (and most of the time, acted) like butter wouldn't melt, Isla had a sassy reputation. I hugged her, overwhelmed by the scent of her shampoo. Warming vanilla with a hint of spice.

'I like the seeds. Promise.' I put one in my mouth, trying to smile as I chewed it.

'Suck-up,' Rory mouthed in my direction. 'She *never* eats the healthy snacks in board meetings. This girl is a Rolo fiend through and through.'

With most of us having grown up in London (with the exception of Maeve, who'd moved around a lot and therefore had a non-accent), Rory's Geordie accent stuck out like a sore thumb. It was one of my favourite things about him. A comforting nod to the North, reminding us that there was life outside this city we loved. Adrian was also Northern – a Scouser who had been studying in Leeds when he and Maeve had bonded over the brutality of their course. He squeezed Maeve to him now.

'I *wish* this one would offer me a Rolo occasionally.'

Maeve rolled her eyes. 'Dark chocolate is brain food. Look it up.'

'It's time, guys,' Isla said, clapping. 'Time for some classic organised *fun*.'

Rory groaned, but he was only kidding. Without Isla's forethought, none of our plans would ever reach execution. I was meticulous at work, but I let that slip as soon as I left the office, and Maeve had her head in the clouds too often to coordinate her own calendar. Isla was now handing out sturdy-looking sombreros, not like the ones I'd have been inclined to pick up from the pound shop. She didn't do anything half-arsed, even if it was an amateur cooking competition.

'This is excellent news. I've always loved a surprise hat element to an evening.' Maeve grabbed one, trying to manoeuvre it over the space buns she'd twirled her tight curls into. Rory had just as much of a task trying to fit one over his own hair. Isla pulled out a bottle of tequila and clinked a shot glass against it.

'Let night two of *Come Dine With Me* commence. Give us anything less than a nine and I'll bring poison ivy home from the shop and put it in your duvets. Margarita anyone?' She started pouring shots, instructing Joe to rim the glasses with salt. The rest of us blinked back. For someone with a job that radiated soft energy, Isla managed to give floristry an edge.

'How *does* one rim a glass with salt?' Joe wrinkled his nose. 'Swap with me?'

They switched places seamlessly, with the ease of two people who had grown up together.

'Joe doesn't know how to rim his glass.' Rory threw a mocking glance his way, pretending to take notes. 'That's another point docked.'

My brother rolled his eyes. 'A win doesn't count if you win by dirty tactics.'

'They're not dirty. They're fair.' Rory was still pretending to write. 'Pumpkin seeds, below-par snack.'

Isla smacked him with a tea towel.

'Don't stress, it's pointless expecting him or Penny to appreciate a healthy snack,' Joe said, rubbing Isla's shoulders. 'Maeve and Adrian are medical professionals, they understand nutrition.'

Adrian laughed. 'I have heard rumours that both of their respective cupboards at uni were a walking advertisement for Heinz beans.'

Joe joined in: 'If we'd offered cheesy puffs in fancy bowls, we might have got a ten from them. Shall I whip up some chicken nuggets?'

'See what you've done?' I shot Rory a look. 'We're the butt of every joke.' I choked back another handful of seeds to prove a point.

'Fifty quid says she spits those out.' Rory wiggled his eyebrows at me.

'I'll raise you sixty.' Maeve pinched my arm lightly. 'Although, we've now triggered the competitive streak. She'll eat the whole bowl.'

I swallowed, raising my arms in victory. 'Screw all of you.'

'I really do think that would ruin the friendship dynamic we've worked so hard on as a group.' Rory hid behind his sombrero as we all started chucking pumpkin seeds his way.

3

'And another landslide victory to moi.' Ella held up her green smoothie triumphantly, adding another check mark to her tally.

It was a stupid competition that had started a few weeks prior to launch, when we'd all been so hellbent on finalising every detail that we'd consisted of 99 per cent caffeine, 1 per cent human. The rules were simple: make the most of your Pret subscription and consume the most drinks to get your next month's subscription free on Level's expenses. As far as employee incentives went, it was proving to be pretty successful. I'd banned Rory from participating after he almost body-slammed me on his way into the office, too desperate to add a tally to his name.

Dexter fanned his nose. 'I would *not* want to be Darcy. All those smoothies you consume have got to come out the other end at some point.'

Harriet snorted, barely looking up from her Itsu and the crime novel she had been devouring. 'Relationships are all about compromise.'

Ella, who often looked to Harriet for back up (we all did), clapped. 'Say it louder for the people in the back! You're just bitter that your measly two Americanos a day couldn't beat my total.' She took a long glug of the smoothie to prove her point.

It was lunchtime on a Monday, and everyone was surprisingly energetic, the product of a good week of downloads. It was my favourite part of building a company from the ground up: how much everyone genuinely cared. Rory had burst into the office this morning laden with bulk-bought custard doughnuts to celebrate. My enthusiastic group email had paled in comparison, but I was used to being bad cop. Rory had good cop laced through his veins. He chose this moment to walk back into the office, two Diet Cokes in hand. He chucked one in my direction with no warning, and I scrambled to catch it, shooting him daggers.

'How are we all?'

Dexter high fived him on his way past. 'We were discussing the sad fate of Ella's other half.'

I winced at the phrase 'other half' – a personal bugbear and one that came up quite frequently in the world of dating apps.

Ella pouted. 'Dexter is just jealous that I've experienced real-life success with a dating app. How is your lizard doing?'

Dexter crumpled up his napkin and threw it at her. 'Peggy is an *iguana*. And she's doing brilliantly, thanks for asking.'

Rory was watching the camaraderie, one eyebrow raised. 'I feel like I've massively missed something here.'

Harriet filled in the gaps without looking up from her book.

'Not that I don't wish Level was my relationship origin story,' Ella continued. 'Link is a sad side effect of having met her a few years ago, in a lonely, Level-less world.'

I decided to chime in, swallowing a bite of pasta salad first. 'You are solid proof that apps *can* work. And if Link can produce a relationship as steady as yours, just imagine what Level can do.'

Rory had come to a halt, leaning on one of the desks and cracking open his can. I was still hesitant to open mine, aware that my white jeans probably wouldn't survive an explosion.

Dexter pointed his fork at me. 'If you're so confident, boss, why aren't you using it?'

This was the downside of employing people you'd known a long time – Dexter had been our friend during the university days, and he had *plenty* of experience in ribbing me.

Before I even had the chance to register his jab, Rory had jumped in. 'Penny? Come on, she'd never test the goods herself.'

Everyone laughed – including Harriet, who had pulled out a bookmark, deeming our chat more interesting now that we were mocking my dating history. I tried not to feel offended. I wasn't a *complete* loser. I'd dated, I just . . . hadn't in a while. We'd been *busy*. I didn't have time for grown men looking for a substitute mother, or emotionally unavailable men trying to get me to doubt my self-worth. But it didn't mean I *couldn't* date. I narrowed my eyes at the sight of Rory laughing along with the others.

'Is that a challenge?'

Rory whipped his head round mid-laugh. 'What?'

Aha. Maybe I didn't have to be straightlaced, workaholic Penny. Maybe I could surprise the team now and again. Maybe *I* could be the custard-doughnut-buying, product-testing kind of boss.

'If that's an official team challenge, I think I just might accept it.'

Rory was the one person in my life I looked to when I needed someone to challenge me. He looked momentarily thrown that I was giving it back.

'I was only kidding —'

Dexter interrupted. 'Don't ruin this for the rest of us, Snory. Penny using Level? I might cancel my streaming subscription.'

'Funny.' I thought about the logistics of inputting my likes and dislikes, waiting for the matches to load. I reckoned I could box it off whilst brushing my teeth or waiting for my pasta to cook. 'Challenge accepted. Watch me Level up.'

I didn't necessarily believe that the challenge would be successful, but it was worth it for the look on their faces. Like I'd gone out for lunch and had a brain transplant.

Ella was beaming. '*Yes, Penny.* This is the post-launch spirit we need.'

Rory was communicating to me via facial expression again. This one said 'Do I need to take your temperature?'

I ignored the look.

'You hate dating. Are you feeling okay?' He came over and laid the back of his hand over my forehead.

I brushed him off. 'Hilarious. But no, I'm serious. I might as well start practising what we've been preaching.'

'Well, this is gonna be good.' Dexter went back to his computer, signalling the end of our slightly elongated lunch break. 'Let the games begin.'

***

Rory pulled me as soon as everyone had wandered back to their desks, groaning at the prospect of another four hours' work. There weren't enough doughnuts in the world to erase that kind of pain.

'Any other life-altering decisions I should know about?' He straddled his desk chair, scooting into the middle of our shared office and staring at me over the top of my computer. 'Decided to throw caution to the wind and never write a to-do list again? Suddenly woken up with a desire to climb Everest?'

I grabbed my planner, half ignoring him. 'It is *not* that big of a curveball. I can't put off dating forever.'

He narrowed his eyes. 'There's being open to dating, and then there's using Level and reporting back to the whole office. It was just a joke, Pen. Don't feel you need to prove this point.'

I sighed, scribbling another task in my planner that I'd woken up in the middle of the night thinking about. Being a borderline workaholic was my thing, but this was different. My office dignity was at stake. It was time for Penny's spontaneous era, a concept that I knew Joe would find particularly hilarious.

'I'm a multi-tasker, Ror. It's in my blood. In fact, I'll do it right now.'

He was staring at me, taken aback. There were not many things that left Rory McCarthy speechless. The first part was easy; of course I had Level already downloaded onto my home screen. I clicked 'set up profile' and input my details, turning the screen so that he had full view. *Penny Webber. 26. Computer programmer. South-East London.*

'Computer programmer.' Rory blinked back at me. 'The app is supposed to be *honest.*'

'I *am* a computer programmer. No one has to know that I'm a CEO too. I don't want to scare anyone off.' I recoiled at my own words. *See?* There it was already, one of the things I hated most about dating. Already trying to temper myself.

'There, done. Complete. Penny is online dating.'

I still had the questionnaire to fill out, but the hard part was done. I could do it later whilst I was waiting for the kettle to boil, and by 5 p.m. there would (hopefully) be six perfect matches waiting for me. Maeve was going to lose her shit. Rory went back to his desk, shaking his head.

'You could try it too, you know.' I smirked at him when he turned around. 'First one to have a successful date wins. You haven't dated since Lottie.'

Rory was usually the first person to get competitive, especially where I was involved. I readied myself with a comeback.

'I don't know – this is your adventure, not mine.' He shrugged, running his hand through his curls. 'I'm not really in the mood for it at the moment.'

I was completely thrown off. 'What, dating? You're always in the mood for it.'

I couldn't count the number of times he'd stopped by my uni room between the hours of ten in the evening and one in the morning, five-pack of Sainsbury's chocolate chip cookies in hand (the fluffy, gooey ones from the bakery), ready for a first-date debrief. We'd discuss every element of his night, from the awkward hello to the slightly alcohol-induced kiss goodbye. There had been a particularly good one in first year where he'd been so nervous, he'd walked out without remembering to pay. Maeve and I had never let him live that one down. It had become less frequent over the years, and things had been a bit vague after his breakup with Lottie, but still, he'd never been *not in the mood for it*. Dating was, for all intents and purposes, our life's work.

He was halfway out the door now on the way to a meeting. 'People's interests can change. Want me to take this one for the both of us and make notes?'

Our finance meetings happened biweekly, and they were my least favourite. No one ever warned you how much your workload changed when you became a company owner rather than just someone with an idea.

'Have I ever told you I love you, Rory McCarthy?'

He nodded, saluting me before heading off into the meeting. I opened Level again, tempted to box off some of the questions whilst I waited for my emails to load. I stared at the first one. Would I prefer dinner, or an activity-based date? I thought about the reality of playing minigolf with a stranger and wanted to bang my head against my desk.

'Hey boss.' I jumped, turning my phone face down as Dexter came into our office. 'Ready to talk about the coding for the voice notes?'

I grabbed my notebook. 'Absolutely.'

We'd been brainstorming for weeks about what a new level within Level might look like, and we were leaning towards a way to exchange voice notes even before you saw each other's faces. There was something so revealing about the way people spoke, and how they spoke about the things that mattered — or didn't matter — to them. Other dating apps were starting to incorporate voice notes too, so we needed to get ahead of the curve. I tried to imagine what I'd say in a voice note; Maeve would go on a rant about burnout in the workplace, Rory would probably do an impression from *The Office* (US version) . . . Who was I when I wasn't at work? And who would be my own perfect match? One thing was absolutely for sure: if our algorithm for love couldn't manage to partner me up, what could?

4

Another useless reply lit up my screen.

'This is hopeless.' I turned my phone over on the kitchen counter with disappointment, taking the hair claw clipped to my belt and pulling my hair up in a knot. It had been a particularly humid day in the office. 'It's a good job you're getting this out of your system, Mum' – I gestured to the bowl of wedding cake batter – 'because you won't be making one of those for me in this lifetime, I can assure you.'

Mum paused her fondant moulding to pat my shoulder, getting orange dye all over my white T-shirt.

'Really?' I said, frowning. 'Did that not seem inevitable to you?'

She ignored the jab, focusing back on the fondant. 'I've got some Vanish in the cupboard, I'll sort it after I've managed to get the shape just . . .' She leaned back and squinted at her creation. 'Does this look like a carrot to you?'

The fondant shapes were a little stumpy. 'Maybe a Chantenay?' Or something phallic that I *definitely* was not voicing to my mother.

'You're right. More length.' Her tongue was stuck out in concentration; not the most hygienic visual. Her apron had illustrated cupcakes on the chest, with glace cherries for nipples. Mum was 53 going on 15 when it came to her sense of humour. But nipple apron or not, she was a damn good baker. Baked goods had been a constant during our childhood (the other children's birthday cakes *paled* in comparison to my own replica of Barney the Dinosaur), but it hadn't been until two years after the divorce that she'd taken the plunge and applied for a loan to open her own shop. Flash forward thirteen years, and it was the go-to bakery in Greenwich. Last week I'd had to queue for twenty minutes to get cookies for a team meeting. Family favouritism? Our mother didn't know her.

'Explain the carrot thing to me again.'

She stopped what she was doing to stare me down. 'Penny, the first rule of professional baking is to never be judgemental about customer requests.'

I was pretty sure she'd made this rule up after the first time she'd been asked to make a penis cake for a hen do. Funnily enough, that custom cake didn't make it onto the Fondant & Flour Facebook page.

'Me, judge? Never. Now explain the carrots.'

Mum sighed. 'Apparently, the bride wants the top tier – carrot cake – to have a fondant bride, groom, and five miniature bunnies to represent her childhood pets.'

'Presumably Cotton Tail and friends are no longer with us?'

'Yes, Penny. Dead rabbits. Dead rabbits that came with photos so I could "reimagine the likeness". Happy now?'

I tried and failed to stifle a snort. 'Extremely.'

Last month she'd taken an order for a birthday cake that looked like the rear end of a baby, for a baby shower. People were so weird. Some cake places only took on specific custom orders, with hefty guidelines, but Mum was not one to discriminate. Her website emphasised 'ANY orders welcome' and I was convinced that some people saw that as a challenge. Fondant & Flour had grown significantly since Mum had started it from our kitchen counter, and she'd recently expanded from a takeaway-only bakery to a sit-in café, complete with her childhood dream of a lilac coffee machine. As much as she took care with every bake, the bigger projects were her favourite, and she tended to bring most of the wedding cakes home where she could work in peace. In her eyes, it was the most stressful kind of cake to make. It needed near silence, something that working in the back of a café, where the sound of screaming babies in buggies often filtered through, did not provide. Caroline Pearson was the first female entrepreneur of the family. It was obvious where I'd got the bug from.

'So remind me' – she was sticking her tongue out again, concentrating on shaping two tiny bunny paws – 'why is this hopeless?'

It was Thursday evening; three days since I'd set up my profile on Level. By the time I'd collapsed on our sofa on Monday night, my six matches had rolled in like clockwork. I'd been way too busy on Tuesday – back-to-back meetings followed by pizza with Dad – to even think about it, but one jab from Dexter yesterday morning and I'd immediately clicked the icon. From then on, it had been an absolute disaster, which probably wasn't the best endorsement of my own creation. To be honest, I was at my wits' end with it. *None* of my six profiles seemed to want to engage in actual adult conversation. I showed Mum my phone.

'Well, firstly,' she said, pulling her glasses up from their chain (we'd tried to tell her that this wasn't a look, but Mum thrived on ignoring her children), 'if I understand this right, you haven't even talked to all of them.'

I looked at the screen. 'Well, no, but Patrick and Matt have been enough to put anyone off. It's like talking to a brick wall.'

She squinted. 'Why is "Matt, 27" only responding to you in puns? You weren't even talking about cheese here.'

'*Exactly*. He works in a deli, I think.'

'Good God.' She smirked down at her cake batter. 'I know that as the mother of a dating app creator I probably shouldn't say this, but I'm so glad that I've avoided men since the divorce.'

I groaned. 'Don't remind me. How can I be a career woman if I'm having to check my phone for cheese puns, or' – I checked back at my brief conversation with Patrick – 'questions asking me if my bum is worth the wait? We were supposed to have weeded these problematic guys out!'

It was at that exact moment that Joe walked in, Isla behind him.

'Did I really just walk in on you talking about your arse with our mother?' Joe scrubbed his hand over his face. 'I am way too tired for this.'

Mum flicked icing sugar in his direction. 'Nothing I haven't seen before. In fact, I was one of the first people to see —'

He groaned. 'I'm going to have to stop you right there.'

Isla handed Mum the delivery clipboard she used when helping out with cake deliveries before pulling out one of the kitchen stools next to me. 'Seven very happy customers, Caroline. The woman with the engagement cake burst into tears at the front door. And Pen, I think you have an excellent bum — the perfect mix of round and perky — definitely worth the wait.' She looked at my phone. 'Tell "Patrick, 29" that he just has to be patient. Sorry, who is Patrick, anyway?'

She stared harder at the screen. '*Wait.*'

'Yes, yes. It's what you think it is.'

Isla's eyes lit up as I filled her in on the office-banter-turned-challenge. Joe had disappeared upstairs, fresh in from a shift at the hospital and likely making the most of Mum's fancy shower gels. He pretended to complain, but I knew he liked smelling of peaches.

'Okay, this is exciting. Don't look at me like that — this is going to be *fun*.' She pouted at my expression, taking over my phone and tapping at the screen. 'Can I have a go?'

'It's not a ga —' I started to resist, but it was too late and she was already typing.

Mum winked at me from where she was scooping batter into three large tins. Isla was like the nosy older sister I'd never had. It hadn't taken long when she'd arrived on the scene for her to slot into place. In a little over a few months, it was like she had always been there. She was the baby of her own family, with two older sisters in their late thirties and early forties. Both had fled London when they'd decided to start a family, and as far as I knew, she barely saw them. Her sisters were tied together by proximity in age and a shared childhood that Isla hadn't really been a part of. I had been ecstatic at the prospect of a new sister – if they didn't appreciate her, I'd happily have her. Besides, Joe had never been very good at sleepovers and midnight feasts, and Isla had been more than happy to binge-watch *Dawson's Creek* with me and pile up our mugs with an army of mini marshmallows. In her teenage years, it had been common knowledge that as soon as Isla turned 18 her parents would move abroad, something they'd been wanting to do since they were in their twenties. So by the time 18 came, Isla was well and truly a Webber, if not by marriage then by everything but. She'd jumped at the chance to help Mum with the business; nowadays she worked as a florist a few doors over, and I knew they liked to spend their tea breaks together, gossiping. Like Mum, creativity was in her bones. Joe and I were better with the practical things. Anatomy and computers, we understood (respectively). Give us a bunch of roses or a fondant carrot, and we crumbled. It was why Joe and Isla were a perfect mix of personalities. She was the light relief he needed at the end of a long day, and he made sure they never let their TV licence run out.

'Hey, this one isn't too bad. He's even typing out the word "you" instead of shortening it to one letter.'

Isla turned my phone back to me, reuniting me with Matt and his puns.

'The bar is clearly on the floor, Isla, if that's what we're celebrating.'

She rolled her eyes. 'There's something really sexy about a man who chooses full sentences over "WUU2".'

Joe came downstairs then, freshly showered and out of his scrubs, smelling suspiciously like a fruit salad. He stopped behind Isla, rubbing her shoulders. 'I wish I'd known it was that simple to impress you.'

She sniffed. 'I mean, I'll still take the flowers and the cups of tea in bed, thank you very much. I was just making the point for *Penny*. Keep the big gestures coming.'

Joe laughed awkwardly, and I forcibly avoided Mum's eyes. Sunday was the day set for the biggest gesture he'd ever made, and every time I saw my brother he looked more nervous than the time before. He was usually quite jittery – a mixture of work stress, long hours, and enough caffeine to sink a ship to try and counteract those things – but this week he was even more on edge than usual. Only Joe could build an engagement up for over ten years and then feel nervous. Isla would say yes in her sleep. I would bet our entire projected revenue for Level on it.

'Any particular reason why we're talking about this?' Joe peeked at my phone.

'Penny is dating again,' Isla said, then explained the challenge to Joe.

'Are you now? And here, I thought you were destined to be the fun spinster aunty.'

Mum pointed her piping bag at me. 'I wouldn't rule that out.'

'I'm sat *right here*, guys.'

'She can still be the fun aunty. Just the fun aunty with wild dating stories from her youth.' Isla took the phone from me again. 'They can't *all* be write-offs. There are four men here just teeming with untapped potential.'

I stared at the list of remaining contenders. Jake, Sayanm, Isaac, and Nico. I wasn't holding out much hope.

'I bet Rory is loving this.' Isla exchanged a look with Joe.

After teasing me as much as the rest of them to begin with, Rory had actually massively backed off from the whole thing, not taking part in Dexter's daily banter. I said as much. 'I think he's scared I'll finally become the fun boss.'

Isla raised her eyebrows. 'Yeah. I'm sure that's it.'

'Any cake going spare, Mum?' Joe had clearly lost interest in our boy drama. 'And what the fuck are those?'

Mum sighed, passing him her tin of cake offcuts that she saved for whenever we visited. 'They're rabbits, Joe. Dead rabbits.'

He almost choked on the chunk of vanilla sponge he'd shoved in his mouth. 'I swear, this household gets more batshit every time I visit.'

5

As soon as Maeve's face appeared in the frosted glass, I could tell she'd clocked my expression.

'Oh no.' She pulled open Isla and Joe's front door to let me in. '*Another one?*'

Indeed. Another one. Another bad date. I just nodded, sighing as I threw down my bag next to their side table (a side table that I had knocked my hipbone against *many* a time).

'Not today, Satan.' I threw a finger up at the sideboard and made my way into the living room, where Isla was giving it her all on a dance mat.

'How bad was it?' She was breathless, not looking round and barely missing a beat.

'Well, she's speaking to the furniture' – Maeve ignored the look I gave her as she grabbed a third wine glass from the kitchen cupboard – 'so that should tell us everything we need to know, really.'

The closing beats of 'I Kissed a Girl' sounded, and Isla collapsed on the mat, huffing.

'New dance mat?' I gestured to where she was in a heap on the floor.

'Yes. A present from me to me.' She stretched forward, grabbing her wine and taking a glug. 'You don't date a doctor without learning the importance of "moving your body", and there is quite frankly no way that anyone is getting me to go on a run to improve my cardiovascular health. We went running together a few weeks ago and it was almost the end of our relationship. I don't know how you put up with him on your runs, Penny. I almost lobbed my water bottle at his head.' I tried not to laugh. 'So, I bought a dance mat on eBay instead. Was it really this hard when we were kids? I almost threw my back out during 'Everytime We Touch', but it's the energy Cascada deserves.'

Maeve had joined me where I'd slumped onto the couch. 'Definitely not, but she will test you like that.' She waved at me to go on. 'Well, what happened?'

I flopped my head back, staring at the ceiling. 'It wasn't quite as bad as the first one.'

Isla cheered. 'See! That's something.'

'Isla. Date one literally ditched before chipping in on the bill. I paid for an ugly man's steak. I'm not sure there *is* a bigger insult than that.'

It was true. Jake had been a complete and utter loser from the moment he sat down. And clearly not the sharpest tool in the box; *everyone* knew that 'my boiler is broken and I need to leave immediately' was an excuse. I was no hypocrite, and I stood by my principle that the bill should be split evenly down the middle. *Not* paid by one party. Especially if that party was me. He'd also clearly been threatened by the fact that I'd founded a company. Not hot.

'I'm pretty sure it could have been worse. Yes, you paid for his steak. But he could have been a serial killer.' Maeve rubbed my shoulder reassuringly, even though her words were anything but.

'Because *that's* the kind of talk that'll get her on another date.' Isla rolled her eyes.

Maeve was always on hand to scare us after she'd watched a new true crime documentary. Once, after she'd described one of them in detail at a girl's night, Isla had woken Joe up in the middle of the night to go to the toilet with her, scared that a madman would be waiting when she got there. My brother had banned Maeve from sharing her crime obsession with us after that.

'Yeah, thanks for that. The only thing worse than my date would have been getting slaughtered in the back of his car. Brilliant. I'll remember to tear out a few strands of my hair just in case next time.'

Isla was scrolling through the list of old-school pop songs on the TV, finding her next target. She kept flitting between Nelly Furtado and Anastacia. 'Have you ever thought that you might be manifesting bad energy on these dates?'

I blinked. 'No.'

She turned at that. 'Yeah, because you're *radiating* positivity right now.'

The only bad thing about having a pseudo big sister was having a pseudo big sister.

'Okay, so we'd already established that date one with Jake the Flake was a write-off.' Maeve brought the conversation back round. 'But what was bad about Sayanm?'

Sayanm. Match number four, and tonight's date. His chat had seemed relatively normal (*and* he'd been the one to start it, a rare win, I was learning) and it wasn't dry enough to make me want to slam my head against a wall. He was a basketball coach in his spare time, which made up for the fact that he was an accountant during the day. And when we'd unlocked our photos, his had been perfectly fine. Even if one of his photos had been with his Mum, which, in hindsight, set the tone.

I winced. 'Okay, so this time *I'm* the dick. But he was a bit of a . . .'

Isla nodded. 'A wet lettuce. It happens.'

Maeve snorted.

'He *told* me that he doesn't have much luck with "the ladies". Which is fine! Every "nice guy" says that. But then he let it slip that his Mum vets the profiles of his matches.'

Both of them winced in sync.

'It's always the men who handle balls who don't have any.' Isla topped up my wine. 'But the good news is that these stories are *character-building*.'

She was mocking Maeve's new favourite phrase. It turned out that she liked to give us the same kind of motivational language as she gave her 12–18-year-olds. Rory had suggested a swear jar to stop her from saying it, but I wasn't convinced it would work.

She threw a pillow at Isla. 'Don't be an idiot.' Pause. 'It *is* kind of character-building, if you think about it.'

I thought about the date – a bottle of wine in an old-fashioned pub. It had taken precisely twenty minutes for me to gather that cargo-short-wearing Sayanm, who had Star Wars fan art as his phone background (that he'd explained in great detail), was not going to make it to a second date. *And* he hadn't ordered the gherkin on his burger. Sacrilege.

'Oh yeah, people who don't get the pickle' – Isla shuddered – 'are the same kind of people who say toothpaste is spicy.'

'A definite ick.' Maeve stabbed an olive with a toothpick. 'Oh well, onwards and upwards.'

Between two bad first dates and two conversations that had been a waste of time, I wasn't sure I had it in me to pursue the final two matches on my profile. It was hard being Level's biggest cheerleader when it couldn't even come up with the goods for me. I hadn't even opened the final two profiles, scared that they would prompt an existential crisis about the app.

'I'm not sure I have the time to carry on.' I was fully in whinge mode, but I didn't care. 'I feel like I well and truly gave it a go. The work lot can shove it. Penny is not the problem here. The *men* are.' I finished my glass of wine. 'More please.'

Isla dutifully topped me up, abandoning the mat to come and sit on my other side to create an Isla-Penny-Maeve sandwich, squeezed on their second-hand sofa. 'You know, if dating was easy then everyone would be coupled up from the off. It just takes one to sweep you off your feet.'

I wrinkled my nose and Maeve intercepted. 'The day Pen gets swept off her feet, I will go naked to a hot yoga class.

We'll settle for someone who makes you laugh, as a starting point.'

'Yes, but how am I meant to know if I'm laughing because *they're* funny, or because *I'm* a hoot?'

Both of them rolled their eyes and fell back laughing.

'*See*?'

'Okay, okay, pass it here.' Maeve held her hand out for my phone. 'I'm going in. Match five, here we go.'

I passed it over. 'If you could also write out my "no thanks" text to Sayanm, I'd much appreciate it.'

She rolled her eyes. 'On it – I'm a master of the gentle let-down. Are you this hands-off at work? I'm surprised Rory puts up with it.'

Rory was out with Joe and some other lads tonight, trying an all-you-can-eat pizza place in the middle of Soho and probably psyching Joe up for the proposal. Everyone was in pre-party mode – the only one of us who was not aware that we'd all be drinking champagne at the pub on Sunday was the bride herself. Adrian had cancelled last minute because of some work stuff that he was needed for in Hull, and whilst Maeve hadn't made a big deal of it, I could tell she'd been in dire need of a girl's night.

'Obviously, I am not like this at work. Although this *is* starting to feel like a second job. Do you have any carbs lying around, Isla?'

'Didn't you just eat a burger? *With* pickles?' Isla was getting up, used to my appetite.

'I did, but that was a whole hour and a half ago. I need comfort carbs now.'

She pulled a bag of tortilla chips out of the cupboard along with some salsa and guac. 'I always do our regular food shop, and then an extra shop to satiate you and Ror. He came around the other day and polished off a whole *box* of eclairs.'

Maeve and I gasped at the same time.

Isla realised what she'd said. 'Okay but you *can't* tell Caroline. I didn't have time to wait in her queue! I told you, I need emergency rations at the ready with you two. You're like a Dyson!'

There were very few things Mum was strict on, but betraying Fondant & Flour was one of them.

'If you hotfoot it over here with those chips and dip, I might consider my silence bought.'

I shovelled a few stress mouthfuls in before Maeve interrupted, killing my appetite.

'Oh, look, Isaac messaged back in under a minute.'

'*Promising.*' Isla nodded.

'Do I really want a man who is glued to his phone?'

Isla shoved me. 'I've seen you playing Candy Crush when you don't think we're looking.'

All three of us leaned in to read the conversation.

```
Me: Hiya. How are you doing?
```

'Hiya?' I looked at Maeve, appalled. 'Really?'

She flipped me the finger.

```
Isaac: Hey. Weirdly enough, I was just
about to message you.
```

I didn't call bullshit out loud, just registered it internally. Maeve started typing.

Me: Not sure if I believe that, but I can work with it. So Isaac, what do you do?

I nudged Maeve. 'Fair play. You channelled your inner Penny.'
'This isn't my first rodeo. Ooh look, three dots already.'

Isaac: Chemistry teacher at a high school. I literally work in chemistry. How much of a catch does that make me?

I snorted involuntarily. *Not bad Isaac, not bad.*
'Okay, I think I can take it from here.' I snatched the phone back, not wanting Isla to jump in with a crude joke.
I saw them exchange a look behind my head.
'Just because I'm sending a message, it does not mean you can start planning my wedding.' I left out that in a matter of days, wedding planning would begin regardless. And it wouldn't be for me.

Me: I'll be the judge of that. If you talk about Bunsen burners the whole time, it might kill the spark.

Isla groaned. 'This girl is beyond help, Maeve. Want to see who can get the best score on 'Left Outside Alone'?'
She was already on her feet, heading towards the dance mat.

'You have no choice in the matter, my friend.' I patted Maeve's leg. 'Off you go, soldier.'

I watched them enter competitive mode, bending muscles I hadn't bent in years, each of them trying to tap their back foot quicker than the other.

'Watch me crush you like a grape, Maeve!' Isla was already panting.

I would *much* rather be watching the two of them than be sat opposite a guy who didn't even check if I wanted his gherkin. Double entendre *not* intended.

6

Maeve and I were sitting in front of Maeve's giant antique mirror (Rory had *not* taken too kindly to lugging it up three flights of stairs when we'd first moved in), passing palettes and compacts between us like we had back in uni. Some things had changed since we were 18 – we spent less time in dressing gowns, had long sworn off Lambrini and we'd finally invested in a garlic crusher – but most things felt exactly the same. We still ate dry toast straight from the toaster when we were hungover, and we were a well-oiled machine when it came to getting ready. I knew that *technically* you weren't meant to share make-up, but we'd been using each other's lipsticks for years and nothing drastic had happened. I grabbed my eyeliner from one of the make-up bags, checking my phone for what felt like the fiftieth time.

Maeve watched me out of the corner of her eye, mostly concentrating on twisting pieces of hair into tiny braids. 'I take it we haven't heard from the future Mrs Webber yet, then?'

I sighed, rooting for an eyelash curler. 'Nada.'

'Mae? How does this look?' Adrian's voice increased in volume as he wandered through the living room and into

Maeve's bedroom. He fanned his hand down the length of his body, showing off a crisp white shirt and chinos. I wasn't the only one in this household who turned to my best friend for fashion advice.

'Looks hot.' She gave him a thumbs up in the mirror.

'You didn't even look.'

She whipped her head round. 'I *did*. Grouchy much?'

I did the typical British thing and pretended I was not in the room. Adrian wasn't even supposed to be here; he'd made a last-minute decision to get a train and had arrived in a stinker of a mood after a diversion at Doncaster.

He perched on the end of her bed now, beer in hand. 'Fine. Forget it.'

Maeve shot me a look under the pretence of passing me her mascara. Long distance meant hours spent on trains, leaving both of them susceptible to strikes or delays and a long list of things out of their control that could threaten to ruin their precious time together.

'Anyway . . .' I took it upon myself to defuse the situation, wishing Ror was here to make a stupid joke. 'Crisp, anyone?'

I held out my share bag of Wotsits.

Adrian snorted and took an obnoxiously orange cheese puff from the bag. 'Any update from Joe?'

'Negative.' I leaned back on my palms. 'Maybe he's wussed out.'

My phone vibrated.

'Okay, if he asks, I didn't just say that.'

I opened up my phone to a text from Isla in the group chat.

You're looking at the future Mrs Webber!!

The text was accompanied by a photo of her and my brother, Isla's slender hand sporting the ring held up between them. I could see candles in the background, softened by the sharpness of both of their faces pressed up together, flushed and happy.

'Why do I feel like I might cry?' Maeve was squinting at her own phone. 'God, their living room looks like the world's biggest fire risk right now. One wrong move and we *won't* be celebrating tonight.'

I poked her. 'That's not very "think positive" of you, Dr Bellarby.'

Another text came through, this time from my brother just to me:

Joe: Success! Couldn't have done it without you – see you at the pub? There's a pint with your name on it.

I grinned as I typed my response. My brother was getting *married*.

***

'Wow, Caroline, you've really outdone yourself.' Maeve made a beeline for the buffet table as soon as we arrived, pouncing on Mum, who was still laying out baked goods. She'd been working overtime to produce doughnuts spelling out 'Just Engaged', each shaped like their individual letter. She'd also made oatmeal raisin cookies, Isla's favourite (the only downside of having her in the family, because what kind of psycho has raisins in their favourite cookie) and chocolate shortbreads, which were Joe's.

'All in a day's work.' She brushed her hands together, smacking Maeve on the bum when she tried to pinch a cookie. Maeve and Isla were on the same wavelength about oatmeal raisin. It was horrifying.

The pub looked fantastic; Mum and I had managed to string fairy lights around our designated section of the room, and we'd pinned up transparent balloons filled with pastel confetti.

'You guys have done such a good job she might ask you to plan the big day.' Maeve beckoned Adrian over from where he'd been hovering by the door, typing on his phone.

'Quick, Mum, make it look shit.' I was only half joking. I wasn't sure there was room for Wedding Planner on my CV.

We were among the first few here – Isla's sisters were at the bar with glasses of lime and soda, whispering to each other and gesturing at the décor. I rolled my eyes. I'd received a terse email from the elder of the two, telling me that they couldn't stay long due to babysitters, and had Joe not thought about proposing at lunchtime instead? I hadn't replied.

'Well, well, well.' I knew the Geordie accent like the back of my hand, feeling Rory's hands on my shoulders before I saw him. He swayed me from side to side. 'Everyone ready for the wedding of the decade?'

I looked up at him. 'You do know that this is the engagement party, right?'

He pouted as he started to walk away from me. 'But I brought my fascinator and everything.'

Adrian seemed to perk up at the sight of another guy, and they made their way to the bar, catching up.

'He has been in such a mood from the moment he arrived.' Maeve was chewing on her lip.

'A couple of beers and he'll be golden. Travelling's a bitch isn't it?' I nudged her. 'Speaking of – drink?'

She nodded, and we were about to follow the boys when I saw Dad walk into the pub. 'Be there in a sec, okay?'

'I'll get you a Corona. Say hi to Bill for me.'

I met him at the entrance, feeling the anxiety coming off him in waves.

'Hey kiddo.' He gave me a big one-armed squeeze. 'You look nice.'

I looked down at my lilac jumpsuit; a step outside of my comfort zone, encouraged by Ella on a random lunch break a few weeks ago.

'Thanks, Dad. How are you?'

I gave him a once-over and he raised an eyebrow. 'Eating three meals a day, promise.'

'Sorry, force of habit.' Regardless of who was to blame for the breakdown of their marriage, our dad was still our dad, and he'd suffered the most for it in the end. When we were kids, Joe had been a complete mummy's boy, but I'd followed my dad around like a shadow. That closeness had never dwindled, even during the worst of it when he'd stay in the office until after I'd gone to bed. Every morning when I woke up, there would be some kind of treat on my bedside table. A rubber shaped like a rainbow, or a packet of mini Jammie Dodgers. When I went to university, he sent me off with bags and bags of fusilli and Dolmio. I lived in fear that those things were all he ate nowadays too.

'Well, I promise. Made a ham and cheese omelette last night, food of the gods. Been painting the bathroom today. You'll have to come and see it. Joe, too.'

I didn't think Dad was ever going to get out of the mindset that Joe and I needed a specific reason to come see him. I'd explained a hundred times that wasn't how it worked.

'All right, Bill? Extra lime wedge in there, just how you like it.' Rory stepped up behind us, his own beer in one hand and a pint of Diet Coke in the other. Dad had gone sober a few years back, which had been a massive relief to both me and Joe.

'Thanks Rory.'

Rory nodded, and I felt a warm current of affection for him. The boy really did pay attention. 'Cheers to at least one of the Webbers rustling up a nice little nest.'

The affection cooled, and I smacked his arm. 'You're not funny.'

Rory hooked his arm around my neck and pulled me in, planting a quick kiss on my head. 'We can be nest-less birds together, Pen, don't you worry.'

'Not if the app works out for me.'

Rory cleared his throat. 'Ah yes, that.'

Dad clinked his glass against Rory's pint. 'You two are ridiculous. Where's your mum?' He craned his neck. 'Are they doughnuts over there?'

'They are.' I shot him a look. 'But if you eat one before Isla and Joe get here, I think she might go into cardiac arrest.'

He patted his chest, pretending to look wounded. 'What do you take me for?'

I gave him another look, remembering the arguments caused by biscuits consumed straight from the oven back when he lived with us.

'I swear on Cookie's life I won't steal any baked goods. Anyway, I'm going to go and say hello.'

Cookie was Dad's rescue beagle with a reputation for howling. He'd found a dog sitter for the evening. We both watched him head over to my mum.

'Oh, Bill.' Rory squeezed my arm. 'He looks good, Pen.'

'He does.' I nodded, watching him catch Mum's elbow and pull her in for an awkward hug. Over the years they'd learnt to be civil – well, Mum had learnt to lower her cold front – both of them realising that they were always going to be present in one another's lives. I knew it took a lot out of my dad, and he was one of the main reasons I couldn't stand the thought of dating; look what it could do to a person. He'd been career-driven in his youth, making plenty of money and climbing the ladder at the detriment of his marriage. Now he didn't even seem that interested in work, content to do the bare minimum during his nine to five and potter around his flat on the weekends doing DIY. I couldn't understand, and I didn't ever want to.

'One Corona.' Maeve appeared in front of me again, already halfway through hers. 'Ask and you shall receive.'

I took a swig, watching Rory as he mingled across the room, flirting with Isla's florist friends. 'Are you seeing this?'

He was leaning in and saying something to make them laugh, the two of them inching closer to him. Like he'd sensed me staring, he looked up at me and winked in a 'what can I say, they love me' kind of way.

'I am indeed. Our Rory, the undeniable flirt.'

Adrian had joined us and was watching too. 'And why not? He's single. Best part about it.'

I winced, watching Maeve's hackles immediately rise. 'What is *that* supposed to mean?'

Adrian shrugged. 'Nothing.'

Her expression had crumpled slightly, but she picked herself back up.

'Penny gets territorial over Ror.' She nudged me. 'Has done ever since we were in first year. He'd head out on first dates and she'd spend the whole evening speculating about how bad it might be going.'

'That's *not* true.'

Maeve blinked back at me.

'It's not!'

'I'm not caving in to your therapist eyes.' I looked at Adrian, who had one eyebrow raised. 'Either of you.'

Especially since what she was saying *wasn't* true. I wanted both of my best friends to find love, and I'd been friends with Lottie, Rory's ex. Maeve didn't know what she was on about. A cheer went up on the other side of the room. Isla and Joe had emerged through the double doors, both of them leaning into the excitement and beaming.

'Saved by the bell, ey?' Adrian nudged me as we all made our way in their direction, ready to celebrate.

I rolled my eyes, following the crowds to congratulate the happy couple.

7

'I honestly think she thought it was a prank at first.' Joe spoke around a mouthful of shortbread. 'Fuck, these are good.'

I wasn't sure Mum would appreciate his language, but I knew she'd appreciate the compliment. When we were tiny, she'd let us cut shapes into her traybakes, buying a mega box of cookie cutters and letting us go wild. Joe always ended up with an alphabet of biscuits (predictable and boring), but I'd mixed it up every time, bringing butterfly shortbreads to school in my lunchbox one week and aeroplanes the next.

'That's what you get for cling-filming your bedroom door.' My brother and his now fiancée were notorious for their ongoing prank war. We'd all been dragged into it on multiple occasions, Rory getting a flour-filled balloon to the head once when Isla thought it was Joe coming through the front door. He couldn't hear properly due to flour cloggage for a whole week.

'So, how did you convince her that it wasn't a decade-long prank?'

He smiled. 'I think the ring did it. After that it was just tears of joy. You may even say I nailed it.'

I rolled my eyes but I didn't doubt it. Isla had burst into tears at an RSPCA advert last week.

'Well, as much as our relationship is based on a mutual understanding that we can only be sarcastic to each other, I'm proud of you.' I held out my bottle for a clink. 'You're officially even less of a screw-up.'

'Who is less of a screw-up?' Rory excused himself from a conversation with Mum's friend Angela to tune into our conversation, swaying ever so slightly.

'Not you, that's for sure.' I stole the drink in his hand, replacing it with my empty one. 'Thanks.'

He pulled a face at me, pointing at Joe. 'And you, my friend, congrats. Everyone knows that wedding flowers cost a fortune, and you've picked just the fiancée to cut that cost.'

'*Does* everyone know that?' I quipped.

'Take a day off, Pen. Go text the latest lover boy of yours.'

Rory was just trying to hit a nerve, but he didn't know that I actually *did* have a text from Isaac waiting for me. Match number five. We'd only exchanged a few texts – I was notorious for opening messages and forgetting about them until I was nudged – but I didn't hate the conversation. I was saving his message for later, when I could give it my full attention. Rory was staring at me now, challenging me.

'Lover boy, was that what you said? Sorry, I couldn't hear you over the sound of me kicking your ass in this bet that I couldn't take on Level.'

Joe was watching us verbally joust. 'I thought tonight was supposed to be all about me.' He was joking, but it was enough for Rory to pull him into a conversation about stag do ideas.

Marriage had come up enough times in the pub for us to know that Joe and Isla wanted a 'sten' (a stag and hen do all in one). I imagined Rory drinking through a penis straw and wearing a pink cowgirl hat. It brought me great joy.

'Hiya, sis.' I'd barely had the chance to speak to Isla since they arrived, but she edged her way over to me now, cheeks flushed. She had the 'J' doughnut in her hand, a huge bite taken out of it and a tiny splodge of pink icing on her top lip.

'This is the best day ever.' She sighed. 'All that waiting was worth it.'

Joe paused his conversation with Rory, who took the opportunity to head to the bar. 'I heard that.'

She offered him some of the doughnut and he wiped the icing away from her lip. 'You were supposed to. I was almost a geriatric bride for a second there.'

Isla was only kidding; I had no idea why she was so loyal to my idiot brother, but she'd been in it for the long haul – engagement or not. I'd had to stop her many a time from describing to me in great detail how much she fancied him. That was where I crossed the line. I was already scarred from the knowledge that some of the nurses compared him to Mason Mount. England matches were ruined for me forever.

'So, do we have to prepare ourselves? Is your sweet Isla era over? I suspect you could be the bridezilla to end all bridezillas.'

She was wearing a glittery gold dress that shimmered with the force of her shaking her head. 'If I become a bridezilla, you have permission to cancel the wedding. We've had our fair share of hellish brides come into the florist, and I would rather walk down the aisle naked than be one of those.'

Joe rubbed his hands together. 'Sounds good to me.'

I coughed. 'Before I *vomit*, I'm going to find Maeve.' I took a quick look around. 'Anyone seen her?'

Isla shrugged. 'I think she went outside with Adrian.'

No doubt he was getting an earful after his performance tonight. I left them to it, mingling with the same florists Rory had been flirting with earlier. They were speculating about how Isla would plan a wedding, calling dibs on doing her bridal bouquet. I didn't have the heart to tell them that if I knew my soon-to-be sister, she'd handle all of it herself.

My phone started to ring, Rory's name popping up. I answered.

'Rory, your laziness has hit new heights. Are we not in the same room?'

He didn't immediately laugh like I'd expected. 'About that . . .' He sounded surprisingly sober. 'I'm about to get on the Tube. It's Maeve.'

There was a small wail from his end of the line.

'Wait, what? Where's Adrian?'

Another wail.

'Listen, I'm literally about to go underground, but do you think you can sneak away too? We've got a bit of an issue and you need to come home.'

I didn't think twice about ducking out of the pub; everyone was too tipsy to notice my absence, and Joe and Isla would understand if I sent a quick message. 'Okay, give me fifteen minutes. I'm coming.'

★★★

Over the years, we'd developed an unspoken rule when it came to emergencies. If we were able to drop everything, we would. We'd only had to use it on a handful of occasions – when Rory's dad had gone into hospital after a minor car accident in second year, and when Maeve had failed a really important exam – but there was a system in place for a reason. I'd barely inserted my key into the front door before it opened seemingly of its own accord.

'Shitting hell.' I pressed my hand to my chest.

Rory stood in front of me, massaging his temples like he was warding off the beginnings of a headache. 'Sorry. Thought for a second it might have been that dickhead.' He paused, his chest rising and falling dramatically. 'I was ready to give him a piece of my mind. He literally left her on the kerb outside the pub.'

I was beginning to piece together what might have happened. I followed him through to the living room, where Maeve was sitting on the sofa, knees tucked to her chest and panda eyes in full force.

'Hey Mae.' I dropped my bag on our rug and sat beside her, rubbing her back. 'What's going on?'

Maeve was not a wailer. She was usually more of a quiet weeper – very in touch with her emotions, and able to keep them under control. But now that she'd laid eyes on me, heavy sobs were (I presumed) starting all over again. 'He dumped me.'

It was jarring to have my suspicions confirmed. I exchanged a look with Rory – one that said 'what on earth is our plan of action?' before wrapping Maeve up in my arms. Rory joined us, his long arms easily bringing us both into the hug.

'We've got you.' I rubbed my best friend's back, feeling the weight of her sadness. 'We've got you, I promise.'

With Maeve in between us, I could communicate with Rory over the top of her head. She hiccupped against my chest.

'Why?' I mouthed it to Rory.

He shrugged. 'No idea.'

I tentatively pulled back to gather some more information, so that I knew what we were dealing with. I'd become an expert in other people's heartbreak over the years. Was this a small tiff that could be repaired overnight? Or a bigger rift that had been widening over time?

'Did he say why?'

Maeve rubbed her eyes. 'The distance. He said he's been thinking about it for a while, and the' – she took a moment to inhale a jagged breath – 'the engagement just reminded him how far away we were from that.'

I frowned – there was no solving long distance overnight. Not when both of them loved their jobs as much as they did. You couldn't close the gap between London and Hull with a click of your fingers. Adrian was supposed to be her *one*, as she'd phrased it in the past. And now he wasn't.

'I tried to reason with him, but there was no changing his mind.' The wails had subsided a bit now. 'It just feels so *sudden*.'

Neither of us knew what to say. Heartbreak was just so colossally, completely *shit*.

'You know, maybe this is for the best.' Rory pulled her into his side, giving her a big squeeze. 'Long distance has been stressing you both out for a long time. Not able to live fully in either place.'

She recoiled. '*I* didn't mind that.'

Maeve was blinded by sadness right now, but I knew that wasn't true. Every other Friday after work she'd had to trek to King's Cross with her suitcase, and come back on Sunday evening never feeling rested enough to start the new week. She'd struggled to bond with his friends as she was never involved in the inside jokes, and it had got to a point – like today – where both of them often arrived tired and cranky. Sometimes, all the will in the world didn't seem like enough. I went to the fridge and got a bottle of cheap chardonnay. She took the glass I offered her and downed it.

'Let's just take this one day at a time, okay?' I poured some for myself, and Rory headed to the fridge to grab a beer. Wine gave him the worst hangovers. 'All we have to do right now is get through tonight.'

Maeve nodded. 'I can do that.'

I pulled our fluffy throw over the three of us, grabbing the TV remote so that we could find the most distracting, psychologically disturbing show from Maeve's watch list.

'And you know,' Rory said, squeezing her hand, 'this is going to be *character-building*.'

She snorted. 'You absolute prick.'

I grabbed her other hand, squeezing it just as tight. This situation was almost enough to stop me ever texting match five back. Heartbreak was *not* high on my personal to-do list.

8

I closed the door lightly, holding my breath and trying not to wake my sleeping best friend. Maeve had tossed and turned all night; it was a good thing I slept like a log. It was one of the reasons I'd wanted to live with a flatmate instead of living alone; I was screwed if a fire alarm went off in the early hours. Well, that – and being able to share the Deliveroo order fee was a godsend.

'Boo.'

I jumped out of my skin. 'That's the second time you've skyrocketed my blood pressure in less than twelve hours.'

Rory was sitting at the kitchen island, already suited and booted and drinking a cup of coffee. I stared pointedly at the mug he was holding – my favourite mug from Oliver Bonas with the intentionally wonky handle and the tiny yellow stars on it, to be exact. Last time I'd had a favourite mug – a decade-old, faded one that had come free with a Mini Eggs Easter egg when I was a teenager – he'd managed to chip it during a vicious game of Monopoly. I eyed him suspiciously.

'Just so you know, that mug cost over ten British pounds.'

He looked at it. 'Really? It looks like my niece made it. Yours is ready too' – he pointed to a second mug – 'and we need to leave in ten minutes.'

'Thanks.' I went over and started adding a shit ton of sugar. 'I wonder if the matches between the eyelids trick actually works.'

'Long night?' Rory winced as I added a third teaspoon of sugar.

'Well, I doubt if she – or I – got more than three hours.'

He'd slept in my bed whilst I'd shared with Maeve. It wasn't unusual for Rory to spend the night; he had an emergency stash of deodorant and boxers at the back of my wardrobe. It *was* unusual for him to get the whole bed rather than the couch, and I'd silently cursed him at 3 a.m. when I was wide awake under Maeve's gingham duvet.

'Ouch. I could kill Adrian, I really could.'

'I think probably not the best course of action. You're too pretty for prison, Ror.' I dashed back into my own room now, eyes zeroing in on the work outfit I'd had the foresight to pick out yesterday before the engagement party. I brushed my hair back into a hair claw, twisting the strands so it looked like an intentional style rather than overdue a hair wash. A slick of eyebrow gel and a brush of mascara later and I looked semi-presentable. When I got back to the kitchen, Rory was busy doodling on a Post-it note.

'What's that?'

He looked up. 'Just a little "you've got this" note for Maeve.'

I followed him to the coffee machine, where he was sticking it. Surely enough, it was a note of encouragement, complete with a tiny illustration of Maeve as a superhero, cape and everything.

'Bet you wish you'd taken GCSE Art like me.'

I touched the tiny doodle cape, smiling. 'Sometimes you do surprise me.'

'I'm the gift that keeps on giving.'

We heard Maeve stirring in her bedroom.

'Murder plans aside, I have literally no fucking clue where this has come from.' He kept his voice down. 'Have you heard from him since?'

I shook my head, although I'd been so wrapped up in Maeve's crisis that I hadn't even charged my phone last night. So much for replying to Isaac. He'd probably moved on to another match. I plugged my phone in now, ready to fire off some apology texts to Isla and Joe.

'I did think he seemed on edge last night,' Rory was still musing, 'but I assumed it was the train journey.'

I took another big swig of coffee before packing my bag. 'I think that was the final straw.'

'Doncaster train station has a lot to answer for. Right, you ready?' Rory started towards the door.

'As I'll ever be for a finance meeting.' I downed the rest of my caffeine, grabbing my phone on the way. I had one text from Dad, checking I'd got home okay, and some drunken messages from Isla and Joe in the group chat. Nothing from Isaac, which was unsurprising since it was my turn. I quickly responded to him, knowing that I wouldn't get another chance until this evening. We were having a conversation about food markets in London. I was team Spitalfields all the way, obsessed with the viral crumble stall where you could get *all* crumble, no fruit. He had declared himself more of a Borough guy, prepared to stand in an hour-long queue for mushroom risotto. I could work with that. Within seconds of my response, I had a notification from Level.

Congratulations! Next level with Isaac unlocked.

Shit. This was big.

'Penny Webber, don't make me get the DLR without you.'

'Sorry, sorry.' I raced after Rory, loading up Isaac's profile so that by the time we stepped onto the Tube, I could immediately start scanning his photos. Not that I was shallow. I wasn't. But there was no denying that it mattered, at least a little bit.

'What are you doing?' Rory leaned in so close that I could smell the coffee on his breath. 'Are you on Level?'

I pushed him away gently, too engrossed in Isaac's photos to start debating my dating life. Up until now, I'd known more about what his Labrador looked like than what *he* looked like (sleek black coat, a bit on the tubby side, a childhood pet who was finally slowing down in her older years). Now, I could see him in all his glory. He had five photos uploaded to his profile: one that someone had taken across from him at a restaurant (I squinted – it looked like pie and mash, five bonus points); one with what I presumed was a best friend, looking flushed and happy; one with him and the Labrador; another one with friends; and then one in front of a Christmas tree, elf hat and all. It was a good selection of photos that said sociable but dependable, interesting but not wild. He was averagely built, with a hint of muscle and short brown hair. In two of the pictures he was wearing reading glasses.

'Looks like a catch.' Rory was still staring at my screen. 'Even if he does wear an elf hat pretty badly.'

I stared up at him; when we were standing side by side on the Tube, he towered over me. 'Don't be bitter because you thought I wouldn't see the challenge through.'

Rory scoffed. 'That isn't the reason.'

Aha. I started to say: 'Oh, so you admit it, then?' before the buzzing of my phone pulled me out of the conversation.

```
Isaac: At last, the mystery is over.
```

'So predictable.' Rory pressed the button for the doors to open at Bank. 'I wonder how many times he's used that one?'

I ignored him, smiling at my screen against my better judgement.

***

Despite the flurry of downloads when we'd launched, Level wasn't yet in the same realm of popularity as some of the other dating apps on the market. Loyalty took time, and we were still very much in our fledgling phase. When we'd been in the very initial stages of the app – and by that, I mean sitting on Rory's bed with an A4 refill pad – money had felt like Monopoly cash. Nothing felt real yet. Years later, when we felt our pitch was spot on, we'd presented at a crowdfunder and gathered enough interest to get things off the ground. Now we had to prove we were worth every investor's time. In Harriet's experience, partnerships with other start-ups were an effective profile-builder, and we were also conscious of any new investment: brands who had spotted our launch and wanted in on the action. Between the core team (Ella, Harriet, and Andrew – our accountant) we had biweekly meetings to make sure we'd never go bankrupt. And luckily for us, the team understood that as much as we liked owning a business, Rory and I had always had a passion for the programming.

'Okay.' Harriet held up her iPad, scrolling through a press release. 'I think this new app, GetThere, is one you guys are going to feel passionately about.'

I'd looked over this one in the email she'd circulated ahead of the meeting: an up-and-coming app that compiled all the available transport in a certain area, so that anyone travelling home at night (or any time of day) could make it there safely. They'd started testing it out here in London to make sure every Tube, overground and bus route was accounted for, looping in taxi companies for the final leg. Once they'd cracked London, their plan was to widen the coverage to include the whole country.

'There hasn't been a lot of press coverage so far, since they haven't even officially launched yet, but what there *has* been is overwhelmingly positive.' Harriet pulled up the logo, a little lilac bus. 'I think our users would benefit from this.'

I could tell from the look on Rory's face that we were on the same page.

He went first. 'I'm in. I think it's a great idea.'

'Ella?' Harriet panned around the table.

Ella, who had been tapping her pen against her chin, nodded. 'I think the ethics of the app align with ours, and the work we've been doing to verify each user that downloads Level. A safe night out is a good night out.'

She was referring to the extra level of protection we'd added to the coding a couple of months ago: a verification process upon sign-up, requiring you to take a live photo. The app then used facial recognition technology to verify that you were the same person as in your uploaded photos. It was one of the hardest parts of the app to nail down but had been a non-negotiable for both me and Rory. Nothing was worse – or more potentially dangerous – than a catfish.

I threw my hat in the ring. 'I like it. I'd use it, and I'd recommend it to my friends. People need to feel that they can safely make their way home from a first date.'

Andrew, who very rarely spoke up unless it was absolutely necessary, interrupted. 'I think it's a wise decision. Start-ups banding together to promote safety might draw in some new investment.'

'Okay, it's unanimous. We'll reach out to them. And now,' Ella moved onto the next point on the agenda, 'for the weirdest offer of the week.'

On the agenda we'd received yesterday, this item had been extremely vague, simply titled 'Discuss New Opportunity'. When a point on a meeting agenda lacked detail, it usually meant that either Rory or I wouldn't be the biggest fan.

'I'm on the edge of my seat.' Rory shuffled forward to emphasise his point. 'Which one of us was the reason that this was the vaguest agenda point in history?'

Ella coughed. 'We've had some contact from the team at Link.'

We didn't even have to look at each other to speak in sync. 'NO.'

'Whatever it is' – I looked to Rory for backup – 'solid no.'

'That's what I thought.' Ella chuckled. 'Worth a shot. They were very keen to discuss a small investment in the company.'

'That makes literally no sense.' Rory sat back in his seat.

Link was the most popular dating app in the UK, as deter-mined by their number of downloads (*not* by number of five-star reviews). It was also the app that had kick-started our research into creating an alternative, and was our biggest competitor. It made no sense for them to want to invest.

'Press-wise, I'd be worried about what it might say about our integrity.' Harriet said, wincing slightly.

'Okay, so a resounding no to that one.' Ella exchanged a look with Andrew. It must have been a considerable amount of money that they were willing to offer. Tough shit. I'd rather our company collapse than accept help from them. 'That's the last point on the list. I'll make contact with GetThere, let them know that at the very least we'd love to meet the team.'

'Make sure you tell Link to kiss my ass too.' Rory stood up. 'You coming, Pen?'

I stood up, saying bye to everyone and following him out of the room. 'You do know what a professional meeting is, right?'

He grinned. 'I've seen Ella and Harriet sink enough pints in the pub to know that they won't be offended. And Andrew will be too focused on the money we might have just lost to care if I swore at the end of the meeting.'

'True.' I rolled my neck, the tiredness catching up with me as we made a beeline for the coffee machine. 'That was weird, right?'

Rory pressed the button for a black coffee. 'Weird, but irrelevant. We know where we stand.'

We watched the coffee drip from the machine in silence for a few seconds.

'Any news on finding Prince Charming?' Dexter came up behind us, clasping his hands to his chest. 'We placed bets that you'd have given up by now.'

I shot him the finger, his jabs momentarily distracting me.

'Any news on that code we asked you to fix last week?' Rory was joking, but it was clearly a shutdown.

Dexter rolled his eyes and went back to his desk, calling out behind him. 'Remember when you were the fun one?'

Rory passed me a coffee, pulling his phone from his back pocket. 'I'm going to ring Maeve. See you later?'

He must have caught my expression because he stopped in his tracks. 'Don't worry about it, Pen. It was probably a spur of the moment offer from a team that only knows how to design an app badly.' Rory touched my elbow lightly. 'Forget about it.'

But Level was our whole world, and it *was* weird that Link had wanted a piece of it. I didn't stop thinking about it for the rest of the day.

9

I climbed the steps out of the Tube station at London Bridge, narrowly avoiding an elbow. The culprit didn't even pause, just continued shoving her way up. I refused to believe anyone was in that much of a rush, and I was a Londoner born and bred. Maeve answered on the first ring.

'Penny, I literally spoke to you half an hour ago.'

It was good that she sounded exasperated; that felt like progress. If she was getting annoyed by us all checking in, she was feeling better. She'd given herself a talking to last night after a solid week of moping; watching a psychologist psychoanalyse themselves had been weird the first time she'd ever done it, but I was used to it now. You just had to leave her to it, safe in the knowledge that the advice she'd give herself was miles better than what you could realistically offer.

'It was actually thirty-five minutes ago' – I got my bearings, momentarily distracted by the homemade pasta in the window of Padella – 'and I will not apologise for being a helicopter parent. Are you *sure* that you're okay about this?'

A heavy sigh from the other end of the line. 'Sure about my best friend going on a first date she's excited about? Yes, I'm quite sure.'

Excited was a strong word, but I didn't correct her.

'Plus, Isla is *right here*.'

There was a shuffle on the other end of the line, and then Isla chimed in. 'Right here indeed. Armed with a box set of *The O.C.* and *all* the bags of Cadbury-related joy that Tesco Express had to offer. Go have fun.'

I pictured the two of them wallowing in the post-breakup chocolate haze and almost jumped back on the Tube.

'And no,' Maeve said, reading my mind, 'you aren't invited to our pity party. I will quite literally barricade the door.'

Rude. I said my goodbyes and hung up, pulling up Citymapper to try and find the pub that Isaac had suggested. I was an East London girl – I still needed a map from time to time. The pub was small and cute enough for a date, and I settled into a faded leather booth at the back, favouring the privacy. I'd spied on and judged enough first dates in restaurants to know that as soon as the general public got a whiff of awkward icebreakers, they would listen in for the rest of the evening. I took a quick look in my phone camera, tilting my chin to double check for any embarrassing bronzer smudges or bits in my teeth. Would he recognise me from the app? Both of my previous first dates had – that was quite frankly the only success; everything that followed had been downhill from there – but there was always the risk that your set of photos was a bit *too* far from your day-to-day look. Maeve had perked up at the opportunity to get me dressed up for a night out, which I'd decided to let her take control of. She'd chosen a red pleather skirt and black bodysuit combo, with gold hoops, hair up, and a pair of black, heeled ankle boots. I was hoping the finished product said 'fun and flirty, but not up for being pissed about'. Maeve had assured me that it did, but she'd say anything to get me to abandon my neutrals.

'Penny?'

I looked up, halfway through re-reading the wine list. Isaac was standing over me, leaning on the table and rocking on his heels, waiting for confirmation.

'That's me.'

His profile did not do him justice.

Trying to forget that I was absolutely shitting it, I jumped up to hug him. The embrace itself was a solid 8/10 (the man was built, but not so built that it felt like meeting a concrete wall), but things went south when I pulled away. I felt the abrupt tug as my earring caught on the threading of his jumper, leaving us stuck together. I tugged a little bit further, but it only left us more stuck. *Could the ground actually swallow people up?* I prayed.

'Excellent start.' Isaac looked at me sideways, his eyeballs straining to make contact in our predicament. 'Interesting tactic to ensure that I didn't take one look at you and leave.'

I snorted. 'Right back at you. These threads are *suspiciously* loose.'

He laughed, gingerly trying to extricate my earring. 'There goes the entire date. Is there an ick kicking in?'

It was hard not to laugh. Isaac sat somewhere between confident and self-conscious, a good balance of the two. 'You're on thin ice, but I reckon you've got another chance left in you.'

'Aha!' He pulled himself gently away from my ear. 'Fixed it, with not only the jumper and the earring intact, but also my chances. What'll you be drinking?'

His accent was strong and he was so clearly a Mancunian. He was wearing his glasses; damn it, I was a sucker for glasses.

'Rosé please. With lemonade,' I requested quickly before he had the chance to call me out, smirking at his menu instead.

I was a historic lightweight, and although drunken dates could be fun, I had no interest in making myself look any more of a fool than I had done in the last two minutes.

Whilst he was at the bar, I texted Maeve quickly to report that he didn't seem like a murderer – our six-year-long rule for when the other one went on dates. Granted, I hadn't used it in a while. She texted back immediately.

Maeve: Excellent news. Now leave me to my Seth Cohen and have fun.

'They asked if you wanted ice. I went for it.' Two glasses were plonked down in front of me, one full to the brim with several cubes of ice.

'A risk-taker, I like it.' I fished a few out, adding them to my wine.

'So, Penny.' He leaned forward, elbows on the table. 'I have to say, it's really good to meet you after all the intrigue.'

I fought the urge to ask him whether a voice note feature would have stepped up the mystery. This wasn't work.

'Am I worth the wait?'

He held up his pint for a cheers. 'Very much so.'

We settled into comfortable conversation, building on the snippets we'd exchanged over the past week. It had never come naturally to me to be an open book, but I was resisting less than usual, which was a start. I told him about Joe and Isla's engagement, and the ridiculous sten do that I assumed Rory would pitch for.

'The first thing I said to my mate, when I saw your photos, was that you looked like you had a close-knit group of friends.'

I smiled at the visual of him with his friends, poring over my photo of the six of us in Madrid last year, drunk on sunshine and sangria. It was one of my favourites ever.

'Yeah, they're the best. You know when spending time with people doesn't drain your battery at all? So you fully assessed my photos, then. What did you get from the rest of them?' I sipped my drink, well aware that I was fishing for a compliment. I really did need to know if the photo of me asleep on the beach was on the wrong side of funny. Isla was adamant that it was.

'Your photos are great, but to be honest I was hooked before that. As soon as we started talking, I abandoned my other matches.' He shrugged. 'That's probably very uncool of me to say.'

I didn't think it would go down well to admit that he was the fifth of my matches that I'd pursued, so I told a white lie.

'Not uncool at all. I was the same. I don't have time to be messaging six people at once. When would I eat, or sleep?'

This part, at least, was true. I wasn't in the market for another full-time job.

Isaac grinned, emboldened by my response. 'You're actually the first person I've met from Level. I downloaded it as a bit of a joke, to be honest.'

Did this stray into the immoral side of dishonesty? As far as Isaac knew, I worked in computer programming. But he had no clue it was for the very app that we were discussing. Oh, and that actually my best friend and I built it.

'How so?' I bit my lip and decided to crawl further into my web, considering this flow of conversation a valuable nugget of market research. Rory would have done the same thing — a benchmark with which I judged a lot of my decisions.

'Well, there's a new app every week at this point. One of my mates sent me the link, and I was a bit put off at first. Stripping back the dating experience seemed so old-fashioned, like something my parents would have done. But it was nice. In this weird digital age it kind of felt more real.'

I fought the urge to ask him to slow down, so I could type this on my phone notes. Would it be going too far to use it as an official product review?

'I imagine that was the aim.' Now that I was in the web, I might as well stretch my eight dishonest legs a bit. 'How much can you actually know about your compatibility with someone based on a photo of them pouting in a mirror?'

Isaac snorted. 'You're not wrong. I'd never thought about it that way, but you're right. What made you download it?'

I hesitated, before scampering full-force down the path of deception.

'Oh, same sort of thing as you. My friends dared me to download it, really.' *Technically* true, if by friends I meant colleagues. And by download it, I meant finally use it. It had been downloaded on my phone the second it went live on the app store.

'Classic.' Isaac nodded, accepting the lie without a second thought. 'Another drink?'

I glanced down at my empty glass, surprised. Time was flying by; I'd expected to stay an hour, two at most, and then to head back to the flat, ready to collapse onto the sofa and settle into an easy evening with the girls. Instead, I found myself wanting to stay. There'd been no misogynistic comments or offensive stereotypes. No calling his ex-girlfriends psycho, being rude to the bartenders, or saying that he didn't believe in tipping. It was going suspiciously smoothly. Maybe Level *did* actually work.

★★★

It took about ten seconds from me walking through the door for them both to pounce. Isla was wearing silk pyjamas, her hair in dressing gown curls. I took that as confirmation that she was staying the night; she had been known to go home in her 'comfies', but this was pushing it.

'*So?*' She linked her elbow through mine, leading me into the living room where I could see evidence of a very successful pity party.

I pinched the last chocolate button before glancing briefly at Maeve, who narrowed her eyes. 'You'd better not be considering downplaying any happiness because of me.'

Maeve had given both of us – particularly Isla, with her post-engagement glow – a strict talking to about hiding our joy. Apparently, it wasn't healthy for us to push it down, or for Maeve to live in a world where no one talked about it. She'd forced Isla to tell her everything she'd missed from the latter half of the engagement party. Maeve was staring at me now, daring me to hide anything from her.

'Okay then, yes, I think I had a good time.'

Isla pulled back to look at me. 'You *think*?'

I thought back to how quickly the evening had passed, and how he'd pulled me in for a hug at the end of the evening. He smelt like mint and fresh air (which was *rare* in this city).

'Fine, *I know* I had a good time.'

Both of them squealed in harmony.

10

Sometimes, even when you've known people for so long that you thought they couldn't possibly do anything to surprise you, people do things that surprise you.

'Are you *sure* this is what you want?' Mum was historically a very easy-going woman when it came to how we wanted to live our lives, particularly in her post-divorce, open a bakery era. But right now, she was not hiding her expression well. An expression — slightly wrinkled nose, skin a bit pale — that said, 'I don't think this is what you should want'.

Isla paused, midway through a monologue about risotto versus ravioli.

'What? Ravioli?' She fixed us with a stare. 'No, I'm not sure. That's the whole point of this conversation.'

I saw Mum shoot Joe a look. He was cramming the end piece of a garlic baguette into his mouth, refusing to meet her eyes. Dinner at Mum's house was a biweekly tradition, one that had started as soon as we were all in London again. Joe's shifts at the hospital meant that sometimes you didn't see him for days at a time; having a date in the diary ensured you'd stay on his radar. It was the only item in my calendar that I treated as sacred. Plenty of other plans I sacked off for a late night in the office, but this was immovable. Only in exceptional circumstances.

Isla continued to stare at Mum, finally clocking. 'You mean the whole *wedding*?' There was an awkward pause. 'I haven't just said this on a whim, Caroline.'

Under the table, Joe gave me a gentle kick. I knew what it meant.

'I think what Mum is trying to say,' I said, pushing lasagne around my plate, 'and I'm not trying to bring the vibe down here, but is it logistically possible to plan a wedding in two months?'

This was the bombshell that Isla – mainly Isla – and Joe had dropped on us over slow-cooker lasagne. They wanted to get married in June. *This* June. Which meant that we were only two months away.

Joe finally looked up from shovelling food into his mouth. The man ate like every meal was his last. 'Isla's done her research. Ow.' He shot her a look. 'We've both done our research.'

'Obviously it won't be a fairy tale wedding' – Isla was on her phone, pulling up pictures of rustic table settings – 'but that's not what I want. I don't care about all of that stuff, I just want everyone I love to be there, and I just want to be married to Joe. God knows I've had long enough to think about this.'

It was the right comment to throw into the equation, because Mum's expression softened.

'That's a really nice idea, honey. If it's what you want, then give us a list and we'll crack on with it. I've been thinking about your wedding cake for over a decade.'

I spoke through a mouthful of cheesy goodness, earning me a scathing look from her. 'Didn't you have a Pinterest board for your wedding?' I had vivid memories of Isla pinning photos of dresses and veils when we were teenagers.

'I did . . .'

Another thought came to me, and I butted in to ask the question that Rory would have done, had he been here. 'Is this a roundabout way of telling me I'm going to be an aunty?'

My brother coughed, choking on some garlic bread. 'No, that's definitely not it.'

Isla was looking put out. Which was hard to do, because she had that eternal-sunshine energy. It was like kicking a puppy.

'Sorry, sorry. Cynicism not welcome. I think it's a great idea.' I dug deep for some romantic optimism. 'You've been together since the dawn of time, it's not like anyone needs to get used to the idea of you as husband and wife. Mum's right. Tell us what you need us to do, and we'll do it.'

From across the table, my brother mouthed 'thank you'.

'I really appreciate that.' Isla was beaming again. 'I knew we'd be able to convince you both. After all, you're our family.'

It spoke volumes that Isla saw her fiancé's mother as someone she needed to convince, rather than her own. 'I'm thinking twenty-eighth of June, which *will* be a time crunch, but I've been making some calls. This gorgeous venue in Hackney has a cancellation on that day.'

She looked way too ecstatic about this, given that a cancelled wedding could never mean anything good for the original party. I said as much.

'They mentioned something about cold feet . . .' Isla remembered herself. 'Which is obviously *very sad*, but some things are meant to be. Like us, on the twenty-eighth of June. I've found this pair of second-hand wedding shoes on Vinted that I just love, and I've been watching YouTube videos on how to make your own bunting.'

I listened to her chatter about invitations and confetti for a minute, watching how animated her facial expressions became when she spoke about being tied to my idiot brother forever. To me, the idea of sharing your life with someone was terrifying. I *loved* having my bed to myself, and not having to wait for someone else to wake up in the morning. Getting the ultimate decision on every takeaway, and jamming all of my free time with efforts to see my friends. But Isla and Joe made a shared life seem like the most exciting thing in the world.

'I know you think ragu might be the more universally appreciated decision, but my heart says it's overdone.'

They were back onto the main course dilemma. One of her friends' husbands had offered his catering company at a mates' rate, and the menu was clearly playing on Isla's mind. Ragu ravioli or saffron risotto. Joe was firmly team ravioli, on the basis that saffron was a risky ingredient, but I wouldn't have been surprised if she sent an email to all of us with an anonymous voting system. Isla loved things to be fair.

'I don't think we need to take the entire universe into consideration,' I chipped in, speaking around another mouthful of pasta.

'And *you*,' Isla said, smiling at me, 'I have another question to ask.'

She pulled out a small gossamer bag from her pocket, barely managing to contain her excitement. Joe was smirking into his bowl. 'The wild Penny is a skittish creature, likely to run a mile at any mention of the word marriage. So now we see her outside of her natural habitat . . .'

He was doing his impressively realistic Attenborough impression.

Isla thumped him. 'Stop! It's a special moment. Here you go, Pen.'

I put down my fork, opening the bag to reveal a tiny vintage locket. I'd always loved hunting down antique jewellery; the older and more previously loved the better. The obsession had started with a gorgeous emerald that I'd inherited from my maternal grandmother and wore around my neck without fail every day, and from there it had only grown. My jewellery stand was full of hidden gems I'd picked up over the years, a fact which Isla knew from the number of times I'd dragged her with me. This locket was a worn oval made of silver, and I ran my fingers over the mottled metal.

'This is gorgeous.'

Isla clapped her hands together. 'Read the back.'

I did as she asked, turning it over and reading the intricately engraved letters. It read 'Maid of Honour?' and the photo inside was a tiny one of us both on New Year's Eve five years ago, sparklers in hand. I'd been home from Edinburgh for the week spanning Christmas to New Year, and Isla had spent the entirety of it with us. I'd been heading back to university a couple of days later, so we'd made the most of the evening, the three of us staying up in the garden with a bottle of red wine until way past midnight. I knew that, technically, my loyalties always had to lie with Joe, but I loved Isla (even her morning affirmations and the way she put chia seeds in everything).

'Are you serious?' When she nodded, I sniffed. 'I would love to.'

Joe was smirking. 'Is that *raw emotion* I'm seeing?'

I flipped him the finger.

'Before you decide to flip me off again, guess which groomsman you'll be paired with?'

Joe had been one of those annoying people that had *never* been short of friends, at any stage of his life. But no one had ever clicked quite like him and Rory, who was one year older than me, placing him square in the middle of two siblings. I squealed.

'Whatever you do, don't let him give a speech. You know what free champagne does to that man.'

Joe grinned. 'I do, and that's why he'll be firmly instructed to not start drinking until *after* his best man speech.'

I clapped my hands together. 'Oh shit, *really*?'

This was going to be so much fun. Rory and I lived for a project to co-organise, and we'd been itching for something new now that Level was out in the world.

'Obviously. Everyone knows the best man and the maid of honour walk together.'

Isla's smile was wide, her food forgotten. 'We couldn't think of two better people to do it.'

I held back from texting Rory in the middle of dinner. 'Have you asked him yet?'

'Not yet.' She poured herself some water. 'And obviously, you'll be allowed a plus-one. I didn't want to be too hasty and put Isaac down on the list.'

This was the problem with hanging out with die-hard romantics. I'd been on one date with the man. Well, two, if you counted tomorrow morning. We were having a Saturday morning walk along the Southbank, with a stop off in Borough Market for doughnuts and coffee (he didn't know that yet, but I was not the kind of girl who left date planning to a man). It was highly unlikely he'd be my plus-one at the wedding.

'Give the invite to someone else. I won't need it.'

Isla gave me a warning look. 'What have we said about being pessimistic? I'm going to grass you up to Maeve.'

'*No.*' I'd reached my limit when it came to lectures about love, intimacy, and 'opening ourselves up'.

Joe shrugged. 'Well, you and Rory both have the choice to bring someone. He might actually need it. What's the name of that girl he started seeing?'

He looked at me for confirmation, but my face couldn't have been anything but blank. *The girl he'd started seeing?*

'It begins with an M . . . Maisy, it's Maisy.'

This was complete news to me. I racked my brain for any memory of Rory mentioning a first date. There definitely hadn't been a late-night debrief over chocolate chip cookies.

'He hasn't mentioned her.' *Weird.* 'In fact, he distinctly said he wasn't "in the mood" to date.'

They exchanged a look.

'Oh. Weird. Anyway, I'm making the call.' Isla moved swiftly on, and was scratching something down on the page.

'Saffron is too risky, Joe, you're right. I'm going with the ravioli.'

Joe was still tackling the rest of the lasagne in the middle of the dinner table, tearing off another piece of bread. 'See? Told you. How about garlic bread?'

Mum stared him down. 'I didn't raise a man as intelligent as you to not think through the risks of serving garlic bread to an entire wedding congregation.'

I laughed along with them, trying to hide the hurt I felt at not being in on a clearly well-circulated secret.

11

There were many things I'd decided I would *not* do during my lifetime. At the top of the list was skydiving (voluntarily plummeting to your death) and eating oysters (why eat something that looks like phlegm when you could eat pizza instead). Somewhere on that – admittedly, long – list, was yoga in a park. I had the flexibility of a number two pencil. And yet . . .

'We're going to start off today's session with some gentle flow and internal clarification of our intentions.' The instructor, a perky young woman who I would have put somewhere between 20 and 25, raised her arms slowly above her head. 'Fingertips to the sky, everyone, and gently push up onto your toes. Inhale slowly, and exhale as we bring our feet solidly back down to earth.'

Someone, somewhere, was laughing at me. And it could very well have been the teenage boys standing thirty feet away, camera phones at the ready.

'You don't look very relaxed.' Maeve spoke through the side of her mouth, her eyes barely open and her face slack with blissful, relaxed energy.

'That's because I'm not,' I hissed back. 'I'm pretty sure that we're about to become a meme. The laughingstock of every year eight classroom.'

My best friend didn't even bat an eyelid, bringing her feet 'back down to earth'. 'Life begins when you don't care what people think, Pen.'

Yeah. Right. I closed my eyes and focused on the instructor, who was now telling us to stretch (sorry, *sweep*) our arms diagonally over our heads. It was incredible really, having lived with Maeve almost consistently since I was 18, that I'd managed to last this long without being roped in to yoga of any kind. But despite gradual progress on the heartbreak front, I'd heard sniffing coming from Maeve's bedroom this morning when I'd gone to the kitchen to grab a cup of tea. Heartbreak was not linear. And Adrian had returned some of her belongings to her, courtesy of Royal Mail. No one wanted to receive a selection of thongs, an electric toothbrush, and the latest Richard Osman in a surprise package. Which was how we'd ended up here.

'You know' – Maeve opened one eye as she stretched – 'I think this might be the nicest thing you've ever done for me.'

'Even nicer than the time I caught the pigeon?'

She snorted, and then poked me in the ribs when we received an irritated glance from the woman in front of us.

'I've never been told off during yoga in my *life*.' Maeve narrowed her eyes. 'This is your influence. But yes, even nicer than the pigeon.'

Our first houseshare in Edinburgh had been a complete dump, but it had windows that opened so wide that they were almost at risk of coming loose from their hinges. And after a year in university halls, where they practically barricaded the windows, we'd made full use of them in the summer months. Until a pigeon flew into Maeve's bedroom. An excited pigeon, who did a lot of flapping. We'd been on a night out the previous evening, and I and my (extremely rare) one-night stand had shot up in bed at the sound of Maeve screaming. Instead of a knight in shining armour, it turned out that I'd accidentally shagged the biggest wuss to ever exist, and I'd ended up catching the bird in a tea towel whilst he cowered behind Maeve. She'd done my washing up for a month as a thank you, and the guy went home *very* shortly after the morning's escapades.

'The pigeon-catching was a spur of the moment reflex. You really had to *think* about booking yoga in the park.'

A thought I was beginning to regret, as I watched the instructor slowly bend herself into a pretzel shape on her mat. I tried to imitate it, before giving up and going for foetal position so I wouldn't be seen shirking on the back row. This Saturday morning session in Finsbury Park had a good turnout, so I was hopeful that I could get away with the bare minimum. My attitude towards almost nothing, except cooking and yoga.

'Really, though, it means a lot that you'd risk becoming a meme for me.' Maeve had mastered the pretzel and was speaking to me through a gap in her arms. '*Especially* when you have to go straight to your date, with potential yoga sweat.'

I felt my heart rate increase. The second date. I genuinely couldn't remember the last time I'd been on one. What did people talk about when all the obvious small-talk opportunities had been used up?

'I think I'm safe from exerting enough energy to activate my sweat glands.' I raised an arm up so it looked like I was participating. 'You'll be all right, though, whilst I'm gone?'

She nodded. 'It was a shock. Who expects to receive their underwear in the post? But I'd rather a clean break than a messy one.'

I nodded. Messy breaks were the thing of nightmares. At least, if Bill Webber was anything to go by.

'Besides, he never said I had to post *his* stuff back. And I am *definitely* keeping the Phoebe Bridgers vinyl that he lent me.'

I laughed quietly to avoid the stink eye from the instructor. 'That's the spirit.'

I mustn't have looked convinced, because she continued. 'I'm going to be alone for an hour, max. Rory is meeting me for ice cream after he's finished at the climbing wall.'

Rory had really stepped up in the aftermath of Maeve and Adrian's breakup, spending more time with her than he had maybe ever. If anyone was going to have the goss about his date, it was Maeve. I entered stealth mode.

'How is Rory? I haven't seen him much this week.'

Maeve smirked. 'That's what a jam-packed dating life will do to you.'

I choked on my next question. Well, *that* had been easy. 'Dating life?'

'Erm yeah, remember? Hot chemistry teacher? Meeting him at 11.30?' She shot me a weird look. 'That shouldn't be new information. Has the blood rushed to your head? You've been sat in foetal for a while.'

I sat up, ignoring the glares from around me. 'Jesus, I thought yoga people were meant to be full of serotonin. I'm aware of hot chemistry teacher, thank you very much. I meant Rory.'

She suddenly became very interested in her downward dog. 'Oh, right. Yeah.'

I copied her, shuffling my mat so that I was right by her face. 'That's all I get?'

From the front of the room, the instructor encouraged us all to slowly return to our feet for final stretches. I held my arm behind my neck.

'I think he's been on a couple of dates. Nothing ground-breaking.' Maeve closed her eyes. 'You know what he's like. Give it one more date and he'll have found some minor reason to call it off.'

She had a point. Ever since his breakup with Lottie, he'd found every reason under the sun not to let things get serious with anyone else.

'I can't believe he didn't tell me about that.'

She rolled her eyes. 'If we sent round an alert every time someone went on a date lately, we'd never be able to relax. Anyway, aren't you going to be late for this date?' She checked the time on her phone as she rolled up her mat. 'It's past eleven.'

I looked at the time on my own phone. 11:10. Shit.

★★★

Isaac was staring at me, and not in a smitten 'I *need* to get my hands on you' kind of way.

'What?' I put my doughnut back in its brown paper bag. 'What are you staring at?'

He laughed. 'It's just, have you been outdoors this morning?'

I froze. Maybe my half-hearted downward dog *had* activated my sweat glands after all. I tucked some hair behind my ear and tried to take a subtle sniff. The coast was clear. Dove deodorant was all I was getting. Isaac reached over and pulled a leaf from my hair. Oh.

'I didn't realise I was dating such an outdoorsy type.'

Dating? Were we *dating*? Fear crept up my spine.

'You are not dating an outdoorsy type.' I would lie about my career, but not this. That was how you ended up on a hike, pretending you enjoyed sleeping in a tent. 'You're on a second date with someone who would do anything for their friends.'

I hoped he didn't take offence at my slight correction. We weren't *dating*.

'How's your doughnut?' I took a bite of mine again, the chocolate oozing out. Isaac had gone for vanilla (I was trying not to hold it against him).

'Phenomenal, as always.' His tongue caught the sugar on his top lip.

'Did you ever play that game at birthday parties? Where you had to resist licking your lips the longest?'

I tried it now, swerving the sugar crystals accumulating above my lip. Joe had been awful at that one, a lot happier when playing pass the parcel. He'd hated the messiness of the sugar – I laughed as I shared this with Isaac.

'Are you close to your brother, then?' Isaac picked up on my comment as we started to walk again, passing a busker who was playing a cover of 'Here Comes the Sun' and had encouraged a small crowd to stop and get their phones out.

I thought of Joe, who'd sent me a text this morning asking for advice about colour palettes. I got the sense that he was in *way* over his head with this wedding. As maid of honour, I had a feeling I was going to be looped in on a lot of minor wedding debates that I didn't fully understand. I said as much to Isaac.

'Wow, maid of honour. My sisters would not trust me with that kind of responsibility.'

He had two sisters – one in university, and one fresh out of it.

'I'm lucky that Joe and I get on so well now that we're adults. Our circle of friends is really close.'

Or so I'd *thought*. I felt a bit guilty about how distracted I'd been for the first half of my walk with Isaac, forgetting my own coffee order and accidentally ordering one without sugar, and then walking off before we'd even paid for our doughnuts. My conversation with Maeve had completely thrown me off. I'd almost missed the stop on the Northern line on the way over here.

'So' – I took a swig of my coffee and winced at the bitterness – 'tell me about the kids you teach. I have no idea how you have the patience.'

As soon as I mentioned his job, Isaac beamed. 'They're not that bad. We've all been 14, haven't we?'

I winced, harking back to pre-puberty Penny. 'Braces and frizzy hair. The worst.'

'Classic. Mine was acne and being the shortest in my form. Devastating. Being 14, and 15, and 16, is the worst thing in the world. You don't want to stick out too much, terrified of saying the wrong thing. Unless you're the kid acting out for attention, which is a crisis in itself. It's the most confusing time, being a teenager, so I think they can be forgiven if sometimes they struggle to annotate the first line of the periodic table. Is it really the end of the world if they didn't get the chance to do their homework? Probably not. I'd rather win them over with genuine joy than threaten them with detention. You should have seen their faces last week when we tried electrolysis.'

I wracked my brains to remember anything at all from my own Chemistry GCSE. I came up blank, and my expression must have said it all.

'I'm not expecting you to know what electrolysis is.' He nudged me. 'But seeing their faces light up when they produced something out of nothing, that's the magic. It's why I wanted to teach. I remember my high school chemistry teacher because he made us *want* to learn how things worked. I'd like them to remember me for the same reason.'

Why was hearing someone talk about the things that they were passionate about so sexy? Isaac's cheeks were flushed, so happy and willing to talk about his students and the progress they were making. It was a rare thing in adulthood to find people who were so excited about their work. Ambition was one of my non-negotiables.

'I really like how much you like your job.'

He grinned. 'I really like how much you like that I like my job.'

I scrunched my paper bag in my hand, popping it into a bin as we passed. When I turned back to walk with him, he'd come to a stop, a small smile on his face. We were halfway down the Southbank, the Thames glittering in the April sun. It was a perfect location for a first kiss and I was surprised to find that I actually *wanted* it to happen.

'I'm really glad I met you, Penny,' he whispered in my ear, closing the space between us before he finally pressed his lips against mine.

I kissed him back.

12

Isaac: So, do I get a chance at date three?

Me: Mm maybe, I'll think about it if you make it worth my while ...

I typed out a wink emoji and then thought better of it. There was flirty and then there was thirsty, and you should *never* risk giving a man that kind of power over you. I'd felt unexpectedly hopeful after date number two, and I was still acclimatising. My WhatsApp immediately sent me a notification. Maybe I *wasn't* the thirsty one.

Rory: Look at this thread. Made me think of the debriefs. Can almost taste the chocolate chips and you shouting at me for getting crumbs on your duvet.

I followed the link to a Twitter thread about a really bad first date, where a woman had been told she looked a little too much like his sister. I snorted. People were ridiculous.

'Well, well, *well*, if it isn't Little Miss Smitten. I don't think I've seen you smile at your phone like that since you got a fully stamped Nero card.' Joe came out of his front door, closing it behind him. His hair was damp and he was wearing a track-suit, an overnight bag of clean scrubs thrown over his shoulder. Today was his final night shift, and he looked exhausted.

I shoved my phone in my pocket, choosing to let him believe he was right, and that Isaac's texts had been what I was smirking at. Why ruin Mr Know-It-All's day? 'I'm just a girl, begging her big brother to shut up.' I knocked my shoulder against his, noting his eye bags and feeling a rare wave of affection.

'Luckily for you, I might. Isla warned me not to tease you about it, said you're like a rabbit in the headlights and must not be startled.'

I glanced up to the street-facing window in the living room of their second-floor flat. Sure enough, she had her face up against the glass, waving when we made eye contact. She had green goop all over her face, which I could only hope was a face mask.

'How's the wedding planning going?'

Joe raised an eyebrow as we started walking. 'Excellent deflection there. But yes, who knew wedding planning would be more stressful than working in A & E? Give me appen-dicitis and sutures over seating arrangements any day.' He exhaled. 'Who knew so many people wanted to rent a photo-booth on the same day? I spent an hour and a half on the phone this morning only to be told we couldn't have it. Sorry. Rant over.'

I waved him on encouragingly. 'No no, rant away. You have approximately six minutes until we get to Dad's. Lay it on me.'

Joe didn't need telling twice, talking a mile a minute about wedding breakfasts and canapés and several other phrases that I could never have imagined him using. The menu was *almost* nailed down, and the cake was in hand with Mum. The venue was booked, but it was a blank canvas and everything inside it needed to be hired. It sounded like a logistical nightmare.

'And trying to cram conversations with Isla about all of these things around my night shifts is an absolute pain in the arse.'

That language was more like him.

'I very wrongly assumed that Isla would just get on with it.'

I shot him a withering look.

'I know, I know. Apparently, me choosing table names for the reception is going to smash the patriarchy. I've got samples of the bloody ravioli for my 1 a.m. dinner.'

This made sense. One of Isla and Joe's main love languages was food; right from the off, Isla had identified night-shift packed lunches as the way to support my brother through a career that was worlds away from her own. She made a weekly menu that she stuck to the fridge, and you could pretty much always guarantee that Joe had been sent off to work with lasagne or a burrito or something else that he loved. Today, it was his wedding dinner for breakfast. For Joe, twenty minutes in the break room with his headphones in to scoff his dinner was the glorious marker of a night shift halfway done. He religiously listened to the same radio station he'd been following since we were teenagers, battling it out for the radio in Mum's car. It used to drive her mad – first, the argument over who got to sit in the front (always Joe), and then the argument about what we listened to for the ten-minute journey to drop us off at Dad's flat. Life had been easier when we'd both been given portable CD players for Christmas, and I could happily hum along to Girls Aloud's 'Sound of the Underground' from the backseat.

'Anyway, enough about ravioli. Which is excellent, all rants aside. How is Maeve doing?' His jaw clenched slightly. Even though he'd considered Adrian a close friend, he'd adopted Maeve as an extra sister a long time ago.

'She's getting there.' I filled him in on the postal delivery of her belongings. 'Ups and downs.'

'Wow.' He let it sink in. 'Just full of surprises this guy.'

Although he hadn't vocalised it (at least not to me), I knew Joe had been hurt by the breakup too, after reaching out to Adrian and getting nothing back. It terrified me, the thought of a breakup splintering my group of friends. There had been no question in this case about where the chips would fall, but what if it happened to someone a few years down the line? If it happened to Joe and Isla? We didn't have a protocol.

'Her confidence has definitely been knocked. But fear not, I have stepped up.' I told him about yoga in the park – from which I still had a bruise on my bum cheek. I spared him the details about that.

He shook his head as he pressed Dad's intercom. 'Penny Webber. You've had a serious personality transplant lately. I would have paid good money to see you trying to stay upright in a tree pose.' He clocked my expression. 'What? I've been known to do a yoga class. Have you got cake in there?'

Joe gestured to the tote bag I was carrying, which contained a lemon drizzle loaf from Mum. It said a lot about our parents that even though they didn't live together and rarely spoke, we always arrived at Dad's flat with some sort of treat.

'I have indeed. You know the drill.'

'Who is it?' Dad's voice finally crackled over the intercom. Cookie was barking in the background; I'd purposely worn light-coloured trousers – one meet-cute with a beagle was all it took to be on fur patrol. That dog was a *shedder*.

'Dad, we *just* texted to tell you we were on our way.' I smirked at Joe. 'Let us in, I'd rather not get mugged for my baked goods.'

'Cake?' The front door opened. 'Why didn't you lead with that? Come on in.'

It took precisely five seconds for Dad to snatch the Tupperware out of my hands. He was always happier to see a box from Mum than he was to see either of us. He lifted the lid, beaming at the sight of the perfectly glazed loaf. His favourite. I'd spent eleven of his birthdays in the living room, all four of us crowded around a lemon sponge. She'd never missed a birthday since – aside from the first year mid-divorce – even if she wasn't there to help him blow out the candles.

'How are you both doing?' He squeezed me carefully in order to protect the box, and then did the same for my brother, the hug lasting a solid ten seconds before he led us through the front door of his ground-floor flat.

When Dad had moved out, I'd been prepared for the cliché of an extremely depressing, prison-looking abode. And for the first six months or so, it had lived up to expectations (I'd very pointedly given him a warm lamp for Christmas, a not-so-gentle nudge towards the land of the living, rather than just surviving). A year post-divorce he'd started painting the walls and changing the previous owner's curtains, and by year five he'd adopted Cookie. The real turning point had been sobriety. Dad might never have recovered romantically, but we were getting there with everything else.

'Not bad, Dad, not bad,' I said, clocking the huge Hello Fresh box on his kitchen table. Every single time we'd visited for dinner, we'd either ordered pizza or been served beans on toast.

'I know, I know. Long time coming.' Dad patted the box. 'First up is a lentil masala. I don't think I've ever touched a lentil in my life.'

I could feel Joe's eyes on me.

'How's the app going, love?' He passed me a Diet Coke.

'Good. We're getting a steady number of downloads, no horrendous reviews yet.'

He offered a can to Joe. 'I was actually a bit tempted to download it myself.'

I almost spat out my drink but managed to save it, eyes watering as it went down the wrong way. 'You want to *date*? *Online*?'

This was major news.

'Don't be silly, I'm a bit old for that.' Dad rubbed his hand over his — now practically bald — head, blushing. 'Just to see what it's all about. Support you.'

My eyes almost watered again, nothing to do with the Coke. Joe got there first.

'I've never seen you volunteering yourself for stitches, Dad. I'm quite frankly hurt.'

'Very funny. I get a bit bored sometimes after work, in this flat all night. Older people can'' — he searched for the right word — 'use it, can't they?'

It had never factored into the marketing plan for Level, but it was designed for anyone who didn't want to waste time. Maybe we needed to make it clearer that all ages could find love on Level. I made a mental note to discuss with Harriet tomorrow.

'And is it easy to use?' Dad had pulled his phone out now. It did not escape my notice that the app had already been downloaded. I watched our little green icon appear on my father's screen.

'What prompted this, then?' The unspoken question here was 'why is now the right time to finally start moving on?'

We'd spent the best part of our adolescent and now adult lives despairing that Dad was pining after Mum to no avail. Now that he was finally expressing an interest in finding someone else, it felt a bit alien.

'Like I said, it gets quiet round here. It can be slightly isolating at times, and that seems a stupid thing to feel when my own daughter has created an app just for that.'

I felt a bit touched, even if I did have to resist the urge to intercept and say that actually, people didn't *need* to date to feel less lonely. I wasn't entirely sure how I felt about being responsible for my Dad getting back on the horse.

'You getting engaged, Joseph,' Dad said, finally looking up from his screen, 'made me realise that life is too short to live in the past. I don't want to be the man that everyone feels sorry for.'

'We don't —'

He shot me a look. 'I might be getting older but I'm definitely not getting thicker. I know your Mum and I reacted differently to the divorce. She didn't look back —'

Joe tried to intercept but Dad shushed him.

'You don't have to sugar-coat it, son. I know that your mother dealt with it better and I've been the sad ex-husband. Well, until now.' He squinted at the screen, which was asking him to set up his profile. 'What is this? Penny, I don't think I've taken five photos of myself in my entire fifty-three years combined.'

Joe was staring at him like he'd sprouted antennae. I intervened before we caused offence. 'It's okay, I got one of us three at the engagement party. I'll send it to you. So that's one out of five.'

He nodded. 'I'll do this later. No rush when you've been on your own for fifteen years, is there?'

I tried to imagine Dad using Level. The replies we usually got from him started and ended with a thumbs up and an 'OK', so I couldn't imagine his chat being particularly enthralling. He'd found Mum in a time before apps. They'd met in a bar when they were students, after Dad had accidentally thrown a dart in the direction of the table where Mum and her best friend were sitting. Apparently, he'd charmed her, but that was hard to imagine now. Maybe he'd just lost his game.

The conversation had moved on, Joe telling Dad about the short time frame for the wedding and arranging a time for them to go with Rory – who had accepted his role as best man with *much* enthusiasm, and the promise of an excellent last-minute stag do – to be fitted for their suits.

★★★

As soon as we got outside, we both started talking over each other. I conceded and let Joe go first.

'I would rather treat one hundred gobby patients on my ward than have to field questions once he starts using that app.' When I laughed, he stopped in his tracks. 'I'm not kidding. The app is your brainchild, your problem.'

'Well, *that's* not very in the spirit of supporting our father as he takes his first steps towards moving on, now, is it?'

We started walking, aware that in a couple of minutes we'd go in different directions – him to the hospital for his night shift, and me back to the overground.

Joe shot me a look. 'Like I said, your app, your problem.'

'Okay *fine*, but if he starts asking me anything about sexting, it's on you.'

We shuddered simultaneously.

13

'Answer it, answer it!' Maeve had snatched my phone from my hand and was waving it around. 'Date three is on the horizon, baby.'

I rolled my eyes, answering Isaac's call.

'How was dress shopping?' I smiled involuntarily at the sound of his voice. This wasn't the first time he'd rang; apparently, Isaac was an over-the-phone date planner.

'We found it. Or rather, she found it. Maeve, Mum, and I just sat around all afternoon drinking mimosas.'

It was true. We'd been tasked as the wedding dress team, lazing on the sofa in the changing room and giving brutal honesty (which Isla had specifically asked for) at every new dress. Mum had stepped in at the last minute to be there – Isla's own mother was on a non-refundable weekend away in rural Spain – and her sisters (the two other bridesmaids alongside Maeve and me) hadn't been able to find babysitters in time. An excuse I had my suspicions about. We were T-minus fifty-two days until the big day, and Isla had tried on seven dresses, all the way from meringue to mermaid, before falling in love with a simple A-line with tiny little diamantes scattered in the skirt, providing a subtle shimmer. It was the kind of dress that would absolutely lend itself to the sunshine in June. It was gorgeous.

'I'm sure that you were suitably supportive even in your drunken state. It sounds a lot more fun than my afternoon spent marking papers. Who knew thirty mock papers could give me such a headache?'

Next to me, Maeve was mouthing 'invite him to the pub', but I gave a sharp shake of my head. After Adrian, anyone we dated would need to go through a tough initiation before we let them into the circle of trust.

'So, I was actually ringing to organise our third date. What do you fancy? I was thinking dinner at a little Spanish place I know in Waterloo? Amazing red wine. But I'm open to any and all ideas.'

I didn't have to look at Maeve to know that she would be gesturing wildly about communication and effort. I smiled. 'That sounds great. I'm free this Friday?'

'It's a date.' Isaac was smiling, I could hear it. 'I imagine you're on your way to celebratory drinks at the pub?'

Again, I fought the urge to invite him. We'd only been on two dates, and part of me was worried about unleashing the wolfpack on him. I didn't want them to start assessing or passing comment until I'd made up my own mind. What would they think of straightlaced, sensible Isaac? What would Rory – who lived and breathed fun – think of him? Not that it *should* make a difference what Rory thought. That was irrelevant, *obviously*.

'I am indeed on my way for a pint. What's the point in having a wedding if you can't celebrate every milestone?' Our local was in sight now, an old man's pub that was equidistant to all of our flats. Isla had stayed behind at the boutique to finalise a couple of things, but everyone else was en route. Saturday nights together were generally held sacred. It was a selfish bonus that we had Maeve every week now, rather than just one in two.

'Well, have a lovely evening and report back on the goss. I love a wedding.'

I knew from our first date that he'd been the ring bearer at his parent's wedding; way too young to have been sinking pints, but a cute visual nonetheless.

'Well, you never know, you may get an invite to one sooner than you think.'

Okay, I had *definitely* consumed too much prosecco to be talking to a man over the phone. Maeve slapped my arm, raising her arms in a party motion.

Isaac laughed. 'Yeah, maybe.' There was a pause. *Oh shit. Why on earth had I just said that?* I didn't even really mean it.

'Anyway, go and have a drink for me and I'll see you on Friday. I'll text you the details when I've booked it.'

We ended the call, promising to see each other in six days' time. The plus-one faux pas aside, I was excited to see him again. It felt new, the fizzing in my stomach.

'Go *Penny*.' Maeve beamed. 'Someone is beginning to catch a few feelings.'

The blood ran from my cheeks. 'I am *not*.'

'Right, okay.'

I ignored her and led the way into the pub.

★★★

As soon as we made our entrance, Maeve made a beeline for the toilets, having made the mistake of breaking the seal back at the boutique. I joined Rory at the bar.

'Hey stranger.' I was going for the sneak attack, trying to make him jump. He was wearing a faded sweatshirt from our university days, his hair still damp from the spell of rain we'd had. That man had never carried an umbrella in his life.

'Heard those boots clacking a mile off, Webber. Nice try.' He turned and handed me a pint, our hands overlaying in the exchange. We both stared down, neither of us moving for a second until he cleared his throat, causing me to pull the glass from him as he went back to nursing his own drink.

'How did the big dress excursion go? Successful?'

I ignored the weird moment, plastering an unbothered expression on my face to match his. 'Very successful. Dress has been secured, and I'm not giving *any* hints.'

He smirked. 'It's only the groom that's meant to be in the dark. Or have you mistaken me for your dashing older brother?'

I took a swig of my pint and pulled a face. 'Gross.'

'And what about your dress? The maid of honour is the second most important, no?' Rory was teasing me, the corner of his mouth upturned.

'No progress as of yet, not that I'd tell you anyway.'

He leaned on his elbows, closing the distance between us. 'You tease me, Penny.'

I swallowed. What was going on? Dating was clearly messing with my head. I was beginning to think *everything* was flirting.

Rory had laughed off his comment, running his hands through his curls. 'I'm telling you, this Isaac fella is a lucky man.'

I felt a weird flash of irritation. 'It's been two dates, I'm not betrothed to the guy.'

'I hope not.' Rory exhaled.

I stared at him, confused, and he immediately realised what he'd said. 'You know, because of the office bet?'

'Right.' I narrowed my eyes. 'It's probably nothing anyway. Dating has never been my strong point before, so I don't see why it would be now.'

I caught Maeve's eye as she came out of the toilets and gestured to a booth in the corner. Booths screamed sticky leather to me, but she loved the intimacy of them.

'Pen.' Rory put the tip of his finger under my chin and swivelled me round to face him. 'Don't do the thing.'

I jumped to my own defence. 'What thing?'

'The thing where you push people away because you're scared of getting hurt.'

The accusation was so far from true, I actually laughed. 'I don't do that.'

Rory nodded. 'I'm just saying that –'

'Hello, my favourite little dream team.' Isla pounced on us, finally arriving with Joe in tow. From the hiccup, I could tell she'd caught up with Maeve and me and finished off the bottle of prosecco.

Rory dished out their drinks. 'We'll be over in a second.'

I tried to follow my brother, who winked at me, but Rory stopped me in my tracks. 'Oh no you don't.'

My pint sat on the bar, begging to go for a walk and join its friends in the booth. The sticky leather booth. I sighed. 'I'm not scared, Ror. I just don't want to waste my time.'

He nodded, hands in his pockets. 'Right. And the sky isn't blue.'

We were in a momentary stand-off.

'Not every breakup ends with fifteen years of loneliness and refusing to change a pair of drab curtains. I promise. Look at Maeve.'

I did as he instructed even though it had been rhetorical. She was laughing her head off at something Joe had just said, dangly boob earrings back in her ears again.

'I know that. I know.' My voice sounded small.

Rory picked up the drinks again. 'Just think about it, okay? I've known you a long time, and I know that you're just as scared of letting someone in as you are of getting appendicitis in the middle of the night.'

It was a niche fear, but still very valid. We'd had a code in first year, a sequence of knocks I would bang on his neighbouring wall if I woke up in a panic.

'I promise, whatever happens, you'll always have me.'

I swallowed. How did some people manage to see the parts of you that you didn't even show to yourself?

'Anyway.' He nudged me in the direction of the booth. 'It's time to get good and sticky on that leather over there.'

I shuddered. 'Don't remind me. Look at those perfectly clean wooden chairs on the other side of the room.'

Rory shook his head. 'Maeve is still in her heartbreak quota I'm afraid. She makes the rules. The bright side of getting dumped is that if it did happen, we'd let you have the wooden chairs as long as you liked.'

I rolled my eyes, following him over.

Maeve patted the space next to her. 'We've just been having a very important discussion over here.'

Joe nodded. 'Possibly the most important aspect of this whole saga,' he said, wincing as Isla elbowed him, 'is entirely out of our control.'

Ah. The sten do. I'd spent years working side by side with a dreamer, forever the more practical when it came to shared projects with Rory. The man had no concept of limits, and this was no exception to the rule. He immediately jumped into the conversation now, and I willed him not to bring up his initial idea of us all flying out to the Maldives. I wasn't sure airlines accepted magic beans as currency nowadays.

'We have some tricks up our sleeve.' He tapped the side of his nose. 'But it will be a joint endeavour, of course. Exactly as you specified.'

This part of the plan was Joe and Isla's only condition. No splitting of the sexes.

Isla beamed. 'Goodbye horrid traditions, hello epic friend adventure.'

I winced at the word epic – we only had fifty-one days to plan this thing. Less than that, because the sten had to happen *before* the wedding, but not the night before. Joe's other condition.

My brother rubbed his hands together now. 'Excellent. Any more clues?'

In reality, we were between ideas. Rory's ideas were slightly wilder, from a luxury holiday abroad to an afternoon of go-karting (which I knew Isla would detest). I was more on board for a weekend in a cosy lodge, with plenty of booze and a hot tub on the decking. This mismatch of ideas was usually our way when it came to brainstorming. Little by little, each of us would give, until we had a perfectly reasonable compromise. We'd perfected it to a fine art over the years.

I shot Rory a look across the table that said 'we cannot let them know how undecided we are, given that it's in seven weeks' time' and he nodded imperceptibly.

'No can do, Joseph. No can do.' Rory sipped his pint. 'You've picked the best team in the world to plan your final weekend of unmarried life, just trust us with it.'

Maeve rolled her eyes. 'They're doing that creepy thing where they speak to each other without speaking.'

'We do not do that.'

Joe, Isla, and Maeve just looked at me.

'Okay, whatever. We've got more pressing things to discuss anyway.' I'd been waiting for the right moment to pounce on this, and now felt as good a time as any.

All four of them looked at me expectantly.

'How's the dating going, Rory?' I narrowed my eyes at my best friend, trying to communicate that I was *not* happy to have been left out of the loop.

It wasn't often that you caught Rory off guard, but he looked like a deer in the headlights.

'How did you −'

Maeve held up her hands, clearly assuming that she'd let the cat out of the bag and not my brother, who was looking extremely relieved. 'Guilty. But I was blinded by heartbreak, so I can't be held responsible for my actions.'

I watched Rory's face flicker almost imperceptibly with betrayal. 'Traitor.'

He didn't elaborate, choosing to focus on the beermat in front of him, tearing it up into tiny pieces. After all his criticism of *my* dating approach, here he was, staying silent.

'So . . .' I waved my arms in front of him. 'Come on. Share with the group.'

He exchanged a look with Maeve, and there it was again. That sinking feeling of being on the outside of something.

'I've been seeing this girl, Maisy, for a few weeks. It's nothing major.' He shrugged it off. 'Just dipping my toe back in again, seeing what Level has to offer.'

So he *had* chosen to download the app, even after he'd said he wasn't in the right headspace. What had changed his mind?

Isla pounced. 'And what is she *like*? We need details.'

I watched him squirm, cheeks flushed and so far from the usual Rory performance. 'She's a vet. Really cool, chilled.'

A vet? Really cool? Chilled? It felt like a dig somehow. No one in the history of Penny Webber had ever called me chilled. There was a slightly awkward silence.

Maeve stepped in to break it. 'Well, I've met her, and she seemed lovely. Gorgeous red hair. Who wants another drink?' She stood up. 'Rory, help me?'

She all but dragged him away to order with her, immediately putting an arm around him and whispering something in his ear. What the *hell*? If he was dating someone, then I had definitely misread our body language at the bar. I was losing my mind. The other two seemed none the wiser, launching into a conversation about table runners. I kept my eyes on Rory. *What was going on?*

14

I stared down at my unopened message. This was *exactly* what I'd been afraid of.

Maeve met me at the sink and I passed her the toothpaste, the Hello Kitty toothbrush that she'd bought me as a joke already in my mouth. 'Ticks can't turn blue out of sheer willpower, you know. He'll text back, I promise.'

I didn't say anything, my mouth full of minty suds. But also, because I didn't trust myself not to say something completely miserable. Isla had told me we were supposed to be 'nurturing Maeve's persistent optimism', which was code for 'Penny, stop saying every man is trash'.

'Pen?' Maeve put her hand over mine where it was gripping the sink.

I spat. 'I'm fine, I'm fine. In the grand scheme of things, thirty-six hours is not that long.'

Maeve winced before soldiering on.

'This paranoia is a bit rich, coming from someone who once left me on read for a whole week.'

Now it was my turn to wince. 'It was *one time*. And you were in the Caribbean!'

The bright side of Maeve's parents not being able to settle anywhere for longer than a few years – the reason Maeve's accent was a complete *non-accent* – was that she'd spent many a Christmas Day on the beach. Webber Christmases, on the other hand, could be total chaos. Particularly after Mum's friend Angela had started tagging along, children, ex-husband, and now grandchildren in tow. There had been no time for texting, it had been all hands on deck.

'Luckily for you, forgiveness is essential for psychologists.'

I didn't buy this. 'Adrian?'

Her expression darkened. 'He's still on my hit list. Aren't you late for work?'

'I'm going to say you had a crisis and I had to delay. Don't tell Rory otherwise.' I moved into the kitchen and started packing my laptop into my bag, grabbing a banana and a Trek bar.

'Telling the truth is also essential.' She followed me in. 'Go, and don't stress. You know when you're next seeing Isaac. He's probably just busy with work. God knows you can relate to that.'

I sighed. 'Fine, I'll ignore the obvious evidence and tell myself he's busy. Happy?'

She nodded. 'Besides, you'll ruin the third-date sex if you overthink this.'

Oh God. Third-date sex. I couldn't remember the last time I'd had to get a razor out in preparation for one of those. Not that I had any obligation to do that. Was it a better statement to leave the razor gathering dust in my cupboard? Yet another pointless thought that would circle around my mind during work today. I wasn't entirely sure this was a dilemma I could bring to a board meeting. Andrew would go into cardiac arrest if we strayed from budget to bikini lines.

Maeve poured us both a coffee. 'Anyway, even if Isaac is a loser, you still have the best housemate in all of London. See you later? I was thinking I might make tacos.'

I grabbed the sugar, dumping heaped teaspoons into my travel mug.

'Music to my ears. I'll bring the guac.'

★★★

As soon as I walked into the office and was met with an enthusiastic round of applause, I knew something was going on. I definitely hadn't spilled coffee down my white shirt, I'd checked (it happened often enough that a daily check in the mirror in the lift was essential), so it had to be something else.

'All right, boss?' Dexter greeted me with a devilish grin, halfway through making a chain out of paperclips from the stationery cupboard. The garland almost spanned the entirety of his desk. 'How's the dating going?'

One of the designers on the other side of the room tried and failed to hide a snicker.

I raised an eyebrow. 'Clearly a lot better than your work ethic.'

Dexter was probably the only member of our staff that I could talk to like that, bar Rory. Our lead programmer had come out of the womb a sarky bastard.

Ella strolled out of the office now, immediately flushing when she spotted me. 'Oh, hey Penny.'

She too kept her eyes on me. I felt like an exhibit at London Zoo.

'Is someone going to tell me which office joke I'm the butt of this time?'

No one spoke, although there were a few more titters. I ran through the possibilities in my head. It was possible that I was about to walk into my office and see my desk covered in wrapping paper. I couldn't rule out a stupid prank, and it *had* been known to happen. Usually only on the first of April, though. Another thought occurred to me.

'Did you hack my Level profile?' I played it cool, refusing to give Dexter the satisfaction and trying not to let on how humiliating it would be if that was the case. I didn't want anyone in this office to have access to my poor flirting attempts.

'As tempting as that obviously is,' Dexter said, adding the final paperclip to his garland, 'we were actually listening when we had the GDPR training.'

I snorted. Likely story. These people heard the words 'training' and translated it into 'an excuse to completely zone out of work'. Last time we'd given them a course, they'd ordered pizza to the office and taken it as permission to put their feet up for an afternoon. I'd been slated for weeks for requesting a ham and pineapple.

'Okay, so what is it, then?' I zeroed in on Ella, who I knew for a fact would be the easiest to crack. It took a previous teacher's pet to know another, and I hadn't pestered my high school teachers about missed homework for nothing. There was no way someone who lined up their pencils every morning, and who baked cupcakes for the office 'just because', wouldn't break under the pressure. 'Ella?'

It took literally seconds to fluster her. 'I think you should probably just speak to Rory. He's in your office.'

I could see him behind the glass wall, leaning over his laptop and studying something on the screen. Dexter heckled me on my way over there. 'Leave the door open, would you?'

I flipped him the finger and closed the door behind me, hearing a series of groans as the rest of the office became background noise.

'What on earth has got into them?' I dumped my bag on the floor, walking over to my desk that sat opposite Rory's on the other side of the room.

He looked tired, his shirt crumpled. The man didn't own an iron and wouldn't have known how to use one even if he did. 'They're being ridiculous. It's nothing.'

I took a swig of my coffee, wincing. Why did they make travel cups so effective? What was the point if it never reached a drinkable temperature? 'Okay. Well, it's obviously something. Dexter is literally unable to wipe that grin off his face.'

Rory didn't look up from his screen. 'This random lifestyle magazine wrote a piece about "the creators behind a hot new dating app".' He said the last part in air quotes, his feelings towards the piece evident through his tone.

I had never quite understood people's obsession with app creators. Particularly dating app creators. No one was queuing up to hear the life story of the creator of the latest viral game about birds, but for some reason, the personal lives of those associated with dating apps were fair game. It didn't help that Michael Broadhurst, the founder of Link, had milked the PR opportunity for all it was worth. A two-part Netflix documentary had aired a few years ago, focusing on his rise to success, and how it had all started when he'd met his wife. From then on, he'd set out on a mission to help people in the masses have their own romantic encounters. Blah blah blah. I just didn't get the obsession.

'What's the angle? Have they exposed my permanent singledom?'

This, I could deal with. It wasn't a secret that I'd devoted my early twenties to Level. If anything, it could make our users trust us more, to know how far our dedication stretched.

Rory laughed, but it fell a bit flat. He still hadn't made eye contact. 'Not quite. It's *Influence* magazine, if you want to read it. They've tagged us on Twitter.'

I'd never been an avid Twitter user, not quite sure why the general population would want to hear my opinions on pointless topics. But I did have an account, which I saved for the post-midnight brain rot scroll before bed. I'd never even tweeted, and my username was @PennyW3B97. How had they found me? I scrolled through my mentions – of which there were quite a few more than the usual zero – locating the tweet and clicking on the relevant article.

When Penny Met Rory: On the Same Level All Along

I skimmed the paragraphs, groaning. 'Where do they get this bullshit from?'

One of the comments named our university halls, and how we'd met when we were 18 and fresh out of sixth form. Where did they get this kind of information? I ran through my mind, trying to think of anyone who might have snaked us out for a quick fix of cash.

Finally, Rory glanced up from his screen, closing the lid on his laptop and coming over to my side of the room. 'It's annoying, you're right. But I mean it's not a ridiculous theory to draw, is it?'

A thump on the glass outside made us both jump. Dexter was on the other side, holding a printout of the article.

'I'm going to frame this and put it next to the fridge. We're all so proud of you two.'

Unfortunately, our office was not Dexter-proof. The sad reality of setting up a new office with a small budget.

'You're not funny.' I scolded him.

'Will you sign it for me?' He faked an angelic expression.

I added it to my to-do list to send round another batch of dull mandatory training especially for him.

'What do you mean?' I turned back to Rory, who was ignoring Dexter.

'Well' – he ran his hands through his hair, picking up my coffee and taking a sip, not even flinching at the temperature – 'firstly, this is disgusting. That's a hot milkshake, not a coffee. And second, it's not the most ridiculous theory in the world, that we might be dating. Or at least be *a little more* than friendly. We've spent a lot of time together over the years.'

I thought of the other day at the pub, and became suddenly aware of our proximity right now. Our faces were centimetres apart, and the rest of the office was only on the other side of a glass wall.

'Right. It makes sense.' I was reassuring myself more than anything, and I watched his Adam's apple bob as he swallowed. 'It's good to be realistic about the conclusions people might draw. Even if they're false.'

Because they *were* false. I was almost definitely sure. I'd spent more time with Rory than I had with anyone else for the best part of a decade. I'd slept in his bed at university, and I'd used his toothbrush on countless occasions when I didn't have mine to hand (even if I'd never told him about it – he was weird about dental hygiene). And nothing had *ever* happened. Ever.

'Yeah. Completely false.' Rory hadn't broken our eye contact.

I broke first, slamming my laptop screen closed and forcing down a swig of scorching hot coffee. 'An article spouting a pack of lies. What's new?'

I stared down at my desk until Rory went back over to his. *What the hell was going on lately?* I took my jacket off, suddenly warm.

'I wonder what lover boy is going to think about this.' Rory was swinging his house keys around his finger, swivelling on his chair.

I scoffed. 'What is *Maisy* going to say about this?'

That shut him up. I took it as confirmation that neither of us wanted this article falling into the wrong hands.

15

'Penny!'

I hadn't even pushed on the door before Mum spotted me, drowning out the sound of the little bell overhead. Fondant & Flour was usually almost empty following the mid-morning and lunch rushes, which made it the perfect time to take a late lunch and visit Mum.

Angela was leaning on the counter, flipping through a magazine.

'Come join us.' Mum's glace cherry nipples were the first thing I noticed as she beckoned me over. 'You were just the person I wanted to walk through that door.'

I was instantly suspicious. She typically put her blinkers on once she got in the zone. Joe had come in once for cookies and she hadn't clocked who it was until he'd handed over his card.

'Happy to see you too –' I barely had the chance to finish my sentence before she threw me an apron and produced a piping bag from underneath the counter. *Ah. There we go.*

'And here I was, thinking that you were just thrilled to see me.' I gave Angela a half hug as I shrugged the apron on. She was currently sporting a lilac 'lob' that I hadn't seen before. Angela had been in a midlife crisis as long as I'd known her. 'What have you two been gossiping about?'

I'd witnessed my mum with her friends and a bottle of sauvignon blanc enough times to know when she was having a full-on debrief. My mother had the most vibrant social life of all of us; if she wasn't at her weekly bridge tournament, she was at book club. And if she wasn't there, she was round at Angela's.

'Always thrilled to see you. But even more thrilled to have an extra pair of hands. Especially when my assistant baker called in sick this morning. I need you to pipe cream into these butterfly cakes. Go wash your hands first.'

She didn't wait for confirmation that I *could* give up my time to pipe some cakes. Things must have been desperate if she was asking me to step in; I was usually relegated to back-office administration or taking the bins out. Baking had never come easily to me, no matter how many times she'd propped me up on the kitchen counter with a mixing bowl. All her efforts had produced was a 7-year-old girl who was addicted to licking the spoon.

'I have a job, you know.'

Angela squinted up at me, her reading glasses on the table next to her. 'What's the point in being a CEO if you can't take an afternoon off?'

'To Penny, an afternoon off is a fate worse than death.' Mum passed me over a cup of tea. She wasn't *wrong*, per se, but that was just because there was always something Level-related to be done. Or so I told myself.

'Fine, fine. You have me for an *extended* lunch, but that's it!' Why did I constantly feel like I had to prove people wrong lately? I fired off a text to Rory letting him know I'd be taking a little longer than expected. He sent back a GIF of someone collapsing from shock, which I deliberately ignored.

'Where do you want me?' I washed my hands and tied my hair up, grateful at least to have a menial task to occupy my mind. Today was Friday, the day of my third date with Isaac. Or, the *supposed* day of our third date. I still hadn't heard from him, not since Saturday afternoon. I had however, heard from my own stupid app, churning out a meet-cute even though we hadn't spoken in days. It had popped up on my phone last night whilst I was scrolling in bed:

Congratulations! Next level unlocked: You and Isaac would have met at a wine bar in Shoreditch.

Which was two dates too late, and only succeeded in rubbing salt in the wound. I wasn't going to need that meet-cute now. Even Maeve had conceded that it wasn't looking good at this point. My cheeks flamed at the thought of everyone knowing I'd been ghosted.

'Make sure you pipe the first centimetre or so onto baking paper.' Mum watched over my shoulder, close enough that I could see the light sheen of sweat on her upper lip. 'The initial pipe is never the best.'

'If you're going to trust me, trust me. I can pipe some icing onto a cake.' I waited for her to back down. She did.

'That's rich coming from the girl who gave me five rounds of "amends" when I baked her birthday cake last year. And also, it's *buttercream*, not icing.'

When Mum felt like it, she gave as good as she got.

I turned, feeling bad for snapping. 'Sorry. Bad day.' I considered it. 'Bad week, actually.'

I wasn't actually sure which aspect of my week had been worse; the fact that I was almost definitely getting ghosted, or the fact that loads of people on the internet were conspiring about my love affair with my best friend. Everyone in the office was still riding on the hilarity, but I was over it. Even if it *had* caused our downloads to shoot up. And I was probably being paranoid, but I could have sworn that Rory was avoiding me. He'd been hanging out in the main office a lot, pulling up a chair to work with Dexter or having meetings with Ella in her office rather than ours. *And* he'd been going on lunchtime walks to the sandwich shop that was almost twenty minutes away. No one did that for fun.

'That looks good.' Mum gestured to the buttercream I was piping in each vanilla sponge. 'So, tell us what's bothering you.'

This wasn't the first time that I'd come to the bakery for advice; usually on my way home from work when she was just closing up. It was the adult version of sitting at the kitchen island after school, nibbling away at my lip until she prodded me to let it out. Before I could second-guess myself, it all came spilling out. The dating challenge, Isaac, Link trying to muscle in.

'Oh, honey.' Mum signalled for Angela to rub my back, her own hands stuck in a ball of dough. 'You put so much pressure on yourself.'

Angela nudged my tea towards me. 'Trust us, finding a partner is not the be-all and end-all. Seriously.'

Angela had been divorced three times. Neither of the women in front of me had time for men right now.

'It's not that I even want one' – every time I closed my eyes and imagined losing three nights of my week to a stranger, I shuddered – 'but what if there's something wrong with me that means I can't get one?'

Mum started laughing, and then immediately stopped when she noticed that I was blinking back tears. 'Well, for starters, Pen, we can't say for *sure* that something hasn't happened to Isaac. He might be dead in a ditch.'

Angela stepped in. 'Probably *not* dead in a ditch.'

I wasn't a monster. I was almost definitely sure I would rather be ghosted by Isaac, than for him to be lying in a ditch somewhere. *Almost* definitely sure. 'I should never have agreed to download the stupid app in the first place.'

I saw them exchange a look before Mum stepped in. 'Honey, the app isn't stupid. It's men.'

Angela pressed the palms of her hands together. 'Amen.'

'Actually,' Mum said with a mischievous glint in her eye, 'I don't mean that. *Some* men seem to be worth a second glance. Have you been doing much scrolling on Twitter lately, Ang?'

Angela gave me a knowing look. 'In fact, Caroline, I *have*.'

Ah. It was now glaringly obvious what they'd been gossiping about before I walked in.

'If you're talking about the article . . .' I went back to piping, anything to avoid their eye contact.

Angela interrupted. 'We are. We are talking about the article. We want to know what's going on with you and that boy with the eyebrows.'

I stifled a snort. 'Absolutely nothing. You should know better than to ask me that.' I pointed the piping bag at Mum.

'Should I?' She popped a teacake in the toaster. 'It's not the furthest leap for them to make.'

'Seriously?' I accidentally squeezed the bag too hard, one of the cupcakes exploding from the pressure.

She narrowed her eyes at me. 'Watch it. Those sponges are a good batch.'

I checked that she was fully focused on the teacake again before sliding the ruined cupcake underneath the counter for me to take home. If I was going to wallow, I might as well wallow in sugar. I'd already tasted a tiny bit of the buttercream; *real* vanilla, the kind where you could see black flecks from the beans.

'You're not getting out of this that easily.' Angela gave me a withering stare. 'Spill the goss, Penny. We're old. We live for this shit.'

I sighed. 'Nothing is going on. This is why you two shouldn't be allowed social media accounts! I think you'd know if I was secretly in love with my best friend.'

'That's what the word "secretly" implies, Penny.'

She had a point.

'I'm dating' – admittedly, not very well, but still – 'he's dating. We're both dating, and definitely not each other. He's my *friend*.' I said 'friend' very slowly, for emphasis.

'I was best friends with my third husband for ten years before we decided to give things a go.'

Mum intercepted. 'You divorced him because you had no sex life.'

'*Mum.*' I cringed. 'You've got *customers.*'

She let out a laugh. 'They know who they're dealing with, love.'

She handed the teacake to Angela, who immediately started picking out the raisins. 'You could do a double Webber wedding. Really cut down on the costs. I've heard that loads of ministers are more likely to say yes to a last-minute wedding if they can double up on marriages. Does it work on a commission basis, do you think?'

The temptation to turn the piping bag into a rapid-fire buttercream weapon was increasing.

'Funnily enough, I don't think a double wedding is on the cards.' I huffed before putting the final touches to the last cupcake. 'And voila. Any other jobs I can do whilst you exploit my need for mother–daughter bonding time?'

She shook her head. 'Sit down and drink the rest of your tea. I might not be the world's best agony aunt when it comes to matters of the heart, but I do make a cracking brew.'

I did as I was told, cradling the mug.

'How long can you stay?'

I shrugged. 'Rory's fine holding the fort for a bit.'

'Rory, Rory, Rory . . .' Angela picked out another raisin, making a little pile on the side of her pink scalloped plate. Why on earth had she asked for a teacake if she was going to do that? It was now essentially a bread roll. 'That boy certainly comes up in conversation a lot, doesn't he?'

Don't pick up the piping bag again, Penny. You're a grown, responsible adult.

'Leave her alone. She's a woman on the edge.' Mum wiped her hands on a cloth. 'So, what are you going to do about tonight? Just turn up?'

I groaned at the thought of being stood up. 'I genuinely don't think my brain will let my legs walk over there. It's too embarrassing.'

I'd made this decision somewhere between piping cupcake one and twenty. There was *no* way I was giving Isaac the satisfaction of that.

'Pen, it's not embarrassing. But I do understand.' She took one of the cupcakes and slid it onto a plate, knowing exactly what I needed.

I stuck my index finger into the buttercream, scooping it into my mouth. 'Who would have thought. A son who's marrying his first ever girlfriend, and a daughter who is more inclined to marry her laptop.'

She laughed. 'You're being dramatic, Penny.'

Angela pulled out her phone. '*Speaking* of dating, look what I spotted during my morning swipe.'

I took one look at the screen and immediately wanted to crawl under one of the tables. It was Dad. On Link. Not Level.

Mum looked completely taken aback. 'It's taken you until *now* to mention this?'

Angela threw her hands up. 'I didn't know how to tell you! Did you know anything about this?' She turned the spotlight towards me.

'Well, obviously I wouldn't have encouraged my father to download my main business competitor.'

I would be having words with him about that later.

She nodded. 'Fair point.'

Mum was trying to make herself look busy. 'But you *did* know he was thinking about it?'

I pretended not to hear her, suddenly extremely engrossed in the gingham apron I still had tied around my waist.

'Penny?'

I threw up my hands. 'Fine. I did know he wanted to date again. He spoke to Joe and me about it last time we went round.'

It was rare that I managed to surprise my Mum. But I could tell that on this particular occasion, I had. Her features immediately creased, before her expression settled into one of mild disinterest.

'Oh, really?'

I stared at my tea, willing someone to ring me with a work emergency.

'Did he like the lemon cake?'

I tried to make eye contact with her, but she'd turned away from me to restock her fridge with cans of Diet Coke and San Pellegrino. The blood orange kind.

'He practically started salivating at the sight of it.' I paused. 'I don't think it's anything serious.'

Mum's lips were white. 'It's okay, you shouldn't have to play it down.'

Angela was standing, getting her umbrella out. 'I'd better go and pick up little Lola from school.' Angela's first grandchild was her pride and joy. 'Besides, this feels like a family affair.'

Mum protested. 'I'm *fine*.'

'I know, I know. But it's still strange, even after all this time. If I don't go now, Lola will think her Nanny has forgotten her. Don't work yourselves too hard, do you hear me?' She turned her attention to me. 'Both of you.'

I gave her a quick wave as she headed out the door.

'Mum? Are you okay?'

She seemed to shake herself out of a moment, already moving onto the next task and disappearing into the kitchen. A few seconds later she reappeared with a tray of pastries, and the haunted look was gone.

'I'm fine. Like Angela said, it's a weird feeling. Don't tell me anything else about it, I'd rather not know. The world is small, I bet I know half the women my age that are on the app.' She handed me a croissant. 'Want to take one of these back for Maeve?'

I let her spread raspberry jam onto the pastry, sensing that she needed to keep busy for a minute. The café was quiet, and aside from a brief interlude to box up four butterscotch cupcakes for an elderly woman (for the grandkids, she'd assured us, like the owner of a bakery was going to judge anyone for too much sugar) it was just the two of us, stirring cups of tea.

'Really though, Pen,' she broke the silence, 'I want you to know that you're bigger than any boy trouble. Any of it.'

I knew she was referring to both Isaac's radio silence *and* the article.

'Maybe you have the right idea.' I slumped on the counter. 'Maybe I should just ignore all of it. Focus on work.'

After all, I'd learnt it from the best.

16

I grabbed another glass of prosecco without a second thought.

'You're my new favourite person.' The waitress was already moving on, but gave me a weary smile on her way to offer her tray to a group of older men (because of *course*, this room was teeming with them).

It was Tuesday, weirdly early in the week for a corporate mixer. It was the kind of event where Rory and I usually divided and conquered; he handled the small talk, I handled the business chat. Today, I just wanted to get drunk. My phone buzzed.

Maeve: Oh, Pen. I'm sorry. At least now you know, though?

I downed the dregs of glass number three and smoothed out my maroon leather trousers from where they'd creased lightly in the taxi. Maeve had informed me last night that red leather trousers were a power move, that screamed 'don't you dare ask my male business partner questions instead of me'. Since she was the expert in all things psychological, I'd decided to trust her. I typed out a quick response.

```
Screw men. Seriously. Screw Adrian and
Isaac and all the other shitheads.
```

It was four days since my date with Isaac. The word 'date' being used in the loosest way possible, given that the date had never happened. I'd spent Friday night knee-deep in egg fried rice and reality TV with Maeve, and then I'd chased up on Saturday afternoon – a whole week since our last text – only to be met with silence until about twenty minutes ago. I'd hidden my phone screen from Rory and Harriet, who'd been on either side of me, too embarrassed to admit to my dumping on a weathered leather taxi seat.

```
Isaac: Hey, sorry for the radio silence.
Been a really mad week. I've been thinking
about everything and I do really like you,
but I've been talking to another of my Level
matches and I think our connection might be
deeper. I'm sorry.
```

I reread it again, getting more and more fuelled up. A *deeper connection? I thought you were only speaking to one of us!* I grabbed another glass from another tray. *Why* did men chat such *shit?* There had been no need to lie; dishing out six matches was the whole point of Level. It was to be expected that someone could be talking to multiple people at once. So why *lie* about it? I'd assumed that by taking on the challenge of using Level, I was signing myself up for wasting my time. I hadn't foreseen total humiliation. Maybe the app just gave people another excuse to screw each other over. Were six perfect matches too many? Ridiculous, given that my app couldn't manage to spit me out one reasonable human being.

'On the good stuff, I see.' Harriet appeared beside me, the click of her heels audible from a mile off. She clocked my expression. 'Everything okay?'

I nodded, not trusting myself to speak. 'Mhmm.'

Harriet was a mother. She could read you like a book. I felt her eyes giving me a once over. 'Right. I definitely believe you. Rory looks like he's killing it over there.'

I spotted him on the other side of the room, chatting to two women. The four of us – me, Ror, Harriet and Ella – had spruced ourselves up in the office bathrooms after lunch before hightailing it over to London Bridge where the mixer was being held. Rory had bought a new suit for the occasion; sleek, fitted and navy. He pushed his shirt sleeves further up his forearms now, revealing the product of his lunchtime gym breaks.

I cleared my throat, not wanting to dwell on him shame-lessly flirting. Could we not take him anywhere? 'Forget him. Look at our other social butterfly.'

Ella hadn't wasted time once we'd entered the room either, immediately making a beeline for someone she knew from a previous role – they were on the same netball team, apparently. We both watched her act out what looked like a netball goal, face animated.

Harriet shook her head, smiling. 'That girl is a force of nature. Those women speaking to Rory are the creators of GetThere.'

At that, my attention was piqued. GetThere had agreed to an initial meeting with us regarding a partnership. Clearly – I watched Rory gesture wildly – my co-founder was sealing the deal.

'It's good to see more women in here than last year.'

Harriet nodded. 'We're getting there. A lot more than when I first started out, believe me.'

The more I read up about GetThere, the more I wanted to rally behind them. And not just for our own sake – a partnership encouraging users to get home safely would be phenomenal for our brand – but also for my own. And Maeve's. And every other woman in my life who waited up for an 'I'm home!' text at the end of the night.

'He's a bloody natural.' Harriet laughed as we watched Ror win them over. He was making them laugh, with swooping hand gestures that could only mean one of his ridiculous anecdotes. He'd been the same at house parties during university, winning strangers over with stories that left you thinking 'how could that possibly be true', but believing him nonetheless. He came to the end of his story, a little bit out of breath, whilst the two women – Katie and Kirsty, if I remembered correctly – gave him a lowkey round of applause. I could see, objectively, why he got so much female attention at things like this. He was charming but not sleazy, fun but not obnoxious. I squinted, trying to work out what he saying. I was pretty sure that if *I* was Maisy – the ever-mysterious Maisy that he hadn't elaborated on and seemed to avoid talking to me about – I wouldn't have been happy about this. Harriet was still watching too.

I took another swig from my glass. 'Are you about to tell me to put my charisma hat on too?'

Harriet was the queen of knowing what was best for our reputation, and the queen of a gentle nudge.

She gave me her side-eye now. 'As if. I came over here because I can't be arsed buddying up with some of these idiots in suits. You don't need to be the loudest person in the room Penny, a lot of ground-breaking ideas go on in that brain of yours. The majority of the men in here would cower if they met you in the boardroom.'

I smiled, touched. And she was *right*.

'How are you finding this thing anyway?' Harriet was tucking into a prawn cocktail, somehow managing to keep her lipliner completely intact. She held up a finger when I went to answer. 'Hang on. Neil is in the middle of a twin-sister meltdown emergency. I told him we should never have bought them different Barbie dolls for their birthday. Yoga Barbie with the top knot is *clearly* the best. I'm 37 years old and even I can see that.' She tapped furiously on her phone, a woman on a mission.

Neil was Harriet's husband, a sweet but quiet man that we'd met at last year's Christmas party. He'd been in charge of school pick-up today, and Harriet had predicted in the taxi on the way over here that somewhere between carrot sticks and dolls, he'd encounter a snag.

'Okay, I'm back with you. Crisis averted.' She nodded for me to go on.

'I'm scoping it all out before I swoop.' This was not true. I was actually scoping out the safest place to sit in a corner and steal a full bottle of prosecco. What was the point in glasses? They just slowed you down.

'That's exactly what I used to say before I walked into a nightclub.' Harriet flagged down a waiter, who was offering canapés to the crowd. I took one without thinking.

'This looks *disgusting*.' I offered the oyster to Harriet, who slurped it back, making me gag. 'Where are all the mini pizzas at? The sliders?'

'I think they're that way' – she pointed out of the front door – 'take a left and you'll find yourself at the 6-year-old's birthday party.'

'Hilarious.'

Harriet took my arm as she watched me neck a freshly filled glass. I was usually the sensible one in the office. 'Are you *sure* you're okay?'

I was well aware that I was a glass past fully in control. 'Yes, of course.'

She took my arm. 'You sure?'

Oh God. I felt tears prickling at the back of my eyelids.

'Shall we go to the toilets?' Harriet steered me in the direction of the swanky bathrooms near the entrance, rubbing my shoulder. 'It's okay. Nothing wrong with a wobble.'

I downed what was left of my glass and let her half drag me to the toilets. As soon as we got inside, I pulled myself together, getting out my red lipstick and reapplying to distract myself. The tears had surfaced now, running down my cheeks, and there was no way of stopping them.

'Oh, Penny, what is it?'

I hiccupped, the rest of the prosecco racing to my head. 'I'm worried the app doesn't work.'

Now that I'd spoken it out loud, I started crying even harder.

'Shit.' Harriet was filling up a water glass from the tap. 'You're meant to be the easy one. It's like my twins; one of them always cries in public, the other one is a sweet little angel. Here, drink this.'

She passed me the glass, gesturing for me to take more than the tiny sip that I did. 'Let's not make any hasty statements about our company.'

I glanced at my reflection, which looked a little manic. My hair had come out of its half up, half down hairstyle, framing my face with unruly, random pieces of hair.

'Harriet.' I reached out and grabbed the front of her dress.

She paled, taking a sip of water herself. 'Yes?'

'I'm being serious.'

She nodded. 'I know, that's why I'm worried. Penny Webber doesn't *do* unserious.' She took a breath. 'The app *does* work, Penny. We've just fixed the glitch, and –'

I interrupted before she could continue. 'I don't mean *technically*. I mean' – I waved my arms around – 'our ethos. About the perfect match. The concept doesn't work. We designed an algorithm for love, and it's full of shit.'

'Oh crap.' Harriet started rifling through her bag. 'Phone, phone, phone . . .'

'Who are you calling?' I watched out of the corner of my eye, leaning in really close to the mirror and trying (again) to maintain a steady hand and fill in the outline of red. Wow, they weren't kidding when they said that bubbles had an immediate effect.

'I'm calling Rory. This is a code red.'

I laughed and held up the lipstick. 'Did you say that on purpose?'

Harriet shot me a look. 'Just keep applying and don't say any more career sabotaging statements. I've got make-up remover in my bag, just hang on a minute.'

It only took a few seconds for Harriet to locate her phone, and she shuffled into the corner of the bathroom, pressing a few buttons and sighing heavily when she didn't immediately get an answer.

'Okay, he's useless. What's the point of having a phone if you don't bloody check it?' She regrouped. 'New plan. Get it all out now, whilst we're on our own in here. Tell me why the app is full of shit?' She pinched the bridge of her nose. 'I cannot believe I just said that to my boss.'

She was right; we were on our own. It was one of those venues with a million different toilets dotted around the place. Plenty of locations for people to duck out of a conversation and spit their oyster into the toilet bowl. Or at least, that's how I'd interpreted it.

'The app doesn't work. It's just like the rest of them. Shallow people searching for shallow connections.'

Harriet was all but getting into brace position. 'Is this about you saying you'd date? Because I don't think anyone will mind if you call it off.'

I showed her the text. 'Four of my matches, Harriet, were complete duds. And this one was a complete waste of my time too.'

She winced, reading. 'I'm sorry, Penny. It's really hard when you like someone and —'

'This isn't about me *liking him*.' I thought for a moment. 'Okay, it's a teeny bit about that. But it's actually about more than him. It's proof that Level fundamentally doesn't work.'

I was trying my best to communicate eloquently, even with the prosecco buzz ringing in my head, but I was sure she was getting the gist.

'We said we'd create something that went "beyond the surface", but now that I've tested it out, I don't think that's even possible. Which makes us just as fraudulent as every other option on the market.' I hiccupped again. 'My prosecco consumption doesn't make this any less true, by the way.'

Harriet was nodding along, anxiously checking the door to the bathroom and double-checking that there wasn't anyone in the cubicles. 'I really don't think you can base your faith in a lifelong project on one bad set of dates.'

'But that's the thing, Harriet.' I went into one of the cubicles and slumped on the closed seat. 'It *wasn't* a bad set of dates. On the surface, Isaac was everything that I would have expected our app to serve to me. I just thought it would be a little bit more accurate. I thought we'd cracked the code for love, and it turns out we haven't. I don't even know what love is. How *ridiculous*, for a permanently single woman to pretend that she ever did.'

'Oh God.' She crouched down beside me. 'This is the alcohol talking.'

I accepted the sip of water that she was offering to me again. 'Is it? Or did we just spend *years* creating something that doesn't work?'

'Penny.' Harriet tilted my chin up slightly. 'Take it from someone who did a lot of dating before she settled down, one bad date does not mean that a dating app doesn't work. That's why you give people six matches, right? Not every single one is going to be your soulmate.'

I scrunched my nose in disgust.

'Sorry, but it's true. Not every match is going to work, but it gives you a better shot than any of those other apps do, that's for sure.'

Her phone started ringing, and I took that as permission to leave the loo.

Yes, she was probably right. But it *wasn't* just one bad date. It was the two first dates before that, and the mind-numbing conversations with my first two matches at the very beginning. We'd laboured over the app's programming. Spent hours and hours figuring out how to calculate one member's compatibility with another, considering factors like their location and time most active (because it said a lot about people's schedules and availability for a relationship, what time of day they were on their phone). Level was supposed to be a breath of fresh air – it was *not* supposed to leave you feeling so lonely.

'Hang on, Rory, one second.' Harriet put one hand over her phone, gritting her teeth. 'Where are you going now? Wait, Penny – stay still!'

I pushed on the bathroom door, so enraged with everything work-related that I didn't watch where I was going, colliding headfirst with someone's chest.

'Oof.' I bounced back, making eye contact with an extremely attractive man. The fizz in my veins crackled. Oh, *hello*.

17

Given that I was five foot six and wearing heels, it wasn't often that I bumped into someone's chest. A someone that was extremely, *extremely* attractive.

'Where are you going in such a hurry?' The mystery man steadied me, keeping a hand on my arm. His voice was deep and his accent was far from Rory's Geordie or Isaac's Mancunian; I would have guessed West London. He looked a bit like a Disney character, his blonde hair artistically wavy and his suit jacket clinging to his arms. And yes, Level was designed to be less shallow, but I was *mad* at it, so I'd decided that for one night only, I was not going to follow its lead.

'Nowhere important.' I smiled up at him, trying to think clearly. *Had I checked for lipstick in my teeth?* It was going to be a miracle if I didn't have Charlotte Tilbury's K.I.S.S.I.N.G all over my face.

He ran his hands through his thick blonde hair. 'One look at you and I'm thinking I need to get a drink and play catch-up.'

I crossed my arms. 'What are you trying to say?'

'That you've clearly got the right idea, making the most of the free bar.' He leaned in conspiratorially. 'Can I tell you a secret?'

I could smell the mint on his breath, and the slightly musky, fresh scent of his aftershave. Scent was the easiest way to fancy someone. We'd done our research in the early days, bitter that technology hadn't yet advanced enough to transfer scent through a screen.

He was looking at me intensely, waiting for my permission.

'Yes, you can.'

He relaxed. 'I hate these things. They make me want to scream. If anyone else comes up to me pretending to care about what I do for fun when all they really want to do is talk business, I'm walking out.'

He grabbed us both another glass, which I gratefully accepted. I'd now gone *fully* rogue. Talking to strange men was the final nail in the coffin.

'Agreed. I'll go with you.' I paused, horrified. 'Not like *that*.'

'No?' His eyebrow was raised, a challenge, and the alcohol had emboldened me.

'Well, maybe if you play your cards right.'

Who was I to turn down the initial advances of a Prince Charming lookalike? Especially now that my dating app had proved to be so fundamentally flawed. Maybe dating apps were out, and organic meet-cutes were in. Either way, I wasn't looking a gift horse in the mouth.

'I'm Daniel.' He held out his hand for me to shake, and when I took it he pulled me in, gently resting his hand on my lower back. I usually hated dominance, but I was three glasses of prosecco past caring. *Someone* needed to take control of the situation.

He moved me gently out of the way of a disgruntled woman trying to get past. 'I think we should probably stop blocking the ladies' bathroom.'

I flushed. 'Great idea. Let's go before my publicist hunts me down.'

In the back of my mind I knew this was unfair to Harriet. All she'd done all night was try and give me the pep talk I probably needed. She was a good friend. I hoped I remembered to tell her that in the morning.

Daniel guided me over to a secluded sofa tucked in an alcove, away from prying eyes. 'Publicist? You must be a big shot.'

My cheeks reddened yet again. 'Sorry, she's Head of Comms for my business, not me. I'm Penny, I work at —'

I prepared the business spiel. That *was* what we were here for, after all.

Daniel interrupted. 'Can I propose an alternative?'

Luckily for him, the copious amounts of alcohol had mellowed me out. Sober Penny would not have stood for that interruption.

'Let's not talk about business. Let's just be Penny and Daniel.' He clinked his glass against mine. 'How does that sound?'

'What makes you think you know me well enough for us to be "Penny and Daniel"?' I narrowed my eyes, suspicious.

'Okay, correction. Let's just be Penny' — he held out his left hand — 'and Daniel.' His right hand mirrored the other, and I forced myself to tear my eyes away from his forearms. And his long fingers.

He pressed on. 'It's exhausting, having to open up every conversation with a LinkedIn bio.'

I knew what he meant. Especially tonight when all I really wanted was to forget about Level. I eyed Daniel's hand again, which was now held out to me for the second time in ten minutes.

'Okay.' I shook it. 'But only because I know a good business deal when I hear one.'

'Attagirl.' He took a gulp from his glass, putting his hand on my knee. 'Tell me something about you that isn't about work.'

I thought hard for a second before landing on exactly the right anecdote. 'Ever since I was in sixth form, I've had this phobia of getting appendicitis in the middle of the night.'

It was true. One of the girls on my English course had missed our morning lesson, and by lunchtime she'd texted her friends and the news spread like wildfire. You could just *wake up* in the middle of the night with a burning appendix out of nowhere? New fear *unlocked*. I tried to let rationale guide me in most areas of my life, but that was freaky.

Daniel was silent for a second, processing the story before bursting into genuine laughter. 'That was incredibly niche. Well done. Weird fear, but well done.'

I tried not to feel disgruntled. When I'd told that to Rory during freshers' week, he'd immediately understood.

He gestured for me to move closer. 'Okay, my turn. This one is really juicy.'

I found myself leaning in so that he was almost whispering in my ear. 'I'm 29, and I've never ridden a bike.'

I pulled back. '*Never?*' I was always incredibly sceptical of people who said this. Most people had been plonked on a bike with training wheels between the ages of 4 and 6.

'Never. It's too late now, I fear. I'm going to be the man who can't ride a bike forever.'

'Alternatively, you could just choose a different anecdote, avoid bikes, and no one would ever be any the wiser. I can't remember the last time it was necessary for me to ride a bike. Unless you're planning on entering a triathlon anytime soon.'

Daniel nodded. 'You're right. I'm just an attention whore.'

I snorted. There was something about this man that was completely unexpected. I probably wouldn't ever see him again after tonight, but maybe that was the whole point. Maybe after a month of bad dates and disappointment, I just needed someone who could remind me what a connection felt like.

'I like your hair.' He twirled one of my waves around his index finger. 'Gives you a sort of wild look.'

If I had a pound for every time a man at a bar had used that line on me, I could sack off my career in app development. I said as much.

'Oh, I'm *sorry*, are my chat-up lines not original enough for you?'

I took his glass from him, finishing it since mine was empty. 'Not nearly original enough, sorry.'

What I wanted to say was that I'd been around dating apps long enough to know every possible chat-up line in the single-man-repertoire. But I held back, given our deal. I was mysterious Penny tonight.

'Does that mean you're trying to chat me up?' I bit back a smile, watching his expression turn to surprise.

'Well, it's not what I expected when I was forced here tonight by my team' – he took my chin in his hand gently – 'but it's a happy accident, I must admit.'

I knew a first kiss when I saw one, and I felt something coil in the pit of my stomach. I hadn't been kissed once in the last year, and now here I was kissing two men in the space of a few weeks. Whoever was writing my story was having the time of their life.

'A very happy accident,' I murmured against his lips before he finally took the plunge, and I melted into the feeling of his mouth moving against mine. His hand traced up my thigh, moving dangerously close to places that definitely weren't appropriate for a corporate mixer.

'What the hell are you playing at?'

Rory's voice cut through the kiss, and the alcohol, and I yanked myself away from Daniel. My best friend was standing over us, Harriet behind him, and he looked *pissed*.

18

As far as I could remember, there had only been three times in our eight years of friendship that Rory had been mad at me. Like *really* mad. The first, when Maeve and I had locked ourselves out of our uni house, leaving all three of us sat on the doorstep in the middle of the night. We'd both been wearing short skirts and flimsy T-shirts – high on the rare August heat and forgetting that summer nights were not comparable – and Rory had given up his jacket, laying it over our legs and sitting in a huff for the whole hour it took for one of our other housemates to get back from their own night out.

The second time had been in the early stages of our partnership, when we'd reached a stalemate over one of the components of the programming. I'd been steadfast in the belief that our app should be completely blind (no names, no bio – nothing) and Rory had stood firm that the only element that really mattered when it came to a blind match was the photos. At least, the only element that might get us a shot at funding. Mine had been a stupid idea, but I'd sat stubborn on the concept for weeks, and we'd tiptoed around each other long enough to question whether the whole thing – and our budding partnership – was a dud idea. Our cold front had ended with Rory caving and letting me run with it, only for me to come back to him a week later with an apology and my tail between my legs.

The third and final time had been last year, in the aftermath of his and Lottie's breakup. They'd been together for over two years when they'd split, and Lottie had been just as entwined in our lives as Adrian had been. When he'd turned up at our flat, looking for a place to stay for the night because they'd decided that he needed to move out, I'd texted Lottie to check that she was okay too. Rory was not an inflammatory person – it took a lot to rattle him – but apparently knowing that we'd been in contact was enough to cause argument number three. It hadn't been a huff like the first time, or a prolonged cold front like the second, but a different kind of anger entirely. He'd been defensive, hurt that I'd reached out to her instead of standing by him.

It was this kind of look in his eyes now, as he stood in front of Daniel and me.

'What the hell are you playing at?'

I immediately jumped up, a rabbit caught in the headlights. Daniel, caught between two relative strangers, took his time rising to his feet, and immediately sprung to my defence.

'Look, I don't know who you are, but she's not doing anything wrong.' He looked at me with a grin. 'She's mingling.'

I knew better than to laugh at the joke, but I had to bite my lip to stop it.

154

'Oh, I'm sorry.' Rory's face was deadpan. 'I forgot that the best way to network was to stick your tongue down someone's throat. Clearly, I've been doing it wrong all evening.'

Daniel straightened up almost imperceptibly so that he was closer to Rory's height. 'Well, if you've been like *this* all evening, I can't imagine you've made any firm business connections. Now, do you mind? We were a little bit busy.'

All credit to Rory, he barely batted an eyelid. 'Right. Busy. Looked important.'

He didn't make any move to leave. Harriet shot me a warning look, one that clearly said 'do something'.

'Look' – the prosecco was catching up with me again and I made a conscious effort not to stumble over my words – 'it was just a kiss. No harm done.'

'No harm done.' Rory repeated the words back to me. His arms were crossed, hands gripping his biceps so tightly that I could see the veins in his hands. I swallowed. Bad prosecco. Bad, bad prosecco. He narrowed his eyes. 'Pen, can I speak to you for a minute?'

Daniel stepped in front of me. 'Mate, who even are you? She doesn't have to go anywhere.'

Even in my current state, I registered how annoying this show of testosterone was. 'I don't have to, but I'm going to. This is my business partner, Rory.'

Again, I didn't elaborate on what our business was. This was all part of the game. A modern-day Cinderella. Should I leave behind my shoe? I was pretty sure I'd stepped in a deconstructed croque monsieur on my way to the bathroom earlier, so maybe not.

'If that's what you want.' Daniel nodded and stepped back. 'Don't let him make any decisions for you.'

Rory barked out a laugh. 'That's rich. Come on, Pen.'

He took my hand, but the grip was firm, not affectionate. Harriet was watching the whole thing like a tennis match, eyes narrowed at my new friend.

Daniel cleared his throat. 'I need to leave anyway. Too many pompous idiots at these things.' The intention behind his words was obvious.

'It was great to meet you, Penny.' Daniel leaned in and kissed my cheek, pausing for a second. 'Can I just . . .' He wiped at the skin just below my bottom lip with his thumb.

Rory dropped my hand like it was on fire. 'Classy.'

I could only assume that my lipstick had gone AWOL.

'Nothing wrong with a bit of smudged red, don't you think, Pen?' I hadn't told him my nickname but he'd clearly picked it up from Rory, who was glaring at him, a thunderous expression on his face.

We all watched him wander back into the crowd, picking up another glass with ease and turning back to raise it in Rory's direction.

'Okay, so that was . . .' I felt a rush of embarrassment for the first time since Rory had appeared.

He just held up a hand, signalling that he needed a minute. He went over to the bar and came back with a whisky on the rocks. He downed it.

'Right. Go on.'

'I think I can hear Ella shouting me . . .' Harriet looked over vaguely to the other side of the room, desperately searching for an out.

I snorted. 'You have permission to leave.'

'Fabulous.'

She strode off, wasting no time in leaving us behind. If this had been any other context, we'd both have found this hilarious. Instead, Rory just stared at me for a second before he erupted. 'What on earth are you doing?'

I looked anywhere but directly at him. 'I've had a really *shit* day.'

His expression softened for a second before he was back on the attack. 'Then come and find me! I was right there, on the other side of the room. What you did tonight was incredibly stupid.'

I reeled back, affronted.

'Who the hell *was* that guy?' He wasn't avoiding eye contact in the same way that I was, looking at me with laser focus.

Something inside me clicked, and I was suddenly just as angry as he was. I hadn't spoken to anyone important about my concerns about Level, I hadn't caused a drunken scene and vomited on someone's shoes. All I'd done was have fun. For once, I'd been carefree Penny. I was starting to forget that she even existed.

'Why do you care who he is?'

Rory paled. 'I don't.'

'You don't?' There was a moment of tense silence.

'I care because this is our public image.' He gathered himself. 'I care because we're still a fledgling company. We need people to respect us. And they won't, not if our CEO gets a reputation for disappearing into dark corners at parties.'

I narrowed my eyes. 'This corner is extremely well lit.'

Rory threw his hands up, exasperated. 'You know exactly what I mean.' He sat down and perched where Daniel and I had been sitting moments before. 'Look. I know you've had a shit week. Harriet told me what happened.'

I briefly considered the betrayal but after all that had happened tonight, I probably didn't have a leg to stand on.

'Don't be mad at her. She had to explain the code red phone call. I thought it was a practical joke at first. Penny Webber does not tend to cause code reds.'

I snorted. 'Does she not?'

'I think the last time was about five years ago, when Maeve called to tell me you'd assumed jelly shots weren't alcoholic.' He paused. 'Isaac's a prick if he can't see how brilliant you are. He'll regret it, I'm sure.'

In getting carried away with a handsome stranger, I'd forgotten all about my motives for getting drunk. Now, that sinking feeling returned to my stomach. Alongside a horrific swirling motion, which I could only hope wasn't about to bring the prosecco earth side.

Rory continued, his voice a little bit firmer. 'But it isn't Level's fault, Penny, it's his.'

'Harriet told you a lot of things, didn't she?' I crossed my arms.

'She's not used to calling *me* in a crisis, that's for sure.' He tilted my chin upwards, looking me right in the eye. 'This is going to feel better in the morning, I promise. Rejection is the hardest thing in the world. Trust me on that one. Now come on, let's go.' He took my arm and pivoted me in the direction of the exit, causing me to stumble slightly.

'Whoa there.' He steadied me. 'How many glasses did you have?'

I'd lost count after the fifth. 'Lots?'

He shook his head. 'What am I going to do with you?'

I considered getting him to drop me off at my flat, lying in bed and being finally alone to process Isaac's dumping.

'Can I stay with you?'

Rory swallowed, and for a moment I thought he might say no. 'Sure. But only if you let me feed you first. You're going to have one hell of a hangover tomorrow.'

I had visions of cheesy chips. 'I am not against that plan.'

He rolled his eyes. 'Didn't think so. Come on.'

★★★

If anything could sober you up, it was shoving chips into your mouth on the Jubilee line.

'Better?' Rory was sitting next to me, occasionally pinching one. He shot me a look when I tried to steer the Styrofoam box away from him. 'I bought these chips, Pen, hand them over.'

He had a point. I passed him the box. 'These have nothing on the cheesy chips and gravy from Tony's.'

I was referring to a tiny fish and chip shop in Edinburgh. The location for many end-of-the-night carb top-ups. By now, Rory's anger had ebbed into mild irritation, and he'd started to warm up again.

'You're right. And now you've pointed it out, they taste like cardboard.' He closed the box. 'Done with this?'

I nodded, stomach sufficiently saved from the peril of alcohol. I was out of any *immediate* danger of throwing up my guts, I was almost entirely sure.

'You're my favourite person, do you know that?' I'd reached the sentimental stage of my drunken cycle, leaning my body against Rory's and trying to manoeuvre around the awkward armrest between us. I felt his sudden intake of breath.

'I do know that. Come on, we need to change.' He led me off the Tube carriage, reaching down to grab my hand and steer me towards the DLR. He'd held my hand a million times, but for some reason *now* I cared if they were clammy or not.

'Let me just . . .' I unlocked my fingers to wipe my hands on my trousers before reaching back for him.

He didn't say anything, but the corners of his mouth turned up.

After hungry Penny came sentimental Penny, and shortly after that, *exhausted* Penny made an entrance. My limbs felt like lead as we walked back to Rory's flatshare. The weight of the reality of tonight's actions began to hit. I was *dreading* facing everyone tomorrow.

I collapsed onto his bed as soon as humanly possible once we'd walked through the door, and he held a finger to his lips, silently communicating that his flatmate Stephen might be asleep.

'You're a piece of work, you know that?' Rory was loosening his tie as he stared at me from the other side of the room. 'Are you going to sleep in those trousers?'

I glanced down at the leather. 'No?'

He rolled his eyes, throwing me a T-shirt. 'Don't say I never give you anything.'

'My hero.' I locked eyes with him, suddenly self-conscious. 'Are you waiting for a show or something?'

Rory laughed, turning round whilst I got changed. I couldn't quite make out whatever sarcastic mumble escaped him as he took off his own shirt. My cheeks flushed at the sight of his naked back, something I'd seen a million times over the years. I stopped looking, reaching down into the third drawer of his bedside table. I wasn't sure how it had happened, but over the years, no matter where he'd been living – aside from the brief interlude of his year living with Lottie – I'd had my own drawer. We'd had too many late nights working on Level for me *not* to have some make-up remover and a toothbrush here. It was the equivalent of his belongings at the back of my wardrobe, just waiting for him to come back.

I scrubbed at my eyes with a cotton pad. 'Thanks for letting me stay here tonight.'

Rory nodded, not saying much. 'I bet Daniel would have let you stay at his too.'

Oh God, we were back on this. The mention of Daniel brought more pressing issues to the surface. 'Are you sure this is okay?'

Rory hesitated as he was taking off his watch. 'Is what okay?'

As much as I'd usually think nothing of climbing into bed beside him, we were grown adults, and something inside me felt like it might be wrong. 'You know, Maisy?'

He nodded, resuming his movement. 'Ah, about that.' I could see the cogs in his brain turning before he came to some sort of decision. 'Look, don't worry about it. It's fine.'

Was it though? I opened my mouth to protest.

'Honestly, Pen, nothing to worry about. I'll fill you in properly tomorrow. Just shut up and go to sleep.'

At that, my interest was well and truly piqued. But he'd shut the conversation down, climbing into bed and checking his phone before setting an alarm and placing it face down. He had historically always taken the left side, and me the right. The first time we'd ever shared a bed, after a night out in first year, there hadn't really been an excuse. My room was right next door. But we'd decided that we were too tired to walk even five steps further, and curled up in his bed instead. The number of nights we'd slept together had decreased over the years, but I still felt just as safe lying beside him. I took his word for it that we weren't about to make a hugely immoral error and got in next to him, shuffling to make myself comfortable.

'Rory?' He'd switched off the light, so I spoke into the darkness.

There was a second of silence before. 'Yeah?'

'I'm sorry about tonight.'

From across the sheets, his hand reached for mine, squeezing it. 'I think I'll find it in my heart to forgive you. But I'm not protecting you from Dexter tomorrow.'

I snorted. 'I think I can handle it.'

We settled into silence again. Rory hadn't moved his hand, rubbing the back of his thumb over mine. The contact fizzed underneath my skin. I didn't dare take a breath, not wanting to ruin the moment.

'And just so you know' – I heard his head turn towards mine, even if I could barely make it out in the dark – 'Isaac's an idiot.'

I nodded, already on the way to forgetting about the man who'd ghosted me. 'Yeah.'

'He didn't deserve you.' After a second he finally moved his hand from mine and turned away. 'Night, Penny.'

I felt the loss of his body right next to mine and shivered immediately. Being as sneaky as I possibly could, I edged closer by a few inches. Rory was like a furnace, his body heat radiating out from his side of the bed.

What would happen if I reached over there?

I blinked back the thought, rejecting it as soon as it crossed my mind and rolling away instead. The duvet would have to do, heat wise. I tucked it right up to my chin. *What was wrong with me?* I'd had way too much prosecco tonight. Any girl would have felt attracted to the man who'd fed her chips on the Tube and given her a T-shirt. It was a sad girl's instinct, right? Also, I'd kissed *far* too many people lately. The urge was bound to still be in my system. This wasn't about Rory. I ignored the urge to scoot over a few inches again and buried it deeply.

Rory's breathing hadn't evened out yet, so I knew he was still awake.

Our backs weren't actually touching, but I could feel the almost-contact as if we were pressed together. I rolled even further away, staring at the ceiling and trying to count sheep, deliberately pushing all other thoughts but fluffy white farm animals out of my brain.

I needed to get it together. For the sake of Level. For the sake of a friendship that had lasted just a couple of years short of a decade. Some things were too important to ruin with unsavoury thoughts. Rogue Penny had dug her claws in, but I could flush her out of my system.

I listened to the sound of both of us breathing in sync until sleep finally came.

19

When I woke up the next morning he was already gone. There was a note on his bedside table letting me know that he'd headed to the office but that he would cover for me if I was late. Everyone told me that the best part of owning a company was that no one would argue if you didn't show up on time, but I'd never once arrived after 9 a.m. I checked my phone. 9.03. Great. I jumped into action, ignoring the pounding in my head. The later I was, the worse facing the music would be.

Rory had left a granola bar on the kitchen table, next to a glass of water and some painkillers, and a note that said 'Consume all please' in more of his messy boy handwriting. I did as I was told, this time, running my fingers through my hair and using my limited supply of third drawer belongings – a mascara, some lip balm, and a spare pair of knickers – to make myself look a bit more human. I yanked the leather trousers back on, pulling one of Rory's white T-shirts from a hanger and going for the oversized, tucked-in look. His wardrobe mirror revealed two obvious eye bags. No amount of concealer was hiding those bad boys. This was going to have to do.

By the time I got to the office, I was sweating profusely from my time underground – and I was pretty sure my sweat was 90 per cent alcohol. Any and all efforts to look presentable had been erased.

All right, Penny, you can do this. I took a deep breath in. *Everyone gets hanxiety. Even if it's never usually you.*

'Morning!' I bit the bullet, pushing on the door and strolling in with my empty coffee cup in hand. If I acted like nothing had happened yesterday, maybe everyone would follow my lead.

'Morning boss.' Dexter looked up briefly before getting back to his computer. Odd.

A few of the others said hi, barely glancing in my direction. Okay, even by regular standards, this was weird. Manifesting did *not* work. This was not my doing.

I made a beeline for the coffee machine, desperate for my next hit of caffeine. This coffee was going to be so sweet it'd make my dentist squirm. Dexter met me at the machine, bringing his mug over for a refill.

'Just so you know,' he was basically whispering, 'Rory told us he'd cut the Christmas party budget in half if we mentioned it. But I *cannot* get through today if I don't make at least one joke. Let me have it?'

Ah. Now everything made sense. I waved him on. 'Go for it.'

He turned, getting a mini prosecco bottle out of the fridge. 'Hair of the dog?'

I groaned. 'You won't be laughing when I vomit all over your shoes.'

Dexter stepped back. 'You wouldn't.'

'One more prosecco joke and those New Balances are going to be green, not white.'

He shuddered, filling his mug and backing away. 'Jokes aside, I thought it was kind of iconic. Way to show off your new personality transplant as of late. Kiss a rando at a party.'

The memory clung to me like a bad smell. In broad daylight, I could see how it might not have been my finest moment.

'I thought I heard you come in.' Ella came out of her office. Even though we'd been at the same event, she looked perfectly put together. She'd even done her staple eyeliner wings. 'I left you alone with Harriet for literally one hour. What on earth happened?'

Clearly, Ella was the only member of this office who'd taken no notice of Rory's threat.

Harriet was looking slightly sheepish over at her desk (or, as sheepish as you *can* look with your hair in a slicked-back ponytail, wearing a pantsuit). She held her hands up. '*You* hired me because I can spread news like wildfire. Secrets go through me like a laxative.'

Dexter gagged. 'Can we go one second in this office without someone threatening to release bodily fluids?'

I held up my hands. 'Harriet, that secret was fair game. And Ella, yes, I did have a meltdown in the middle of a mixer. But we all make mistakes.'

She nodded, getting the message loud and clear.

'And Dexter, for the love of God, drink that prosecco or get it out of my sight.'

Dexter, who was back at his desk taking out his headphones, grinned. 'I don't need telling twice. Consider me drunk.'

All things considered, I'd survived the first five minutes unscathed. And everyone who worked in a close-knit office knew that the first five minutes were always the hardest. I stirred an extra spoonful of sugar into my coffee.

'You're going to give yourself even more of a headache doing that.' Rory was leaning in the doorway of our office, watching me stir. 'This must be some kind of record.'

'Nope.' I tapped the spoon on the side. 'My record is five sugars the day after Glastonbury.'

We'd gone as a group of six last year; multiple days of torrential rain, mud baths, and tents so flimsy that by the final night all of us were crammed into the last one standing. We'd barely got ten minutes of sleep between us, and had spent the next evening collapsed on our sofas with a Domino's order so big that I felt I had to justify it to the delivery man.

I followed Rory into our office, trying to forcibly remove any memories from the night before. I'd woken up in the night with my entire body curled around his, draped over his bare skin, having scooted over in my sleep. I'd stayed there for a minute, before jumping back to my side when his breathing had broken its pattern. Thank *God* he'd been asleep.

I cleared my throat. 'Anyway, thanks for last night.'

He collapsed on one of the bean bags we'd bought for the space between our desks (studies showed that comfy seating produced more effective brainstorms. And by studies, I meant entirely made-up ones). Rory was much less suited and booted than he'd been last night, wearing jeans and a grey Nike hoodie. The only suggestion that whilst I was absolutely hanging out of my arse, he might have been suffering a little bit too. 'Anytime. How's the head?'

I fell into the other bean bag. 'It's been better.' I took a deep breath, desperately wanting to address what had been on my mind since last night. 'So, do you think Maisy is going to mind that I stayed over?'

Rory ran his hands through his hair. 'Oh. That.'

I waited impatiently whilst he chose his words, seconds away from jumping across the bean bags and shaking him. 'I'm not dating her any more. Nothing to worry about on that front. Fizzled out before it had even really got going.'

I tried to pretend that this wasn't big news, stirring my now lukewarm coffee.

'Oh, right. Interesting.'

Fizzled out? I was overcome with the need to know why. How could I bribe Maeve into getting the gossip for me? Why didn't I feel like *I* could ask him about this?

Before I had the chance to expose my nosiness, Ella knocked on the door. 'Sorry to interrupt, but you've got a delivery, Penny.'

A delivery guy came in behind her, placing a huge bouquet of flowers on my desk. Pink roses and huge yellow sunflowers, with foliage bulking it out. It was *beautiful*.

'I didn't order those.'

Rory whistled. 'No shit.'

Ella pulled the door almost shut. 'Well, it says your name on it.' She shrugged.

'Someone really wants to send a message.' Rory was staring at the bouquet. 'Are you going to put us both out of our misery? The suspense is killing me over here, Pen.'

'Right, yeah.' I manoeuvred myself off the bean bag (not easy, especially when wearing leather). Reading the label, I pulled the little notecard out of its envelope.

'*Holy shit.*'

Rory didn't budge; the only sign he was even interested was the slight flicker of his eyes in my direction. 'Isaac already regretting his move?'

I read the notecard again to make sure I'd read it right.

Last night was fun. Do it again sometime?
Daniel x

The same Daniel who didn't know my last name, or where I worked. I explained last night to Rory; the whole shtick of not telling each other any of the details.

'Wow. And now this has turned up at the office.' He hummed the tune to Jaws until I screwed up the envelope and threw it in his direction, making sure to save the notecard with his mobile digits written in the florist's handwriting.

'You're going to ignore it, right? I'm not kidding, Pen, that's creepy as fuck.'

Was it creepy? Or was it romantic? My cynicism was so strong that sometimes I wasn't sure what was genuinely a red flag. And it *had* been a good kiss. Maybe sometimes you could put up with a few red flags. Show them off, like decorations on a sandcastle.

'I don't know. It *was* a genuine meet-cute. How often does that happen?'

'Can you honestly call him pouncing on you when you came out of the ladies' bathroom half-cut a meet-cute?'

I scoffed. 'He didn't *pounce*. I walked into him.'

I hadn't had an in-person meet-cute since my first year in London, when I'd accidentally taken some guy's latte instead of my own. At least, I'd *thought* it was a meet-cute, until I'd spotted the ring on his finger. These kinds of opportunities only came up once in a blue moon.

'There might be a completely innocent reason for this.' I gestured to the flowers. 'At least I know he isn't a *complete* stalker, or he would have known I'm a tulips girl.'

Rory was staring at me, unconvinced. 'All these years you remain a complete cynic, and now suddenly we're excusing a man who is *really* channelling Christian Bale in *American Psycho*?'

I stuck my tongue out at him, rearranging the flowers and leaving the notecard in my desk drawer. Rory was overreacting, *right*?

***

'He did *what*?' Isla sipped her cocktail – something fruity, something pink – before leaning in over the table and putting her hand on mine. 'I know you hate when I say it, but everything –'

I rolled my eyes. 'Everything does *not* happen for a reason.'

She threw her hands up. 'Then explain why the *exact* veil I wanted appeared on Vinted last week.'

'Coincidence.' I slurped my own cocktail, a non-alcoholic Moscow mule. 'Purely coincidence.'

Maeve, who had been staring into space next to me, shook her head before giving her input. 'People like to think everything happens for a reason in order to give their life meaning.'

I snorted. 'Well, aren't you the bringer of doom.'

Adrian down-days were getting rarer and rarer to the point of extinction, but today was an exception. She took one of the three shots she'd lined up in front of her. We hadn't intended our after-work drinks to include shots – I was absolutely *not* in the headspace for alcohol after last night – but there had been no dissuading her.

'Well, I firmly believe it does. If that translates into me trying to give my life some meaning, then so be it.' Isla took one of the shots herself. 'Maeve, finding ex-boyfriends on dating apps is a rite of passage. Put the shots down.'

After weeks of resisting, Maeve had finally downloaded Link (Rory and I were trying not to hold it against her), in an obvious attempt to try and see if Adrian was dating. A couple of nights ago I'd caught her dropping her location pin right next to his flat at 2 a.m., in a desperate attempt to catch him (without being caught herself).

'I mean, *look* at this one' – she held up her phone, showing us a photo of her ex-boyfriend grinning from ear to ear on the streets of Rome – 'I literally took this photo. I bet, if you zoomed right in on his eyeballs, you'd see me.'

I gently pried the phone out of her hands. 'Which we're definitely *not* going to do.'

'And written on my forehead' – Maeve was trying to grab the phone back – 'would be the letters M-U-G.'

Isla shot me a look, and surreptitiously stole another one of the shot glasses, dumping the tequila into a plant pot. Maeve was too busy wrestling with me to notice.

'Anyway, enough about that prick.' Isla slid my mocktail over to Maeve to placate her. 'Back to business. He left flowers on your desk? And his *phone number?*'

Maeve relented. 'I will agree to shelve my wallowing, but only because I need to know if we're dealing with a creepy stalker or a Richard Curtis-level romantic gesture.'

'It's still up for debate.' I tucked Maeve's phone into my back pocket and played with a napkin, tearing it into tiny pieces. 'Rory is firmly on the side of creepy stalker.'

'Shocker.' Isla rolled her eyes. '*I* think it's romantic. It was a corporate event. He probably just asked at reception. Plus, this is the perfect way to get your confidence back after the almost-ghosting.'

I winced, my pride still not recovered. 'Alternatively, maybe I should buy a double lock for our front door.'

'Penny' – she flicked me with her straw, getting gin in my eyes – 'must you always be so pessimistic?'

I held the heel of my hand to my eyelid. 'Thanks very much for that. And yes. I must. In fact, Isaac has cleared me out of all optimism for the next twenty-six years.'

Maeve clinked her one remaining shot against my drink. 'Cheers to that.'

Isla sighed. 'And here I was, thinking that tonight might be *fun*. Silly me.'

'We can't all have hot doctors waiting for us at home.'

I shoved Maeve. 'That's disgusting. I shared a womb with that doctor.'

'Not at the same time, though. Which counts for something.'

Isla scrunched up her nose. 'Are psychologists meant to be this messed up?'

'No.' Both of us said it in unison, matter-of-factly.

'Speaking of my hot doctor' – Isla winced – 'sorry, Penny. Is the sten booked yet?'

It was a miracle that I'd managed to do anything productive today, but Rory and I had finally sat down together, booking out a meeting room and coming to an agreement about the most important part of our maid of honour slash best man duties. We'd compromised on the lodge with a hot tub in the Yorkshire Dales, where the boys would spend an afternoon go-karting, and us girls would go for a Taylor Swift-themed bottomless brunch. Isla was a diehard. I'd nailed this.

'We may have booked something, but no spoilers, sorry.' I tapped my finger against the side of my nose. 'I'm taking it to the grave. Or, to the opening moments of the hen do. Whichever comes first.'

Maeve, who was in on the secret, patted Isla's hand. 'I can read you like a book. I promise Rory isn't going to force you to abseil down a cliff, or almost drown in a kayak.'

My sister-to-be looked incredibly relieved.

'Good, because I haven't been sleeping well. I've had visions of us all camping in the middle of nowhere with only matches and Super Noodles to keep us going.'

174

It was a good job we'd never shown her the rough list of original ideas.

'I'm offended that you thought I'd let it come to that.' I stole my glass back from Maeve and tipped the last of it down my throat, crunching on the ice.

'I know what you and Rory are like with each other. I've never known two people so obsessed with compromise. It's like you get so stubborn about pleasing the other one that you lose sight of the goal.' She tilted her head. 'No offence.'

Maeve was nodding along with Isla. 'It's true.'

I was still way too hungover to argue. 'Well, I can promise that there will be no Super Noodles at your hen do.'

She nodded and launched into a monologue about her homemade confetti. Isla was glowing with pre-wedding excitement. The universe had been good to her. I looked down at my bag, where I could see Daniel's note peeking out of the inside pocket, eleven digits beneath his name. My own little weird universe moment.

'Penny, are you even listening?'

I shrugged off the thought, tuning back in and offering my opinion on oatmeal versus shell napkin holders, pushing it to the back of my mind. I had *no* idea what I was going to do about that phone number.

20

I squinted at the track in front of me, my brother barely a speck in the distance.

I cupped my hands and yelled. 'Joe, come on. This is a supposed to be a bonding activity.'

The speck got bigger and bigger as he jogged back towards me.

'Pen, how can we bond when you're miles behind?'

I flipped him the finger. 'We don't all have freakishly long legs.'

He wasn't even that much taller than me; five foot eleven to my five foot six. We'd both inherited Mum's tall genes – Dad was five foot eight at a push, and Mum had always been slightly taller, the one to reach the top shelf at the supermarket. I had to admit, I'd been a bit concerned about Dad's height hindering him on Level (once I'd got past the betrayal of him downloading Link too), but he'd texted me a few days ago to let me know that of his six matches, three had messaged him first. Research showed that women messaging first was an anomaly; it was hard thinking of other people seeing your dad as a catch.

'Fine, I will take the bait and jog at your pace. Oh, look' — he pointed at the ground — 'a snail just overtook us.'

I rolled my eyes. Despite my aversion to outdoor yoga and twisting my body into unreasonable positions, I did enjoy running. I was by no means good at it, but we'd started running together in March with the goal of feeling confident enough to join parkrun. It came a lot more naturally to Joe than it did to me.

'Do you feel the stress falling off you in waves?' I kept my focus straight ahead on the dirt track in front of me but directed the question at him.

'A little bit.' He pulled a fruit gum out of his pocket and threw it into his mouth. He'd been watching *way* too many running videos; I didn't think you needed sugar boosts when you were barely running 5K. 'Between work and the wedding, I could do with my stress being cut in half and then some.'

One of the main reasons we'd started this in the first place had been to try and combat some of the stress Joe built up after a string of shifts at the hospital. It was hard for the rest of us to comprehend the kind of things he saw on a daily basis, and whilst Isla helped with her lunch boxes, I had stepped up to bat and offered to be his running partner. Well, mostly to support him, but also because the lift breaking in our office building earlier this year had almost sent me into cardiac arrest.

'I hear Dad is having major luck with the ladies,' Joe said as he steered us around the curve in the path. Our usual route was through Greenwich Park, heading up towards the old naval college and following the park's trails.

'Indeed. He asked me for a glossary of acronyms that people use in texting nowadays. Try explaining DILF to your own father.'

Joe snorted. 'I'd take a glossary any day. I'm meeting him for a pint to "go over dating etiquette".'

I slipped the straw that was built into my running vest into my mouth to stop from laughing. The vest was a ridiculous but practical gift that Rory had bought for me when I'd started running on a regular basis.

'It's probably because he knows you've got tons of free time, what with being a doctor and having a short-notice wedding to plan.'

He snorted. 'Absolutely. I was just getting bored, looking for something else to throw into the mix. Why *not* remind my dad to slip a condom into his wallet.'

I was horrified. '*He did not ask you that.*'

'No, he did not. But I like to catastrophize sometimes.'

'Do you think that's genetic?'

'Quite possibly.'

I tried to pace my breathing. It was hard when your running buddy wanted to chat. 'Well, make sure you tell him that they expire. We don't want any accidental half-siblings.'

Joe pulled a face. 'I think "Mary, 59" is probably past child-bearing. But I'll tell him just in case. One little sister was quite enough.'

I squirted my water pack at him. 'Life got ten times more interesting when I was born, and you know it.'

I tried to imagine Joe as an only child and immediately failed. He'd lived for playing pranks on me, hiding in the wardrobe for over an hour once just so that he could success-fully execute the jump scare. I'd been 6 and had needed a change of clothes afterwards.

We ran in silence for a few minutes, my breathing ten times louder than his. I checked my Fitbit: twenty-seven minutes and thirteen seconds. It was at this point that I always started to fantasise about the bacon butty at the end – like a mirage, I could almost taste it.

'So, what's left on the wedding checklist?'

Joe groaned. 'Remind me never to let someone convince me to plan a wedding in two months again.'

'*Are* you planning on getting married again?'

'Fuck, no.' He checked his own watch. 'This first one has shaved about ten years from my life expectancy. It's becoming glaringly obvious that Isla's side of the family are willing to do absolutely zero to help.'

I winced. It had been a topic we'd all darted around, without actually saying it. Her sisters weren't even coming to the sten do.

'They'll be first in line for the free bar, but God forbid they actually help us source a hundred chairs for the ceremony.'

I let him rant, sensing he needed it. By the time the big day came, all of these kinks would be ironed out – and if they weren't, by then it wouldn't matter. Isla was far from a bridezilla; she just wanted to be married to Joe. Anything outside of that was a formality.

'Does it bother Isla? Her family?'

Joe shrugged, bracing his hands on his knees as we came to the end of our route. 'She says not, but I'm not sure I believe her. It's a bloody good job that Mum basically adopted her the minute I brought her home.'

I smiled at the memory. I'd been sat at the kitchen table doing homework, and Isla had been visibly nervous. Mum had been baking overtime, presenting Joe and Isla with cookies and flapjacks the minute they'd walked through the door. It was a good job Isla had a sweet tooth. She'd chatted to Mum for ages whilst Joe had helped with my equations. We'd still been in those fragile years post-divorce, navigating a new landscape where Dad had to meet Isla separately (and wasn't around as much to help with my homework). Isla had arrived at a time when we'd needed something new.

'Well, I, for one, am extremely glad that we were able to steal her.' I took a long glug of water. 'She makes an excellent bacon sandwich post-run.'

★★★

I rooted around in my bag, crouching down to try and find my keys and wincing from the indigestion. I'd inhaled Isla's breakfast treat way too quickly for someone who was increasingly discovering the delights of acid reflux in their mid-twenties.

'Come on, come on . . .' Why was it that the second you needed to find something in your bag, it migrated to the unreachable depths? I pried some old chewing gum from the bottom of an ancient lipstick. My desk was the epitome of organisation. My handbag . . . not so much.

'Gotcha.' I stuck my key in the door, immediately hearing Rory's voice coming from the kitchen.

'I don't know about that. Seems like a huge risk.'

I paused, halfway through the door. My gossip radar went off. *What* was a huge risk? I stayed still, trying not to breathe too loudly.

'You're an idiot if you don't think that now is the right time.' Maeve's voice chimed in, soft but firm. 'She needs to know. We can't keep it from her.'

Keep it from her? It took all my willpower not to burst in. Call it a sixth sense, but I had a feeling that this was *not* a conversation I was meant to be overhearing.

Maeve continued, and I heard the fridge shut. 'Tea? Come on, Ror, don't look at me like that. I don't like keeping secrets from my best friend. Particularly when it's something I think they deserve to know.'

Shit. I could feel my heartbeat in my ears. Now it definitely wasn't just a sixth sense — if they were talking about their best friend, there was only one person in the running.

Rory cleared his throat. 'She's got enough on her plate. It's going to stress her out. And yes, but don't put any of that oat shit in it.'

I stifled a laugh.

'You're going to have to start paying rent for this semi-skimmed. We only ever buy it for you and Joe.' The sound of a spoon clinking against a mug tinkled through the airwaves. *Stop dawdling over cups of tea and tell me what this secret is, for God's sake.*

'Besides' — the clinking stopped — 'this isn't a board meeting or a deadline. It isn't about having too much on her plate. This is good news, Rory. Don't you want to be happy?'

'What a stupid question. Thanks.'

I imagined her passing him the tea, giving him one of her best 'do what I say or else' looks. I'd been on the receiving end more often than I'd liked.

'It was rhetorical. I know you want to be happy. *I* want to be happy, and this is blocking my path. Just get the hard part over with. It won't be as bad as you're imagining, I promise.'

My legs tensed; delayed cramp from our ten miles. All I wanted was a hot shower, but I didn't want to miss out on any gossip.

'Can you tell her?'

Another sigh from Maeve. 'No, I can't. Obviously. Now come here.'

There was an immediate shuffling, and then silence. You know that classic icebreaker: what superpower would you choose? I closed my eyes tight and prayed that I would suddenly develop X-ray vision. What *secret* were they talking about, and why had they gone quiet? This was a real head–heart dilemma. On the one hand, I wanted to run in there and demand to know what was going on, but my head knew that I might miss out on important intel by rushing in too soon.

'I promise,' Maeve was speaking quietly now, and I had to strain to hear, 'it's going to be okay. She might be terrified of love, but she'll come around.'

I reeled back, affronted. Terrified of love? That was harsh. I wasn't terrified of love. Scared maybe, a sprinkle of fear that loomed every time someone suggested a date, but I wasn't *terrified*. There was a difference. Anyway, why *were* they talking about love behind my back?

'Rory,' Maeve's voice got closer and I sprang up, ready for an Oscar-worthy performance of someone who had just this second got back from their run, 'I'm in this with you.'

I froze, almost dropping my keys. *I'm in this with you.* Wait, were Maeve and Rory *seeing each other*?

21

It was all I could think about. When I had finally walked into the living room they'd frozen, panicked expressions on their faces. I'd watched them like a hawk all evening, sitting in between them on the sofa whilst we ate Indian takeaway and used Rory's dad's Netflix login (because who was paying for their own any more?) I waited for some sure-fire giveaway that my suspicions were along the right tracks; some sign of the shift from friends to lovers. I'd felt itchy with unease, which I'd decided was definitely the reason I'd crumbled and texted Daniel to ask if he wanted to meet for coffee. My head was all over the place. I'd tried to imagine my reaction if Rory *had* decided to come clean about their secret relationship. Would I have been happy for them? They were my best friends. I'd been third-wheeling for over a decade now with Joe and Isla, and it had never bothered me with Adrian and Maeve, but this was *Rory* and Maeve. How had this even happened? Was Maisy even real? Mai-sy wasn't a far cry from Mae-ve. And the only person who'd supposedly met the mystery redhead was Maeve herself. It had kept me up all night, and I was already regretting the decision to say yes to this coffee date.

'One oat milk latte.' Daniel pulled out the chair opposite me, placing a mug down. It had tiny giraffes all over it.

I'd suggested a coffee shop not too far from the flat – the kind of space with houseplants in every nook and cranny, and items on the menu like 'beetroot latte' and 'rosehip chai'. I couldn't imagine many people were out here ordering shots of vegetables in their caffeine hit.

'Thanks.' I cradled the mug, rubbing one of the giraffes affectionately.

'Don't say I never treat you to anything.' Daniel started stirring a sweetener (gross, potential red flag) into his own mug. He was just as put together as the last time I'd seen him, only this time he was in a checked shirt rather than a suit and tie, leaving it wide open so that you could see the fitted white T-shirt underneath.

He nudged the pot of sugar packets in the middle of the table closer towards me. 'With all the sugar a girl could dream of.'

Okay. This was getting weird.

'How do you know that I take three sugars in my coffee?' I tried to play it off as a light-hearted joke, but I couldn't help it; my suspicion was clear.

Daniel sipped his own coffee and winced. 'Definitely should have let that cool down first. I make the same mistake every time. You said you liked sugar at the event last week? We were having a conversation about controversial opinions, and you said that your business partner can't stand the number of sugars you add to your coffee. I didn't know the exact number, but I guess now I do.'

Oh shit, I did remember saying that, somewhere between the copious glasses of prosecco. I was jumpy, on edge for so many reasons (most outside of Daniel's control), but I couldn't shake off the fact that I was almost 100 per cent sure that whilst I had forgotten about mentioning my affliction for sugar, I hadn't mentioned Level. Not mentioning it had been the foundations of our maybe meet-cute.

He was staring at me now, head slightly tilted.

'Are you okay, Penny?'

I liked the way he said my name – drawing out the 'Y' so that it sounded more lyrical, and less like your neighbour's cockapoo (which was a comparison that one of my bad dates had made, believe it or not.)

I decided to bite the bullet – maybe we'd be laughing about this in years to come, bringing it up as a funny story at our own wedding, the type of anecdote that was destined for a speech. Rory had already pocketed an anecdote about Isla thinking that a hamstring was a type of sandwich for his upcoming best man duties.

'I guess I'm kind of confused about the flowers.'

Daniel smiled. 'Roses and sunflowers.'

I snorted. 'Not *what* they were, just . . . How did you find out where I worked?'

There was a second of silence before Daniel burst out laughing. 'Penny, did you think I was stalking you?'

'Why are you saying it in the past tense? I still do.'

He set down his Americano. 'I was intrigued by you at the event, so I asked at reception. Said I'd been chatting to you and was interested in making a connection. They thought I meant business, but what harm is a little white lie?'

I couldn't help it, I flushed involuntarily. 'And they just gave up that confidential information, did they?'

He tried, and failed, to suppress a smile, before moving on. 'I'm pretty sure that we were all meant to be wearing those ridiculous name tags anyway, it's just that I resisted, and you probably lost yours somewhere on your journey from sober to very, very drunk.'

I blushed again, but this time not because he'd been flirting.

'Any more questions to rule out my potential stalker tendencies?' He clasped his hands on the table. 'I'm an open book, Penny, quiz me until you're blue in the face.'

I was pretty sure I believed him. Somewhere early on in my memory of the evening, I could recall Ella chucking name tags in our direction before she swanned off to mingle. If I remembered correctly, I'd dropped mine into a plant pot on my way to the ladies.

I took a big mouthful of coffee, buying myself time. 'I don't know what you expected me to think.'

He smirked. 'I expected you to think "how romantic, the guy I snogged in a conference hall has sent me sunflowers and roses".'

'I've been told that I'm an incredibly sceptical person.'

'Which makes perfect sense, given your career choices.'

We were playing a verbal game of tag, and I couldn't deny that I was enjoying it.

'It takes a sceptical person to create a dating app that doesn't have any of the bullshit in it.' Not that this theory stretched to Rory, who *always* erred on the side of optimism. We were yin and yang, a perfect match.

Daniel nodded. 'I haven't used Level, but I've heard about it. It's a good idea. I bet your marketing team have had a field day with the concept.'

He'd clearly done his background research.

'So, would you?'

He took the beat to lift his mug to his lips again. Very nice-looking lips. If I remembered correctly, extremely soft lips, not like the higher-than-acceptable percentage of the male population who thought that they were above Vaseline.

'Would I what?'

'Use my dating app.'

'Well, that depends, Penny.' He gave an almost-laugh.

'On what?'

'Whether you'd definitely be one of my matches. I have a feeling we could have a lot of fun together.'

I grinned down at the dregs of my latte. If I was completely honest, I'd come here under false pretences. But now that I was here, I wasn't having an *awful* time.

'Well, that also depends.'

He leaned closer. 'On what?'

'Whether you're planning on sending bouquets to any of my other undisclosed addresses.'

'Just the one.' He patted his pockets. 'Turns out sunflowers aren't as cheap as they were when I got my first girlfriend a bunch from M&S in sixth form.'

'You haven't bought a bunch of flowers since sixth form?'

Daniel leaned back in his chair. 'You don't give a man a second to breathe, do you?'

I tucked my hair behind my ear, smiling. 'Let's just say my quota of naivety is up for the year. Hence the getting hammered at a work event.'

'Ah, I see. Well, his loss. It certainly worked out well for me that night.' He paused. 'That is, until your business partner waded in.'

A flash of protectiveness hit me. This was clearly my 'fuck it' man. My rebound into the world of not taking things too seriously. But I wasn't going to throw Rory under the bus, regardless of the things he wasn't telling me. I changed the subject.

'You've clearly done your homework on me. Why were *you* there that night?'

It had dawned on me sometime during our conversation that I actually knew nothing about this man. He knew where I worked, how many sugars I took in my coffee, and had met my business partner (if not under slightly fraught circum-stances). The split between us wasn't equal, and it was bothering me.

'Fair enough.' Daniel crossed his arms, leaning on the table. 'I work in app development too, but we're very much in the beginning stages. A photo-sharing app. I can't give too much away. You know how it is.'

He tapped his nose. I was unimpressed. 'I'm going to need more than that.'

Daniel laughed. 'Imagine my surprise. We're hoping to rival Instagram.'

I blew out a breath. 'Big ambitions.' It was one thing to hope to rise up in the dating-app sphere, another to aim for one of the biggest players in the world.

'It's my dad's company,' he continued before I could make any rash judgements. 'And no, I didn't just get the job because I'm his son. He'd never hire a weak candidate, regardless of who they were. I actually applied under a pseudonym.'

I hated to admit it, but I was impressed. 'Surely when you got to the interview stage —'

Daniel coughed. 'Again, I have a feeling it might have worked against me, not in my favour. He wasn't on the panel, and no one wants to hire a daddy's boy.'

'They clearly got over that. What is it you actually do?'

'I'm a programme designer.'

Part of me was jealous that my date — somewhere along the way, that's what this had become — was still in the trenches of app development. The fun stuff.

'A CEO and a programme designer walk into a bar . . .'

He laughed, looking relieved to no longer be under the line of fire. 'And what might have happened in that bar, Penny? If the CEO's business partner hadn't interrupted them?'

'I couldn't possibly say . . .'

Because while it may have been out of character, I knew right then that I'd have slept with him that night, had Rory not appeared. It was what the universe would have wanted. And there was still time.

22

Rory: Were you in the office today? I didn't see you. In and out of meetings.

I winced. I'd rushed out of the office on the dot, and he knew it. I also had a text waiting for me from Ella asking if I was okay; I was a chronic overstayer, even nailing down my perfect office dinner (a nutritious combination of McDonald's chicken nuggets and the egg fried rice from the Chinese takeaway down the street). Rory and I had spent many an evening in the office long after everyone else had gone home, debriefing about the day and trying to come to unanimous decisions. But the tables had turned since last week; I was no longer bothered if Rory was avoiding me, because I was definitely avoiding *him*. It was all part of my mission to avoid three eventualities. The first, that Rory would bite the bullet and tell me about his new relationship with my other best friend. I didn't think I was emotionally ready for that conversation. The second, that he *wouldn't* tell me, and I'd be left feeling an even bigger sense of betrayal. And third, that he'd devote the whole day to ripping into Daniel, who had ended

up not being a bad date. Or a bad kisser. And I wasn't ready
to justify that to Rory. All three eventualities were bleak, so
I'd done the sensible thing and chosen complete avoidance
instead. Healthy. Maeve would have been proud. I typed out
a response to him because I couldn't drop *completely* off the
radar.

Me: Must have just missed you. Busy levels
have hit the roof.

I nibbled the cuticle of my index finger. He was going to
see right through this. He replied instantly, the three dots
appearing as soon as my message had sent.

Rory: No problem. See you tomorrow.

Or not. He had bigger fish to fry – or get home to – than
me avoiding him for twenty-four hours. It wasn't unusual for
me to go off-grid if I was immersed in something. I closed
the chat, scared of going home to him and Maeve and instead
fleeing to Mum's.

'Mum?'

I turned my key in her door, listening for the tell-tale signs.
If she was in her kitchen baking, then I'd be able to hear her
humming softly to herself or the whirr of her KitchenAid. If
she was in her living room, I'd be able to hear Classic FM,
her background music of choice as she read one of the many
courtroom thrillers on her shelves. I'd already noted her car
in the driveway, so she was here *somewhere*. I couldn't hear

either of the giveaways, so I ventured further in, dropping my bag on the kitchen table and grabbing a chocolate chip cookie from the plate in the centre. Still warm. The plot thickened.

'Mum?' I tried again, breaking the cookie in half and stuffing it in my mouth as I headed up the stairs. She'd been known to take naps at odd hours when she had a lot of orders. Apparently, it was easier to decorate cakes at midnight than it was during the normal nine to five, and she *did* have a highly important cake on her mind at the moment. We had reached the point where wedding preparation was all anyone could talk about. Between making bouquets for other brides at work and then getting on with her *own* wedding preparation, I was pretty sure even Isla was tiring of it. God knows how anyone managed to talk about a wedding for the length of a normal engagement. Last week it had been the politics of the seating chart. Did it make sense to stick Aunt Zoe on the table next to Uncle Steve, when they'd had a row last Christmas over who made the best stuffing? It was doing my nut in.

I ventured across the landing, a bit spooked by the silence and fully prepared to just wait downstairs with my laptop until she emerged. 'Hi Pen!' Her voice came from behind her bedroom door and I jumped out of my skin before narrowing my eyes. She was sniffling, I was sure of it. Even more sure because I'd inherited my ability to hide my tears *from* her. I pushed open the door slowly.

'Mum, you okay?'

She was sitting on her bed, a blanket draped around her shoulders and a cookie in hand. *That* should have been the dead giveaway; whenever we'd been sad as children, she'd immediately jumped into action and baked a batch of chocolate chip. And she didn't use the classic chips either, instead chopping up generous servings of Dairy Milk and making sure every bite contained a huge piece of chocolate. I blamed her for my sweet tooth. Her cookies had always sold instantly at our primary school charity bake sales.

'Hi Penny.' Mum shook the blanket off, trying to pretend that I hadn't just walked in on her crying. 'How was your day?'

I knelt on her fluffy cream duvet, kicking off my loafers so I could get further on without getting told off (old habits die hard). 'You're not getting out of this that easily.'

'Right.' She finished off her cookie.

As a child, she had known *exactly* when to push me, and when to leave me alone. I pushed now, and she didn't need another nudge before letting it spill.

'This is going to sound *crazy*,' Mum said, swivelling slightly to face me, 'but I downloaded your app.'

I tried not to let the surprise show on my face, but seriously, *what the fuck?* Both of my parents had clearly been on crack. There was no other explanation.

'Any particular reason?'

She laughed. 'Too much time on my own with fondant carrots? Does that count?'

I leaned my head on her shoulder. 'Partially. Dead fondant bunnies would get anyone in their own head.' I waited for her to elaborate, knowing that she would.

She leaned her head back against the headboard, her curls that were so similar to mine softening the blow. 'I wanted to be able to understand your work, so that I could brag about it at the wedding.'

'And?' I knew there was more to it – a quick Google would have put her mind at rest about that.

'And part of me wondered if it might match me with your dad.' She blushed. 'That's ridiculous, isn't it?'

It *was* a bit ridiculous, but I knew better than to say that. Ever since their divorce, it had been Mum who had stood firm, never wavering. Never once looking back.

'Do you' – I couldn't believe I was saying this out loud – 'want to get back together or something?'

She snorted, her sniffling slowly grinding to a halt.

'No. There were a million good reasons why we split up. Of course, there were the little things,' Mum smiled to herself, 'he used to browse the baking section in Waterstones, just to take a picture of a new recipe and send it to me – but they weren't enough to keep us together in the end.'

I laughed despite the sentiment. 'He would just put the book back and leave? Classic Dad.'

'I never said he was perfect, Penny, far from it. And I don't know if you remember this, but when you were little you had this phase of only eating chicken dippers and alphabetti spaghetti.'

I did remember this. Or maybe I didn't, but it was fresh in my consciousness because of how often Joe liked to bring it up.

'We all ate the same thing, mainly because I couldn't be arsed making something different for your dad and me. Looking after you was tiring enough' – she elbowed me softly so I knew she was kidding – 'and your dad used to spell out messages on my plate. Sometimes stupid things just to make me laugh – like that time he spelt "shit" and then Joe wouldn't stop saying it. But sometimes he'd spell out "I love you" in alphabetti spaghetti, and it seemed like the most romantic thing in the world.'

Obviously we both knew that family dinners had stopped happening shortly after the chicken dipper phase, when Dad's office hours radically increased, but that didn't mean it wasn't a good memory.

Mum sighed.

'But those aren't reasons to keep a marriage afloat when it's sinking. I know that. I just thought maybe your app *didn't* know that.' She shrugged. 'But even your app could see the cracks.'

I couldn't pretend to understand the complexities of a divorce, but I did understand the sting of rejection.

'The app isn't always accurate, Mum. Just because he isn't on your list, doesn't mean you weren't well matched. I promise.' I moved closer to her on the bed, so that I was lying against the headboard too. 'Level is not the be-all and end-all of compatibility.'

She leaned her head on my shoulder. 'I told you it was silly.'

'That's definitely not silly. I can guarantee I've cried to you over more ridiculous things. Remember the time I cried for three hours when my helium balloon flew off?'

Mum laughed. 'Yes, but you were 5 years old.'

A moment of silence before she spoke again, her voice much smaller this time. 'Have I set a bad example for love?'

My reaction was immediate. 'Of course not.'

'Penny.' She looked me dead on. 'Tell me the truth.'

I thought back to their marriage, but more specifically the aftermath. Mum's constant mantra that independence was the most important thing in the world. The decade-long black cloud that had fallen over Dad.

'I mean, maybe a bit.' I sighed. 'But clearly it didn't stop Joe, did it? So maybe it's a me problem.'

She gave me a little shove. 'Joe was that little bit older when we separated. He saw the bigger picture before any of us did.'

I remembered Joe squeezing my hand under the kitchen table when they'd told me that they were splitting up. Whispering in my ear that it was a good thing.

'He's always been annoyingly mature.'

Mum nodded. 'Mature beyond his years. Another thing I worried about when he was little.'

My mum was a lot of things, but I'd never thought of her as a worrier. I said as much.

'Where do you think you got it from? Until the divorce, your dad never worried about a thing.'

We sat in silence for a minute, and I mulled over what she'd said.

'Mum, the only reason I'm single is because I haven't found the right person. I'm in no rush. I just haven't met them yet.'

She smirked. 'Penny.'

I squeezed her shoulder and moved the conversation along. 'Besides, if there's one thing I absolutely learnt from your divorce, it's that a woman doesn't need a man to be successful. Why do you think I wanted to start my own business?'

I had very vivid memories of lying stomach down on our kitchen floor, drawing plans for my own business whilst Mum danced around me. It was in the very early days of Fondant & Flour, when everything was just barely getting off the ground. I'd considered opening my own florist (didn't think through my horrific aversion to pollen), an open-air cinema (overdone) and had even drawn the plans up for a restaurant (bold, given that at the age of 12 I could barely fry an egg). It'd taken a while to find my calling, but I'd only ever tried to find it because I'd watched Mum find hers.

She smiled. 'How did you become the one who knows how to cheer *me* up?'

'I'm very wise, if you didn't know.' I pulled out a second cookie that I'd squirrelled away in my pocket. 'You can pay me for my time in baked goods.'

'I'll make a note of that.' Mum sat up a little bit, taming her hair into a ponytail with the scrunchie she kept permanently on her wrist. 'But seriously, Pen, I don't want you to think that love isn't worth a shot. And definitely not because me or your dad made you think that. Promise me?'

I looked down at her phone, to where she was deleting Level. Was there *anything* my app could actually do right? In the real world, with real emotions instead of a testing lab, did the algorithm produce perfect matches? Or did it just breed doubt?

'You've been the best role model a girl could ask for, Mum.'

She shot me a look. 'That's not a promise.'

I squeezed her, giving her one of the hugs she used to give us as kids. The kind of hug that meant you couldn't breathe as easy, but instantly made you feel protected. 'I promise.'

23

I rubbed my eyes, trying to avoid smudging my mascara, and stifled a yawn as I pressed the button in the lift. I'd stayed at Mum's last night, only leaving to grab dinner for us and a sentimental can of alphabetti spaghetti, which I'd presented with a flourish. I'd even conceded my own TV preference so that she could lose herself in *Death in Paradise*. I felt protective of her in a way that was new, in the same way I'd always felt protective of Dad, who had texted me a thumbs up and smiley face emoji in response to my question about how his second date had gone. Unsurprisingly, given the quality of the stimulus, I'd fallen asleep on her sofa, waking up in the early hours of this morning with one of her huge, knitted throws over me.

'Morning, boss.' Dexter saluted me from his desk. We were the first to arrive. I'd had to trek back to my flat painfully early to grab a change of clothes, only allowing myself five minutes under the delicious hot steam of the shower so that I could get into the office on time. The sooner I arrived, the sooner I could lose myself in a task and feign busyness to Rory. I'd caught Maeve texting in the kitchen the night before

199

last, grinning at her phone whilst she waited for the kettle to boil. As soon as she'd noticed me, she'd put her phone face down on the table. The plot thickened, and I was pretty sure I was spot on about the narrative. I looked into our office. Rory's jacket wasn't on the back of his chair. Success.

'Any progress on the compatibility glitch yet?' I straddled the chair opposite Dexter. You could tell a lot about each of our employees by what they chose to keep on their desk. Ella had a Polaroid of her and Darcy, an industrial-sized hand sanitiser, and more often than not, a packet of Love Corn. Harriet had a tiny fan, hairspray, and a box of Maltesers. Dexter had a Lego houseplant and an endless supply of Red Bull.

'Every time we test the new system, it fails. We're on the sixteenth attempt.' He sighed, deflated, combing his hand through his hair. 'It's connecting the compatibility rankings from user to user that doesn't seem to be working.'

On the whole, our app had launched with very few glitches. We'd been prepared to weather much worse storms than our most recent glitch: some users appeared to be matched to someone, only for the other person not to have the match appear on *their* profile. Dexter could appear as a compatible partner for me (hypothetically – he liked sushi and video games way too much for us to be destined to be together), but for some reason, I wasn't currently appearing on *his* profile. Connecting users, ironically, was harder than it looked. I leaned over his laptop, scanning the current report.

'Have you tried looping back to the sequence that we used here?' I pointed at one of the old sequences, from a previous attempt. A bit of tweaking and I was sure it could work. I'd had the conundrum stuck to our bathroom mirror for the past week, staring at it for two minutes every morning and night whilst I brushed my teeth.

Dexter paused, thinking it through. 'That might be worth a try, actually. I'll give it a go this morning and report back.'

It felt good to flex my programming brain a bit. People in business didn't tell you how everything changed when you finally launched. Sometimes I missed those all-nighters at university. It had seemed glamorous in theory, but I was learning that maybe I didn't need glamour, just the chance to be creative.

'Oh, and by the way,' Dexter said without looking up, 'that just arrived for you.'

I looked over at my office, where I could see a brown paper delivery bag from Gail's on my desk. *Surely not again.*

'You really landed on your feet, snogging that mystery man.'

I thumped him with the newspaper I'd grabbed on my way into the building. 'Shut up.'

As extra as it was – getting daily office deliveries – I was starving, so I had my fingers crossed that there was something edible in there. Something buttery and warm. I'd been texting Daniel on and off since the weekend – he was a pretty consistent communicator, choosing real words over GIFs and always assuming I got his jokes, rather than mansplaining (it was a low bar). He was incredibly flirty, and he *wanted* me, which was a nice change after Isaac.

I read the label on the front of the bag under my breath. 'One extra-large, extra-hot oat milk latte, and one cinnamon bagel with butter. Thank you, dating gods. You know I deserved this.' I immediately delved into the bagel, moaning when the sweet cinnamon came through. 'I could definitely get used to this.'

'Get used to what?'

I jumped out of my skin, completely unaware of Rory's presence behind me. I quickly wiped the crumbs from around my mouth.

'Jumpy much?' He walked over to my desk, pulling the to-go cup out of the bag and reading the message printed on the side. I had my fingers crossed it wasn't anything flirty.

'*Penny*,' Rory started reading. '*Don't worry, I didn't forget the sugars. Look in the bottom of the bag. I still think you're sweet enough, Daniel.*'

He pulled a face. 'God, this guy is embarrassingly persistent. Does he not take no for an answer?'

I didn't respond, feigning ignorance and taking the drink from him.

'Wait a minute.' Rory hung his jacket up. 'You called him, didn't you?'

I pretended to be extremely interested in my – colour-co-ordinated – sticky notes, tabbing up some of the meeting prep I'd done last night whilst I was sitting with Mum.

'Oh, for God's sake, Penny. That guy was a sleaze.' Rory crossed the room, his steps heavy. Looking at him up close, I realised that even in the depths of my suspicion, I'd missed him.

'I'm pretty sure sleazes don't send flowers and lattes to offices.'

He shot me a look. 'I think that's *exactly* what they do to get what they want. Did you order the penis straws yet?'

I snorted despite myself, making a note to order the goods for the sten do, which was fast approaching. 'Quite the conversational diversion.'

'Is it? I imagine there's quite the overlap in the Venn diagram for men who pester women in offices, and novelty penis straws. It's obnoxious. Why do the rest of us need to be involved?'

I bit back a comment about how he was only irritated because he didn't feel like he could parade *his* new fling around the office. My rush of affection for him was dwindling fast.

'What's got into you? You met him for precisely one minute before you made him feel uncomfortable enough to leave.'

'Let's not get into this, shall we?'

We worked in silence for approximately ten minutes, both of us passive aggressively slamming down our coffee cups and typing like we might accidentally break the keys.

He sighed. 'I just . . . didn't think he was good enough for you.'

I wasn't quite ready to bury the hatchet. 'You don't know him.'

'Neither do you.'

'I think that's the point of dating. If it isn't, then we *massively* misunderstood a major part of our careers.'

He rolled his eyes. 'Very funny. If this company does go down in flames, I'd start writing your stand-up set if I were you.'

He was joking, but it hit a nerve. We weren't on the lookout for investors just for fun; it turned out that there was a *lot* of expenditure in the first few months of a business launch.

'Anyway,' I said around a mouthful of cinnamon-y goodness, 'good enough or not good enough, I hadn't eaten this morning.'

Rory looked up from his laptop. '*I* could have bought you a bagel, Penny. It isn't ground-breaking stuff. Shall we go?'

Ella was ready and waiting for us with another batch of potential partnerships, waving through the glass of our office.

I took the second half of my bagel for the road. 'Ready as I'll ever be.'

★★★

Under the table, Rory squeezed my hand, our frostiness momentarily forgotten. When it came to our personal lives, apparently all bets were off. But in here we were a united front.

'I think we really need to consider it.' Ella clicked onto the next slide, showing us the information about our competitor – their monthly downloads, their public image – that everyone in the room already knew by heart. First rule of launching a brand in a competitive market: know who you're up against. Second rule: don't jump into bed with them. Which was exactly why Rory and I were avoiding a partnership with Link like the plague.

'What about the interest we had from *Influence* magazine?'

Rory might have been desperate, but he was also correct. After their condemning article about our secret love affair, they'd been in touch to enquire about further collaborations. 'And didn't we also get something from that sex-toy company?' He stood firm.

'The sex-toy brand didn't want to invest, just to cross-promote.' Andrew was scribbling in his A4 refill pad as we listened to Ella. 'Same with *Influence*. People just aren't investing like they used to. Most people want to wait a bit, see how the app does. We have nothing in the same *realm* as the offer from Link. Right, Andrew?'

Our accountant nodded. 'It would be enough to tide us over for at least six months, and by then, we'd be out of the woods.'

I didn't think I'd ever heard Andrew speak so many words at once. He adjusted his tie, embarrassed.

'What will it do to our reputation if we accept investment from the main reason we created this app in the first place?' Rory wasn't backing down.

Harriet jumped in. 'It won't be ideal, but I can explain it away. This happens in tons of markets – if anything, it's a sign that they believe you're on the same playing field. We might hate them, but people respect them.'

Under the table, Rory gripped my hand tighter before taking his clammy palm and rubbing it on his legs. I didn't have to ask him to know what he was thinking. A month ago, when they'd first pitched to us, I'd felt the same thing. Now, I wondered if it wasn't such a bad idea. Link were the leaders in our market, and they knew what they were doing.

Like Harriet said, if Link wanted a piece of us, then we were a piece worth having. And at the end of the day, we were all doing the same thing. Milking human connection.

'Penny? What do you think?' Ella was staring at me over the table, her eyes slightly narrowed like she was trying and failing to read me. I thought of the photos on her desk, and Dexter's Lego plant. This was a *business*, and we had to protect it. Protect their jobs, protect *ours*. Maybe sometimes you had to sell your soul to the devil in order to survive.

'Well . . .'

Rory's foot knocked against mine three times. It was our secret signal, devised a few months into our friendship. Three touches meant a code red, and neither of us played it except for in extenuating circumstances.

I might have been about to drop a bombshell, but I pulled back. 'I think we should give these opportunities for cross-promotion a chance. See if they stir up any further interest.'

It went down like a lead balloon.

'Are you sure?' Ella looked disappointed in me. I was pretty sure *I* was disappointed in me.

I swallowed. 'I think if we're playing the long game, this is what's best for the company.'

Harriet nodded, and I could feel Rory finally relax even if my own body remained rigid with anxiety. Did *I* think it was what was best for the company? I wasn't sure.

I picked up my laptop. 'Are we done?'

When Ella nodded, I took it as permission to leave, heading straight to the toilet to splash some cold water on

206

my face. Things were heating up when it came to pressure from the rest of the team. And I understood. It was a tough time to launch a business, and sometimes you had to make tough decisions. I was just undecided on what those decisions were.

24

'Okay, so you chop, while I fry these off.' Maeve pointed me in the direction of the massive heirloom tomatoes she'd picked up at our local deli this morning. She'd started going on 'hot girl walks', arriving back at the flat with paper bags full of new finds. I didn't hate it, *except* when I was expected to cook with the goods. The word 'cook' being used loosely.

I eyed the knife. 'And if I accidentally chop my finger off . . .'

'Then we're screwed, at least until Joseph arrives. I only know how to fix minds. But you're not going to do that, because you're going to *look where you're going*. Penny!' – she gestured wildly in the direction of the knife I was wielding – 'Don't look at me, look at your heirlooms.'

I pouted and got chopping, trying my best to achieve the rustic Italian look that we were apparently going for. The dreaded evening had finally come around: our *Come Dine With Me* attempt. It was really only a formality, since Joe and Isla had smashed it out of the park. Even though I was *extremely* suspicious of my best friend, I was still rather thankful to be her sous chef instead of working alone. A happy side effect of Adrian's departure. I was just glad to not have to put my friends through the 'help yourself' fajitas I'd been planning. The Old El Paso kit could remain at the back of the cupboard.

'Rory told me about the meeting this week, about Link?' Maeve said it casually, but I whipped my head around. We may have been bonding over our three-course spectacular, but I had not forgotten about her almost-definite secret affair with the man in question.

'Yeah.' I didn't elaborate, leaving her open to putting her foot in it.

She tipped a mountain of onions into her frying pan, adding some garlic. 'I know how both of you feel about Link. That's a rough call to make, I'm sorry. Rory was pretty frustrated when I spoke to him.'

I prickled, even though it was perfectly normal for news to reach her through him. I wondered when he'd told her about it. Had it been in person, whilst I was mere metres away in my bedroom? Or had it been whispered down the phone, late at night? I'd been paying attention to Maeve's movements after I went to bed, but I hadn't heard anyone sneak in, and she'd been in every night this week, playing Candy Crush on her phone and watching *Schitt's Creek*. She'd been more available than ever before. I clearly wouldn't make a great detective, because she'd evaded my every attempt to fish for details.

I sighed, taking out my frustration on the pile of diced tomatoes in front of me, practically chopping them into pulp. 'It wasn't great. He's really stressed about it.'

See? I know him too.

'And you're not?' Maeve was staring at me sceptically.

'Of course I am.'

In reality, I wasn't particularly stressed about Link. But I *was* stressed about everything else, and what we were going to do if we didn't take their offer. It seemed to be the week for telling white lies in this flat. 'But it could have been so much worse. Besides, this is basically an endorsement.'

That's how I'd been choosing to see it, anyway. In a worst-case scenario, giving some of our company to Link wasn't the end of the world. It was barely one chunk in a share bar of Dairy Milk. And the fact that the offer was even on the table showed that Link saw us as a bar of Caramel, not just a bar of Fruit & Nut. I said as much to Maeve.

'I guess I see your point, even if I do think Fruit & Nut reigns supreme. You know Rory – he's life or death when it comes to Level.' She gave me a pointed look. One that said 'I thought you were too'. When I didn't react, she went back to her prep. 'Your analogy is making me wish we'd chosen chocolate torte over tiramisu.' We both stared at the pile of sponge fingers that were lying on the worktop. Changing the menu last minute would tip me over the edge.

'When you're done chopping,' she said, eyeing my pile of decimated tomatoes, 'can you add them to a glass bowl, drizzle with olive oil, and then get soaking those sponges with espresso from the machine?'

I was consistently impressed by people who could cook. I looked at a recipe, and all I saw was gibberish. In the end we'd gone for an Italian theme (Maeve had taken one look at my fajita kit and sighed), after Rory's seaside and Joe and

Isla's Mexican. It was basic, but the food would be good, and that might just be enough to carry us through. Maeve was making some sort of elaborate chorizo pasta dish as well as most components of the dessert; I was on bruschetta duty, and coffee dunking. It was a well-matched set of tasks. We worked in silence for a while, only stopping to either ask questions (me) or bark orders (Maeve).

'So . . .' Maeve finally broke the silence, not looking up as she poured a dash of cream into her sauce. 'You saw Daniel. Rory told me.'

'Anything you two haven't discussed this week?' It was a catty remark, and I instantly regretted it.

She looked hurt. 'Well, if *you're* not going to tell me . . .'

I put down the jug of espresso I'd been making. 'I'm sorry. Long week. I did end up calling him, we went for coffee on Saturday.'

Maeve didn't look thrilled. 'Do you think you'll see him again?'

Which really was the question of the moment. Was I going to see Daniel again? Probably. I *deserved* to see what was under those clothes.

She wrinkled her nose. 'TMI.'

Oops. Had I said that out loud? 'Nothing in the entire history of our friendship has ever been TMI.'

Not even the time that she'd lost a condom and had to go to A & E to retrieve it. *That* had been a fun escapade.

'Yeah, well, there's a first for everything.' She laughed it off. Now that I thought about it, I wasn't really in the market for a detailed description of *her* sex life at the moment either.

'I just want a bit of fun, after the Level disaster.' I shrugged. 'If you can't have a bit of fun in your mid-twenties, when can you?'

Which was exactly how I was justifying it to myself. It was like a reward for testing out the app. A very handsome, charismatic reward.

My best friend visibly softened. 'I know that Isaac hurt you.'

'Isaac *offended* me.' I corrected, swallowing the unexpected lump in my throat.

'Right. Offended, not hurt.' Maeve was trying not to smile. 'Well, regardless, I agree. You do deserve some fun. But just remember who you are, Penny Webber.' She was picking basil leaves from her plant on the kitchen windowsill, adding them into her pasta sauce. 'Sorry for that initial reaction. It's been a *really* long week.'

I jumped on the chance to quiz her. 'Why? What's going on with you?'

I willed her to give me something – *anything* – about what I'd overheard at the weekend. We'd been in the same room plenty of times this week. Plenty of opportunities to be honest. Maeve was my person, and I trusted her with my life, but right now the secrets were nestling into the foundations of our friendship, and for the first time in a long time it felt unsteady.

'Work is *horrible* at the moment. There are too many patients that I want to help for longer than six months.' Her face crumpled momentarily. 'It's hard not to bring it home, you know? Adrian was a great distraction for that.'

My bad-friend status hit me like a punch to the gut. 'I'm so sorry, Maeve. I know how much you care about your patients.'

I felt awful that I'd forgotten to check in on her.

'It's just' – she tasted the sauce – 'that needs more salt . . .'

'Maeve.'

'Oh, right, it's just hard, losing the one person who understood my job completely.'

I imagined not having Rory in the office. No one wanted to sit on a bean bag alone. 'I'm sorry.' I went over to her and rubbed her back. 'I've taken my foot off the pedal with the Adrian stuff.'

And I *should* have considered her lack of a person to lean on when it came to her job. Sometimes I took for granted that Rory understood all my work woes in great detail.

She turned and leaned her head on my shoulder for a second. 'You're only one woman. *And* you did yoga in the park for me.'

'I know.' I dunked a sponge in coffee, trying to hold myself back from shoving it into my mouth. 'But I'm not just here for extracurricular activities. You can talk to me.'

About anything, I wanted to add.

'It's fine.' She'd shaken off the almost-breakdown, focusing on her sauce. 'Adrian is clearly long gone, and it only hurts now because work is hard. I chose this job. And most days I'm really glad I did. That moment when I manage to push through a teenager's barriers and connect with them during the hardest period of their life so far is my favourite thing in the world. Some weeks, though, it does just feel very lonely, carrying other people's problems around.'

The buzzer for our flat went off repeatedly, making us both jump.

'Don't worry about me, I'm fine. Just an occupational hazard. Go and get them, I think we're almost ready.' She chucked a necklace made of fake garlic bulbs at me. 'Take these. That way, it won't matter if it's them at the door, or vampires.'

I laughed, not sure I felt okay leaving mid-conversation like this. I wanted her to feel like she could tell me anything. Even the secrets that left a hollow feeling in my chest.

She paused, opening a packet of rigatoni. 'Joe will beat down our door once he smells this pasta, you know that, right?'

I did. My brother was a fiend when it came to pasta.

★★★

'I have to say, I was sceptical about this.' My brother stabbed another piece of rigatoni with his fork. 'But this is fucking delightful.'

Maeve smiled, her brief interlude of sadness earlier forgotten, pointing him in the direction of the hob. 'I'm going to choose *not* to take offence at that. There are extras over there.'

So far, the evening had been somewhat of a success. My bruschetta hadn't killed anyone (yet), the wine that I'd been tasked with picking up was going down a treat, and the seating plan I'd cunningly devised when everyone had arrived was bearing the fruits of its labour. I'd deliberately placed Rory and

Maeve at opposite ends of the table; if there was one thing I'd learnt from Isla and Joe, it was that love knew no bounds at a dinner table. And a longing look could say more than close proximity ever could. I'd watched season two of *Bridgerton*. Joe and Isla were on either side of Rory, and I was right by Maeve. That way, I could check she was okay, monitor them both for longing looks, *and* avoid Rory and conversations about Link and Level at the same time. In my brain, there was a full-on stealth mission occurring. My brother and Isla were blissfully unaware, running us through several elements of their big day.

'How are the speeches coming along?' Joe waved his fork stuffed with tubes of pasta at the two of us, flicking a spot of red sauce onto our tablecloth. 'Written something beautiful enough to make even Isla's mum cry yet? Ow.'

I snickered, having seen Isla's foot jab him under the table. Isla's mum had a reputation for being a bit frosty – from the glimpse of her I'd got at Isla's twenty-fifth birthday a few years back, barking orders at one of the waiters at the restaurant, it was a mystery to me how Isla could have been related by blood. I'd once seen her run over and help a waiter when the plate he was carrying was clearly way too hot.

'I've got something up my sleeve.' Rory tapped his nose. 'Can't reveal too much, though. Don't want Pen stealing my thunder.'

In all honesty, I *hadn't* yet come up with anything to say, and it was keeping me up at night. My faith in love wasn't exactly at an all-time high.

'Well, I can't think of two people more perfect for the job.' Maeve poured a mountain of Parmesan on her food. She'd been known to make waitresses sweat in restaurants, holding out until the last minute to say stop as they continued to grate cheese on her food. 'The love experts.'

I snorted without thinking. 'Yeah, right.'

Rory shot me a weird look across the table before he shook his head, grinning at Maeve. 'Your faith in my speech is much appreciated.'

They exchanged a look, which I tried my hardest to decipher.

'I, for one, cannot *wait* for our weekend away.' Isla poured herself – and Joe, instinctively – another glass of wine. We'd caved and given them a small hint about the sten last week after relentless questions, and it had appeased them for the time being. 'I need some time off. Work is horrendous. If I get as bad as some of these bridal parties, shoot me.'

'You're the most relaxed bride I've ever come across.' I sent her a reassuring look. 'I don't think you have anything to worry about.'

Joe nodded. 'Not even the peony disaster upset her.'

Ah. The peony disaster. Isla's very own peony supplier had told them that they couldn't provide enough peonies on that short notice. She hadn't batted an eyelid, but we'd all known that for a florist, having your favourite flower on your big day was important.

'And you were the coolest about the bridesmaid dresses.' I patted her hand. 'We're forever in your debt for that.'

Her approach to bridesmaids had been very liberal. She wanted us all to feel comfortable, so as long as our dresses fit into her pastel theme, she'd said she didn't care about colour or style. Her sisters had gone for a pastel lilac and blue, Maeve had chosen a green, and I'd gone for a soft pink. Together, we'd look like a rainbow, which was exactly what she'd been going for with the whole wedding theme.

'Ta–da!' Maeve had left the table a couple of minutes ago, returning with our tiramisu, which she placed in the centre of the table. 'Sponges lovingly made by my sous chef.'

Rory smirked. 'You do know that saying Penny helped to make it reduces our willingness to eat it by 27 per cent, right?'

I pulled a face at him, serving myself first to prove a point.

'If Level doesn't work out, I definitely have a career in the kitchen ahead of me.'

His face dropped. 'Why wouldn't it work out?'

There was a moment of tense silence around the table whilst I decided how to defuse. 'It was a joke, Ror. I know it'll work out.'

He shook it off, nodding and accepting the bowl of dessert that Maeve held out to him. She placed a hand on his shoulder, leaning in and whispering something in his ear. No one else batted an eyelid, but I'd zeroed in on it. Another strike in favour of my theory. Everyone else tucked in, but Maeve was staring at me weirdly from across the table.

'What?' I mouthed at her.

She shook her head and went back to her food. 'So, how does everyone feel about charades?'

The mood lightened again as all three of them groaned. I nodded along, realising how precarious this tangled web of relationships had now become. This was *exactly* what I'd always worried about.

25

I lingered outside the restaurant, checking my emails and making use of the minutes until Daniel arrived. Was there anything worse than being the first to show up for a date? One of our housemates had been stood up in first year, and the image of her standing outside Turtle Bay in her kitten heels haunted me to this day.

Emails replied to, I turned my attention to the menu on the exposed brick wall outside the restaurant. He'd booked a table for two at an Italian restaurant near Covent Garden, a place I'd had on my London list ever since moving back after university. You practically had to be royalty to get a table – either that, or you'd had the foresight to book months in advance. I had no idea how Daniel had managed to get a table with only a week's notice, but I wasn't going to argue. Even if I *had* stayed up until one o'clock this morning trying to find him on social media. The man was a ghost. There just *wasn't* a Daniel Grayson online who lived in London and worked in app development. Unless he'd completely changed his look, and had shaved off a goatee recently. He'd mentioned that he tended to avoid social media unless it was for app research, and clearly he was telling the truth. I shook my head, reading through the many bowls of pasta on the menu.

I'd just decided on the fettuccini when I felt a tap on my shoulder.

'Penny?' I glanced up, expecting to see Daniel, even though the accent didn't quite match.

My blood ran cold. Isaac.

'Oh, hey.' I didn't give him more than that to work with; he could sweat this one out.

He shifted from one foot to the other, clearly uncomfortable. *Mission accomplished.* He was wearing the same outfit – deep red jumper and dark jeans, with a long lightweight grey coat over the top – as he had on our first date. I wondered if the jumper still had the same pull in the right-hand corner, where my earring had caught.

His expression morphed from abject horror into one of forced friendliness. 'This is weird, right? Are you eating here?'

Of all the restaurants in London. This was karma getting me back for ever thinking I could mess with the fate of other people. How had *Isaac* got a table? The only logical conclusion was that it must have been booked well in advance. As in, whilst we were still dating. I resisted the urge to narrow my eyes.

'Yeah, I am. I've got a date.'

He smiled. 'That's great! Look, Penny, I felt really bad about what happened between us.'

I imagined he'd lost about ten seconds of sleep to it. 'What happened between *us*? You mean when *you* organised a date and then *you* left *me* hanging.'

His mouth fell open a little bit. 'I just —'

'You just what?' I smiled, hoping my eyes revealed how *not* friendly I was being. 'Look, Isaac, I would have understood if you'd told me. I'm too busy to waste my time prepping for a date that's never going to happen.'

By this point, he'd paled. 'You can't help it when there's a spark elsewhere. That's the whole *point* of that app.'

Boy did I know it. And he clearly wasn't getting my point. I was glad to find that I didn't feel hurt any more; this was a man who ghosted women unless they pestered for a response and if I was honest, he had a permanent cowlick. The only thing left wounded was my pride.

'Well, you're welcome.' I smiled.

'For what?'

Okay, it was petty. But I'd said I wasn't *hurt* any more, not that he didn't still piss me off. 'I'm assuming she was one of your other six matches, on Level?'

Isaac was obviously confused, wondering where I was going with this. 'Yes, but —'

'Well, you know how I said I worked in app development? Level is my app.' I held out my hands as if I'd just produced a paper flower from my sleeve. 'Virtual Cupid, here in the flesh.'

His expression told me one thing for sure; there was no way he'd seen that article about Rory and me. He looked mortified, but he recovered quicker than I'd anticipated. 'Ha–ha.'

'Nope, 100 per cent not kidding. Enjoy your date.' I pulled out my phone again, reading Ella's response to the email I'd just sent and making a mental reminder to tell her not to work after six. Isaac clearly felt uneasy, like he wanted to ask me to elaborate. Tough shit. I'd wanted a bit more of an explanation too. I hoped it was all he could think about over his spaghetti bolognese.

'Penny, hi.' *Thank fuck*. Daniel had popped up behind us, pulling me in to kiss me on the cheek. Perfect timing.

Finally, Isaac sprung back into life. 'Okay, well I'm going to go.' He looked awkwardly between us, clearly doing the maths and realising that I hadn't, after all, been hanging out on my own for the past few weeks.

'Nice seeing you, Isaac. Enjoy the food.' I watched him go into the restaurant, meeting a woman at the bar and kissing her on the mouth. When she turned back to the drinks menu she was holding, he looked around, his eyes fixing on us one more time. 'Who was that?' Daniel squeezed my side.

'No one.' He didn't need my baggage, and I wasn't really in the mood to give it. 'But, how do you feel about *not* eating here?'

Full credit to him, he recovered quickly from the conversational whiplash. 'Whatever you want. Let's do it.'

★★★

Forty minutes later and we were sitting on the Southbank, eating cheese toasties bigger than our heads.

'I think I'm approaching a cheese coma.' I groaned as I took another bite. 'Whoever decided that cheddar and mozzarella wasn't enough, and that they needed to add Red Leicester too, was a *genius*.'

Daniel was mid bite, and he nodded. 'I can see why you're the woman in charge at work. This was a great move.'

I marvelled at the impressive cheese pull when I took another bite. 'Who needs pretentious pasta when you can stuff fries into your toastie?'

I did as I'd described, only clocking Daniel's expression when I came up for air. 'Not that I wasn't looking forward to pretentious pasta.'

He cleared his throat. 'No, you're right. Even if we might be slightly overdressed.'

It did look kind of ridiculous; both of us sat on the ground and clearly dressed for somewhere fancier. I'd worn one of my own dresses for once, a red slinky number that I saved for the minimal occasions where a guy was guaranteed to take it off. I'd paired it with tiny gold hoops and black heels with gold detailing. Maeve had gone out after work so I'd dressed myself without her help, and I was pretty pleased with the end result. Daniel was wearing a black shirt and chinos, and I could smell his aftershave when I leaned in to pinch one of his fries. There was no denying it; the man was hot.

'I'm sorry that we swerved the restaurant. I know the reservation was probably ridiculously hard to get.'

He smirked. 'Not when you know the right people.'

Who did he know? I ignored the slightly obnoxious tone. It *was* a flex to secure a table there at the last minute. My thumbs itched to try and find his social media footprint again.

'Anyway, this is much better. I won't ask about the guy you were trying to avoid. Don't want to kill the mood.'

Everyone at work said that the golden dating rule was to not bring up someone you'd previously dated. Unless it was an icebreaker about your worst first dates (Rory and I had led that icebreaker on our first day in the office as a full team – Ella had won. She'd once sat across from a woman for two hours who'd picked her nose 'secretly' behind her menu. *Gross*). But I wasn't looking for a relationship from Daniel, and it wasn't like I'd been in a relationship with Isaac.

'Just a man who ghosted me.' I polished off the final bite of my toastie. 'A man I met on my own app, can you believe that? Level really did me dirty.'

Daniel laughed. 'That's rough.'

'Yep.' I took a swig of Fanta. 'You probably should know, though, that I'm not looking for anything serious.'

I was 99 per cent sure that the feeling was mutual – it was like an unspoken agreement. But I'd heard enough horror stories to know that it probably *should* be spoken.

As predicted, Daniel was on board. 'The best mindset for dating. I'm having a lot of fun with you.'

'I'm having fun with you too.' I smiled when he slid an arm around my waist. 'I've actually never had one. A relationship, that is.'

For the first time ever, when I said it out loud, I felt a bit self-conscious. What had started out as a badge of independence now felt a little bit like something I had to hide.

'I'd like to say I didn't know that already,' Daniel said, reciprocating my embarrassment, 'but I did a quick Google of Level and–'

I groaned. 'I forgot. Plastered all over the internet for everyone to see.' There was no way I could hide that one, even if I wanted to. I cursed *Influence*.

'I wouldn't say *all* over the internet. I'm sure there are some dark corners that don't know about Penny Webber's relationship status.' He shot me a smile, and I was happy to have had the conversation defused with a joke.

'I just haven't found that spark yet. I'm not even sure I know what that spark is meant to feel like.' I debated asking him why he was a social media ghost, but I didn't want to give him the satisfaction of knowing about my own internet stalking attempts.

He nodded now, finishing off the last of his food.

'A dating app was a rogue move for someone who actively avoids dating.'

There it was. The age-old question.

'It's not that I actively avoid it.' I looked out at the river, not wanting to make eye contact in this moment of vulnerability. 'I just don't value it like other people do. But if people *are* going to search for it, I want it to be safe, and fun, and more likely to pair people up according to actual compatibility. I'm still a fan of the old-fashioned meet-cute, and I wanted to create something that felt as close as possible to that.'

Daniel was listening intently. 'How do you recreate an online version of a ladies' bathroom meet-cute?'

I flushed. 'Not the sexiest location, I'll admit.'

He moved his hand up my leg. 'No, but those leather trousers were sexy as fuck.'

224

I knew what the look in his eyes meant. And I was in the mood to let off some steam.

'How do you feel about going somewhere and drinking something that isn't out of a can?' I held up my Fanta.

Daniel kept his hand where it was, squeezing. 'Count me in.'

★★★

We chatted about mindless topics all the way back to Greenwich on the overground, even though both of us could feel that the air was charged. I might have been allergic to commitment, but I was not allergic to having a little bit of fun.

'Yeah, we're working on something new. An evolution.' Daniel was asking about the future of Level, and I filled him in as I fished for my keys inside my bag.

'It's a good job you're only looking for a fling.' Daniel leaned against the front door whilst he waited for me to find them. 'Sounds like you're working overtime at the minute.'

He was right. Between the app and the wedding, time was tight. I'd spent many an evening in bed with my laptop and a glass of wine (even if I didn't condone it for anyone else in the team). But it wasn't just now; work was always full on. It was the reason Rory and Lottie had finally split – he hadn't seen it coming, but the long hours had finally tipped her over the edge. He'd been gutted.

'Oh, is that what this is?' I laughed at his expression. 'But yeah, it's not for the faint hearted.' I finally found my keys, jamming them in the door.

Daniel nodded. 'I'm sure.'

I opened the door to see Rory on the other side of it, just about to leave. I froze for a second, like I'd been caught doing something wrong, even though he was the one at our flat unexplained. He looked like he'd been punched in the gut, but quickly rearranged his expression to one of mild interest. I knew this man like the back of my hand.

'Hey Pen.' He smiled at me, his lips tight. 'Hi mate.' He stuck his hand out in Daniel's direction. 'Sorry about the other week. I'd had a bit to drink.'

Daniel eyed his hand for a tense moment before taking it. 'No harm done.'

Rory looked between the two of us, Daniel's hand resting lightly on my waist. 'Clearly. I was just leaving – see you on Monday?'

I nodded, exchanging another look with him. It was weighted. There was so much unsaid between us at the moment – what was going on with Daniel and me, what was going on with him and Maeve (even if he thought I was none the wiser), what was going on with our company – and part of me wanted to beg him to stay and ask Daniel to leave. I'd never felt this distant from him before. I sent him a tele-pathic message, willing him to understand.

He seemed to read my expression perfectly, because he reached out and gently brushed my chin with his thumb, leaning over and kissing my forehead, before confirming quietly 'We're good. See you at work.'

Daniel was staring at my forehead as Rory walked away, one eyebrow raised. 'Marking his territory much?'

I scoffed, brushing off the incredibly misogynistic language. 'I'm not anyone's territory.'

'Right. You know what I mean.'

I didn't. I turned and watched Rory head downstairs, a pang of sadness settling in the pit of my stomach. Daniel was already taking his coat off and making himself at home.

26

As much as I wanted to make things right, I didn't see Rory for three days after that. It was like playing a game of whack-a-mole, one of us always disappearing into thin air the moment the other needed us. I'd tried to catch him in the office, but due to a last-minute tech roadshow that Harriet had dragged him to, he'd evaded me yet again. We'd played rock, paper, scissors over text to decide which one of us would stay at the office and which of us would go on the road, but in a landslide victory my rock had overpowered his scissors three times in a row. I'd got to stay in the comfort of my own home and watch TV with a tub of Pringles, whilst he'd had to spend two nights in a hotel (not the punishment he made it out to be, given how great a hotel full English was). The office had been quiet without him, but we'd finally fixed the programming, overriding the bug and linking all users together in a huge web of Level. It was the kind of breakthrough that Rory should have been there for, all of us high from the rush of eventually cracking a code. By this point, I was practically aching to see him.

'I'll get it!' I shouted it to no one in particular, rushing down Mum's hallway to get to the front door and yanking it open.

'Hey.' Rory smiled, bunch of roses in one hand. 'Long time no see.' I fought the urge to squeeze him tight, gesturing for him to follow me down the hall.

'Are they for me?'

He laughed. 'If you play your cards right.'

I feigned a swoon.

'Only kidding. You fixed the Level bug without me, and I can never forgive you for that.' He kicked off his trainers. 'They're for Caroline. I'm hoping it'll be a subtle hint that she can repay me in cake.'

I rolled my eyes and pointed to the kitchen, where Mum was holed away working. 'She'd give you anything you wanted, you know that.'

Rory nodded. 'I do know that. You're not jealous, are you, Pen? I could get you an obnoxious bunch of roses and sunflowers instead if you'd like.'

It was the only acknowledgement of Daniel, and the last time we'd seen each other.

I rolled my eyes and pushed away the niggling feeling at the pit of my stomach. It was probably the yoghurt that I'd eaten two days past its best before.

'Are you ever going to let that one go?'

'Never.' He left me, striding confidently into the kitchen even though he was beyond late for the tuxedo fitting going on in the living room.

'Everything okay in there?' I rapped my knuckles on the door and closed my eyes, not wanting to see more of my male relatives than I'd bargained for. 'Rory just got here, he's in the kitchen with Mum.'

I felt rather than watched myself being jostled, flinching at the surprise contact.

'Does he think we all just sit around waiting for him to be free? Some of us need to be back at the hospital tonight.' A pause. 'Pen, you can open your eyes now. No chance of seeing Dad naked.' Joe smirked when I warily opened them.

He was right, Dad was fully clothed and dressed to the nines. It still made me feel emotional sometimes, seeing him in our childhood home. The last time he'd been here was when Joe had finished his stint as a junior doctor, and Mum had thrown a party to celebrate – complete with cupcakes decorated to look like every part of the human body. And I mean *every* part. Her vulva cupcake had been particularly realistic.

'To clarify' – Dad swigged his Diet Coke – 'at no point this afternoon have I been naked.'

I cringed at the visuals, and so did Joe.

'Thanks for that, Dad.' I held out my own Diet Coke for him to clink, which he did.

'Speaking of Dad naked,' I murmured to Joe, who pulled a face, 'any news on the second date? All I got was a thumbs up and a smiley face.'

My brother tipped his head back before gulping his beer (alcohol-free, he hadn't been kidding about the shift – and sometimes we liked to join Dad in solidarity). 'I believe they're going to a wine bar tomorrow night. But that's all I got. Second date good, third date on the horizon.'

Men. I'd have to quiz my dad when he was done getting his suit altered. The tailor was working on his sleeves now, pinning them slightly higher.

'What did I tell you? Worked a *charm*.' Rory came in, holding a cupcake over his head like a trophy. He offered me a bite, which I accepted. Raspberry buttercream. Delicious.

I spoke through my mouthful. 'Would it not have been more cost effective to just buy some cake?'

He sent me a weary look. 'Clearly, you don't know the first thing about killing two birds with one stone.' He stuffed the final bite into his mouth. 'The perfect tuxedo measuring fuel, if you ask me.'

Joe waved him in the direction of his tux, which was laid out on the couch with a little name tag on top of it written in gold script (100 per cent Isla's influence). 'Which is why you only brought one in for yourself?'

'Did you buy roses for Caroline?'

Joe sighed. 'No.'

He flipped the finger at my brother. 'Exactly.'

Rory picked up his tux, and I immediately batted him away. 'Go and wash your hands. I know you, and there is buttercream lurking somewhere.'

He inspected his hands. 'You clearly don't know me that well then, do you?'

I pointed to a smudge of pink that he'd missed on his wrist.

'Ah, fuck off, Webber.' He made his way out the door, pausing to kiss the top of my head. 'Thanks. As always.'

I watched him go, shaking my head and losing my battle with a smile. When I turned, Joe was staring at me. 'What?'

He turned something over in his mind before apparently abandoning it. 'Nothing. Now get lost, this is a male bonding experience.'

I moved through to the kitchen, leaving the men (plus the weary tailor) in the living room. Mum was hard at work, sat at the kitchen table icing some butter biscuits by hand. It was her new venture; a way of stretching her skills. At this point, she had cake and cookies down to a fine art. You didn't hone a business for over a decade without getting seriously good. But something she'd been talking about for years was learning how to delicately ice biscuits, like the kind you saw in Biscuiteers. Last Christmas I'd bought her a ticket to a professional decorating class, and Joe and Isla had bought her a starter kit with all the tools she'd need. Now, after a series of shoddier attempts where you couldn't quite tell if it was supposed to be a sheep or a cloud — or in Joe's case, if you thought one of her snowmen was a pair of tits — she was on the verge of a breakthrough.

'Don't tell me,' I said, watching her steadily loop the green icing around the outside, 'is it going to be a monstera leaf?'

She glanced up, her hair piled on top of her head in a leopard print scrunchie. She had a smudge of green icing on her forehead. 'I must be getting better! These are a batch for a new plant shop in Hackney. They're having a launch party this week and they've ordered two hundred.'

'Bloody hell, you won't be able to do anything else!'

She snorted. 'I've got the rest of the team on monstera duty too, don't you worry.'

'I didn't realise you'd progressed to actually selling the biscuits.' I pinched a tiny offcut; whenever she made a batch, she always baked the bits that didn't make the final shapes. I popped it into my mouth, the butter base instantly melting on my tongue.

'I decided it was time. I'm doing a discount for businesses or parties that want to try them out whilst I'm still in the earlier stages. Next week we're doing a batch of sunflowers for a charity event.' She stuck her tongue out in concentration as she took a different shade of green, creating the veins of the leaf.

'So.' She pounced on me as I sat down, pulling out a chair and staying well away from the icing. 'How was date two?'

I hadn't actually discussed my second date with Daniel with anyone. Maeve and Rory weren't his biggest fans, and everyone at work was still miffed that I'd given up on finding the love of my life through our app.

I picked up one of her icing bags, squeezing a blob onto my finger and licking it. Mum shot me daggers. 'It wasn't a *date*, not really. But . . .'

I trailed off, thinking about the other night.

'But . . .?' Mum looked up from her biscuits.

'But it's good to have a distraction from work.'

And by work, I meant Link. And Rory and Maeve's affair.

'Penny, not everything has to be about work.'

I looked pointedly at the mountains of iced biscuits she was working with.

'Put the kettle on, smartarse.' She nudged some more offcuts towards me. 'I've been saving these for you.'

I popped another delicious piece of biscuit in my mouth and got up to fill the kettle, pulling out her favourite mug (it had Best Mum written on it, and Joe had bought it after he'd backed her car into the driveway gates two weeks after he'd passed his driving test. Kiss-arse).

'I've been at this for hours. Make it a big one.'

I did as she said, waiting for the kettle to boil and looking into her garden, which was small but organised. I spotted a new gnome — something she'd started collecting when we moved out — this one with deely boppers on its head. I had no idea where she found them.

I pottered around the kitchen, grabbing the milk and putting her mug next to her.

'Thanks. Do you want to see something I've been practising?' She got up, wiping green icing from her fingers.

'Is it a masterpiece?' I followed her into the utility room, cradling my own mug, one I'd made at a pottery painting café when I was 6.

'Now, I wouldn't normally do a practice run for a wedding cake . . .' She gently lifted the protective covering from a three-layer creation. 'But quite frankly, I've never felt this nervous about a cake in my whole career. Not even when I was asked to do one for that influencer.'

I held my breath for the reveal, my suspicions about what was under the covering confirmed.

'Ta-da!' Mum backed away from the cake, which was *gorgeous*.

The bottom layer was covered in a soft pastel pink butter-cream, which ombre-ed up the cake, getting lighter and lighter by tier until you reached the top. There was gentle gold foiling, and a tiny fondant Joe and Isla on top, balancing on a swing set. They were in their wedding outfits, bar a scrub cap sticking out of Joe's pocket, and a flower behind Isla's left ear. It was beautifully simple, and utterly them. It was incredible.

'Mum, this is the best cake you've ever done, without a doubt.'

She smiled, spurred on by the validation. 'This bottom layer is Joe's, the jam sponge. Then this one in the middle is the white chocolate for Isla.'

I could smell the white chocolate from where I was standing. If it was a practice, surely we could have a slice? I said as much.

'Not a chance. At least, not yet.'

'What flavour is the top layer?' I resisted the urge to swipe my finger through the white buttercream.

'They gave me free rein on that one, so I've tested a coconut and lime. And judging by the batter, I have a feeling we're onto a winner.'

I gently reached out and touched the top of the swings. 'Isla is 100 per cent going to cry when she sees this.'

'That's why she absolutely *can't* see this one. They both need to wait until the big day.' Mum started covering up the cake again. 'Besides, this isn't perfect. I could do much better with the foiling, and Joe's nose looks a little bit too much like when he broke it playing football . . .'

She rambled on, covering the cake and pointing out its imperfections. I placed my hand over hers, steadying it.

'You did a great job, Mum.'

And, watching how much love she'd poured into this project, into the two of us growing up, I wasn't just talking about the cake.

27

I was no stranger to an early wake up. My alarm went off like clockwork at 6.30 every morning, ready for me to dive into the shower and bagsy the first bathroom slot. But 5 a.m. was *too far*. I registered my phone ringing somewhere in the back of my mind (I was deep into a dream about winning the Apple Design Award), but chose to ignore it. Whoever it was could wait. The phone stopped, and I snuggled further into my duvet. *Thank God for that*.

There was a blissful minute of silence, and then it rang again.

'Oh, for fuck's sake.'

I dragged myself out of bed, rearranging my vest top (why *was* it that you went to bed with both boobs firmly secured, and then you woke up the next morning with them on opposite sides of the room?).

'Hello?' I picked up, glad that it had at least sounded like a greeting and not what I really felt like saying: 'Piss off'.

'Penny?' It was Rory.

Immediately, my brain reeled off a long list of potential panic-worthy scenarios.

'What's happened? Who is it?'

'Nothing, nothing. Sorry, I should have led with that. Everyone is fine.' I could hear him pacing, imagining him doing laps of his tiny living room.

'So what is it then?' Rory was not like me; his alarm usually went off at 7.30, a whole hour later, ready for him to rush his shower time and cram some cornflakes in his mouth before running out the door. I literally shuddered at the thought.

'It's Level.'

I pinched the bridge of my nose. Level. Of course it was.

'I woke up about ten minutes ago because my phone wouldn't stop *buzzing*.' Rory sounded audibly stressed. 'There's been some kind of security breach on the app.'

Shit. In all fairness to Rory, his 5 a.m. call was justified. For app developers, this was a worst-case scenario.

I started moving whilst we spoke on the phone, lining up an outfit in the pitch black. 'How bad is it?'

We'd put *so* much work into making it watertight. Or so we'd thought.

'I can't tell yet.' I could tell he was also rushing around on the other end of the line. 'I think someone managed to get past our identity verification system.'

I inhaled deeply. This was not good. Yes, there was a TV programme called *Catfish* that, for all intents and purposes, made a joke of the whole thing. Yes, it was funny to joke to your friends that the guy they've been talking to might really be under five foot with a mullet. But actually, catfishing could be dangerous. And we'd prided ourselves on being a safe dating app, with a foolproof method of setting up a profile. I swore.

'Can you get into the office early? I think we need to do some damage control. I've already texted Ella and Harriet.'

I ran to the bathroom to brush my teeth. 'I'm on my way.'

★★★

When I arrived an hour later, I was second into the office. Ella lived just outside of Wimbledon, and had already texted to say that the Northern line was experiencing severe delays. Harriet lived outside of London (as families tended to do, once the parents decided that it wasn't a viable option for their kids to not know what grass felt like) so would be a while. Rory was standing in the kitchen, stirring a coffee and looking into space. It had spilled over the sides, leaving a tiny puddle on the worktop.

'Ror?' I waved my hand in front of his face.

He shook his head. 'Sorry. Went to bed at one, and four hours is *not* enough.'

I had told him many times over the years how important eight hours was, but it didn't seem like the right moment to bring it up again now. The time on his laptop, which was lying open on the counter next to his coffee, said 6.15. I would have yawned if I hadn't been hit by an adrenaline rush.

'Thanks for coming in.' He slumped against the worktop. 'This is so bloody annoying. I thought we were untouchable when it came to security.'

It broke my heart a little bit, seeing him look this defeated. To my knowledge, this was the first time Level had ever let him down. Even when we didn't know whether we'd ever find funding, Rory had been unfailingly positive. I was an old timer by now, when it came to wanting to press delete on the whole thing. I fought the feeling, taking charge.

'Well, clearly not. But we don't fully know what we're dealing with yet. That's the priority.'

I pulled his laptop towards me, taking a sip of his coffee and wincing. No sugar.

'On it.' He moved to the sugar canister, getting another mug out for me without second-guessing.

I found the thread on Twitter, which wasn't hard. All you had to do was type in 'Level', and you were directed to a user profile for a girl called Polly. Nineteen thousand followers. 'Polly' had tweeted the following at one o'clock this morning:

@PollyOSullivan: What will it take for dating apps to take safety seriously?

'Identity verification systems' are complete bullshit.

When someone had asked what happened, she'd replied:

@PollyOSullivan: Imagine turning up to meet your 'perfect' 24-year-old match and finding a fifty-something-year-old man sitting in the corner of the bar, watching you.

The exchange had sixty replies and had been retweeted over a hundred times.

'Shit.'

That engrossed in reading the chain, I hadn't noticed Rory come up behind me, his breath hot on my neck. 'I know. Fuck.'

I shivered, my skin burning at the surprise contact. *Breathe, Penny, breathe.* What was up with me?

I closed the screen and manoeuvred my chair to increase the space between us, trying not to look him in the eye. 'Okay, so it's not ideal that she seems to be an influencer. How did this happen?'

'I have absolutely no idea.' Rory rubbed at his eyes. 'We've got to talk to Dexter and Harriet.'

As if the universe had decided to finally give us a break this morning, we heard the office door open. 'Hello? Where are you both?'

We exchanged a look of relief. Harriet. 'In here.'

She strode in, heels clicking against the tiles. Her hair was in another slicked-back ponytail, and she was wearing red lipstick. I looked down at my own outfit, which consisted of a white V-neck (that could well have come from the dirty laundry basket, if I was completely honest), a pair of old grey jeans and my Air Forces. I'd left my hair in its wildest form, and Rory looked similarly rumpled, in a hoodie and black jeans. I was pretty sure there was a toothpaste stain on them. We both stared at her. There was *no way* she was the sleep-deprived parent among us.

'What?' She patted her hair self-consciously. 'I find the best way to start handling a crisis is to present yourself like there isn't a crisis at all.'

'Clearly' – Rory gestured between the two of us – 'we have exactly the same motto.'

I pulled a face at him. 'Do I not look like I'm dressed for a crisis?'

'Your T-shirt is on inside out.'

I felt behind my neck, my fingers trying and failing to make contact with the fabric tag.

'Need some help?'

I thought of his breath on my neck a moment earlier. 'No. I mean, thanks but I'm fine.' I finally made contact with the tag. 'Oops. I got dressed in the dark.'

'The second way I like to start handling a crisis,' Harriet said, pulling a stool up to the worktop and taking out her own computer, 'is for you two to stop bickering, or whatever it is that you do.'

Her fingers flew across the keys.

'How on earth are you this awake?' I had been about to make her a coffee, but it was clear that she was wired without it.

'I have twins, Penny. Twins. Once you've seen what I've seen, nothing feels like a true crisis any more. And when you've been woken up at three o'clock every morning to banish the monster under the bed, time becomes meaningless.'

Her eyes tracked her screen as she took in the thread.

'Okay, so first of all, we need to reach out to Polly and check that she's safe.' Harriet pulled out the A4 notebook that she carried everywhere with her, writing up a list of bullet points. 'Then we need to issue some kind of statement and hold ourselves accountable for what went wrong. Reassure people that we'll be doing everything in our power to ensure that this doesn't happen again. The worst thing we could do is pretend that it wasn't our fault. I've seen companies sink faster than a ship when they do that. But before we do any of this, we need to get Dexter in, to see if he can figure out what *did* go wrong.'

I watched her work, impressed. My phone was already in my hand, Dexter's WhatsApp chat ready and open (the last conversation we'd had was about him stealing my last cereal bar from the staff cupboard. It had been a long day, and I hadn't been amused). 'On it.'

Rory had started growing stubble over the last few weeks, and he rubbed his chin now, deep in thought. 'Do you think this is game over?'

I felt heartbroken on his behalf. I knew how much this meant to him. I reached out and rubbed the skin between his ear and the beginning of his beard. 'We've got this, Ror.'

He relaxed under my touch, making eye contact and leaning his head into my hand. I broke the stare first, unnerved. *Why was I feeling this way?* This was *Rory*. And more importantly, there was a *Rory and Maeve*. I needed a breather. This morning's stress was clearly getting to me.

Harriet was still scrolling through the thread, narrowing her eyes and jotting things down in the notebook. 'Penny's right. This is your first rodeo, so I completely get that it feels like the world is going to end. The memory of the internet is infinite, but the attention span of users is short. I think it will blow over in a few days. With the best will in the world, dating apps still rely on the goodwill of people. There are so many online dates going wrong. As long as we're doing as much as we can to show that we're trying to prevent disasters, we should be fine.'

Rory inhaled. 'If you say so.'

'My only worry,' she continued, helping herself to his coffee and taking a long sip, 'is what any potential partners might think. It's not brilliant for a brand-new company to have a social media storm so early on. But we'll cross that bridge when we get to it.'

The two of us exchanged a look, able to read each other's mind. Level was not in a position to lose connections. We were at a crucial point in the trajectory of our company, and this was not part of the plan.

28

Of all the aspects of Level that I'd thought might defeat Rory's optimism, I'd never imagined it would be a 50-year-old catfish.

'My brain is so tired I'm struggling to remember how to chew.' He was currently slumped over his kitchen counter, miserably taking on a huge slice of pizza. He'd ordered one with triple the portion of pepperoni, so you could barely even see the cheese. We'd been ordering pizza for years and it was his favourite thing in the world, but currently it looked like every bite was painful.

'Who knew that launching Level would be so difficult?' I chose the slice with the biggest crust and dipped it in barbecue sauce.

'The romcoms make entrepreneurship look so dreamy.' His tone was heavy on the sarcasm, but there was very little humour there.

We'd been in crisis meetings all day, working with Harriet and Ella to compose a media statement, and then working with the programming team to get to the bottom of how our facial recognition technology had failed us. Dexter had finally figured out what had happened; apparently, there were apps that could distort facial recognition, confusing the system. Our system needed to be tighter, so those kinds of creeps couldn't get in. It made me feel physically sick that our app could put someone in any kind of danger. Even more so that someone would go to that length to cheat the system. The risks involved with online dating had been one of our main motivators for building a new app. This proof that even Level wasn't invincible only added to my niggling list of doubts about how likely it was that we were actually helping people find love. Polly had quieted down on social media and we were now talking to her over email, trying to smooth over the situation. Harriet had absolutely smashed it today.

I picked up a second slice. 'Well, on the bright side, that article about us is a fond memory of the past now.'

He shot me a wry look. 'It was only you that thought being connected to me was the worst thing in the world.'

I jumped to my own defence. 'Not the worst thing in the world.' I dipped my crust again. 'Getting stuck in an airport for twenty-four hours would be worse. Or standing in quicksand.'

He threw his own crust at my head.

'Hey, assault by crust is still assault.'

Rory rolled his eyes. 'Did you manage to get any pizza sauce *not* around your mouth by the way?'

I felt my skin flush before reprimanding myself – this was *Rory*. He'd seen me in my post-hangover state many a time over the years.

'It's my new method of repelling men.'

'You're going to need something better than that,' he mumbled under his breath.

'What was that?'

'I said, things not going well with Daniel, then?'

'They are,' I said defensively, trying to subtly wipe the sauce away. 'But it's not serious, it's just . . .' I trailed off, not wanting to spell it out.

'Oh, for God's sake. You're ridiculous, come here.' He reached over and pulled me towards him, causing me to stumble into the space between his legs. He inhaled sharply as he dabbed at the corner of my mouth. 'There.'

Neither of us moved. Desire curled in the pit of my stomach and for a hot second I didn't ignore it. *What if?* Rory's hand was still on my hip, and it tightened.

His eyes flickered up to mine, trying to read me.

'Pen?' His voice was thick.

And then I remembered a little thing called *Maeve*. Our best friend in the world. I really needed to get over my fear and ask them both what the hell was going on.

I sprung away from him like he was on fire, spinning around to go and get a glass of water and catch my breath.

When I turned, Rory was clearing his throat. 'It's been a long day.'

'Yeah. Yeah, exactly.' I didn't wait for further excuses, just blindly agreed. Whatever *that* was, it was a symptom of a long, stressful, emotion-driven day.

'Oh, hey guys.' We both jumped when his flatmate Stephen walked in.

I had never been so happy to see someone in my life.

'Hey Stephen.' I gestured to the pizza box. 'Have you had dinner?'

Rory's flatmate worked in finance and had no real interest in being best friends with Rory, which suited them both fine. After Lottie, he'd needed a drama-free place to live until he figured things out, and this had been perfect. When Stephen wasn't in work, he was hovelled away in his room playing computer games. The odd occasion where they shared a beer and watched *Love Island* or *Match of the Day* was as far as their friendship went, but I liked him. Particularly in this very moment.

He grabbed a slice from the box. 'You guys are my heroes. Triple pepperoni, I respect that.'

All three of us chewed in silence, but the food tasted like cardboard. My brain was fried. Work, Daniel, Rory . . . *Maeve*. Shit – Maeve. I was going to hell.

'You guys have been on the phone a lot this week. Big week at work?' Stephen made an effort at conversation, grabbing a beer out of the fridge.

I was instantly confused. 'On the phone?'

'Yeah,' he spoke around a mouthful of pizza. 'I've been up gaming until the early hours and all I can hear is this one chatting away.'

Unless I'd had an out-of-body experience, that definitely hadn't been me on the receiving line. I didn't say anything, leaving Rory to fill in the gaps.

'Oh no, not work related.' Pause. 'That wouldn't be Pen, she's a stickler for an eleven o'clock bedtime. It was a fucking nuisance at uni.'

They both laughed, and I pulled a face at him. But what I was really thinking was that I'd just been presented with some mightily damning evidence. And just minutes after a moment of *something* between the two of us. I thanked whoever worked up above for intervening.

'But still, incredibly long week at work.' The cloud passed over Rory's expression once again.

I wished I could do something to wipe it away.

Stephen immediately detected the tone change. 'Oh shit. Everything all right?'

I jumped in. 'It's going to be fine. We've got a brilliant comms team.'

It worried me, how I felt hardly anything when it came to our work crisis. My patience with the app was running out. When Stephen grabbed another slice and went back into his room, I took the plunge with something that had been playing on my mind.

'Do you ever feel like we're out of our depth, with the app?'

Rory snapped to attention. 'What do you mean?'

I tore a strip of cardboard from the box, fiddling with it. 'Our team is still really small, and there's only so much we can do. A more experienced team could –'

He held out his hand. 'Please tell me you aren't suggesting what I think you're suggesting.'

I wasn't even sure what I was suggesting. But a very well-established dating app had expressed an interest in us. 'What if we just asked their team for some advice?'

'Penny.' His tone was a warning. 'This is one bad day. We are not stooping that low.'

I fought the urge to explain that, for me, this wasn't the first bad day.

'I just think —'

'Penny, *no*,' he snapped. Although he hadn't quite raised his voice, the tone told me not to press further.

I went quiet. Rory never snapped at me, not like that. Both of us settled into awkward silence. Everything that had happened in the last fifteen minutes was new territory.

'You're right.' I backed down.

Rory's expression softened and he repeated the mantra from earlier. 'It's been a really long day.' He must have been feeling guilty about snapping, because he reached out and grabbed my hand. 'Want to get incredibly beaten at Mario Kart?'

It was a clear olive branch. In complete honesty, I had a banging headache, and after all that had just happened (or not happened) I really needed to lie down. But he looked hopeful, and I knew that thrashing me at Rainbow Road would be just like old, simpler times. It might make us feel better, and it might remind me why heated moments with Rory were an *extremely* bad idea. For so many reasons. I'd stay for a couple of races, but I could not afford to stay *over*. Who knew what would happen if I did.

I squeezed his hand. 'Pass me the remote. It's on.'

★★★

When I finally got home, Isla and Maeve were sitting on our sofa, painting their toenails with those weird foamy dividers separating their toes so that the paint didn't smudge. After an hour of getting beaten at Mushroom Gorge, the contrast between our evening activities was comical.

'Hey guys.' I dumped my stuff in the hallway, wandering through and perching on the arm of the chair.

They were watching a romcom, and from the three seconds I'd witnessed of Jennifer Garner prancing around New York with a fluffy hair slide and pink fur coat, I was pretty sure it was *13 Going on 30*.

'You two are pretty much fulfilling every girly sleepover stereotype right now.' I pointed at their bottle of rosé.

Maeve looked up from where she was painting her pinkie with a bright neon orange. 'I'm not even sure if this is technically a hostage situation you've just walked in on.'

Isla pulled a face. 'You weren't saying that when I walked in and offered to cook you dinner.' She pointed to a pot on the hob. 'There's leftovers if you haven't eaten.'

'It's really good, I have to say. Even if it did come with a hidden condition of watching a Nineties romcom and partaking in a pillow fight.' Maeve laughed when Isla pouted.

'There was no pillow fight involved. I just needed some female companionship. Anyway, there's some over there if you want it. No pillows will be required, I promise.'

I slid from the arm to the hollow at the end of the sofa, resting my head against the cushion behind me and closing my eyes briefly. 'I'm good, I ate at Rory's.'

There was a pause before Maeve spoke. 'You did? I thought you guys were dealing with a work crisis?'

I opened one eye, aggravated slightly by her tone of surprise. Rory was still one of my closest friends, secret relationship or not. 'Yes, we were. Then we grabbed food when we couldn't work any longer. What's the issue?'

'Nothing. *Right, Maeve?*' This time it was Isla who spoke.

Maeve backed down, holding up her hands in surrender. 'Sure. Right, so you can either choose between some odd sort of London-pollution-bogey-green' – she held up one bottle of nail polish – 'or blood-of-your-enemies-red.'

Isla snorted. 'OPI should hire you.'

'I don't think I'd get them many sales.' Maeve was still holding the choices up. 'Any thoughts?'

I had only a few thoughts for the day left in me, and they mainly consisted of my head hitting the pillow and not rising again for a solid ten hours. And maybe that weird moment of tension we'd just had.

'It's been a long day. I'll pass on the salon experience if that's all right. Why the emergency girls' night?'

My soon-to-be sister sighed. 'Joe had another night shift, so he left at seven. So I started going through all the RSVPs for the wedding, and I got out my sewing machine to do some more of the bunting, then I just . . .'

I exchanged a look with Maeve, who answered for Isla. 'She's having her pre-wedding wobble. I'm pretty sure it's a textbook milestone. And that's not the psychologist in me talking, that's the woman in me talking.'

'A wobble?' I kicked my shoes off, sinking further into the warmth of the flat. 'What do you mean, a wobble?'

I had visions of Joe on his own at the altar, jilted.

Isla shoved Maeve with her unpainted foot. 'I knew we shouldn't have told her.'

Maeve waved her off. 'If Penny was about to get married —'
I intervened. 'Unlikely.'

She nodded. 'I agree, unlikely. But if you were about to
get married, you'd have a wobble too. Change of any kind is
terrifying. Ask any of my patients. Well, don't. We have confidentiality for a reason, and that reason is so I don't go to jail.'

'You wouldn't fare well in jail. Although the orange *would*
match your new toenails.'

Isla looked stressed. '*Guys*. Do you ever shut up?'

'No.' I answered honestly. 'And I'm existing on pure adrenaline at this point, so it's probably worse than usual.'

Maeve rolled her eyes. 'Anyway, Isla was having a wobble.'

'It's not that I'm scared about marrying Joe.' Isla twisted her
fingers, nail polish forgotten for a moment. 'I'm just scared about
the after. Engagement was this huge, exciting thing on the cards
for *so* long, and I've loved the pre-marriage bubble, and I just
don't want that piece of paper to make us, well, boring.'

I really didn't mean to invalidate her concerns, but I couldn't
help it. I burst out laughing.

'Well, that is really encouraging.' Isla's tone was dry.

'Sorry, sorry.' I rested my head on her shoulder for a second.
'It's just that you two could *never* be boring.'

Maeve nodded along, solemn. 'This is what I said. We
wouldn't let ourselves be friends with boring people. It's a
rule we have.'

'I walked into your house the other day to meet Joe for
our run and you two were skidding around the house having
a NERF fight.' It was a true story. I'd almost been taken out
by a tiny blue bullet.

'This is true.' Isla pondered it for a second. 'Is marriage boring?'

I thought of my parents, for whom marriage had certainly *not* been fun. It was the only real benchmark I had. I shot Maeve a look, willing her and her nuclear family to pick up the slack.

'My parents still make pancakes together every Sunday. Always have. And when they walk anywhere, they hold hands and my dad swings my mum's arm even though he knows it winds her up. Marriage is what you make it. And I'm pretty sure NERF guns are allowed through the marital door.'

Nailed it. Isla's face lit up. 'See? This is why female companionship was necessary. I asked Joe if he thought we were boring and he reminded me to take the bins out whilst he was at work.'

Men. With comments like that, he almost deserved to be left at the altar.

'Isla, you're the epitome of human sunshine. Boring runs in the opposite direction, I promise. And if it makes you feel any better, you have to take the bins out whether there's a ring on your finger or not.'

She grinned, leaning her head on my shoulder this time. 'And that's why you're my maid of honour.'

I looked over her blonde hair to Maeve, who gave me a thumbs up. Today was a day for fighting fires, and I had about ten seconds of industrial hose pipe left in me before I passed out.

29

Daniel traced a figure of eight on my forearm with his fingertips, both of us dozing in the sunlight that was streaming in
from my bedroom window. I willed him to stop; my semi-con-
scious state a great distraction from reality. All of last
night – texting him, inviting him over – had been an effort
in occupying my mind with something else. It hadn't worked
for long.

'Your coffee is going to go cold.' He nudged my leg with
his ankle. *Damn it, Daniel.*

I gave in and sat up, taking the mug that he held out to
me. 'Thanks.'

He'd dashed out into the kitchen in his boxers about twenty
minutes ago, and I'd spent the entire duration of the kettle
boiling praying to God that Maeve didn't walk out. I wasn't
in the mood for explaining my situationship with Daniel to
her, and I wasn't convinced they'd be best friends.

'So, what are you doing today?' He took a big swig of his
own coffee. The rules were pretty clear now between us. There
was no expectation that we needed to spend the day together.
Even if I *did* have a cool new bookshop–bar hybrid that I

wanted to check out. I'd have to ask Maeve. Or Rory. Or both. Maybe not both. *Eugh*. I resisted the urge to bury myself back under the duvet.

'I need to tackle my bridesmaid speech.' I groaned. 'The bane of my current existence.'

Probably untrue, but only because there were *several* things plaguing me. The speech was definitely somewhere near the top.

Behind me, I felt Daniel's chest rumble as he laughed. 'Ah. Wedding speeches. Modern-day Satan incarnate.'

At last. Someone who understood.

'Rory is looking forward to it. He's suggested a wager for who can make them laugh the most.'

As always when I mentioned him, Daniel's expression darkened. Only for a second. 'The man obviously cannot be trusted, then.'

I brushed off the comment, which felt slightly more loaded than he made it seem. 'I just cannot imagine what I could say about love and marriage that would blow anyone away.'

Maybe I was building it up in my head. Maybe everyone would be too far gone to even care, and I could recite the entire script of *Bee Movie* and no one would even bat an eyelid. But *I* cared. This was Isla and Joe. It mattered.

'Last time I had to do one, I just talked about how drunk my mate had been on the stag.'

I blinked up at him. Clearly, I was going to find no solid advice here.

'You're not being very helpful.' I finished off my coffee, placing the mug down on my bedside table a little bit too hard.

He held up his hands in surrender. 'Sorry, sorry. Mine was a niche scenario. Had a whole plan but then drank *way* too much prosecco before the speeches.'

I shot him a look. 'Because as we know, I have a *great* track record with free-flowing prosecco.'

Daniel smirked. 'Well, I, for one, did actually think that it was great.'

I sighed.

'No one cares what's said in a wedding speech. Just don't make it too long, and don't mention any of the exes. Surely this kind of thing should come easily to an expert on love.'

The phrase made me want to tear my hair out. *An expert on love. Yeah fucking right.* All of a sudden I just really did not want to talk about this any more.

'Anyway, I'm doomed and have accepted my fate. Let's go make breakfast. I bought hash browns.'

We padded into the kitchen, him yanking on a T-shirt just as Maeve left her room, bag thrown over her shoulder and ready to leave.

'Oh, hey.'

There was a moment of awkward silence before Daniel jumped into action, holding his hand out.

'I'm Daniel. You must be the infamous Maeve.'

Maeve eyed his hand before taking it. I knew everything about my best friend, and I knew when she was holding back an eye roll. My cheeks flushed.

'That I am. Nice to finally meet you.'

Aside from our initial meet–cute, I'd only seen Daniel four times. Once for coffee, once for cheese toasties, and now twice when he'd stayed over. It was hardly unusual that Maeve hadn't been introduced.

'I bet.'

I winced at his response, even if he was joking. Maeve was edging closer and closer to the front door.

'Where are you off to?' I pulled a pan out of the cupboard and busied myself opening a carton of eggs, trying not to seem like I desperately wanted to hear her answer.

'Going to meet a friend for some breakfast. We're trying out a new place in Blackheath.' In true Maeve fashion, she'd clearly fought an internal battle and come out the other side, her voice warmer than thirty seconds ago. 'If I'd known you were making breakfast, I'd have asked you to join us.'

I tried to imagine anything worse than a double date with Maeve, Rory and Daniel. Maybe getting stuck in a lift, but even then, there was an emergency button.

'Sounds delicious. It's a good thing Penny is on hash brown duty.'

I finally turned back around, eggs frying on the hob and my hands now out of things to do. Maeve was staring at me, one eyebrow raised, with a look on her face that said 'we'll be debriefing about this later'. It made me miss her, even though we spent the majority of our time under the same roof. She was wearing a bright sunshine-yellow blouse tucked into denim dungarees, and she had a stream of bangles running up her left wrist. I hadn't borrowed her clothes in weeks. I'd been trudging around London in murky neutrals for a criminal amount of time.

'Well, aren't you lucky.' She narrowed her eyes. 'I've always thought that it's so nice when a man makes the effort. Anyway,

I'm going to be super late for breakfast. Hash brown free, sadly. My friend can't stand them.'

There was so much to unpack there that I wasn't even sure where to begin. But there was only one person I knew in my own life who hated hash browns. I never forgot it, because I always ate his. Rory.

'Enjoy.' Maeve waved to me on her way out, leaving me alone with Daniel. I watched her leave with a lump in my throat. There was a hot man standing in my kitchen, but I kind of wished that it was just Maeve and me, attempting to make pancakes like we had when we first moved in.

'Well, *she* has a bee in her bonnet.' Daniel laughed, sitting at the table. 'Who needs help sticking hash browns in the oven?'

I turned away, not trusting myself not to say something mean.

'Toast duty is still an option.' I pointed to the bag of Warburtons on the counter.

'Right.' I heard the chair screech backward as he jumped up. 'On it.'

We worked in tense silence for a minute, my blood pressure gradually sinking downwards to a normal level. Daniel was humming the lyrics to 'Easy' under his breath, tearing into a slice of white bread with his teeth whilst he waited for the toast to pop.

'So, how's work?'

I fought the urge to throw one of my eggs at the wall. Nothing about this was feeling easy or remotely like a peaceful Sunday morning.

'Let's just say that Level isn't my favourite thing in the world right now.' I filled him in on the Twitter storm, and probably out of kindness, he pretended he hadn't heard about it.

'Sometimes, when our whole life revolves around a project, it's really hard to see the woods from the trees. Easy to hate it just because it's the nearest thing to hate.'

I pondered what he'd said. 'I actually don't think it *is* that. And I don't hate it. I just don't know if what we're doing is that great.'

I spoke quickly, horrified but simultaneously relieved. One benefit of Daniel was that he was so far removed from my work life, I could freely blurt out my concerns without worrying that he'd think bad of me for saying it.

He instantly challenged me. 'What about it isn't working?'

I glugged back my second coffee of the day. 'Well, for all intents and purposes, the basics *are* working. People can log in, receive their matches, and start chatting. It does what basically every dating app says on the tin. But that's exactly what I set out *not* to do. I wanted to create an algorithm for love that actually worked, but I think I've realised I don't even know what that should look like.'

Daniel wasn't looking at me, instead focused on buttering the toast. 'No one expects you to have all the answers, you know.'

My silence must have spoken volumes because he looked up. 'What I mean by that is, could you enlist someone to help? Ask for advice?'

I thought about how my idea to work with Link had gone down like a sack of shit.

Daniel pressed on. 'Sometimes, or at least my dad tells me, it takes the pressure off when you don't feel solely responsible for a company. Didn't you mention that you're looking to sell shares?'

I wasn't sure I *had* mentioned that to him on any one of my mini-rants, but I got so riled up sometimes that it could have happened without me remembering it.

'Maybe.' I dished up the food, creating two plates that I'd lost the appetite for.

'Anyway.' Daniel brushed some crumbs off his hands. 'Enough about that.' He came over and pulled me into a long kiss. My mind was focused on my current problems, but I let it be distracted. His hand crept around my waist, squeezing, and I waited for the tingling sensation to kick in. The same feeling from the other night, in Rory's kitchen. It didn't.

'This food looks great, and I bet it'll still look great in a few minutes.'

I pulled back and tilted my head. 'Is that so?'

Daniel nodded, pulling my body flush against his so that there could be no miscommunication. 'I have a reputation for being ambitious.'

★★★

It had taken forty-five minutes to psych myself up to dial his number. Which was utterly ridiculous. Never, in eight years of friendship, had I thought twice about ringing Rory.

'Come onnnn.' The dial tone kept ringing.

Daniel had left a couple of hours ago, mentioning a trip to the pub with his dad and leaving me to fend for myself with this stupid speech. I'd tried watching *Don't Tell the Bride* for inspiration, but all that had done was make me worry that Joe might have bought a giant inflatable llama to stand at the entrance to the church.

'Hi Pen.' He finally picked up.

I tried to hear beyond his voice, listening out for tell-tale signs that they might still be together. There was nothing.

'Finally! Rory, I need you.' I didn't elaborate for a second, trying to ignore the fizz of electricity that phrase sent down my spine.

'Ah, if I had a pound for every time a woman said that to me –'

'Rory!'

'I'd have a fiver, max. Okay, need me as in you've set the fuse box off again and don't know where the switch is, or need me in a more abstract sense?'

I rolled my eyes even though he couldn't see. 'You're never letting that go, are you?'

'You might as well just accept it and move on.' His breath was slightly laboured.

'Where are you, anyway?'

He took another breath. 'Just this second left the climbing wall. Reached a new personal best.'

I tried not to think about him dripping with sweat. The thought should be making my eyes burn. *Why* wasn't it making my eyes burn?

'What's the dilemma, Pen? You can't leave me hanging like that.'

My blank piece of paper was staring at me, as were the opening credits of my third episode of *DTTB*. 'It's this bloody speech. I can't do it.'

From the other end of the line, I heard him laugh.

'It's not funny, Ror.'

He let out another chuckle. 'Winning this is going to be a walk in the park.'

Clearly, the men in my life were not the font of knowledge I'd banked on them being. 'I'm serious. I am not the right person to speak about love. I don't know anything about it.'

I heard the laughter die down. 'Well, that's bullshit.'

'Sorry, you're right.' I doodled a flower with my biro. 'Let me just go and call up all the loves of my life.'

He cleared his throat. 'I meant, that's bullshit because not everything has to be romantic. You'd do anything for the people in your life. Remember that time Joe had a panic attack after his first patient death?'

I did remember that. Isla had been away in Spain for a flower festival with some of her colleagues, so I'd raced over to their place and kept my brother company until the early hours of the morning.

'Or how about the fact that you never, *ever* cancel on your dad?'

This was also true.

'You love harder that anyone I know, even if you haven't found it in the *traditional* sense of the word. Draw from what you know, Pen, because you know a lot.'

I swallowed the lump in my throat. I took it back. At least one man in my life knew *exactly* what to say. I hadn't had a strike of inspiration, but I did feel a bit less lonely.

'Thanks.' I didn't elaborate, suddenly a bit scared that I might cry.

'You love, and you're loved in return. Promise.' Rory's voice was barely above a whisper, but it got through. 'Want me to come over and help you?'

I considered saying yes for a second, but the waters were just *too* murky right now. I wanted him here, I just wasn't sure why. It was definitely best to leave him to his sweaty, post-climbing activities alone. Definitely. I hung up before I could change my mind.

30

'Ginger shot?' Ella's head popped out from behind the fridge door. She was wearing a sky-blue blouse with daisies on it, her red hair in a side ponytail, holding out a tiny bottle to me.

I eyed it warily. 'If you want me to be able to sit through a whole board meeting, you might want to rethink that offer.'

'Right.' She blinked. 'Maybe you should try a peppermint tea instead. How was your weekend?'

I thought about my night with Daniel, and my fruitless attempts at writing a speech. Even with Rory's pep talk, the moment I put pen to paper my mind had gone blank.

'Nothing much to report. How about you?'

Ella was *always* ready for office small talk after the weekend. 'Well, we started off the weekend with parkrun and pastries, and then on Sunday we'd booked a roast dinner in Clapham after we saw it during our nightly scroll on TikTok . . .'

I let her chatter on, hoping her optimism would wash over me. It might not have been in my own personal realm of possibility, but it was refreshing nonetheless.

'And then last night we started a rewatch of *The Vampire Diaries.*' She finally came to a stop, pausing to neck back her own ginger shot.

'Team Damon all the way.'

Ella pouted. 'But Stefan is the better partner.'

God. I couldn't even choose a suitable fictional vampire.

'Anyway, I'll see you in there. I need to go and prep my presentation.' Ella hurried off to the boardroom, having the decency to look at least a little bit sheepish. I was fully prepared for her to shove Link down our throats again this morning. I wasn't sure how many more times I could say no without caving in to my deepest, darkest thoughts.

'Boo.' Rory appeared behind me, making me jump. 'Penny for your thoughts?'

'Like I haven't heard that one before.'

He shrugged. 'It's an oldie but a goldie. Feeling ready for this meeting?'

It was our usual meeting with Harriet, Ella, and Andrew, but today felt all the more important. Sure, the crisis that we'd thought was a crisis was a little bit less of a crisis now (a mouthful, I know), but we still had a tarnished reputation. There was the odd tweet about how we should never have launched coming through every now and then. And despite Ella's sunshine outlook and her ginger shots, we were in dire need of some financial support.

'As I'll ever be.' I handed him a coffee which he took, gratefully. He was zoned in on his phone screen.

'Another Twitter mob coming for the app?'

Rory snorted. 'Thankfully not. I'm in a virtual Uno war with Maeve, and I feel like I'm jinxing us if I walk through those doors without a strong lead.'

A hot poker stabbed at my heart. Uno war. Maeve.

'I highly doubt the future of Level depends on whether or not you win a game of Uno.'

I watched him tapping the screen. *This* was my chance.

'About Maeve . . .'

He spoke over my feeble attempt to get some answers. 'Boom. Take that, Maeve.'

My phone buzzed in my back pocket.

Dad: Just wanted to say thank you. Went on my third date last night and it definitely beats staying in the house.

Awkward moment with Rory aside, I couldn't help but smile, my faith in Level momentarily restored.

Me: I'm happy for you, Dad. See you soon?

He responded with a thumbs up. I had to admit, I was extremely intrigued by all of this. How had my *dad* got it right on the first try? I texted Joe, asking him if he'd heard the update, before sliding my phone back into my pocket and steeling myself for the meeting ahead.

★★★

'Even though what we're really doing right now is looking for investors, I still think it's wise for us to make friends in the right places and pursue more public partnerships.' Ella clicked to the next slide on her presentation. 'This is SafeTI, an app that's making sexual health check-ups more available, and less of a taboo topic. I know you two like to invest in companies that align with the aims of Level, so I thought that this would be a pretty good fit.'

She clicked through some more slides, showing us the design for the app and pitching how it worked. Ella was absolutely spot on when it came to finding companies whose values aligned with ours. Which made the whole Link debacle even more ridiculous.

'It takes the hush-hush element out of finding a clinic, and compiles all the ways you might want to get tested – an in-person appointment, getting a discreet kit through the post . . .' She pointed to a screenshot of the app's hub. 'And it's working with local councils and healthcare centres to share all results in the safety of the app. No one needs to worry about a text popping up whilst they're in the middle of a meeting, because they get a discreet message telling them that their results are ready within the app. There's also a section about safe sex, including contraception demos, and a breakdown of treatment if people *do* test positive. Making sure people have all the information and none of the stigma, so that getting an STI screening doesn't have to be a scary or embarrassing experience.'

She finished the pitch, sitting back in her seat and looking – even if she would never admit it – smug that she'd made a good choice.

'Well, I think that's a great idea.' Rory had been jotting down notes. 'Could we reach out and ask about some kind of cross-promotion?'

'I think so. I've been chatting with their team about how we might be able to include messaging on our app.'

I was pleasantly surprised. Maybe people hadn't been turned off our company forever.

Harriet looked up from her screen. 'Maybe something along the lines of 'meeting a new partner and falling in love is fun, but it should always be safe'?'

I nodded. 'I'm in. Accessible, safe, and perfect for our users.'

Next to me, Rory smiled. 'We're on the same page over here, boss.'

Ella wrote something down. 'Amazing. I think GetThere are also interested in working with them, so it'll be great to see all three of us collaborating.'

'And reassuring to anyone who saw the Twitter drama that Level is committed to putting the safety of its users at the heart of its strategy. Which is exactly what we should be aiming for with this kind of thing.' Harriet looked happy, which was a good sign.

'Okay, so that's partnerships. But as we all know, our outgoings are a little bit higher than our takings at the moment.' Ella looked to Andrew, who nodded and started putting it plainly and simply.

We needed to accept an investor. It was a non-negotiable at this point. We hadn't taken a penny from anyone since we'd been crowdfunded, and I knew Rory was incredibly hesitant to offer up any slice of our company. I reached my hand under the table to steady his knee, which was jiggling obsessively.

'Unfortunately, the lifestyle brand that hinted at a bit of interest last week has pulled out because of the Twitter scenario.' Ella wasn't looking either of us in the eye. 'So we need to get creative.'

I took the news within my stride. I was not surprised. About that, or about what came next.

'But Link is still persistent. We've had several emails from them over the last two weeks, asking to meet. I think we should.'

I didn't have to look at Rory to know what he was thinking.

'What is it that they want to offer?'

He shot me a wounded look that I'd even tolerated the topic enough to ask.

'Enough to get us out of the shit, and then some.' Harriet piped up.

'Would you be willing to meet with them?' Ella gave me her best doe-eyed glance. She'd definitely been manifesting about this conversation. There was probably rose quartz lined up on her desk.

Rory said 'no' at the same time as I said 'yes'.

'*What?*' He whipped his head around to stare at me like I'd sprouted antennae. 'You've got to be kidding me.'

I took a deep breath before ploughing on with what I had to say. 'I think we should hear them out, Ror. Even just to say no, once and for all.'

Ella's expression was cautiously optimistic, but everyone else at the table was silent. Apart from Rory.

'Penny, this is an outrageously bad idea. And you don't often come up with bad ones. Are you feeling okay?'

This was it. This was my chance to admit that my faith in our project was faltering. To get out what I'd been trying to tell him for days. Link had been exploiting people's vulnerability and need for human connection for *years*, and they'd been doing it well. If I still believed we were doing something radically different, I'd be on the same side of the fence as my best friend. But I *didn't* believe that any more. And we were struggling financially. There was something we could learn from these people, even if we were never going to go out for dinner or clink glasses with them.

'Please. I want to hear them out.'

Rory threw up his hands. 'Well, given that you're the CEO, I think we have to, don't we? I cannot believe this.' He muttered the last part under his breath.

'You're just as much the CEO as me, don't be stupid.'

He shot me a withering look. 'Let's not talk about who is being stupid, shall we?'

Ella, Andrew, and Harriet looked like they wanted to crawl under the table and take cover.

I made an executive decision. 'We'll hear them out. When do they want to meet?'

An awkward pause before Ella started twiddling her side pony frantically. 'Well, you see, that's the thing. They were keen to do it as soon as possible. And I thought on the off-chance you'd agree to it, we needed to strike whilst the iron was hot. And if you didn't agree to it, we could tell them where to stick it.'

'Shit.' Rory got there first. 'They're here, aren't they?'

I glanced behind me, like our sworn enemies might already be watching.

'They're in the lobby.' Ella bit her lip. 'I'm sorry, I just really think this is a good idea, and I knew that if I managed to get you to agree to it, you might un-agree to it as soon as you left the room.'

Rory's eyes were narrowed, but I was kind of impressed. 'That was a good tactic, I have to admit.'

She flushed, taking one look at Rory before quickly looking away. 'Okay, I'll buzz them up. You only have to hear them out for ten minutes, tops.'

Ella and Harriet left the room, presumably to go and get our guests. It took precisely two seconds after the glass door had swung shut for Rory to turn to me and let loose.

'What on *earth*?' His eyes were wild. 'Is this company not everything we were trying to counteract when we started working together?'

I nodded, trying and failing to reach for his hand, which he snatched away. 'Yes, I know. But if we don't get this out of the way, it'll keep coming up. You know it will. We don't want to look scared of them.'

'We aren't scared of them. We just hate everything they stand for.'

Andrew was twiddling his thumbs, pretending to be engrossed in two pigeons outside on the roof. 'Please pretend I'm not here.'

The pigeons started getting down to business. Andrew averted his gaze from them too. I felt a bit sorry for him.

'We *do* still hate everything they stand for, don't we?' Rory wasn't done.

'Yes, of course.' I tucked my hair behind my ear and smoothed down my dress, trying to regain some composure. What I didn't say was that I wasn't convinced I didn't hate what our own app stood for too.

We heard the glass door open again, Harriet coming in and sitting down. She looked stressed.

'Penny, I had no idea, I swear. I'm really sorry.'

Wait, what?

'Penny, Rory, this is the team from Link.'

Three men in fancy suits entered the room and took their seats opposite the two of us. It took a moment for me to realise that I recognised one of them. One of them had spent the night in my bed.

'Hi Penny.'

It was Daniel.

31

There was a beat of silence before anyone said anything. I fixated on a speck of dust that had floated onto one of the obnoxiously red apples in the fruit bowl. The fruit bowl that literally no one except Ella ever favoured over the bowl of M&M's.

'Penny, Rory, this is Michael.' Ella gestured to what she thought was a complete stranger sitting opposite me.

He gave a small wave, having the nerve to grin. *Michael?* Rory had turned in my direction, but I was just as in the dark as he was. What the hell was going on?

Ella ploughed on, completely oblivious. 'Michael is a board member for Link. His dad is —'

'Michael Broadhurst.' I finished the sentence for her, finally meeting Daniel's eyes. 'So you're *Michael* Broadhurst junior?'

I could not believe I'd had sex with a man who had the same name as his father. I felt dirty. What a colossal ick.

Daniel squinted. 'Well, it's Michael *Daniel* Broadhurst. Bit of artistic licence there, sorry.' I wanted to lob one of the apples at his head, and I wanted it to hurt. *That* was why I hadn't been able to find him on social media. He'd lied to me this whole time.

'Look, Penny —'

I cut him short. 'I really don't want to hear it.'

Underneath the table, my hands were shaking. I was *humiliated*. And I wanted to run straight out of this room and all the way back to Greenwich for a hug from my mum. Instead, I cleared my throat. 'Say what you've come here to say. Wouldn't want to derail your master plan.'

Next to me, Rory hadn't said a word, but he rose out of his seat suddenly, pointing a finger at Michael. 'You little *shit*.'

Michael rolled his eyes. 'Here we go. Defending her honour?'

Rory's chest was rising and falling in quick succession, and he took a shaky breath in. 'You have a lot of nerve.'

My ex–catfish–fling ignored him, turning his attention to me.

'Do you think we could talk in private for a minute, just before we do this?' He pointed to his briefcase, which he'd dumped on the table when he'd sat down. I pictured all of the documents in there, documents detailing how he wanted to get his hands dirty with my company, and my blood boiled. I was never dating again. I was signing up to a convent as soon as I got out of this meeting.

'Penny?' He tried again, ignoring the death stares from Harriet and Rory. Even Ella was looking at him in disgust, and she didn't have the full context.

'I don't think that's going to happen, *mate*.' Rory said the last word with venom, and despite everything, despite our argument precisely five minutes ago, I felt his pinkie touch mine. He latched our fingers together, squeezing three times. *I. Got. You.* 'You really don't deserve one second of her time, and I should definitely throw you out' – he looked at the other members of Level – 'but if she's willing to listen, then you have two minutes. Maximum.'

I could feel the anger humming through his body, just by the contact of our pinkie fingers.

Everyone in the room seemed to hold their breath, and I watched Daniel's eyes narrow.

'Okay, fine. Let's get to it.' He hooked his laptop up to the big screen. 'We've been watching what you've been doing for about a year now, and I have to say, we're impressed.'

About a year now. I blinked back the prickling sensation behind my eyes. I'd been such a sucker.

'At Link, we're always looking to make forward-thinking decisions about the future of online dating. Now obviously, we were ahead of the game.' He flicked to a slide which detailed the history of his father's own app, dating back to 2013. 'But times are changing, as they often do in business. We want to make sure we stay ahead of the curve. Now, I know you're looking for investors . . .'

I know you're looking for investors. My brain zeroed in on this as he bulldozed on. I'd leaked information to a snake. A tall, blonde, irritatingly charismatic snake.

'We've been pitching to you for the last few months, offering our investment for a small cut of the company.' Daniel met my eyes (I could *not* bring myself to call him Michael), but he was in full flow now, and I couldn't spot any remorse. 'And that's still on the table. We want a piece of Level.'

Rory snorted sarcastically.

'But we've seen how good your team is, and we've been paying attention to your audience. And now we're interested in more.'

The slide flicked over, showing a screen that hybridised both of the apps. A pit in my stomach opened. Ella's eyes were saucers; clearly, she hadn't vetted this presentation beforehand.

'What is it exactly that you're offering?' More than anything, I was curious. This was our biggest competitor, and they seemed to be so afraid of us that they'd do anything to be in on the action.

'We want to offer a merger of the two companies, to put it in simple terms.' His hands formed a frame in front of him.

'This isn't *quite* what we discussed over email.' Ella stepped in, aware that she'd just allowed a piranha into the boardroom by mistake. 'If I'd known —'

I clasped my hands on the table, but Rory's hand stayed on my leg. He had my back. I took a breath. 'It's fine, Ella, let him speak.'

Daniel seemed emboldened by this. 'Excellent, I knew you had a good head for business on those shoulders.' I felt sick. This man had been in my *bed*. He continued. 'This is your company, your rules. All we want to do is join efforts and be as successful as possible. Our team is bigger and has been doing this a long time. We can offer experience that you may be lacking at the moment. This is Jeremy, who can walk you through the financial technicalities' — he pointed to the man on one side of him — 'and this is Nick, one of our programmers. We'd love to chat a bit more with your programming team.'

It did not escape my observation that everyone sitting on their side of the table was male.

'I'm going to say one thing, and one thing only.' I steadied my voice, which was shaking. I would not give this man the satisfaction of knowing that he'd rattled me. 'Get the fuck out of my office.'

Rory squeezed my leg. 'You heard her.'

I grabbed my phone, hightailing it out of the boardroom and hoping for a moment to regroup and cry in the toilets whilst Ella dealt with the collateral damage. I didn't get the reprieve.

'Penny, wait.' Daniel followed me out of the room, ignoring Ella's protests. Rory met my eyes from where he was rising from his seat. *Do you need me?*

He seemed to sense that I wanted to take back control of this situation myself. I gave a quick shake of my head.

'Penny.' Daniel caught up with me. 'Don't make a stupid business decision based on some fling.'

Some fling? Okay, *I* was allowed to diminish it, but he had some audacity to say that himself.

'You're lucky I'm not calling security up here.'

Daniel scoffed. 'You're being overly dramatic. This is a great opportunity for you and Level, and you said it yourself, you didn't even *want* a relationship. It was just business.'

My blood boiled. 'Business? I don't think it counts as business if one party doesn't even know what's on the table. You getting into my pants and poking around my brain was not business. That was a betrayal. And it will *never* happen again.'

Daniel rocked back on his heels. 'I'm doing you a favour. You're losing faith in the app. Don't pretend that's not true.'

There it was. The real stab in the back. I hadn't just shared a bed with this man; I'd shared information that I never, ever should have. I willed him to speak just a little bit quieter. Behind us, Ella and Harriet were still in the boardroom with the other members of Link. And it looked like they were giving them a royally good telling off.

Daniel followed my eyeline. 'None of them were in on it.'

I raised an eyebrow. 'A lone ranger, are you?'

He glanced down, having the good grace to look a bit sheepish, but only for a second before the steely look was back in his eyes. 'You know what it's like. That constant pressure to do the next big thing. I needed to do something to impress dad —'

'Fuck me.' I folded my arms. 'Why does everything come back to men and their daddy issues?'

Daniel's upper lip curled slightly. 'Right. Well, clearly you wouldn't understand. I saw a chance, and I took it. Sue me.'

He froze, probably calculating whether I could.

'You are full of such bullshit, *Michael*.' I jabbed my finger into his chest and he grabbed it.

'You know what, Penny?' He narrowed his eyes. 'You've been looking for a way out of this company for *weeks*. You might not be telling the truth, but you're glad I'm here.'

I scoffed, ignoring the tiny part of my brain that wondered if he was right.

'If you think you're ever getting into bed with me again, you've got another thing coming.'

He gave a short, sharp laugh. 'Right. I may have been dishonest on the business front, but there are a few lies you've been telling too. I never stood a chance with you longterm.'

I rolled my eyes even though he was definitely correct. 'I have no idea what you mean.'

'Sure. Because that *Influence* article was completely full of shit, wasn't it?'

I paled, hoping Rory was nowhere near us.

Daniel laughed, but it was void of humour. 'And for the record, I thought we were on the same page. It was just sex. No strings. So what if I mixed business with pleasure? You should be flattered that Link wants to work with Level. I *know* you've been doubting Level's ability to make a success of itself . . .'

'Doubts that I *never* would have shared with you, had I known that you were poaching our conversations for business intel.' I pinched the bridge of my nose. 'This is ridiculous. I can't even believe I'm entertaining this conversation.'

'Is it?' Daniel stood up straight. 'I don't think it's ridiculous, and I think deep down that you don't think it is either. I know that Ella had to convince you both to let us up here, and I can't imagine that it was Rory who cracked. At Link we know how to successfully maintain a dating app's popularity. We've been doing it for ten years. You, on the other hand, know how to keep a dating app new and fresh, and you've caught the attention of your audience. I think joining forces is a brilliant next step for both of us. Why should users be diluting their success – and our success by proxy – by flicking between two different platforms? I think once you let me expand on what I spoke to you both about today, you'll agree with me that this is best for your business, and for mine.'

He was a little out of breath from his outburst, tugging gently on his tie, as if trying to force more oxygen down his throat. I imagined tightening it.

'It doesn't matter how I feel. I started this as a project with my best friend, and you'll never convince him that this is a good idea.' I lessened the distance between us. 'You can let yourself out.'

'Just for the record' – Daniel caught my shoulder on the way past – 'I might not be able to convince Rory, but there's one person who could. And we both know that it's you.'

I walked out of the room and didn't look back.

32

Rory slammed the boot shut, having successfully stacked enough food for five people as well as Isla's excessively large suitcase in there like a game of Tetris.

'That was impressive.' Maeve squeezed his arm, heading to the other side of the car to climb into the passenger side. She'd called shotgun this morning whilst we'd been running around throwing things into our cases (well, *I* had been running around, Maeve had been packed for days, her suitcase stacked with packing cubes and outfits categorised by activity). I'd been all too happy to let her be passenger; I still had no idea where I stood with them both, and Rory had excused himself to call her as soon as Daniel had left the office. It seemed we all had someone to turn to in our darkest moments, except both of mine had decided to create a private members club.

'You okay?' Joe hovered near me whilst the other three manoeuvred themselves into the car. Isla had agreed to go in the middle since she was the shortest, and I'd let her. It was her wedding, after all.

'I'm fine.' I smiled up at him, repeating the same phrase I'd had on autopilot since Wednesday. I felt like one of those teddy bears with the recorded voice box inside, destined to only say the same thing for years and years until I fizzled into non-existence.

My brother had an infuriating ability to read my mind. 'As you keep saying. Just not sure I believe you.'

I looked at Rory, who was busy straightening the sat nav in the front seat. 'It was a shock. I'm still a little rattled.'

His eyebrows rose, and he was right to be sceptical. I *wasn't* in shock. I'd had time to process everything. Including the complete humiliation – processing *that* had involved a lot of red wine – and the offer from Daniel. Or whoever he was. It was a real head–heart dilemma; before the version of myself with a horrendous track record when it came to dating, I'd been the version of myself who'd dreamed of starting a successful company. And that Penny had a horrible feeling that the offer on the table from Link required more than immediate dismissal. I'd doodled a pros and cons list in my planner, making sure to slam the pages shut when Rory walked in the room. I had to be *sure* it was what I wanted before I said anything.

'I know when you aren't saying something, Penny.' Joe squeezed me into his side. 'I've known you my whole life, unfortunately.'

I rolled my eyes. 'Is there a pep talk at the end of this?'

'Yes.' He gave me one final squeeze before letting me go. 'You're too independent for your own good sometimes. Let us in.'

He was right. I knew that. I planned on letting Rory in, just as soon as this weekend was over. This sten do had taken too much planning to let Daniel ruin it now. I'd even borrowed

Maeve's pink cowboy boots for our bottomless brunch. This weekend needed to be perfect. I just needed one thing to go as I'd planned it.

'Joe, I'm fine. Our dance with the devil is done,' I said, hoping he couldn't detect the white lie. 'This is your weekend. Forget about Level.'

'Fine.' He pulled a face. 'As long as you promise that Isaac and Daniel haven't put you off dating forever. I'd rather not have to buy you a hip flask so that you can fulfil your lifelong destiny of being the fun aunty to my children.'

I snorted, whacking him on the arm. 'I would be the best fun aunty this world has ever seen.'

He nodded. 'I know. You'd be *too* good at it. You'd give Aunt Sarah a run for her money.'

Aunt Sarah was Mum's sister, notorious for slipping us a tenner and a Werther's Original under the table, even now, when we were 26 and 28 respectively. She owned a nasty Jack Russell called Milo (although tell her that he was nasty, and you'd be crossed off the Werther's list), and dyed her hair a different colour every time we saw her.

'Are you two coming, or shall we just drive to Yorkshire and leave you here?' Rory stuck his head out of the driver's window. 'My sat nav says five hours and eleven minutes, and I'd like to get moving, if that's quite okay with the two of you.'

I stuck a finger up at him, but his excitement for our road trip was endearing. In his eyes, aside from being absolutely livid with Daniel, everything was back to normal. Link was finally out of the question. Ella hadn't brought it up since, and everyone else in the office was treading on eggshells (for once in his life, Dexter hadn't passed comment). The merger was quite clearly a no-go. For everyone but me. The only thing I considered a complete no-go was ever going near Daniel again. If they could sort us a deal with him out of the picture, I might just consider it. My palms felt clammy at the thought of breaking this period of peace, but it was time to come clean about everything. Rory deserved that.

'Right, we'd better get on the road before Mr Organised Fun starts throwing Percy Pigs at us from the driver's seat.' Joe squeezed my shoulder. 'But you're okay?'

I nodded. 'Promise.'

'Okay. Mum told me that if I didn't look out for you this weekend, then she'd make my ears big on the wedding cake.'

He said it with such sincerity that I didn't doubt that it was true.

★★★

After six hours in the car and a mind-numbing game of I Spy, we had finally made it to Yorkshire. And listen, I *loved* London. I loved that there had never been a shortage of things to do in the school holidays, and that Mum and Dad had taught us to memorise the Tube system before any of the other kids. I knew my Northern from my Piccadilly before I could even spell the words. But despite the hidden merits of being a Londoner my whole life, I couldn't deny that in terms of green space, it had *nothing* on Yorkshire. We were deep in the Dales, and there wasn't a skyscraper in sight.

'Is it just me, or does the air smell different here?' Maeve stepped out of the car and stretched her legs, joining the three of us who had desperately fought for the door handles in order to uncrumple ourselves from the back seats.

'Of course it smells different.' Isla took a deep breath and pulled her cardigan tighter around her. 'It's untouched.'

Joe put his arm over her shoulders, rubbing her arms. 'I bet after two nights here, we might be able to blow our noses and it not be black.'

'What a *lovely* thought. So glad you verbalised that one.' I pulled a face, getting the booking confirmation up on my phone.

We were staying in one of their wooden lodges, complete with a hot tub on the decking and a wine fridge big enough for the number of bottles that Maeve had shoved in the boot. Joe and Isla had the master bedroom, for obvious reasons, Maeve and I were sharing a bedroom with two singles, and Rory would be sleeping in the living room, where the sofa pulled out to reveal a double bed. It was going to be cosy, but that was the point of this weekend. One last hurrah before – let's be honest – nothing changed. My brother was hardly bachelor of the century.

'It says we need to put this code into the safety deposit box, and the keys will be inside.' I pulled up the email from Wendy, who I'd been conversing with since we'd booked.

Rory joined us, slinging his arm around my shoulders. 'What would we do without you taking on the lion's share of the work this weekend?'

I recoiled. 'I *offered* to take over the driving halfway. I'm not losing maid of honour points because you don't trust me.'

'It's true.' He jabbed me lightly in the ribs. 'No rental car insurance is bulletproof enough to take the Penny risk. Not after the supermarket car park incident of 2018.'

The others laughed, the incident a running joke. I'd been having a *really* stressful day at uni – it was hand-in day for our undergrad dissertation – and my head hadn't been in the game. I'd almost been rammed over by an elderly woman's trolley in her haste to get some broccoli, and when I'd arrived back at the car someone had parked scarily close to me, leaving me to drive straight into the back of them whilst my radio played old-school Mika. I'd called Rory, who had been about to leave for Newcastle to visit his parents for the weekend, and he'd delayed his trip to come and rescue me. Ever since then, my driving had been the butt of every journey-related joke.

'It was *one* time, on a really stressful day. And everyone in London drives so infrequently that surely we get a quota for –'

Rory interrupted. 'Isla, you hardly ever drive. Have you ever body-slammed a car?'

'Well, no, but –'

'Point proven. Sorry, Pen, the joke stays.' He leaned into my ear conspiratorially. 'Don't worry – I quite liked being the knight in shining armour. Think it suited me?'

I rolled my eyes, ignoring the shiver I felt at his breath hot in my ear. 'You called The AA and drove me home.'

'Exactly. And Her Majesty knighted me the very next day. Come on, we're being left behind.'

He gestured to the others, who were laden with bags and wandering over to lodge number seven, our home for the weekend. I grabbed a bag of snacks and my overnight holdall. This was going to be fun. As long as no one brought up Level, or Link, and I managed not to speak my mind about Rory and Maeve (now was not the time). Easy.

33

'Are you awake?'

I was turned to the wall, desperately trying to force myself back to sleep despite the sound of the birds outside (how had I gone twenty-six years without realising how *loud* birds could be?)

I mumbled the word 'unfortunately' back to Maeve, who sounded far too awake for – I glanced at my phone screen – 7.30.

'This is our weekend of relaxation. Why don't you try, oh, I don't know, *relaxing?*'

I didn't need to turn over and look at her to know she was pulling a face.

'I'm just excited. When do we get to spend time like this, all together?'

I thought of all the nights in the pub after work. 'All the time?'

'Oh hi there, killjoy. I meant, when do we get this kind of time when Joe isn't rushing off to save lives, and you two' – she didn't have to specify who she meant – 'aren't worrying about one Level-related thing or another? It's nice, that's all. I want to make the most of it.'

She was right about adult friendships; it was rare to have everyone fully present.

'Okay, I'll concede.' I turned over, facing her. She was on her side, beaming at me over the gap between the two beds. 'You have my full attention, even if it is the crack of dawn.'

'Brilliant. Meet you in the hot tub in ten?'

I nodded – albeit slightly hesitant at the thought of getting into a bikini when it wasn't likely to be anywhere near a temperature I approved of for that kind of activity – watching her spring out of bed in her rainbow pyjamas. Deep, deep down, I knew that we could all do to be a bit more like Maeve.

'Morning, grump.' I could hear her mumbling to Rory in the living room, presumably trying to wake him too. She got a groan in response.

'How often do we get to be together like this?' I heard her repeat the same spiel to him, and he must have reacted similarly.

'Hot tub in ten or you'll be in my bad books.'

A second groan was the only signal that her message had been received.

It seemed that Joe and Isla were given a free pass to sleep as long as they wanted, judging by the sound of my brother's snoring. I tied the straps of my pale pink bikini at the top of my shoulders, swearing when it came undone as soon as I moved. Surely, of all the clothing items, these things should be the most robust. I double knotted it and walked out of the bedroom in a daze. One wrong move on a banana boat in Portugal and this would be at the bottom of the ocean.

'I see you've been forced into an early rise too.' Rory was on the way out of the bathroom in his swimming trunks, mid-yawn and scratching at his chest. His hair was messy from sleep. I deliberately looked away; I was in absolutely no position to be thinking about my best friend in any other way than my *best friend*.

As I turned, the other side of my bikini popped undone, and I scrambled to hold it in place. 'For God's sake.' It was like the universe *wanted* us to feel uncomfortable. 'Can you tie this for me?'

Rory picked up an apple from the fruit bowl, tossing it between his hands. 'And why would I do that?'

'Because I'll be naked otherwise?'

He gave me a funny look before putting the apple down. 'Yeah, I can get it. Come here.'

I edged closer, very aware that aside from the moments when we stayed over with each other and turned too quickly whilst the other was getting changed, this was the most we'd seen of each other in *years*.

He tied the knot, hesitating before slowly tracing his finger down from the top of my spine.

'Penny . . .'

I didn't say anything, but my breath hitched. We were so close to a repeat of the night at his place, and I didn't trust myself. I felt our fingers intertwine as his other hand touched mine. I debated squeezing his hand three times in quick succession. *I. Need. You.*

'Yeah?'

There was a weighted moment, and I didn't breathe, scared the rising and falling of my chest might stop me from hearing the response. His hand still lingered on the bikini tie at the centre of my spine; I fought the urge to tell him to pull it undone.

'Rory?' I twisted to look at him, but as soon as we made eye contact the moment was over. He shook his head out of the daze.

'Trust you to pick the most impractical swimsuit in the history of swimwear.' He moved away. 'You're all good. Unless a tidal wave hits the tub, in which case you might as well resign yourself to public humiliation.'

'Public humiliation? What's that?' I batted my eyelashes, not missing a beat. I'd been so stupid to let it get that far. He'd clearly pulled away for a reason, and that reason was waiting for us outside in the hot tub. *I should have been thinking about Maeve.*

Rory laughed as he grabbed us both a towel from the stack that Wendy had left by the back door. 'You're a pro at that now, I'll admit.'

I headed towards the fridge, trying to acclimatise and copy his complete and utter indifference to whatever that had been back there. 'If we bring mimosas with us, are we less likely to be told off for taking longer than ten?'

He clicked his fingers in my direction. 'And this is why you're the brains behind the operation.'

We wandered out with bottles and glasses in hand, to where Maeve was fully submerged under the bubbles, her head leaning back against the tub.

'Is she . . .?' I walked over to stand above her, sliding back her sunglasses.

Rory sighed. 'She definitely is.'

Despite getting us up at the crack of dawn, she was snoring softly.

'I did try to tell her that the hot tub wasn't going anywhere. Plenty of time for relaxation.'

We watched her for a minute, half expecting her to wake up. She was wearing a neon orange swimming costume, her hair braided.

'She's been having a hard time at work lately.' Rory moved to the other side of the decking to open a bottle of prosecco. 'She doesn't like to lie awake, thinking about it.'

Against my better judgement, I pictured them lying awake together. The two of them having heart-to-hearts and whispering in the darkness. A lump formed in my throat.

'Is she okay?' *Compassion not jealousy. Compassion not jealousy.*

He sighed. 'She will be. Analysing people's brains is a lot easier in theory than in practice, I think.' Rory was staring at her, the level of care obvious. A reminder that they were speaking a language that I knew nothing about.

'Can I ask you something, and will you give me an honest answer?'

He passed me a glass. 'Anything.'

'Are you two . . .?'

Maeve stirred, panicking for a second when she realised she was underwater.

'You're okay.' Rory abandoned our conversation and went over to her. 'You fell asleep in the water. For a health professional, that wasn't very safety first of you.'

I laughed along with them, hoping it was convincing. 'People get way too complacent about their safety when my brother is in the next room.' I handed her a glass. 'Mimosa?'

She took it, rearranging her swimming costume and immediately taking a gulp when Rory poured prosecco into it. 'Well, you know, I never would have fallen asleep if you two hadn't taken liberties with your ten-minute warning.'

Rory shot me a look, hiding a smile.

★★★

'If there is one thing I'm thankful for' – Isla readjusted her pink, heart-shaped sunglasses – 'it's that we are currently debating between pancakes and avocado on toast, and not fighting for our lives in tiny death-mobiles.'

It had become *incredibly* apparent how Isla felt about go-karting. She'd said farewell to my brother as if he and Rory were never coming back.

'I don't think they'd let it happen if it wasn't safe,' Maeve mused, scanning the menu.

'Tell that to the bruised shoulder blades of my childhood.' I winced. Trying to keep up with Joe and his friends at his twelfth birthday had cost me.

'You know what I think is a travesty?' Maeve put her menu down. 'That the only part of bottomless brunch that's actually bottomless is the cocktails. I want to sit here and eat pancakes and maple syrup until the boys have to come and physically peel me from this leather booth.'

She did have a point. Bottomless brunch was misleading if you couldn't order a ridiculous amount of toast.

Isla sipped her pink cocktail, which had strawberry sherbet around the edge of the glass. 'Speak for yourself. They can keep these coming.'

Although we'd kept most of the weekend a surprise, we had told Isla in advance that she needed to pick an era. Her sunglasses and pink shaggy jacket screamed *Lover*. Maeve was covered in stars as a salute to *Midnights*, and I'd gone full *Fearless*, right down to the curls and the cowboy boots. It was a no-brainer; I'd spent way too many nights during university blasting that album. Maeve and I had dedicated a whole evening earlier in the week to making friendship bracelets, which we'd presented this morning with a flourish. They were currently stacked up our arms, and Isla had spent ages choosing ones that coordinated with her outfit. You could be a bride-to-be, but you'd always be a girl at heart.

'I'm going to the loo.' Maeve stood, pointing to the menu. 'Order me a breakfast burrito with extra cheese?'

It took precisely five seconds after she'd walked away for Isla to lower her sunglasses. 'Okay, spill.'

I nursed my own cocktail, which was bright orange. 'What do you mean?'

'I'm going to officially be your big sister in T-minus eight days. I know when you're lying. Something has been up with you for *weeks*.'

I stared at my soon-to-be sister. She was right. She'd been able to read me for years.

'It's about Level.' I squirmed, uncomfortable. 'I just . . .'

Isla put her hand over mine. 'You don't love it any more.'

What? Maybe I wasn't as good at hiding my feelings as I thought I was.

'Ever since I met you, ambition has been your thing.' Isla tilted her head. 'I know when the light leaves your eyes that something has gone wrong. Talk to me. You know I won't tell.'

And I believed her, I did. When I'd lost my virginity in first year, she'd promised not to tell a soul (especially Joe) and as far as I knew, it had never surfaced. So I spilled and told her everything, as briefly as I could given that there was only so much primping in the bathroom that Maeve could do.

'I'm not saying we need to merge with Link.' I sucked back the last of cocktail number one. 'I just wish I could talk to Rory about it more openly.'

Isla nodded, sympathetic. 'This is a hazard of working with someone you love. Do you know how long it took for me to work up the courage to tell your mum that the rosewater pastries weren't selling?'

I snorted. Telling mum she was wrong was like strolling straight into a lion's den.

'I think you need to talk to him.' I didn't have to ask who she was referring to. 'He cares about you more than he cares about the company.'

She shut up abruptly as Maeve came back over, three neon-looking drinks in hand. 'They said something about pink gin and I said we were sold.'

We settled into our usual excited chatter, going over the last items on Isla's – and by extension, our – to-do list. Aside from the actual logistics of picking everything up on the day, and some last-minute wedding favour making (everyone was getting a personalised packet of sunflower seeds), we were down to the final tasks.

'I just need to decide what I want to put in our bouquets.' Isla had the dreamy look in her eye that she always did when it came to flowers. 'Rory told me I should put tulips in yours, Pen.'

'He did?'

She nodded, smiling down at her cocktail. I was touched.

'Speaking of Rory, I can't wait to see everyone all dressed up.' Maeve clapped her hands together. 'I can't remember the last time I saw him in a suit.'

Excitement over sunflower seeds forgotten, I felt a pang in my stomach. Getting all that Level stuff off my chest and telling Isla the truth had been freeing. Maybe I needed to push myself a little bit harder.

'About that.' I stared down at the table, psyching myself up to the glorious opening notes of 'Bejeweled'.

'About what?' Maeve was looking at me, expectant. 'What does Rory in a suit have to do with anything?'

Did I sense a slight defensiveness in her tone? I didn't want to fall out with my best friend. Then again, if she'd read my mind these past few weeks, or been a fly on the wall in Rory's kitchen, or during our bikini moment this morning, we'd be destined for conflict anyway.

Isla patted my hand again, clearly sensing I was halfway to another revelation. It gave me the last spurt of confidence I needed.

'Maeve.' I stared her in the eye. 'I know about you and Rory.'

34

Two things happened at once. One, the waiter arrived with our food, not quite realising what he'd just walked into, arms laden with breakfast burritos and pancakes that I'd pretty much lost my appetite for. And two, Isla and Maeve burst out laughing, Isla wiping tears from her eyes. The waiter looked slightly afraid as he put down our plates.

'Thanks.' Maeve smiled at him, cheeks bright red. As soon as he walked away, she snorted again. 'I'm sorry, Penny, what the *fuck* do you mean, you know about me and Rory?'

'No, don't.' Isla clutched her stomach. 'It hurts.'

I was completely and utterly taken aback. I'd expected anger, denial, and maybe a few tears at being caught out. I had not expected hysterics.

'That is the most ridiculous thing I've ever heard. Sorry, Penny.' Isla speared a banana slice with her fork, spilling over into more laughter and putting it down. 'I literally can't eat.'

Her quota for sympathy and understanding had clearly been maxed out for today.

'Walk me through this.' Maeve finally calmed down enough to eat a mouthful of eggs. 'Walk me through how you got to this insane conclusion.'

I ran over all the concrete evidence in my head. Staying up late on the phone at night, touching his arm at the dinner table, going out for breakfast with a 'friend'. Both of them going quiet when I walked into the room, and Rory being cagey about who he was dating. I reeled off each point, trying not to be distracted by Isla's clear attempts to stifle back another outburst of giggles. Maeve's expression had settled into one of disbelief.

'Okay, so you've been putting these pieces together for how long? And you didn't think to just *ask* me? What the hell? We've been best friends for eight years. I think I would tell you if something that momentous had happened.' She took another bite. 'Also, gross. He's like my brother.'

Isla nodded. 'A hot brother, in all fairness. He's been working out, and it shows.'

Without warning, my mind wandered back to his hands on my shoulder this morning. What would have happened if we'd been completely alone?

'Again, like a brother to me.' Maeve was wrinkling her nose. *Focus, Penny.* I willed the image of Rory's arms to disappear. I seriously had a problem. My sex-supply being cut off after the Daniel/Michael saga was sending my hormones down a rabbit hole.

Now was not the time to be thinking about any of this.

'But he was dating Maisy, and I thought that was code for –'

'"I'm shagging my best friend"? Christ.' She held up her hand. 'We live together, how could I possibly have hidden that?'

This was it; I'd finally cracked. I was losing the plot. 'Well, I didn't think you were hiding it very *well*.'

She'd stopped laughing now, fidgeting with one of her earrings and looking rather pissed off.

At some point during the last five minutes, it had dawned on me that I was very, very wrong. One of my favourite things about Maeve was that when you asked her something directly, she very rarely didn't give you the truth. Even when it came to outfits and you were already late. So now that she was point-blank denying it, even when I'd asked her outright, I believed her. And I felt mightily, *mightily* stupid.

'If it wasn't for Isla's hen do, and the fact that this brunch cost an arm and a leg, I would be furious right now.'

I blinked back. 'But you're not?'

'Oh, I am.' She downed the rest of her cocktail. 'But I'm trying to keep it in check. You've been so self-obsessed lately, Penny.'

Isla was no longer laughing, eating her pancakes and watching us both rally. 'Come on Maeve, that's not –'

I held up a hand. 'No, I have.'

Right now, in the light of day, I could see it. I'd been so consumed by their maybe-affair that I'd missed *a lot*. About her work, about her personal life. I'd been so scared of what I might find if I dug a little deeper that I'd neglected to ask the right questions.

'If you'd been paying proper attention to my life instead of being so unbelievably wrapped up in your own, you'd know that I actually leaned on him for support during my severely painful breakup. Remember that? And now, I'm actually dating a man I met off Level. *Not* one of my closest friends.'

'Oh.'

She barked out another laugh. 'Yes. *Oh*. You've been so tightly wound about whether the app actually works that you didn't pause to ask whether it had worked for me.'

'I didn't even realise you were on it!'

She tapped her foot against the floor. 'And whose fault is that?'

I thought back to my now not-so-concrete evidence. The breakfast date. The giggling at her phone. She was dating, yes, but she wasn't dating Rory. And there was probably more than one person in the world that didn't like hash browns.

'I'm an idiot.' I pushed my cocktail towards her as an olive branch. 'Is it going well? Can I see a photo?'

She took a huge gulp of air, like she'd swallowed down what she had been about to say. I'd surprised her. 'I like him. Level did a reasonable job. We're a good match, I think.'

Well, there was a first fucking time for everything.

'But I'm probably going to end it soon. It's been fun, but it's not forever.' She pulled out her phone. 'Just because I'm showing you this doesn't mean I'm not still mad at you.'

Isla leaned in as we waited for her to pull up the photo. 'We have to let her be in her *Reputation* era right now I think.'

All three of us burst out laughing.

'I really am sorry.' I grabbed Maeve's hand.

She sighed. 'I forgive you. But you have to buy dishwasher tablets for the next year.'

'Deal.' I smiled, the tightness in my chest unravelling slightly.

'So who *was* Maisy?' Isla shovelled another pancake in.

Maeve shot her a look. 'I'll show you as many photos from my Level matches as you like, but I refuse to spill any of Rory's secrets. Have you thought about actually talking to the boy yourself?'

Isla gave Maeve a knowing look in return. 'Right. Shall I go and get another round of drinks?'

I finally let myself tuck into my own burrito, making appreciative noises as Maeve scrolled through her new man's Instagram. Even if, as she was telling me, she was pretty sure she was going to call it off before the wedding.

'If I'm in *any* era, it's *1989*.' She sighed. 'I'm taking inspo from Caroline Webber at the moment.'

I smiled, knowing Mum would be flattered, but I was distracted again. One half of the mystery was clearer, but that still didn't explain the late-night phone calls, or why Rory had kept things from me. Not that I could point fingers at anyone, when I really just needed to get over myself and talk to him. About work. About Link's offer and how conflicted I felt about it. And definitely *not* about anything else. Not the fact that I'd wanted him to work on untying my bikini this morning rather than securing it. Especially when he'd shut the whole thing down, and I now knew it had nothing to do with Maeve. I wasn't ready to open that box. I needed to stay firmly in my best-friend lane. But Isla did have a point; I couldn't put off talking to him about Level forever.

★★★

I'd decided — mostly due to the fact that this weekend was about Isla and Joe, but also due to the massive hangover from brunch — that the sten do was off limits for any more truth telling. The rest of the morning had put the term 'bottomless' to the test, and I was now sure that we couldn't face York city centre ever again. We were one of the bridal parties that made locals roll their eyes, and Isla had *lived* for it, adding a veil to her *Lover* outfit and practically jumping Joe when we'd met them at a more traditional pub afterwards. We'd had a barbecue back at the lodge, Rory burning all the burgers to a crisp and earning — what I could now tell was a completely platonic — telling-off from Maeve. My brain felt peaceful in a way that it hadn't for what felt like weeks, the Maeve–Rory drama put to bed (even if he was oblivious to it all) and my resolve to confront Rory when we got back to London growing every minute. Things were going to be all right.

'I've got a blister the size of England,' Joe was whinging, showing off his heel to the rest of us. We'd spent this morning on a hike in the Dales, and it was abundantly clear that we were a group of Londoners.

'You wouldn't think that you spent most of your working hours on your feet.' Maeve chucked a plaster at him.

'If the A & E ward was uphill, you'd know about it.'

Isla, who was making salad for our pizza night, snorted. 'Don't be fooled, he asks me to rub his feet on an almost daily basis. A fate worse than death.'

All three of us wrinkled our noses respectively, Rory midway to the dining room table carrying the pizzas (delivered from the village nearby – highly recommended by Wendy in our welcome booklet). 'It's a good job that nothing can put me off pepperoni. Come on, it's hot.'

We all made our way over to the table, Maeve tucking an extra bottle of rosé under her arm. Isla, Maeve, and I were already in pyjamas after a long stint in the hot tub this afternoon, and I was pretty sure I'd caught the sun on my face. I was relaxed and completely ready to load up on carbs.

Joe raised a glass and signalled for us all to do the same. 'To Penny and Rory, for organising the perfect sten.'

Everyone lifted their glasses, Rory kicking me under the table and shooting me a smile. Against all odds, with a groom and a bride that enjoyed completely different activities, we'd managed to pull this off. And no one had been involved in a go-kart crash.

'I've got a fun idea.' Isla beamed, a slice of veggie pizza in her hand. 'Why don't you two do a practice run for the big day? Show us a little bit of your speech?'

I clammed up immediately. Isla did *not* need to know that her maid of honour had a blank sheet of paper that she carried in her jacket pocket everywhere she went.

Rory crossed his arms. 'My speech is a thing of beauty. No need to practise.'

I gritted my teeth. 'Me too. Can't spoil the surprise.'

It wasn't that I wasn't committed to the wedding; I'd ordered a white clipboard and had asked the seamstress to give me a demo of precisely how Isla's veil needed to be arranged. But the speech? If anything, I was now even *less* sure about what I wanted to say.

'Okay, okay.' Maeve held up her hands. 'But when one of you gets stage fright and forgets all your lines, I'm definitely going to say I told you so.'

'This isn't a primary school production of Snow White, Maeve.'

She pulled a face at me.

'Maybe not, but stage fright is a given.' Rory spoke through a mouthful. 'There's no shame in wearing a nappy just in case, Pen.'

I flipped him the finger, basking in the glow of everything feeling normal. Everyone slipped into contented silence for a few minutes whilst we ate, speaking only about passing the barbecue sauce or filling up a glass.

'We're out of wine.' Isla pouted at Rory, who was closest to the fridge.

He sighed. 'When I get married, Isla, I'm going to employ you as my own personal Cinderella. Before the makeover, when she was all grubby.'

Despite his protest he ambled over to the fridge, and Isla pushed her plate away, leaning happily on her hands. 'This has been the perfect weekend.'

'That's the wine talking.' Joe pinched a crust from her plate.

'That' – she offered him another – 'and the natural high of being with my best friends. Rory, what's the hold-up?'

We all turned to see Rory leaning against the counter, staring into space.

'What's up, mate?' Joe, despite being several pints in, looked concerned.

Rory was silent for a moment before picking up my phone, which I'd left on the side whilst we were eating. 'Penny, what's this about?'

Even though I had no idea what he was referring to, my blood still ran cold.

'I have no idea what you're talking about.'

He strode over, plonking the bottle of wine in front of Isla – who, sensing the mood, ignored it – and my phone in front of me. The screen was lit up with several messages.

Daniel: Hi Pen. I was wondering if you'd thought any more about what we spoke about? (2h ago)

And then, when I hadn't replied:

Daniel: I know you're a loyal business partner, but this isn't about friendship, it's about business. (3m ago)

Fuck.

35

There was a beat of silence where all five of us just stared at the screen.

'What is he on about, Penny?' Rory didn't sound annoyed. He sounded hurt.

'Let me see?' Maeve swivelled my phone around so that she could read it properly. I winced at her expression.

'I swear' – I laid my hands on the table, shaking – 'that I haven't spoken to him since Wednesday, and I didn't say *anything* to him that day in the office to make him think he could still reach out.'

No one spoke. Not even Rory.

'Come, on Ror, you know I wouldn't do that.'

He wasn't looking at me any more, just straddling his chair and rubbing his face with his hands. 'Do I know that?'

I couldn't help it; I raised my voice. 'I've given everything to Level, why would I go behind your back and sign it away?'

Isla, who was the only person in this room that knew *exactly* where I stood when it came to our company, put her hand on Rory's shoulder. 'She wouldn't, and you know that.'

'I promise, that day in the office I told him where to shove it.' I played with a hangnail under the table, ripping the skin away from my cuticle. It looked like honesty hour was premature. 'But before that, he wasn't *Michael Broadhurst,* board member of Link. Remember?'

Rory was watching me, apprehensive. 'Yes, I do remember telling you to avoid him.'

I blew out a breath. 'And I remember being a grown adult woman who makes her own decisions.'

'Clearly.'

Okay. This was it. My chance to come clean about my feelings towards Level.

'I had started to have doubts about what we were doing. About whether we were actually achieving what we set out to accomplish.' I repeated my spiel from earlier today, and from across the table, Isla nodded at me, encouraging me to continue.

'The thing is' – I was pretty sure that my cuticle was bleeding profusely under the table now – 'people want love *so* badly, and I wanted to be able to give that to them. But I'm not sure any more that an algorithm can do that. And after my most recent experiences, I'm not even sure I know what love *is.*'

They'd all been listening – Joe and Isla intently, Rory sceptically, and Maeve somewhere in the middle. It must have been painful for the rest of them, being stuck in the centre of this.

'Wow, you really don't know what love is?' Rory recoiled. 'You're telling me that you doubted six years of hard work, because a poor excuse for a man ghosted you? Come on, Penny. Come *on*.'

Joe raised a little bit in his seat. 'Rory, mate, don't.'

My brother hated conflict, but he'd pushed a boy off his bike when we were in school, just for calling me names. I intervened.

'It's not just because a boy ghosted me.' I tried to maintain a level of calm. 'And I *tried* to tell you Rory, that day in your kitchen, but you wouldn't listen.'

He shook his head, furious. 'Don't put this on me.'

'But it's *true*.' I felt tears prickling behind my eyelids. 'We had the security breach, and it suddenly became really clear to me that this isn't a game. It's people's lives. And I don't want to play with lives if the app doesn't *work*.'

I stared down at my pyjama shorts, pulling at the blue and lemon striped drawstring.

'I thought I was seeing a guy who I could speak to about that sort of thing. I had no idea who he was, Rory.'

My voice cracked a little bit, the humiliation of what had happened that day in the office still fresh. Underneath the table, Joe nudged my foot. The unspoken sibling understanding kicked in. *If you want me to put a stop to this, I will.*

'She's telling the truth.' Isla poured everyone a glass of water. 'Let's all just take a minute.'

But Rory looked panicked. 'You must have had some serious doubts to spill all of that to a stranger. Where do you stand right now?'

I froze. I hadn't thought past explaining Daniel's text away. But now that I was in the hot seat, I had to continue with honesty. It was the only way out of this with our friendship still intact.

'I'm not sure what I think.'

Maeve got up. 'I think maybe we need to take a breath, and —'

'*How* can you say that you don't know what you think? They want to *merge* apps, Pen, and I know you know what that means.'

He was still using my nickname, which was something.

'If Link takes us over, then it won't be a fair split. I can promise you that. They'd steal our algorithm, take the glory for themselves, and we've not been around long enough for people to remember the work we did.'

Isla nudged a glass of water in my direction and I took a sip, my hands shaking. I did feel a bit like I was in an interview.

'We could negotiate every single term and make sure that didn't happen. I wouldn't sign anything without making sure of that.'

He was shaking his head in disbelief. 'It sounds like you're pretty sure what you want.'

I reached out for his hand but he pulled it away. 'I'm *not* sure. That's the whole point. We need some money right now, and a merger this big doesn't come around very often. They like what we're doing enough to pay a *lot* of money for it. Do you think I want to do business with that man? No. But we may *need* to.'

'I'm aware. I was in the same meeting as you. I just value integrity over money, personally.'

Joe opened his mouth but I shot him a pleading look: 'Don't'. Yes, it was a low blow, but I couldn't argue that it wasn't justified. I was throwing a huge, unexpected spanner in the works. Level was Rory's favourite thing in the world.

'I just feel like a fraud. I don't want to con people into thinking Level will change their lives. Not when I don't think it will.'

Rory scoffed. 'Just because it didn't work for you doesn't mean it won't work for anyone else. It worked for Maeve. Maybe you're just not meant to find *your* person *that* way.'

Maeve immediately held up her hands. 'Don't drag me into this.'

He glanced at her, incredulous. 'I cannot be the only one who thinks this is utter madness.'

She softened, seeing the hurt in his expression. It killed me that I couldn't be the one to move closer and fix it. I was in too far now, I had to see it through.

'It's a shock.' Maeve turned her attention to me, clearly trying to read my mind. I'd let my fear of their affair stop me from telling her the truth too. Now my two best friends in the world were looking at me like they didn't recognise me.

'You might feel differently in the morning, when we've all slept.' She silently pleaded with me, willing me to take it back. But once something like this was out in the open, you couldn't shove it back under the rug.

'I won't.' I traced my fingers in the condensation on the side of my water glass. 'I won't feel differently.'

Rory stood. 'I've heard enough, I think. I'm going to bed.'

'*Rory.*' Now I was the one pleading. He looked at me the way he'd always looked at me, like we were the only people in the room. But this time there was no affection behind it. 'Please can we go somewhere to talk about this?'

His eye contact didn't waver, and for a millisecond I thought he might cave. But then his expression shut down. 'I don't want to talk about this any more. I'm going to bed.'

He walked off, shaking his head as he headed into the bedroom Maeve and I were sharing, slamming the door behind him. Everyone else at the table was quiet. Clearly, I was taking the couch tonight.

Maeve threw her head back. 'Well, that was unexpected.' She grabbed the leftover wine, moving to the fridge to put it away. 'I wish you'd told me how you were feeling.'

I did too. She walked towards our bedroom, glancing at me.

'It's okay. Go.'

She nodded. 'And just for complete clarity, I will *not* be having sex with him.'

Isla snorted, welcoming the icebreaker. Joe looked utterly confused. I watched as she opened the door, murmuring softly to Rory.

Isla came around to my side of the table, enveloping me in a hug. 'Well, better that that's out in the open, right?'

'I'm not so sure.' I stared at the closed bedroom door. The distance between us felt wider than ever.

36

'I am so, *so* sorry about that, Isla.' I slumped on Mum's sofa, defeated.

It was a good job that we'd had to vacate the lodge before nine this morning; any longer cooped up in there with all the tension and I might have combusted. Rory hadn't spoken to me since last night, the only communication an accidental moment of eye contact in the wing mirror. He'd dropped us all off at our flat, and Maeve had headed straight to a yoga class. The remaining three of us had come to Mum's, Joe and Isla clearly gunning for a debrief.

'That definitely wasn't the finale to your hen do that I had planned.'

Isla handed me a cup of tea – something herbal (in other words, gross). 'Oh, would you shut up?'

I blinked.

'That was the perfect weekend. I wore a bikini, drank pink cocktails, and didn't break my ankle on a hike. It's the holy trinity. If I'm worried about anything, it's *next* weekend.'

Joe came in and handed me another mug, switching out the herbal with a normal breakfast tea. I sent him a thankful look as he spoke.

'Rory will probably be over it by then.'

I wasn't convinced.

'And even if he isn't, Rory has taken the best man thing way too seriously to let anything ruin it. I wouldn't be surprised if he's organised a flash mob.' Isla shuddered.

I made a mental note to check that he hadn't *actually* organised one, then remembered we weren't exactly speaking all over again. 'This is so *shit*. I need Rory, and I need to fix this, but we're at a standstill. We fundamentally don't agree. I can't endorse a project I don't believe in, but I don't want to lose my best friend either.'

I sniffled, the weekend's events catching up with me. Now that the cat was out of the bag, I felt more strongly than ever. I couldn't work on the app if it stayed the same, and Rory didn't want it to change.

'Oh, Penny.' Isla moved closer, hugging me. 'You'll work it out.'

And it wasn't even just Rory. It was work, and it was Isaac, and it was Daniel. It was Mum thinking that she hadn't been a good role model, and me not being able to think of a single anecdote for my speech. I hiccupped.

'Why did I have to go and talk to Daniel fucking Grayson?' A tear dripped into my tea. 'Or Michael *Daniel* Broadhurst, whoever the fuck he is. And why did I have to get drunk at that stupid corporate mixer?'

If I hadn't met Daniel or tested out the app, none of this would have happened.

Isla was thinking, her head tilted slightly. 'That's the one thing I don't understand. Why *would* you go to Daniel instead of Rory? Rory's your person. He has been the whole time I've known him.'

I sighed. 'I couldn't vent to Rory just as a friend, could I? When it comes to us, work and personal boundaries are the same. Maybe we never should have mixed the two in the first place.'

Joe squeezed my arm. 'That's not true, and you know it.'

I pressed the heel of my hand to my forehead. 'I just needed to vent to someone who was a complete outsider. And *yes,* I realise how badly that backfired.'

Isla sipped her tea. 'So what is it exactly about Level that's freaking you out? Let's strip back to the basics.'

I took a few deep breaths, trying to regain some control. 'Sometimes owning a dating app feels a bit dystopian. Like some weird episode of *Black Mirror*. I don't want to mess with real people and fuck up their lives.'

She started rubbing my back in slow circles. 'You know what, I get it. It's high stakes. Dating is *hard.*'

I loved Isla, but I was sceptical. 'Not for you two.'

'Not true.' Joe laughed. 'Very much not true. A relationship takes work.'

This kind of talk was news to me, when it came to my brother and his childhood sweetheart.

Isla nodded. 'Particularly when you literally grew up together. We were babies when we met.' She smiled at Joe.

'Trying to figure out if we grew in the same direction was hard, for a long time. But we worked it out.'

I was momentarily stunned. I'd always seen the two of them as an impenetrable unit, bound together by a decade of shared experiences. But it was true, they'd been incredibly young when they'd met. And Joe's career had been a massive sacrifice for both of them.

'Thanks for telling me that.' I sniffed. 'As selfish as this is, it does help to know that people's relationships are hard way before Level gets the chance to come and mess them up.'

Joe smirked. 'This reminds me of that time you dropped your Beanie Baby in the sea, and the only thing that stopped you bawling was me chucking mine in too.'

I smiled despite myself. I'd mourned the loss of that little spaniel for weeks after I'd dropped it in the sea on a family holiday to Bournemouth. 'In my defence, I was 6 years old.'

'Maybe so, but a day hasn't gone by that I don't think about it. Have you seen how much Beanie Babies go for on eBay now? I might as well have scattered my life savings on the beach.'

'We live in London, and you're about to pay for a wedding, so how much would that be? Fifty quid?'

Joe flipped me the finger.

'We even broke up once, actually. For about five days.' Isla was smiling, even though it sounded like the opposite of a happy memory.

'I don't remember that.' I was incredulous. This was *Joe and Isla*.

'Well, it did happen.' Joe scratched his head. 'God, I haven't thought about that in ages. I didn't tell any of you because I hoped it wouldn't be permanent.'

'When was it?'

Isla sighed. 'It was during the final year of his degree. We'd been fighting all the time about our future, and about our compatibility because of that. As soon as we'd decided to end it, I knew it was the wrong decision. I stayed at my sister's house for a week, cried into my granola every morning, and then showed up at his door with my tail between my legs. Turns out "compatibility" doesn't mean shit, because look at us now.'

There it was again, that word. Compatibility. The word that dominated my entire life, seemingly in work and outside of it. What did it even mean? I glanced at two of the people I loved most in the world; would Level have placed them together? Isla was endlessly bubbly where my brother could be a grump, and their careers couldn't be more different (in every single way you looked at it, including their schedules). I wasn't sure that the algorithm would have detected the ways in which they did match; the fact that they both hated fighting and worked hard to communicate how they felt, their affinity for stupid kid's toys and play fights around the house, and the fact that Isla supported Joe's career fully, packing those little lunches with his favourite things every day. An equation for dating could only be so accurate – it wasn't human, didn't get to experience all of the things that made two people compatible *off* paper. Maybe the fun part was taking a punt and seeing whether two people clicked, with no earth-shattering consequences if they didn't. Somewhere along the way, with all the pressure of a perfect match, Level had lost its magic.

'What are you thinking about up there?' Isla pointed to my head.

I leaned my head on her shoulder. 'That real sisters dig deep into their own trauma to soothe each other.'

She snorted. 'Ever the optimist. I know this year has been tough for you, Pen.' Isla was serious again now. 'And I know that you might be doubting a lot of things right now. But don't let one of them be Rory.'

'I'm not doubting Rory.' I grabbed one of Mum's cushions and held it to my chest. 'I've never doubted him. I just don't agree with him on everything.'

From the kitchen, where he was currently rifling through the cupboard for snacks, Joe groaned. 'Our wedding day is going to be like an episode of *The Kardashians*, isn't it?'

I squeezed the fabric tighter, the mere thought of Rory and I walking down the aisle in complete awkward silence making me squirm.

'You're making her stressed.' Isla stroked my hair. 'Don't listen to him. I've caught him watching reality TV when he gets in from work. He'd love it if our wedding turned out to be like an extended episode.'

'It's *soothing* to watch people create drama out of nothing.' He came back around the corner, distributing bottles of beer and Mini Cheddars. Mum would be arriving home with fish and chips any minute now. 'It's like, the opposite of my workday. It's how I de-stress.'

I was learning a lot about my brother tonight. I pulled my legs underneath me, curling up for the night. I'd planned to go home and do some work, but what I needed – shitty TV with my family, and chips drenched in salt and vinegar – was right here.

'Speaking of stress, are you going to tell Mum about your cold war?'

I pulled a face at the terminology. 'No. She already thinks my romantic understanding is damaged beyond repair.'

'Huh?'

'It's nothing.' I brushed the comment aside. 'Just the classic "did my divorce damage my kids?" mentality.'

He nodded. 'Ah, the age-old question. Given that I'm about to say "I do", I think we can safely say I avoided the baggage. Same can't be said for you, though, can it?'

'Too soon, Joe, too soon.' But I was laughing anyway, accidentally getting tea up my nose. My brother was a pain in the arse, but he also knew exactly what to say. Or do, when it came to Beanie Babies.

37

I held my breath as the lift reached our floor.

'You can do this, you can do this.'

I'd officially reached the point of my breakdown where I was talking to myself in the mirror. Next, I'd be having my tarot cards read and only conversing with people whose horoscopes harmonised with my own, condemning the fire signs in case they clashed with my Virgo personality. It had been a sleepless night last night, and I'd been horrified to find that Rory's Aries and my Virgo were *not* signs that aligned.

I brushed an imaginary piece of lint from my blazer and tried to smooth down my baby hairs, walking into the office with purpose.

'Hey boss.' Dexter didn't look up from his computer. 'Feeling rough from the weekend?'

'Something like that.' I looked over his shoulder. 'What are you working on?'

His screen was full to the brim with complex coding.

'Tightening the security. I think it's hacker-proof, but we'll have to test it out.'

I knew Harriet was pushing Ella for rigorous testing of the new security system, well aware that you could avoid a scandal once, but twice was pushing it.

'This looks really good. Thanks, Dexter.' I walked past my own office without daring to look in, dropping in to Ella's instead.

'Morning.' She was spooning a yoghurt pot from Pret into her mouth, an iced matcha ready and waiting on the desk beside her. Prior to the weekend, she'd become an expert in avoiding eye contact with me, mortified about the Daniel incident. I felt the urge to reassure her now.

'You know, last week was absolutely not your fault.'

Ella put down her yoghurt, clasping a hand to her chest. 'I'm *really* glad you said that. I couldn't sleep last night.'

You and me both.

'How did the sten go?'

Clearly, she hadn't yet spoken to Rory.

'Oh, you know. The usual. Plenty of wine, plenty of food.'

'And the hot tub?'

I groaned. 'I think we should get one for the office.' I peeked at some of the paperwork she was going through. Mentally put my big-girl pants on. 'Any word from Link?'

Ella did a double take. 'I thought we never wanted to hear a peep from them again.'

I took a breath before committing to what I was about to say. 'I'd like to see on paper what their terms are. Just to check whether, in theory, it might be worthwhile for us.'

I'd stayed up most of last night after I'd got home from Mum's, unable to switch my mind off. In order to properly discuss everything with Rory, I had to know what we were dealing with. I had to know what my actual opinion was.

Ella had abandoned the yoghurt pot now completely, and her expression was kind of gormless. It wasn't a good look for her. 'So we're genuinely considering the merger?'

I played it safe, not speaking for both of us. 'I wouldn't say that. But I'd like to know more, without having to contact Daniel myself. If that's okay.'

His messages still sat unopened on my phone. There was no *way* I was giving that man the satisfaction of direct contact.

'Of course.' She jotted something down.

'Can you do me a favour and not tell Rory that I asked you to do that? At least until we have the terms of the offer back?'

For the first time, Ella sensed the tension. 'Oh. Yes, no problem. If he asks, though . . .'

'Yeah of course. Tell him if he asks.'

I was really hoping he didn't ask. I stood up, finally feeling steady enough to face the music.

Whatever decision we came to, I needed to work things out with Rory. Who was going to DM me stupid tweets, or send me sudokus that he couldn't finish? We'd been working together professionally for long enough now that, as grown adults, we could surely find a way to figure this out together. I pushed on the glass door to our office, sensing his lack of presence without needing to check. No jacket on the back of his chair, or half-finished cup of coffee on his desk.

I went back into Ella's office, where she'd gone back to her yoghurt.

'Sorry to interrupt again.'

She put it back down, barely concealing a small sigh. 'Where is Rory?'

Ella did her second double take of the day. 'Did he not tell you? He called in sick today. I kind of assumed you'd both just had a heavy weekend.'

I felt a rush of cold sweep through my body. It had definitely been heavy, just not in the way she was guessing. 'Did he say anything else?'

'Nope. Just that he would let me know about tomorrow.'

Fuck. He was avoiding me. Any hope of reconciliation drained from our short-term future, and I felt the warning signs of tears about to flow. I pushed them down, sitting at my desk and getting to work.

★★★

I left the office early, suddenly desperate to see one person in particular. He loped up the hill, two takeaway cups in his hands. Cookie was plodding alongside him, matching his pace instead of racing ahead.

'I'm not getting any younger, and this hill is not getting any easier.' Dad perched on the bench next to me. 'I sensed this was a hot chocolate moment.'

I took the cup gratefully – I'd been sharing hot chocolates with my dad since the divorce, a new tradition found amidst the chaos. We had a regular bench at the top of the hill in Greenwich Park, with a beautiful view of dog walkers and turning leaves and quiet moments in between the hustle.

'Tell me what's going on, kiddo.' Dad put his arm around me and squeezed tight, and I swallowed the lump in my throat that hadn't left since Saturday night when the text had come through.

'Hey . . .' He tilted my chin up. 'Whatever it is, we can sort it.'

This new dynamic was strange, but welcome. I couldn't remember the last time I'd leaned on my dad, instead of the other way around.

He squeezed again, tucking me in like he had when I was little. 'Come on. Tell me.'

For what felt like the hundredth time after so much bottling up, I let it all out. Every gritty detail, from the ghosting, to Daniel's betrayal, to my argument with Rory about work. He didn't interrupt me, knowing that I needed to get to the end in order to take a breath. And when I did, he didn't immediately jump in, instead really thinking about what I'd said.

'It sounds like you've been putting a lot of effort into keeping your partnership with Rory separate from your friendship with Rory.' He finally spoke. 'Have you ever considered that having that bond is what makes your partnership great?'

I hadn't, not for a long time. I'd seen my affection for Rory as something that blinded me from making the right decisions.

'For a long time, Penny, I kept work and home *too* separate.' Dad cleared his throat. 'Staying out too late because I couldn't bear to bring paperwork home, leaving early in the morning to try and get it all done. And I never talked to your mum about it, or explained why I was behaving the way I was. Keeping them separate was my downfall, in the end.'

Hearing him say it out loud stirred memories of staying up until *way* past my bedtime in order to get a hug goodnight. It had been tough on Mum, and over time their bond had weakened to the point of collapse. I didn't want that for Rory and me.

'Don't hold back from confiding in him.' Dad smiled. 'He's one of the best people you've got.'

I sighed, sipping my hot chocolate slowly to avoid burning my tongue. 'My good decisions with men started and ended with Rory.'

Dad approached with caution. 'Do you think you might have been choosing entirely the wrong people? Perhaps on purpose?'

We watched Cookie investigate a new scent, her beagle nose working overtime to get to the bottom of it. I thought back to Isaac, who I had genuinely liked, but maybe not as much as I *could* like someone. And Daniel, who had been a fling from the word go.

'Maybe.' I chewed on my lip. Was I purposely avoiding anyone who might actually have a chance at breaking my heart?

Dad read my mind. 'And maybe you've been doing that because you're scared of ending up like me?'

'Dad, that's not −'

He patted my hand. 'I was careless after the divorce. I should have been teaching you that it's okay for things to change. Instead, I came to a standstill.'

I took another gulp of hot chocolate. 'You weren't in a position to think like that, Dad, and it's okay. We didn't mind.'

'I could have dealt with it a little bit better.' He called Cookie back to us, her nose leading her to wander just a little bit too far. 'My divorce was one of the most painful experiences of my life.' He paused, and I hoped that there was a point to this. 'But only because I hadn't given my relationship my all. You never have to worry about that.'

'I don't?'

He smiled. 'No. You struggle to open up, but once you do, you're the most attentive person I know. You've never let me down, not once.'

I was touched, but he was also wrong. 'I've let Maeve down a lot these past few weeks. And now Rory too.'

Dad sighed. 'A few weeks? That's just a mistake. A few years is a choice. And I had to deal with that the hard way. The risk isn't falling in love, Penny. It's taking what's right in front of you for granted.'

Cookie rested her head on his legs, sensing his discomfort. 'I really appreciate you telling me this.'

He tickled her chin. 'About time I did something useful. Between that and the Hello Fresh meals I've been making, I'm a new man.'

I'd been dying to ask about the dating, and he read it all over my face.

'A new man with a' – he hesitated – 'new girlfriend. Partner? I have no idea what you're meant to call it when you're on the road to 60.'

My heart squeezed. 'So it's official then? That was quick.'

Dad laughed. 'You don't mess around when you get a second chance. I feel happier than I have in years.'

And you could really tell. He'd been making progress anyway, but his skin was brighter, and he'd put on a few pounds.

'I'm thinking I might ask Isla if I can invite Linda as a plus-one to the wedding. I mean, if that's okay with you and Joe?' The suggestion floored me, but only momentarily.

'I think that's a good idea.' And I did. This would throw Mum even more than the dating app, but maybe it was what we all needed. Maybe we'd been stuck in limbo for way too long. I'd been terrified of being vulnerable and really letting someone in, but if Dad could do it all over again, maybe there was hope for me yet. I thought of bushy eyebrows and late-night dinners in the office.

Dad clocked the look on my face. 'I wasn't kidding when I said that sometimes it's right in front of you Penny.' When I didn't say anything, he pressed on. 'Talk to Rory. Figure it out.'

***

'Figuring it out' was one thing in theory, and entirely another in practice. Particularly when the person you were trying to reconcile with had fallen off the face of the bloody earth.

'Pen?' The front door squeaked open, and I heard Maeve drop her keys on the table.

'In here,' I called back from my position on top of my duvet, where I'd been since getting home from my walk with Dad. He'd offered to cook me dinner, but all that emotional deep-diving had drained me, so I'd made cheese on toast and was hand stamping all of the table headers for the wedding instead. Isla and Joe (mainly Isla, I was assuming) had decided on a *Mamma Mia* theme for their tables, since the first date they'd ever been on was to watch it at the theatre. Their honeymoon was also a salute to the story; they were going island hopping in Greece and their final week would be in Skiathos, where they'd planned a whole day trip to Skopelos. Isla had fantasised about recreating Sophie and Sky's duet on the beach, which I'd assured her I would pay serious money to see. Joe hadn't even liked doing the 'Cha Cha Slide' at our primary school discos.

'Wow, you've got a real assembly line going on here.' Maeve appeared, leaning on my door frame.

I glanced at the rows of place cards in front of me, midway through printing 'The Dynamos' on a header for Isla's friends from the florist.

'Got to be efficient. Less than one week to go.'

Maeve smiled. 'Wedding of the decade. I cannot believe they've managed to pull this off.'

I took in her outfit, which was a lemon-yellow corduroy jumpsuit. She had an orange claw clip holding her hair in place, and chunky gold hoops weighing down her lobes. 'Hot date?'

She grinned. 'A first date with someone else. Necked back half a bottle of wine in the first hour, so *clearly* I had some steam to burn off after this weekend.'

I winced. We hadn't directly spoken about it since it had happened. And I knew it was hard for her to go between the two of us.

I carried on stamping, avoiding eye contact. 'How is he?'

She nodded, like 'yep, we're going there'. 'He's not exactly fine. Not yet anyway, but he will be. You really surprised him.'

I nodded. 'I know. I want to fix it, but I want to do what's right by the company too.'

Maeve started taking out her earrings. 'Give him some time to come around.'

I folded my arms over my Snoopy pyjamas. 'How much time is time? Because we've got quite the event coming up, and we *really* need to be speaking by then.'

Maeve attempted to reassure me. 'You're both adults, it'll be fine. He's not going to risk ruining the wedding for this. It's Rory we're talking about. But just give him this week, okay?'

I must have looked unconvinced, because she fixed me with her psychologist stare. 'Promise?'

'Promise.' I went back to my stamping, suddenly exhausted. I'd paid so much attention to not mixing the personal with the professional, and now I'd jeopardised both.

38

I'd been on the verge of pulling my own hair out when he'd finally messaged. It was Wednesday, and I'd been working from home for the last two days, waiting for word from Ella that Rory might be back in the office. And by 'working from home', I meant watching old episodes of *Love Island* and stress-eating chocolate digestives. For someone who'd been a stickler for rules their whole life, taking study leave at its word and using university reading weeks to actually read, this was new territory for me. And, judging by the sea of digestive crumbs around me, it was territory best left unexplored. When my phone finally did ding with an incoming text, my first thought was that it was one of the contestants on my reality show. When they didn't scream out 'I've got a text', I looked down at my screen, which was lit up with Rory's name.

Rory: Can we talk?

For the last thirty-six hours, all I'd wanted was this. I'd been doing ridiculous things like archiving our WhatsApp chat and putting my phone on aeroplane mode just so that

I wouldn't obsess over his lack of response. Now that I was staring at those three dots typing, I felt a bit nauseous. I flopped back on our sofa, steadying myself.

Rory: I can come to you. Seven-ish?

It was currently two in the afternoon. There was *no* way I was getting any more work done today.

★★★

Even though Rory had seen me in various states over the years — the worst being during a particularly bad case of the flu in our final year, when he'd had to feed me buttered toast and Lucozade — I still changed my outfit three times, settling on a loose-fitting beige jumpsuit and my bunny slippers. Who was I kidding? I was in such deep shit that no outfit was going to save me now. Maeve had gone out 'with a friend', which was definitely code for 'going to Isla's to give you two some space'. As thankful as I was, it had only allowed me to work myself up into a frenzy. When the buzzer finally went, I tried not to run over to the door, using the same method I did when I ordered a takeaway and didn't want to look too keen.

'Hi.' He was waiting on the other side, staring back at me, and I felt my body relax. Like it had been tied tight with string and someone had let the end go.

'Hey.'

I used the moment of slightly awkward silence to my advantage, taking him in for the first time in three days. He was wearing jeans and a Nike sweatshirt, his hair slightly messed up from running his hands through it.

'Nice bunnies.' His deadpan expression melted for a second as he took in my own get-up.

'They're *comfy*.' I opened the door a bit wider, trying to ignore the anxiety creeping up my chest. 'You coming in?'

He nodded, shooting me a slightly forced smile and following me inside, closing the door behind him. Maybe this wasn't going to be as awful as I'd built up in my head.

'How have you been?' I instinctively moved towards the fridge to grab him a drink, but he stopped me.

'I'm not staying long.'

'Oh.' I let my hands drop to my sides, deflated. Rory knew how much Maeve hated shoes in the house, but he'd kept his trainers on. For a quick escape.

'I thought you'd come here to talk, that you wanted to figure this out.'

Rory wasn't looking me in the eye. 'I did. I do.'

There was an awkward pause, neither of us sure what to say.

'Listen, Rory.' I spoke at the same time he said 'Penny'.

I tried again. 'I didn't mean for any of that to happen last weekend. I hadn't spoken to him since that day in the office, and he mistook my doubt –'

'That's just it. I'm hurt that you didn't tell me about this "doubt" as soon as it crept in. That you went to him when you could have come to me. We're supposed to be partners.'

I felt a sharp fizzle of anger. Only this time, it wasn't directed at Daniel.

'Do you think you're *that* approachable, Rory? Do you think it's easy to admit to you that I'm not happy?' I gathered momentum, ignoring the voice in my head that told me I'd regret this outburst. 'I can't help how I'm feeling, and I know it took me longer than it should have to admit it, but I'm trying to be honest now.'

'Too little, too late.' Rory shook his head.

'I *tried* to tell you Rory, I really did. But do you know what, I've not been feeling much support from your end either.'

I was out of breath, all fired up now that I had committed to saying what was on my mind.

Rory was incredulous. 'You think I don't *support* you?'

I was in too deep to back down now. 'I think that it's really fucking hard balancing our friendship with work, and I don't think either of us have done a very good job. I feel worlds away from you right now.'

The last few words made him recoil, like I'd physically hit him. This was not how I'd planned this evening. The cans of Dr Pepper – that I hated, but Rory loved, which I'd gone to the corner shop specifically to get – sat unopened in the fridge. The anger drained out of me.

'*How* was I supposed to find it easy to tell you anything? You're Level's number-one fan.'

He winced. 'Right. Except I'm not its number one fan, Penny. I'm yours. I thought that was how this worked. Level is my job. It was never meant to be more important than this.' Rory gestured between us. 'And if that wasn't clear, then we've strayed far away from who we were when we started this project.'

We were now inches apart, every statement loaded.

'I'm not happy with the app how it is.' I didn't break eye contact, willing him to understand. 'I'm not *happy*.' My voice broke.

'I can see that.' His thumb brushed my chin and I fought the urge to trap his hand there. 'And I just wish I'd been the person you turned to when you realised that.'

How could he not see that I'd been trying to protect him? I was nearly crying now, but tried to steady myself by focusing back on Level and not on the man in front of me. 'So where do we go from here?' I placed my hands on the counter.

Rory finally broke his gaze, my change in topic clearly throwing him. He took a small step back. 'If the merger is what you want, then I want you to do it.'

All I wanted was to close the gap between our bodies, but it felt like he was trying to maintain as much distance as possible.

'What do you mean? I thought you would rather die than merge with Link.'

He nodded. 'I would. But I also want you to be happy. So, I want you to take the merger and buy me out.'

I didn't think I'd heard him right, but he ploughed on.

'I've been speaking to Dexter, and I think I want to go back to programming. I want to start something new. Take my share of Level and work on something else. I have a few ideas.'

'But –'

Rory smiled at me sadly. 'At one point, Pen, our visions were completely aligned. But they're different now.'

I felt slightly betrayed that he'd already discussed this with Dexter, who hadn't said a word to me about it, but I guessed that was his point. We weren't each other's soundboard any more. I'd gone behind his back to speak to Ella, who had sent full conditions of Level's offer this morning. It was an excellent offer, if you were willing to fade into the background of your own company.

'I don't want to do it without you.'

He nodded, but didn't say anything.

'Why don't you buy me out instead? It's me who's lost faith in the app, not you.'

Rory looked like he'd anticipated that question. 'Oh, I thought about it, but no. The app is struggling for money. I couldn't afford to buy you out without taking the merger, and obviously I'm not going to do that. You can do what you want with it. Sell it to them completely, if that's what you want.'

I thought about our little team that we'd built from the ground up. I'd never experienced a breakup, but I could imagine that this was what it felt like. My chest ached.

'I'm going to go.' Rory stood. 'Let me know what you want to do.'

I watched him grab his jacket from where he'd discarded it over the chair. I knew where he stood on Level now, but that wasn't the only thing at stake here.

'Are we okay? You and me?' My voice was so quiet I wasn't sure that he'd actually heard it, but he turned slightly, sighing. I placed a hand on his arm, unwilling to let go.

'I'm not sure, Pen.' He looked down at the floor, swallowing. 'I'm not sure.'

My heart broke and I released my grip on him. *This* is what I was so afraid of. What I'd always been afraid of. How someone could just decide to walk away, especially when you needed them most.

He took a step, as if to come and hug me, but changed his mind at the last second. 'I'll see you at the wedding.'

He left without saying anything else, closing the door lightly on the way out. And, in true new-Penny style, I didn't last ten seconds without bursting into tears.

39

'Be honest, have I developed frown lines in the last forty-five minutes?' Isla hissed, pulling me towards her so that I was two inches from her face. She'd just had her bridal make-up done, and she was literally glowing.

'Not a frown line in sight.'

She gritted her teeth. 'Is she genuinely pulling down my bunting? Tell me I'm not seeing things?'

I followed her gaze, to where her mother – straight off the plane and wearing a ridiculously big fascinator – was yanking at Isla's carefully handmade pastel bunting. We'd had some leftover after decorating the venue, so Maeve had strung some up in the bridal suite.

'Are you sure about this colour scheme, Isla?' Her nose was wrinkled. 'It's a little bit, well . . .'

One of her older sisters, who was bouncing a baby on her knee, jumped in. 'Like a 6-year-old's birthday party?'

I fought the urge to take off both my heels and sling them in their direction. Maeve was already on it, chipping in whilst sat in the chair getting her lipstick applied.

'Why *shouldn't* this be like a grown-up 6-year-old's birthday party?' She smacked her lips together. 'Life was better when there were party bags.'

Isla's mum cleared her throat. 'I suppose.'

'My mum made a cracking party bag.' Maeve continued to bulldoze through any awkwardness. 'Ridiculous flavours of Chapstick, neon headbands . . . those were the days.'

There was no longer any room for negativity. Isla's family were staring at my best friend with mild fascination. I mouthed a 'thank you' in her direction.

'You've been so lucky with the weather.' The make-up artist, a friend of Isla and Joe's from high school, pointed out into the garden, where the sun was shining. 'When my sister got married, she spent a ton of money securing a July date and then it rained so hard the gazebo broke right through the middle.'

I winced at the thought. She was right, it *was* a gorgeous day for a wedding. Somewhere else in the hotel, Joe, Rory and my dad were getting ready with the other groomsmen. I'd been trying not to think about that part, wrapping myself up in my duties and ignoring everything that wasn't wedding related. Like Rory, and our ongoing silence. Mum was out in the barn, putting the finishing touches to the cake and making sure that everything else we'd divided up between us over the last few months had gone successfully to plan. It was T-minus one hour until we were due downstairs to walk down the aisle, and I was already feeling nervous. I thought I was due a bit of good karma, but it was well within the realms of possibility that I might trip on a rogue handbag and fly headfirst into a pew. Either that, or Rory might push me himself.

'And we're done here.' The make-up artist framed Maeve's face in a 'ta-da!' motion, and we all cooed over the finished look even though it was identical to every single one of the bridesmaid reveals so far. Our eyes were the focal point; beautiful soft pastel glitters that matched our individual dresses had been applied meticulously. The rest of the make-up was subtle, with a mauve lipstick to finish it off. Every inch of this wedding was bursting with Isla's creativity, from the make-up to the bouquets, which she'd lovingly assembled herself yesterday afternoon. The hairdresser had curled our hair into soft waves that fell down our backs, using Isla's gift to us – a dainty hair slide with tiny gems running all the way down it – to pin a piece back. It was a miracle that she'd had time to focus on the minor details of this wedding – it felt like two minutes ago that they'd dropped the bombshell at the kitchen table.

'Has someone checked the microphones?' I voice-noted Mum, checking things off on my clipboard. We'd been communicating via voice note for the past hour as she'd wandered through the building; it was the modern walkie-talkie. She sent a note back, confirming that the soundcheck had gone well, and adding on a message that said the officiant wasn't too hard on the eyes.

'Only you would be micromanaging from up here.' Maeve shook her head, sipping a mimosa. 'Relax, woman.'

I pulled a face at her. 'I'm maid of honour. It's my job to stress. I won't relax until they've both said "I do".'

'And that' — Isla saluted me from the other side of the room, where her sisters had finally made themselves useful and were helping her into her dress — 'is why I chose you.'

I consulted my checklist, happy to report that we were running on time. Once Isla was in her dress, the photographer was on hand to get some final photos before the ceremony. Isla's final moments before becoming a Webber. And then it was all about the pre-aisle pep talk, which was Maeve's domain. She'd insisted that if there was any part of this day she could nail, it was the motivational speech before we headed downstairs for the ceremony. The only other glaring item on my list, which I was trying my hardest to put to the back of my mind, was my speech. I'd never missed a deadline in my life, but in a Penny Webber first, I was going to have to wing it.

Maeve was looking at my clipboard. 'I wouldn't mention to Isla that you haven't written anything yet.'

'Oh, trust me' — I crossed it out with my sharpie, striking through the letters three more times to make sure it was completely unreadable — 'I won't.'

'I think Rory has memorised his down to a tee —' She winced. 'Oops. Sorry.'

I bit my lip, quickly releasing it so I didn't smudge the carefully applied lipstick. 'No, don't. We have to speak about him. It has to be normal.'

When Maeve had arrived home on Wednesday night, she'd heard me crying and I'd spilled my guts to her almost immediately. I knew it was putting her in an awkward position, so I'd tried ever since to remain painfully optimistic to her face.

'I promise. I'm fine.'

She blinked back at me. 'And I'm not stupid. You're hurting, he's hurting. Sometimes being friends with you two feels like a full-time job. Have your parents spoken yet?' Maeve changed the subject, glancing out the window where we could see Mum talking with one of the guests. I was pretty sure it was weird Uncle Rob. I planned on avoiding him the entire day; no one was a fan of his cheek kisses.

'Not as far as I know.' I watched Mum, so effortlessly graceful as she darted between family members. It was weird to see her all dressed up, no apron in sight, but she looked beautiful in a pale blue pantsuit. 'But I have a feeling that she'll be fine.'

Joe had broken the news to her about Linda's invite to the wedding, sandwiching it between a pretend crisis about some choux buns. She'd been so focused on the pastry disaster that she'd taken it on board like a champ.

'Ta-da!' From the other side of the room, Isla's sisters presented her in her dress. She looked beautiful, and she had tears in her own eyes. My almost-sister had been waiting a long time for this day.

'I hate that you're going to be the prettiest Webber.' I sighed, squeezing her hand. 'It was a good run.'

Isla shoved me. 'You're ridiculous.'

Maeve was fanning her eyes, trying to dry the tears that were threatening to spill over. 'This is definitely the mimosa's fault, don't mind me.'

I rolled my eyes. 'Right, everyone,' I said, clapping. 'It's go time.'

★★★

Once we were downstairs, everything moved really quickly. All the guests were already sitting at their chairs, which had been scattered with gorgeous pink flowerheads supplied by Isla's boss. I could almost breathe a sigh of relief; we'd made it. There was next to nothing that could derail this mission now, and it *had* felt like a mission. *How To Plan a Wedding in Two Months: The Webber Edition.* The photographer ushered Isla away from the rest of the bridal party to get one last shot, and the four of us lined up to wait for the groomsmen. The venue in Hackney was absolutely gorgeous; a blank slate that Isla – along with Mum and Angela's help – had truly made her own. Fairy lights added a soft ambience to the room where everyone was waiting, and I could see a few people turning in their seats, ready to catch a glimpse of the bride. Maeve was at the front of the bridal queue, chatting to Isla's sister. She shot me a subtle thumbs–up. I fiddled with the sleeve of my dress, suddenly nervous; I'd been so wrapped up with my clipboard and getting Isla here in one piece, that I hadn't really thought about what came next.

'Hey.' I felt the lightest touch on my arm and then Rory was right there beside me, the rest of the guys filing in beside their allocated bridesmaid. I had no time to plan something witty, or to think of something interesting enough that it might eclipse the elephant in the room. Maeve immediately burst into laughter at something Joe's colleague, Matt, said to her. Both of us shuffled, self–conscious.

'Hi.' I whispered it back. My voice wavered.

Rory manoeuvred my arm so that I was forced to look at him. 'You look beautiful, Pen.'

I'd been worried about this dress: the softness of the pink, and the elegance of the floor-length number that cinched in at the waist. Just a tad out of my comfort zone. This was no power suit, or red leather trousers.

'I mean it. You do.'

My heart rate didn't know what to do, soothed by his presence and simultaneously terrified that we might mess up this interaction. 'Thanks. You look great too.'

His hair was slightly less wild than usual, and he'd trimmed his beard for the occasion. He must have had a better week of sleep than me, because my eye bags were darker even *with* several layers of concealer. His suit was well fitted, and he'd linked my arm through his, accentuating the hard muscle there.

'I think you can probably put your clipboard down now,' he whispered in my ear as he reached over to carefully take it from underneath my arm. My heart ached at this Rory, the one I knew so well.

'Oh, right. You know I like to plan.'

Rory nodded. 'That I do.'

A flicker of awkwardness passed between us again. I leapt to defuse it.

'Feeling ready for your speech?'

His chest rumbled with a surprised laugh. 'These people aren't going to know what's hit them.' He faced the front as the music started to play. 'Here we go.'

I watched him watch the other members of the wedding party set off down the aisle, a small smile on his face. Something sharp spiked my chest. How had everything between us gone so incredibly *wrong?* We were bigger than awkward small talk; we made fun of people who loved awkward small talk. I stared down at the tulips in my bouquet and felt the prickle of tears; at least a wedding was the one public place where it was absolutely acceptable – if not encouraged – for people to cry. All I had to do was hold it together for approximately twenty more minutes, until they exchanged vows. After that there wouldn't be a dry eye in the house, and I could blend right in.

Isla's sister and another of Joe's friends set off in front of us, and at the end of the aisle, I saw my brother stepping from one foot to the other, blatantly nervous. He looked suave in his tux, and I noticed something tiny tucked into his lapel. *Was that . . .?* I snorted quietly. It was. A tiny NERF bullet. I felt a wave of endearment, watching Joe's face as he waited for Isla to appear. In a crowded room, they'd always been the face that the other one wanted to find. Maeve had finally reached the front and turned to us, eyeing the atmosphere between Rory and me and shooting us both a look. I didn't have time to think about it, because Rory nudged me, signalling for us to start walking. The music hit its crescendo, and behind me, Isla and her dad stepped into place.

This was really happening. My big brother was getting married.

40

'That was the most beautiful wedding I've ever seen. Isla looked *radiant*.' Angela dabbed at her eyes with a lilac handkerchief (sorry, but handkerchiefs were at the top of my list of things that needed to *go*, alongside slow walkers on Oxford Street).

'She really did.' Mum was standing with us in the garden, watching the photographer take photos of Joe and Isla as a married couple. He was getting them to look into each other's eyes, and Joe kept making her laugh by accident so that they'd have to start the whole process again.

'I can't actually believe it.' I vocalised my disbelief. 'My stupid brother. A husband.'

The service had been perfect. All of their favourite people in the same room, Joe only faltering on his vows once – but not on the name, which was the only thing that really mattered, circa 1998 and the Ross/Emily/Rachel saga. We were all in that limbo stage of a wedding, where the reception hadn't started yet and unless you were a member of the bridal party, you didn't have a lot required of you except downing free prosecco. Everyone was outside in the warmth, soaking up the rays and getting steadily tipsier.

'Hi you.' Maeve appeared beside me, two glasses in hand. Her dress hovered just above her knees, a muted sage green that complemented the emerald earrings she'd splashed out on because 'how often do your best friends get married, and why *shouldn't* we be buying our own jewellery?'

She presented one of the glasses to me with a flourish. 'I bring you party juice.'

I wrinkled my nose. 'I'll drink it as long as you never call it that again.'

'I can't promise that, unfortunately.' She pointed to the photographer, who was squinting in our direction and waving us over. 'I think we're being summoned.'

Mum was watching us with amusement, listening to Angela waffle on about sit-down dinners versus wedding buffets (the horror, apparently). I squeezed her shoulder, fighting the urge to stick to her like glue. Whether that was for my own protection – I hadn't spoken a word to Rory since we'd partnered up to walk back down the aisle – or Mum's, I wasn't sure.

'Okay, can we get the bride and groom with the maid of honour and the best man?' The photographer, a rugged-looking man with excess facial hair, navy silk braces over his white shirt and a budding man bun, gestured for Rory and me to step forward.

'Fancy bumping into you again.' Rory touched my elbow, positioning himself as instructed. He was doing that thing I'd seen him do at work events, a polite small talk tactic. My chest ached.

'Fancy that.' I focused on the camera, waiting for the perfunctory click and my permission to leave.

'Smile like you know each other, come on guys,' the photographer instructed, kind of joking but mainly looking exasperated by the whole ordeal. 'Rory, can you put a hand on her waist?'

He did as he was told, his hand slotting into the dip where my dress spilled over my hips. My skin burned under his touch, and I was acutely aware of every single touchpoint between our bodies. I squashed it down and heard him clear his throat behind me. *Click.* I wasn't sure I wanted to see that one.

'Much better. And now one with the whole bridal party?'

Everyone else filed in, laughing as we were forced into various stupid positions so that Isla and Joe would have a whole album of ridiculous poses to mark the best day of their lives. I joined in, my attention completely zeroed in on the feel of Rory's breath hot against the back of my neck. He could have distanced himself from me as soon as the others joined us, but instead he'd remained almost in the exact same position. His fingers still lingered on my hip.

'You all right down there, Webber?' He glanced at me, eyebrow raised. Maybe my fluster hadn't been *quite* as subtle as I'd hoped.

I smoothed down my dress. 'Never better.'

His eyes didn't leave mine, and one side of his grin lifted slightly. I could not stop staring at his mouth, a definite sign that I needed to ditch this glass of bubbly.

Isla turned to me, beaming and breaking the spell. 'Penny. This day is *perfect*.'

She really was the most gorgeous bride. Her blonde hair was framing her face in delicate waves, secured with a tiny braid running across like a headband. The diamantes in her dress shimmered in the sunshine, and her make-up gave her an elegant glow. Joe couldn't take his eyes off her, and I couldn't blame him.

'You know,' she continued to chatter on as the group disbanded, Rory letting go of me finally to go and speak to Mum, 'weddings are the one place where literally anything goes. What happens at the wedding *stays* at the wedding.' Her wink was overexaggerated.

'I have no idea what you're talking about.'

She laughed. 'Keep drinking the free bar and I think you'll get it eventually.'

I watched her go and join her sisters, the post-ceremony energy clearly erasing some of the atmosphere between them. On the other side of the lawn, Mum had been pulled away from Rory to stand with Dad for a photo. Dad said something that made her laugh, and she swiped at his shoulder before smiling again for the camera. Next to me, someone else was watching them with fascination too.

'Hi. I'm Penny.' I held out my hand to the red-haired, middle-aged woman standing next to me. I'd never seen her before in my life, which made me think I knew exactly who she was.

She startled, blushing immediately. 'Sorry, I was just –'

'Are you Linda?' I blurted it out, and it looked like she was expecting it even less than I was. But the elephant in the room needed addressing. At least this bloody mimosa was good for *something*.

Linda — she confirmed it immediately with her raised eyebrows — blushed even deeper, seeming to shrink back into her grey dress. It was an understated shape and fit, like she was trying not to stand out.

'Yes, that's me. Maybe I should go inside . . .' She mumbled it softly.

She was the complete opposite of Mum — hair neatly in place instead of wildly out of it, muted colours instead of bold, shy where Mum was outspoken — but I felt a pull to her. No one should feel out of place.

'You can stand with me if you like.' I grabbed another glass from a passing tray and handed it to her.

Linda looked completely taken aback, and a little over-whelmed. I wondered what had led her here, if she'd had to psych herself up to get started on Level, and if she had any kids who'd been forced to dig through their WhatsApp history and find photos for her profile. I imagined Mum turning up to a wedding where she didn't know anyone, and the thought almost made me grab Linda's hand in solidarity.

'It's really lovely to be here, and to meet you, Penny.' Her features were less 'deer in the headlights' now, and she was smiling, albeit a bit warily. 'I'm a bit nervous.'

'You don't need to be.' I gave her a conspiratorial look. 'We don't bite.'

I'd been dreading this moment — caught between feeling relieved that Dad was building a life again, and sadness for Mum that she had to watch it happen. But looking at her now across the garden, radiant in her independence and her philosophy that actually, not everyone needed or wanted a partner, I felt nothing but pride. For both of them. There was no absence of love here.

She pointed towards Joe, who was being lifted into the air by his friends. 'My son is about the same age as Joe.'

My breath caught in my throat at the thought of everything that was yet to come. But today wasn't about that.

'Do you want to come and meet him?' I clinked my glass against hers. 'Probably best to do it now, before he can't remember where he is.'

She smiled at me, her surprise evident. 'I would love that. If that's okay.'

★★★

For a wedding on a budget with a limited timeframe, we'd managed to make the dining hall look like something out of a fairy tale. The cursive font on the blackboard at the entrance had been written in white chalk, outlining who would be seated where, and when dinner would be served. Each table had tall, white candlesticks that dripped rainbow wax as they melted, bringing a little bit of magic to the centre of the conversations. And there were fairy lights *everywhere*. Our table was called 'Honey, Honey', a salute not only to the ABBA song but also to the nickname that Isla and Joe had adopted in high school. The whole wedding party was seated here. We'd floated the concept of a 'sweetheart table' just for Joe and Isla, but as Isla had aptly put it, they had the rest of their lives to sit next to each other. They were currently making their way around the room, mingling. Isla had changed into a short, floaty white dress that was perfect for dancing – witnessing Joe try to dance later would be one of the highlights of the night – and she had kicked off her heels, walking around barefoot. Something literally only she could pull off. Isla's sisters were at the bar, leaving me, Rory, and Maeve with the other groomsmen. Rory was already well on his way to getting drunk, and the bread rolls hadn't even been dished out yet.

Maeve reached over and fixed his collar, both of us at a loss for what to say as we all settled into awkward silence. Something that was *not* familiar, and did not feel good. Joe's friends were discussing a girl's profile on Link. I felt a bead of sweat roll down my neck. Someone, somewhere, hated me.

'Okay.' Maeve clasped her hands on the table. 'This is ridiculous. It's Isla and Joe's wedding.'

'I'm well aware.' Rory nodded, loosening his tie and taking another long drink. Gone was the soft, attentive Rory from before the service. It was like he'd put on a performance, just to get through it. That, and alcohol always revealed the doors we'd been hiding behind.

'First of all' – Maeve ignored his attitude, pouring him a glass of water from one of the jugs that had been put on the table and stealing the wine right out of his hand – 'you need to sober up. You have a speech to give in a few courses's time – remember that?'

Shit. I poured myself a glass of water too.

'And second, come on you two.' She flicked her gaze between us. 'You have *got* to sort this out. At least just for tonight.'

I waited, holding my breath. 'Do you maybe want to step out —'

Rory's eyes met mine and he quickly looked away. 'I think I'll just see you guys later.'

He stood, stumbling slightly, taking his water with him to the table where Isla and Joe were currently chatting to my parents and Linda.

'Oh, for crying out loud.' Maeve poured herself some more wine. 'This is going to be a long night.'

41

Maeve was tapping her nails against the table, irritated. 'Weddings are *not* supposed to be this angsty.'

I sipped from my water glass. 'Have you seen *Four Weddings and a Funeral? Father of the Bride?*'

I knew she had; we had them on rotation.

'Okay smart arse, correction. *This* wedding is not supposed to be angsty. Isla and Joe are the least dramatic people I've ever met.'

They were still on the other side of the room, Joe dipping Isla for a photo that Mum was taking on a disposable camera. We'd left one on every table, hoping to grab a selection of candid, less polished shots. I could guarantee that at least one of Joe's friends would end up mooning for a photo, leaving a nice surprise for us when we got the photos developed.

'What on earth is he doing?' Maeve threw her hands up as Rory started dancing with one of the florists, twirling her in an almost-perfect circle. A few other people were dancing too, not wanting to wait until after dinner and already moving to the pre-dinner playlist carefully chosen by all of us. My skin prickled at the sight of Rory pulling the florist close to his chest.

'Right. I've had it.' Maeve jumped up, narrowly missing a spillage of red wine on the delicate material of her dress. Her hand reached out for mine, and I didn't think I had a choice in whether I took it. 'Come on.'

I ignored the nosy looks from the other groomsmen as she half dragged me in the direction of the bathrooms, willing the glass of wine in my hand not to spill.

'Are you going to tell me what this is about?'

She stopped for a second. 'If you don't already know, then you're dumber than I thought. Wow, this place is *nice*.' Maeve stroked the gold mirror in the bathroom, momentarily distracted. 'Actually, maybe I shouldn't be stroking that. This is still a toilet.'

The last time I'd been in a bathroom as nice as this one had been at the corporate mixer where I'd met Daniel. At least this time, I wasn't absolutely smashed. I was going to hear every word when I got a talking to, which, looking at Maeve, I was definitely about to get.

'Penny.' She stared me down.

'Maeve.'

'I cannot stand it that you and Rory are having a stand-off on one of the most important days in our social calendar, well, *ever*.'

I shrugged, at a loss. 'It's this thing with Level, it's —'

'Penny Agatha Webber.' Maeve narrowed her eyes. 'This is not about Level, and I'm sick of you both pretending that it is.'

I decided to let it slide, given the fraught circumstances, that she'd just said my middle name out loud. I cursed Mum's addiction to Christie novels every time I had to register for anything serious.

'It *is* about Level.' I folded my arms.

'If it's all about work, why did you get so defensive when you thought Rory and I were dating?'

On the other side of the bathroom door, someone tried to get in. Maeve body blocked it.

'Hey.' Isla's voice was slightly slurred. 'This is my wedding, so this is technically my bathroom for the night.'

'Oh, it's you.' Maeve ushered her in. 'How are you, Isla *Webber*?'

She looked between the two of us. 'Better now that I'm in on this little private meeting.' She rubbed her heel. 'I just need a moment of respite. And a pair of the flipflops we bought for the guests. I think I just stood on a canapé.'

Maeve and I were silent.

'Wait, what were you talking about?' She looked between us. 'I have a feeling this is about to get juicy.'

Maeve leaned back against the wall. 'We were just discussing how Penny is in love with Rory.'

I spat out the sip of wine that I'd just taken, and we all watched it drip down the mirror.

'So she finally admitted it?' Isla beamed. 'I knew the wedding energy would crack you.'

We were going on a *wild* tangent here. 'I haven't admitted anything! What the hell, Maeve?'

Instead of looking sheepish, she just stood her ground. 'Why were you so defensive when you thought I was sleeping with Rory?'

We were wasting precious dancing time, and we were going to miss the bread rolls. I'd been defensive because I didn't want to be left behind, and I didn't want things to change. I said as much.

'You didn't want things to change, or you didn't want Rory to date someone who might actually be endgame?'

'I —' I thought about it. 'That doesn't make any sense. He lived with Lottie. That was pretty endgame.'

Until it wasn't.

'Oh, come off it.' Maeve wasn't backing down. 'That relationship was never going to last, not with you in the picture. She'd had enough of coming second.'

Suddenly, so much made sense. *Especially* why Rory had been so hurt that I'd spoken to Lottie after their breakup. I was getting clammy. I wiped my palms on my dress. 'We're getting off-topic.'

Isla piped up, midway through reapplying her lipstick. 'Penny, this *is* the topic.'

Right. So my brand-new sister was not going to be very helpful here.

'I want you to really hear what we're saying.' Maeve snapped her fingers in front of my face. 'You've been dating low-risk men since the moment I met you.'

I tried to argue, but then remembered my conversation with my father. She wasn't wrong.

'And I get it. It's scary, being vulnerable. But it's holding you back.'

Isla patted my shoulder. 'It's holding us *all* back.'

I blinked, feeling Rory's hand on my hip this afternoon all over again. Remembering our almost-kiss. *All* of our almost-kisses. 'But it's Rory.'

Maeve softened. 'That's why it's terrifying.'

'Oh my God.' I let the realisation slide over my skin. It was *Rory*. It had always been Rory.

Isla and Maeve were staring at me, looking like proud parents.

'Does he —'

Maeve waved her hands in a 'stop right now' motion. 'It's one thing giving you an emotional awakening, but I'm saying nada about Rory.' She massaged her temples. 'Sometimes I feel like I should charge you both for my time.'

'Right.' I was pretty sure I was in shock.

'But please' — she took my face between both of her hands — 'for the love of God, just go and talk to him. I quite simply won't be able to fit you both in if I have to keep seeing you separately. Life is busy. And also, too fucking short.'

'Amen to that.' Isla nodded. 'Now can we please get back in there? First course is coming out pronto.' Isla jerked her thumb in the direction of the door.

'Noted.' Maeve picked up her bag from the sink, grabbing my hand and squeezing it. 'Think about what I said, okay?'

★★★

I followed them out of the bathroom, feeling slightly dazed. *Rory*. I thought I didn't know what it felt like to truly want someone, but I did. I'd always known. Things had been heating up between us recently and I'd just put it down to work-based tension, but it wasn't. It had been a long time coming, and it wasn't going anywhere. Rory wasn't just my work colleague, or my friend. He was my *person*. And I had been a complete and utter idiot.

'I'm going to go and grab my seat.' Maeve followed my gaze to the other side of the room, where Rory was still flirting with one of Isla's colleagues.

'Oh, for fuck's sake.' She squeezed my shoulder. 'Ignore that. Textbook defence mechanism.'

It didn't matter that I was largely at fault here. Seeing him flirt with a stranger *hurt*. Had I been doing the same thing to him for months? While one part of me felt bad about that, a bigger, more prominent part of me watched him flirting and was *mad*. So mad that my cheeks felt hot to the touch. Mad at myself for always, *always* being too scared to let anyone in, and mad at Rory because he'd given up on me at the first sign of conflict and was now flirting with a florist. I had no idea how he felt, but if I didn't say something, I would lose him either way.

'I know I said talk to him, but maybe you should wait until after . . .'

I ignored her, hitching up my dress and marching over in his direction. He saw me coming, eyes widening as he extricated himself from the conversation.

'What the *fuck*, Rory?' As soon as I was in his orbit, angry tears pricked my eyelids.

It didn't take long for him to sober up. 'What's wrong?'

My expression must have been incredulous, because he pulled me in the direction of the entrance to the barn. Once we were outside, he turned to face me.

'What's going on? Are you okay?'

I felt the absence of his hand in mine now that he'd let go. 'If this is about Level . . .'

I scoffed. 'Not everything is about that bloody app, Rory.'

He crossed his arms.

'This is about our friendship, and everything that's −'

Now it was his turn to scoff. 'Right. Our friendship.'

I recoiled. 'Why are you acting like it's the worst thing in the world?'

He sent a look skyward as if asking for strength. 'Because it is.'

'What?'

'I said' − he made eye contact again − 'because it is. It *is* the worst thing in the world, being friends with you. It's also the best fucking thing. And I know those two statements contradict each other, but my feelings for you have been a walking contradiction since the first time you walked into our university kitchen wearing those stupid giraffe slippers that you eventually wore to death.'

His chest was rising and falling as he got more and more angry. There was a fine line between anger and sexual tension, and I was *feeling it*. All the way down to my toes.

'I don't know what you *want* from me, Penny. Do you want me to say it? Do you want me to drive that final nail in the coffin? Sometimes I feel like you're with me on this, and yet you always seem to freak out.'

All of those moments between us, when I'd tried to protect our loyalty to Maeve. The rash conclusions I'd drawn. He had no idea why I'd been backing off. No idea at all. And that was my fault.

'Who was Maisy?' I said it softly.

Rory sighed, staring at me, all the way through to my heart. 'I made her up.'

And there it was. I'd been gathering all of the wrong evidence. Maisy hadn't been code for Maeve, she'd been a protective measure for *him* whilst I was dating all the wrong people. And he'd been turning to Maeve for support, not sex. For someone who prided herself on common sense, I'd been really stupid. Dad's words echoed in the back of my mind. *The risk isn't falling in love, Penny. It's taking what's right in front of you for granted.* I fiddled with the maid of honour locket around my neck, anxious.

'Your fidgeting is really distracting.' Rory pulled my hand away, his eyes searching mine. 'It kept me awake for hours that night.'

That night. The night I'd curled my body around his, when I thought he was fast asleep. He clocked my expression. 'I was awake the whole time, Pen.'

I swallowed.

'I was right there, and I could feel how much you wanted this – how much I *thought* you wanted this – and then you pulled away. Again.'

'Rory . . .' I looked at him. The man who'd always put me first, and who challenged me like no one else did. Who'd been able to get under my skin with wicked resolve since the day I'd met him. Who joked that he had a Penny worry-radar, and who had led me into more house parties than I could count, taking my hand and guiding the way. I felt all my anger melt away, morphing into something that felt even more urgent.

I took his hand, pulling him flush against my body, which was backed against the wall. Three squeezes. *I. Need. You.*

He looked down into my eyes, almost as if he was searching for confirmation.

'Penny . . .' His voice was a low growl.

I nodded once, and that was all it took. He cupped my chin with his hands, pressing his lips to mine. And there was nothing light, or platonic about it. This wasn't a trial kiss. It was hard, and passionate, and loaded with eight years of repressed feelings. I felt the spark zip all the way up my spine. *This* is what it was meant to feel like. And it had been right in front of me all along.

He pulled back, his eyes searching. 'What are we doing?'

A beat passed. I stared at his mouth, already craving the taste of him again. 'You know exactly what we're doing.'

Our communication had been murky as of late, but it was crystal clear now. He pushed me harder against the wall, kissing me like he was starving. 'God, you feel good.'

Desire pooled in the pit of my stomach, and I thought about our hotel rooms, two doors apart. It was incredibly inconvenient that we were in the middle of a family occasion. He wedged his knee between my legs and I held back a pant, well aware that my entire family was mere yards away.

As his lips traced their way down my neck to my collar-bone, I let out a sigh. 'You know, I think it's actually tradition for the best man to go home with the maid of honour.'

Rory pulled back, laughing against my mouth. 'If you keep saying things like that, I might not survive dinner.'

I batted my lashes. 'Things like what? Like everything I'm going to do to you later?'

'Penny . . .' I could see him struggling to restrain himself.

I gave my best angelic look, even though the things I was feeling were *anything* but holy.

His eyes flashed. 'What do I win when my speech is better than yours?'

We'd made a lot of bets over the years, but this time the stakes felt higher than ever before.

I kissed the skin below his ear. 'You get to finally find out exactly what's underneath this dress.'

Rory groaned, dragging me towards the door. 'Come on, I've got a speech to give. And a very important bet to win.'

I let him lead me, unable to hide my smile. This, finally being honest with the man I'd been building a foundation with for years, was much, *much* better than hiding.

42

It came as a surprise to no one that Rory's speech was hilarious. What did come as a surprise, however, was the PowerPoint presentation.

Joe was wiping tears from under his eyes when Rory got back to the table, a smug smile on his face. 'Mate, that was hysterical. I didn't even know we *had* video evidence of Isla falling into that lake.'

His speech had lasted about ten minutes, taking us through a journey of Joe and Isla's most embarrassing moments, both separately *and* as a couple. Matt had stood at the back, filming it and everyone's reactions. For a man who'd consumed a serious amount of alcohol over the course of the day, Rory had really reined it back, putting on a killer performance. I did not have a good feeling about my odds. He walked back to the table, not breaking eye contact with me and mouthing 'pay up'. My skin flushed; I knew exactly what he meant, and I intended on paying in full.

'You are welcome.' He bowed to the table. 'Isla, what did you think?'

She was feigning annoyance, crossing her arms over her chest and narrowing her eyes. 'I'm going to get you back for that. I don't know when, and I don't know how, but I will.'

Rory smiled at her, turning on the charm and dropping into his seat. He casually rested his arm on the back of my chair. 'Then my work here is done.'

From across the table, Maeve shot me a look and mouthed 'oh my God'.

Isla also clocked the movement. 'Maybe that opportunity will come sooner than originally thought. Payback is a bitch, Ror.'

He ignored her, pinching the back of my neck with one hand and passing me the mic with the other. 'You're up.'

Wiping my clammy palms on my thighs under the table, I took the mic. I had been running high on adrenaline all day, and this was the final hurdle.

'You've got this.' Rory whispered it in my ear, making the soft skin underneath my earlobe tickle. 'I'm rooting for you.'

Like always. I shot him a smile, getting up from my seat and facing the rest of the room.

'Here goes nothing,' I joked into the mic, making a few people laugh. Joe flashed me a thumbs up.

For all the weeks I'd spent planning for this moment, I still had absolutely nothing to show for it. My piece of paper was as blank as it had been when I'd started. Our public speaking events for Level had been stressful in the past, but we'd always had cue cards and carefully planned presentations locked and ready to go. This time, I was completely on my own. I swallowed, wincing when the microphone picked up the sound.

'I've known Joe my whole life' – I was completely winging it – 'I know, awful.'

Mum snorted from the table to my left. And looking at her, watching me so intently and willing me to succeed, then down at the people on my table who were so integral to my life, it suddenly came to me. What I wanted to say.

'When Isla asked me to be her maid of honour a few months ago, my first thought was "shit, I've got to make a speech".' I paused to gather my thoughts, letting a few sniggers carry the silence. 'And then I thought, "why on earth would they ask me to write a speech about love?" I have no idea what love is. I've never been in it. I didn't even think I *wanted* to be in it.'

I looked down at Rory, who was watching me with a small smile on his face.

'I've spent my whole career trying to figure out the algorithm for love. How to trap it, and turn it into something tangible so that I could understand it, or at least help other people to understand it. But if there's anything that Isla and Joe have taught me, it's that sometimes love doesn't follow a formula.'

From across the room, Dad was beaming, Linda at his side. Level might not be the answer to a perfect match, but it could give you a chance. And maybe sometimes that was all you needed. I folded up the blank piece of paper that I'd been clutching in my hands.

'The girl who cuts rose stems and the boy who cuts people open might never have been matched by an algorithm, and we'll never know. But they're also the best example of love, trust, and partnership that I've ever seen. From the moment Isla burst into our lives, this eternally optimistic, sunshiney gem of a person' – I glanced at her, hands clasped to her chest – 'I knew that she was the right person for my brother. Who needs someone to remind him of the good in the world.'

I took a breath, trying not to get choked up.

'There is literally no other person on this planet who could put up with my big brother and make him packed lunches every day. Or run around the house having NERF gun battles with him just because it makes him happy. And no offence, Isla, but there is no one else on the planet who would put up with how badly you sing in the shower.'

She tried to protest.

'Nope, sorry. We heard you singing ABBA on your hen do. That shit is horrendous. But Joe puts up with it and you put up with him. Because to you two, putting up with each other has never felt like putting up with each other at all. I've feared falling in love my whole life, but not any more. Because you two make it seem like the easiest thing in the world. So, let's raise a glass to Joe and Isla – who are the real deal.'

Around the room, everyone raised a glass. 'To Joe and Isla.'

I was shaking when I sat back down. Isla grabbed my hand. '*Penny*.'

There were tears in her eyes, and I was surprised to find that mine were prickling too.

Everyone settled into relaxed chatter as coffee was served – yet another element of weddings that I didn't understand. By this point, most people were on their way to being hammered. No one needed to add another stimulant to the mix.

'What are you thinking about?' Rory said innocently as he stirred a sugar cube into my mug with one hand, the other on my knee crawling dangerously higher.

'Well, I *was* thinking about how ridiculous coffee at a wedding is.' I shivered. 'But now I'm thinking about whatever it is you're doing under there.'

He passed me the cup. 'Just giving you a preview.'

Without even thinking about it, I leaned in to kiss him.

'Wow, no soft launch with you two, is there?' Joe's eyebrows were sky high.

I pulled back, blushing.

'I'm happy for you.' Joe held my eye contact. 'I'm proud of you. And I knew the penny would drop eventually.'

I rolled my eyes. 'Hilarious, and as always, completely original.'

Isla was watching the two of us. 'Is this my life now? Stuck between two siblings forever?'

'Yes,' we said at the same time, to an outbreak of laughter.

'You know, I didn't actually think the penny would drop.' Rory murmured it so that only I could hear. 'I'd resigned myself to a life of subpar love.'

My heartbeat skyrocketed.

'I'm not going to say it, don't worry.' Rory tilted his head, watching me. 'At least not yet. I know who I'm dealing with, remember?'

And just like that, a wave of calm blanketed me. Of course he knew who he was dealing with.

'You know, there are lots of things I have yet to teach you about me.'

He grinned, moving his hand an inch higher again. 'I'm looking forward to discovering them. I have a feeling you might need to teach them to me a few times tonight, just to make sure I get it.'

'Oh, I plan on it.' I watched our friends laughing with each other, experiencing the kind of deliriousness that only a wedding could bring.

'You know' – I planted a kiss on his jawline – 'today has turned out nothing like I thought it would.'

He smiled. 'Better or worse?'

This was a game we'd played throughout our degree and into our career. Whenever we hit a crossroads with one of our decisions – whether the interviewee for director had been the right fit for our company, whether the tweak in our dating equation was a good one – we'd ask each other a simple question. Better, or worse?

'Definitely better.' I leaned my head on his shoulder. 'And guess what?'

Rory kissed my forehead. 'What?'

'I know exactly what I want to do with Level.'

Epilogue

Dexter came back to the table carrying five pints, wobbling slightly as he set them down.

'As impressive as that was' – Ella took one, nudging the others in our direction – 'would it not have been less risky to make another trip to the bar?'

Maeve arrived with the other three – one of them a cider and black, for Harriet – balancing them on the table. 'Just for the record, I did also say that.'

Dexter dismissed them both with a scoff. 'This is Level. Taking risks is what we do.'

'I'll cheers to that.' Harriet held up her glass, gesturing for us all to do the same. She was liberated by the fact that she was child-free for the first Friday night in a month, and I was pretty sure she'd just been waiting to start drinking all day.

I shook my head. 'We have to wait for Rory.'

Everyone groaned.

'We get it. You two are attached at the hip now. But I draw the line at not being able to start my pint until the man arrives.' Dexter pulled a face at me, and I pulled one right back.

'He has a point.' Ella took a sip. 'There, I've broken the first rule of cheers. Start drinking, we'll wait until he's here to raise the toast.'

'And this is why you're director. No one makes a decision like you do.'

Harriet had her phone out, checking Twitter. 'It's going down well. Better than well, actually.'

I let myself relax, laughing when Maeve bumped my shoulder against hers. She'd taken a half day to be here, so that she could celebrate the new direction of Level. It had taken us a full two months after the wedding to storyboard and implement the changes we wanted to make to how we marketed our app, but we got there. And the real thing had just launched into the world.

'It feels like yesterday that we were all in this pub, celebrating the launch of Level in the first place.' Ella had her phone out now, scrolling through the comments and shares. 'Time flies when you're having fun.'

I wasn't quite sure that the last six months had been what I'd describe as *fun*. Well, except for the last two. They'd been pretty special.

'Here he is!' Dexter hollered towards the door, where Rory had finally entered the pub. He'd stayed a bit later than everyone else, insisting that he wanted to check that everything was perfect. He knew how important this was to me, and so from the moment I'd floated the idea, he'd made it just as important to him. I watched him look for us, eyes lighting up when he clocked me. It had been two months, but the butterflies were eight years in the making.

'Hey you.' He squeezed into our booth, kissing me.

'What about the rest of us?' Maeve recoiled when he leaned forward. 'Definitely a joke, Ror. Definitely a joke.'

In most groups of friends, this shift of gravity might have been a problem. Not with Maeve. She was happy to be our third wheel, and I was determined to never, ever make her actually feel like one. We'd always been three, and we always would be.

'How did everything go at the office?' I squeezed his leg under the table.

'Everything according to plan. Operation "make Level the first dating app to actively *not* push people towards the perfect match", complete.' He held up his glass. 'Are we doing a cheers?'

Dexter pushed his glasses up his nose. 'Oh, so now the *king* is here . . .'

Ella thumped him, raising her glass to match everyone else's. 'To Level. And to an app that continues to evolve, into whatever we feel it needs to be.'

We all cheered, and I felt my cheeks warm – partially from the alcohol, but mostly because my team had backed me all the way. They'd heard me when I said I was worried about the pressure our messaging – and the messaging of every other app under the sun – was putting on people. They'd responded when I'd suggested a more relaxed marketing plan, which encouraged people to have fun, and to get out there (and get home) safely, with a three-pronged partnership with GetThere and SafeTI. Level now encouraged people to fall in love, but didn't make huge promises about what we could deliver. Our app made dating feel fun, rather than a race to find anyone who fit the bill. As soon as we'd pitched our change in campaign to various lifestyle brands, offers for investment had slowly trickled in, meaning that we didn't need to consider Link's offer to survive. Yes, we'd passed up a lot of money. But taking risks and building concepts from the ground up was kind of our thing.

'I'm proud of you guys.' Maeve fiddled with her boob earrings, which she'd worn tonight as a salute to the original launch party. 'For a lot of things. But mostly for this' – she held up her phone, where our new campaign design was all over her Twitter feed – 'it's really cool. I have a feeling you two are only just getting started.'

I exchanged a look with Rory, and I knew he knew what it meant. It had taken me two months to say the three words that had terrified me for my whole life, but once I started saying them, I couldn't stop.

'Oh, trust me,' Rory said, glancing between us, smiling, 'we are.'

Acknowledgements

Writing Penny and Rory's story was so much fun, but it would never have happened without the love and support of those around me.

My biggest thank you, as always, goes to Meg. My Editor extraordinaire, with the kindest heart and endless patience. Thank you for seeing what I see in those tiny seeds of an idea, for loving my characters as much as I do, and for being the brain behind that tricky structural edit process. I am so thankful to work with you and to be part of our romcom dream team. Thank you to the entire team at HarperNorth; to Taslima and Alice for their brilliant marketing, to Lisa Brewster for my gorgeous cover, and to everyone who helped get *The Dating Equation* to publication (and beyond!).

I started writing this book in the same month that I moved to London and embarked on a career in publishing, and it has been the greatest adventure of my life. Thank you to my team for supporting me as I balance both jobs, to Sian for being my biggest cheerleader and the best friend, and to Christina for going above and beyond to get my romcoms to readers.

In 2020 I wrote a book called *Heartbreak Houseshare*, about a girl who moves into a girls' house to heal her broken heart. And then it happened to me. Thank you to Courtney, Cat and Sarah for showing me just how magic a girls' house can be. There's no one I'd rather share a camembert or sit on the stairs debriefing my day with.

Thank you to Beth and Ross, for making me snort laugh like no one else can, and to Rosie and Adam for trips to the beach and a shared love of tacos and frozen margaritas. To Ciara, who understands me to my core and who I'm so grateful to have met. I hope we'll be chatting over cups of tea (and B&B rocky road) forever. These kinds of friendships last a lifetime, and I count my lucky stars for you all.

Thank you to my Mum for nurturing my love for reading – every inch of my life surrounds me with books, and I have no doubt that's because of you. To Dad, for being the best soundboard for advice and for pushing me to achieve my dreams, and to Rachel and Taylor, who are a beautiful example of love and a great source of inspiration. To my Nana, for reading every book and teaching me to find the small joys in everything, and to my Mama and Grandad, who guide me from above.

And finally, it takes a very special person to support a writer (who by definition, overthinks everything) and I am so lucky to have you, Adam, by my side. Your advice and steady presence ground me and cheer me on, and I'm so thankful our paths crossed.

Harper North

would like to thank the following staff
and contributors for their involvement in making
this book a reality:

Fionnuala Barrett

Samuel Birkett

Peter Borcsok

Lisa Brewster

Ciara Briggs

Katie Buckley

Sarah Burke

Alan Cracknell

Jonathan de Peyer

Anna Derkacz

Tom Dunstan

Kate Elton

Sarah Emsley

Simon Gerratt

Monica Green

Natassa Hadjinicolaou

Megan Jones

Jean-Marie Kelly

Taslima Khatun

Rachel McCarron

Ben McConnell

Petra Moll

Alice Murphy-Pyle

Adam Murray

Genevieve Pegg

Amanda Percival

Florence Shepherd

Eleanor Slater

Angela Snowden

Katherine Stephen

Emma Sullivan

Katrina Troy

Daisy Watt

For more unmissable reads,
sign up to the HarperNorth newsletter at
www.harpernorth.co.uk

or find us on Twitter at
@HarperNorthUK

Harper
North